Magi Journey

ASSYRIA

A story of hope and redemption.

A story of the Magi, the men, and women who saw it all.
The prophecies, the judgments, and the deliverance.

BY

TERRY GARNER

Published by
BrodRo Publishing
Norman, Oklahoma

www.magijourney.com
tpgarner@magijourney.com

Paperback ISBN: 978-1-66780-992-2
E-book ISBN: 978-1-66780-993-9

Book Cover and maps, Nick Bolton on Instagram @rainandcinder
Edited by Teresa Crumpton, Author Spark, at authorspark.org

Contents

CHAPTER 1

The Sign

Scene 1 Persepolis Day Minus 1

The two men and the boy dismounted and proceeded on foot. They were southwest of the Family's compound in Persepolis, Persia. This region of the Zagros Mountains was thinly forested and possessed a good-sized deer population. It also had a fair-sized brown bear population. Navid saw fresh deer scat and knew the deer would not travel far this time of the morning. Navid held out his hand, stopping Yusef in mid-stride. He pointed down at a twig Yusef was about to step on and wagged his finger no. Navid then moved across an area of loose shale and pebbles, demonstrating how to place his feet. Then he motioned Yusef forward again. Navid and Utana were fifty feet apart, moving in a line, with Yusef between them. The deer tracks were faint, but Navid was the best tracker in the Family. He bent down, pointing at a barely perceptible scratch on a rock made by the deer's hoof, and Yusef nodded his head in understanding. Navid was pleased when he saw the light in the boy's eyes and knew he was learning.

Utana stopped suddenly and signaled to Navid. Without moving, Navid could see the still steaming scat in front of Utana, not deer scat. Navid leaned toward Yusef and whispered, "Bear, he's close." They were downwind of the bear, which was good, but Navid slowed, scanning the area thoroughly before he took a step. The three hunters carried their bows with one arrow held in their hand. Navid and Utana nocked their arrow, and Navid indicated to Yusef that he should do the same. They proceeded in line for another half mile.

Navid stopped and slowly pointed to a tree about fifty feet in front of them. There, perfectly outlined in front of the tree, stood a young buck. He was angled slightly, and his head was facing away from them. Navid indicated to Yusef that he should put tension on his bowstring but not draw it yet. Slowly, step by step, they approached the deer. Thirty feet from the deer, Yusef stepped on a dry twig. The deer's head snapped up. Yusef drew and released, but he pulled the shot. The arrow missed the deer's heart and went into the lung. The deer took two quick bounds. Navid and Utana both got off quick shots. Navid's arrow went into the deer's hindquarter, and Utana also hit the lung. The deer bolted, and the chase began. The two men and the boy broke into a run, leaping over felled trees and small rocks. They ran for two miles. Navid breathed in through his nose and out through his mouth, deep, even, steady. He felt the blood expanding the muscles in his legs as he ran. He loved the chase. He saw Yusef breathing through his mouth, gulping air, and saw the boy's stride shortening. Navid could see bright splotches of blood as they ran. The blood splotches were getting closer together. The deer was slowing.

Navid and Utana increased their pace, and Yusef fell behind. They topped a rise, and a half-mile in front of them, they could see the deer limping across a small clearing. Navid and Utana were now at a dead run and closed the distance. Barely slowing, both men nocked arrows and fired two arrows into the deer's heart, putting the poor animal out of its misery. Navid picked out a tree nearby, and the two men dragged the deer to the tree. Navid uncoiled a rope from around his chest and neck; then tied the rope to the deer's hind feet. He threw the end of the rope over a low tree branch, and the two men began to hoist the deer into the air when they heard a blood-curdling scream.

Navid snapped his head around and saw Yusef running at full speed with a large female brown bear in pursuit. Yusef ran to the nearest tree and scrambled up. The tree was barely bigger than a sapling. Navid and Utana dropped the rope and ran up the slope. By the time they arrived, the bear was swaying the tree in huge arcs. Yusef was in the treetop, clinging desperately and screaming at the top of his lungs. Navid and Utana waved their arms and yelled at the bear. Navid yelled at Yusef to stop screaming, and the bear turned and faced the two new threats. Unexpectedly, both men stopped yelling and sat on the ground staring at the bear's feet. The bear stood on its hind legs bellowing at the two men, its maw open wide and spittle flying. Finally, the bear dropped down and continued to shake its head and snort at the two men. Suddenly it lifted its head and began to sniff. It caught the scent of blood, and without a second thought about the three hunters, ambled down the hill to investigate.

Navid looked up and saw Yusef with an idiotic grin on his face and signaled for him to come down.

Yusef's face was red and sweating from the run and the terror of the bear, "Are we going after the bear? What about the deer? Are we going to go get the deer?"

The words tumbled out so fast, Navid could barely understand him. "Whoa, whoa, whoa," he pointed to the valley, "what do you see?"

Yusef almost shrieked, "The bear's eating my deer." He yelled down into the valley, "Hey, that's my deer!"

Navid looked at the boy and shook his head, "That was your deer. Now it's the bear's deer."

Yusef was beside himself, "Let's kill the bear and get my deer back."

Navid sat on the ground and looked calmly at the young man, "We'll wait right here for you. Trot on down there and ask the bear if you can have the deer. Who knows, maybe she likes you. Maybe she'll think it's a good idea. Give it a shot. What have you got to lose?"

Yusef hung his head, "I'm not getting the deer back, am I?"

Navid stood up and put his hand on the boy's shoulder, "Winter is coming; the bear needs that deer more than we do. We had a good hunt, an invigorating run, and a few moments of sheer terror. What more could we want? Let's leave the bear in peace. Now, why don't you fetch our horses, and we'll head home."

The boy grinned at his hero and ran off to get the horses. Navid sat down next to Utana and smiled at his friend.

"Were we ever that young?" laughed Utana

"Yes, and not too long ago," Navid said and laughed back.

Navid was eighteen years old and a natural leader. Long hours spent outdoors had hardened him. Navid was five foot eleven inches with light brown skin, a neat beard squared off just below his chin, and piercing black eyes. His shoulders, back, and arms were corded muscle from endless hours of training with the bow, sword, and Javelin. In the Magi school, he was one of the main arms trainers, but he was exceptional at stealth. Navid commanded the Scouts, a group of twenty-five men specially chosen for their ability to become invisible. Night or day, the Scouts could move almost unseen and unheard. The Scouts learned to endure thirst and pain to maintain their cover for hours if needed. They were the most elite warriors in Persia, and Navid led them. None of the Scouts would ever think of challenging Navid for leadership. Navid dedicated himself to the Family and his men. His honesty and integrity were his cornerstones. At eighteen, he had already distinguished himself in battle and was one of the finest tacticians in Persia.

Utana was a mirror image of Navid, only smaller, darker, and two years older. He was a Scout and Navid's closest friend.

Utana grew suddenly serious, "And yet look at you now. At eighteen, you are the youngest man to be voted onto the Family Council. The truly amazing thing is there's not one person between age thirteen and seventy who doesn't think you have earned the right to be an elder."

Navid blushed, "It was an amazing honor. I never expected the Family to vote me onto the Council at this age. What if I'm not ready?"

"You're ready, and you know it. But what I want to know is what do you want for the Family? Where are we going?"

Navid thought for a moment, "That's the problem, Utana. I don't know if I agree with being satisfied to be a little family with a little school in the middle of nowhere. We could be so much more. Leyla and I will be married soon, and that opens a whole new set of possibilities." (Leyla's father, Baraz, was the Satrap of southeast Persia. Leyla was Baraz's only child, and the Satrapy will pass to her—in actuality, to her husband—upon Baraz's death.)

"There is no reason in the future not to accept the Satrapy and merge the Family into the ruling family," Navid continued. "The school would continue, and the Family would have political influence for the first time.

We have been satisfied all these years just to be servants of the King or Queen. What if we could be more?"

"What of the Messiah, Navid?"

"The Messiah. For five hundred years, the Family has been sitting around talking about the Messiah. We have put out watchmen every night for five hundred years. If He were going to come, He would have come by now. I don't know if I believe any of it anymore, Utana. Jehovah, the Messiah, a bunch of ancient prophets, all that ancient stuff doesn't have anything to do with us today. It's time to move on."

"Scripture is clear, Navid. When Messiah comes, a great light will precede his coming. You know this. Isaiah and Amos faultlessly prophesied God's judgments, and therefore the prophecy concerning the Messiah must also be true. You know this, Navid."

"No one in Israel, and no one in the Family, has heard from God in over five hundred years. That's what I know. Let's say just for argument's sake, He does come. What then? You have heard all the old discussions. The Family is to travel to Israel to meet the Messiah. The whole Family."

"When He comes, Navid, everyone will want to meet Him, to see Him and talk to Him. God's chosen one. No one in the Family will want to be left behind."

"Utana, think it through. Do you think Queen Musa will just let us go? That she will let a possession she values slip through her fingers. The minute the Family begins to move, she will send the Immortals after us. That is a fact. Everything else is speculation, but you can count on one thing, Queen Musa will never let this Family go."

Just then, Navid looked up and saw Yusef approaching with the horses. "I tell you what, Utana. I want you to begin with the Scouts and ask them if Messiah comes, what should we do.

Send a few representatives or the whole Family. You ask them and let me know. I think the answer will surprise you."

"What will the elders think, Navid? I can't do something like that behind their backs."

"You are not doing anything, Utana. You are not seeking to influence anyone. You're just asking them a question. Do this for me, Utana, please."

"I don't like it, but I'll do it for you. I'll start tomorrow. I have the night watch tonight."

Navid looked at him and rolled his eyes. *The night watch*, he thought, *what a waste of time.*

Navid saw Yusef approach leading the three horses. He studied the boy. Yusef was twelve years old, and his teacher, Rahim, asked Navid to spend some time with him. Yusef's father, Danial, was a malcontent and trouble maker. Yusef acted up in class, and Rahim thought Navid might positively influence the boy.

Scene 2 Persepolis Day -0-

"Navid, Navid, come. Wake up, Navid. The elders have called for you."

Navid's eyes opened, but he couldn't understand what his friend Utana said or why he was saying anything at all in the middle of the night. Utana had the night watch; he told him so this afternoon.

"Utana, what are you doing here? What are you doing in my room?" asked a groggy-looking Navid.

"Stop asking foolish questions." He grabbed Navid's arm and pulled him upright. "Get dressed. The elders have called for all the leaders, and for some stupid reason, they seem to think you are a one."

"If this is one of your jokes, there will be no end to the lessons I will teach you in the sword training ground—after the sun rises."

But Navid saw fear and tension in his friend's eyes. "All right, Utana," Navid said finally, "let me pull on my coat." He did and wore a shawl over his head as he followed Utana.

However, instead of proceeding to the door, Utana climbed the ladder to the roof.

"All right, Utana, this has gone just about far enough. Are the elders having tea on my roof?"

"Yes, I think that's where they are," he replied. "Just stop your tongue from wagging for a while; come, and you might learn something."

They stepped onto the rooftop and saw the Council, the elders, and leaders of the Family. The head of the Family, Navid's grandfather, Fardad, stood to Navid's left with eyes fixed on the night sky. Fardad did not seem to notice them come onto the roof. Next to Fardad stood Navid's father, Jahan—huge and burly. Next to him were the Family's military trainer, Kevan, and his son, Marzban. To Navid's right stood Rahim, the school's headmaster, and the horse trainer, Ram.

Navid's stomach gripped into a tight knot. "Grandfather, are we under attack? Has Utana seen a dust cloud on the horizon clouding the stars?" It is the only plausible explanation for such a gathering in the middle of the night.

But Navid's grandfather didn't seem to hear Navid, and then suddenly the older man's eyes focused, and he looked at Navid. "Look," he said, "look to the southwest. What do you see?"

Navid scanned the horizon, looking for anything unusual. He didn't see dust clouds that might indicate the movement of a large group of people. He didn't see fire signs or anything that would bring the elders onto the roof on a night this cold. "I don't see anything," he replied quietly, knowing that couldn't be the correct answer.

"Look higher, Navid; you are looking with your head, not your heart."

"Heart?" *No way, not happening*, Navid thought, *I'm not looking*; he was terrified at what he might see. For five hundred years, the Family watched the night sky for a sign from God that the Messiah had come. Surely that couldn't be what his grandfather meant. Navid stood frozen for what felt like an eternity, but he could not force himself to look up.

Then, finally, his grandfather stepped close to him, and with great tenderness, he placed his hand under Navid's chin and pushed his head up, pointing his eyes directly at a distant star.

"It could be anything," Navid said. "There could be a distant fire, and this is its reflection. The light could be a comet burning its path across the night sky, or it could be any number of other things."

"It could be," Fardad said softly," but look with your inner eye. We have watched it for two hours now. Look at its size; look at its color and brilliance. Plus, it is locked in place; it has not moved in all this time."

Jahan broke in, "We are the watchers, Navid; for hundreds of years, we have studied the stars and the heavens, just as you have for the past eight years. We have cataloged everything we have ever seen. We have seen comets and their tails; great stars appear or wink out; we understand normal things to the heavenly realms. Yet, we have never seen an anomaly like this. So what does your heart tell you it is, Navid?"

Navid's mouth was so dry, his tongue stuck to the roof of his mouth. He could not speak. Around him, the elders stood in silence. It had to be unanimous; he knew that. They waited for Navid to speak, to give the final confirmation of what they already knew. "It's 'possibly' the sign for which we have long waited. The coming of the Messiah." They all knew the prophecy of Balaam, recorded in the book of Numbers, "A star shall come out of Jacob; a Scepter shall rise out of Israel."[1] In Isaiah, they read, "The people who walked in darkness have seen a great light."[2] These men knew the prophecies.

Grandfather stepped close again, put his hand behind Navid's neck, and kissed him once on each cheek and forehead. Tears were streaming unashamedly down Fardad's face. Jahan, the size of a full-grown bear, also stepped close and embraced Navid; it was like being in a vise. Navid thought at least two of his ribs cracked.

Rahim spoke, "It is late, and there's much to discuss. So I suggest we retire, rest for a while, and meet again in the morning. These old bones don't much care for this night air."

With that, everyone left the roof, but Navid told them he would stay for a while and watch with Utana. After a few moments, Utana and Navid were alone on the rooftop and were both staring at the new star; it was unlike anything they had ever seen. They stood in silence for a while, and Navid broke the silence, "You know what this means, don't you?"

"That our world is about to get turned upside down and changed forever. That all that we have planned and dreamed is about to be irrevocably altered. The Council of Elders will meet in a few hours and determine the fate of every man, woman, and child in the Family. Yesterday afternoon, it all seemed easy and clear to me, and now I feel empty and terrified." Utana's voice cracked, and tears ran down his face.

Navid stood with Utana for a while, both of them fixated as they watched the 'anomaly' in the sky. Finally, Navid reached over and gently squeezed Utana's arm. "This is no time for despair, my friend. We have a few hours before the Council meets, so let's think back through everything we know. Help me prepare for the Council meeting."

Utana brightened. "Excellent, Navid, excellent. Let's talk this through," he said.

Navid began, "Let's not leave out anything. Who are we? We are the Magi; we call ourselves the Family because we function together as one family. We descended from the Chaldean/Babylonian Magi. There are other Magi in the Persian Empire from Syria and Assyria, but ours is the last of the Chaldean Magi. Our Family possesses the writings of the prophets of Israel, Isaiah, Jeremiah, and Daniel. The Magi alone, of the Gentile world, have studied all the Hebrew Scriptures, and we worship Jehovah. We have not converted to Judaism. We are secret believers in God; no one outside the Family knows of our beliefs. The Magi believe there is one true God, and He has a plan that includes us, the Gentiles[3]. That plan is the Messiah, as foretold in Scripture, who comes to rule and reign over the world."

"We also know," said Utana, "that the Magi are a valued part of the Persian Empire, and the empire is facing a political crisis. Queen Musa is co-ruler with her son King Phraates V. Queen Musa successfully exiled the children of King Phraates IV, her husband, and then murdered Phraates IV and took the throne. The Satraps, the regional governors, are convinced that Queen Musa has married her son, and revolt is in the air. The Persian ruling class can accept murder but cannot bear incest in the Royal family."

"Excellent Utana," said Navid, "in keeping with that thought. The Magi—versed in military tactics and strategy, literature, history, mathematics, philosophy, astronomy, and astrology—have been the military trainers and educators of Persian Royalty for hundreds of years. The contact with the ruling elites gives us influence and power within the empire. In addition, we select and train the Queen's guard, the Immortals, in one of the most relentless and grueling training camps ever known. There is one way into the training camp, selection by the Magi, and two ways out—success or death. Our friendship with the Satraps and the military puts the Magi in a unique political position. Our influence will significantly impact whether the military leaders stand with the Queen and King or join the Satraps in open revolt. The Satraps are powerful, but unless they can convince the military leaders to join them, there will be no revolt."

"Also," continued Utana, truly getting into the spirit of the exercise, "we alone have a unique recording of history for the past 750 years. We had members on both sides of every political struggle. We recorded the prophecies of Isaiah, Jeremiah, and Daniel, and we participated in the armies that carried out the judgments they prophesied. The Family's scrolls contain all of this knowledge. The judgments against Israel and Judah, judgments against Philistia, Edom, Syria, Assyria, Babylon, Egypt, Ammon, and Moab are all recorded in the scrolls[4]. Then the redemption of Israel from Babylonian captivity by Cyrus, King of Persia, as foretold by Isaiah. And now, after all these years, we have witnessed the fulfillment of the last prophecy, the coming of the Messiah[5]. We will be a part of writing the last scroll."

"Utana, your input has been invaluable. I can't think of any other pertinent facts, can you?" Utana shook his head no. "That leaves us with a response." Said Navid, "What should the Family do now? I see only two possible responses."

"Actually, three," responded Utana, "send a delegation, send the Family, or send no one."

"I accept that in theory there are three potential responses, but the Council would not countenance sending no one. I feel I can make an excellent argument for sending a representative. The single greatest argument for sending a representative is the safety of the Family. There is no doubt in my mind that when the Queen finds out the Magi Family is traveling by caravan to Israel, she will send the Immortals to stop us. Some of us may survive, but undoubtedly she will have to make a strong statement about what happens to those who disobey her."

"I'm beginning to see your point," Utana replied, his face drawn with worry, "and on the other hand, if we successfully make it to Israel, we have no idea how we will be received by either the current leadership or the Messiah. We are Gentiles; we are not Jews. We think we know what

Scripture says, but what if we are wrong? We would be walking into a death trap. You are right, Navid; there is only one sensible choice. You must convince the Council to send a representative."

As Utana finished speaking, the first rays of morning peaked over the mountains to their east. "Wish me well, Utana. I will work to convince the Council, but as you know, I will be up against both my grandfather and father. The Council meeting will be the hardest battle I have ever faced. After you have rested, go and talk to the Scouts, as we discussed yesterday."

"No time for rest, brother. I am heading to the corral immediately. I am going to do more than take an opinion poll. I am going to rally support. The Scouts will stand with you; you can count on that."

Navid and Utana grasped each other's right forearms in a sign of respect and agreement, and Navid descended from the roof.

Scene 3 The Council

As he descended the ladder from the roof, Navid heard the sounds of the household beginning to stir with the coming of the dawn. On the roof, he did not smell the change in the air or hear the first calls of the animals as they greeted the sun. But despite his state of distraction, there was one thing that no 18-year-old male's subconscious is capable of blocking out, and that is the smell of food cooking. The smell of bread in the oven and goat stew on the hearth brought Navid back to this world and banished all thoughts of the potential Apocalypse to come. Ponderings concerning the Council could wait until after eating. He went down to the kitchen; his mother, Asha, and her household maid, Gul, were cooking.

Fahnik, his sister, one year older than him, came into the house after her morning trip to the well. She wore her winter robe, lined with pure-white lamb fleece, which outlined her tanned face. She had a prominent nose, but not disproportionate, that she needed to counterbalance her large, soft, almost-black eyes. Her skin shone with the health of youth and a good diet, and as always, a smile creased her perpetually joyful face. She was not frivolous or foolish; she could not hide the peace and love she felt for the Family, even if she tried. As Navid looked at her this morning, he was amazed, as always, at how much she resembled Asha, their mother, with each passing year. Some man, and he had a good idea who, would be lucky to have her as his wife. But this morning, Navid felt a tug of fear as he looked at her and thought about how the decisions made this morning would impact her life forever.

Pari, Navid's sister, two years younger than him, was already on her eating mat. She was as beautiful as their mother, but a congenital disability had impacted her. She was born with withered legs and had never walked. Her inactivity caused her to be painfully thin, her skin almost transparent, and the gauntness of her face made her eyes appear even more prominent than Fahnik's. Navid loved Pari and felt responsible for her. He never heard her complain or compare her life to anyone else's. She accepted her condition as the will of God and believed she was unique, and God had chosen her for some specific reason. She knew and memorized more scripture than anyone in the Family. Her faith and her prayer life astounded and mystified him. She may not have been angry with God, but Navid certainly was.

Why would God impose such a horrible disability on one so pure and loving, on one who loved Him so much? It made no sense to Navid, and it distorted his view of God and his relationship with Him. Her disability also affected Navid another way; he was two years past the age he should have married. Yes, he knew the woman he would marry and was very attracted to her, but Navid could not bring himself to abandon Pari. After the decisions of the Council today, Navid would more than likely have to address his betrothed much sooner than he wanted to.

Sitting next to Pari on his eating mat sat Tiz, who is a mystery to the family. His mother came to the Family compound twenty-two years ago. She wandered in after a snowstorm near death. She was pregnant when she came and went into labor shortly after she arrived. She was too weak to survive labor, but Tiz survived. No one knew where she came from or anything else about her. A childless woman agreed to raise Tiz, and he became a part of the Magi Family. Tiz's adopted parents both died a few years ago, and now he lives alone. He was six feet tall, four years older than Navid, and built like a young god with broad shoulders, narrow hips, and legs with corded muscles. He was one of the finest warriors in the Magi Family, but his heart wasn't in it. Yes, he enjoyed wrestling with the other young men, not that it was optional, and he loved his time in the field with the Scouts, but these were not his first loves. He was gentle, quiet, and kind, and with either a paintbrush or clay in his hands, he could create sheer magic. His hands were large, perfect for handling weapons. Still, his fingers were long and thin and perfectly suited to creating small delicate details when painting or when sculpting animals so lifelike you expected them to breathe. After Pari was born, it appeared Tiz found his true purpose in life. Tiz became inseparable from Pari after she turned two. That is when it became apparent she would never walk. Tiz was there every day for every activity.

When Tiz began to help with Pari, their father became concerned, and he and Tiz talked at length about his involvement with her. Tiz convinced Jahan that he was drawn to her by her gentle nature and her need for physical assistance. Tiz argued that as Pari grew, it would be increasingly difficult for Asha and the other women to carry her and care for her. Tiz pleaded with Jahan to let him help and devote himself to her care. Unheard of, no one had ever experienced this type of relationship before. Jahan relented and told Tiz we would see how it went; that was fourteen years ago, and the relationship between Tiz and Pari grew stronger and closer each year. Tiz knew there would be obstacles he would have to overcome to assist Pari fully, but he diligently pursued solutions.

Preserving Pari's and the other women's modesty was the first thing to be solved. So he fashioned a hood for himself made of thick material that allowed him to see some amount of light but no details, and he trained himself to walk wearing the hood and to do other simple tasks, such as tying and untying strings. Then, when ready, he showed the hood to Jahan and explained what he intended. Jahan was delighted. By wearing the hood, Tiz could take Pari to the women's areas in the morning, and he could also carry her to the bath and help her undo the fasteners on her robe. From that point on, Jahan had absolute confidence in Tiz, and Tiz and Pari were inseparable.

Only one event terrified the family, when Pari was eight and Tiz was fourteen. Tiz took her to the sports field where the children played and practiced athletic events; although she couldn't participate, Pari loved watching the other children play. Tiz set her in the shade of a few trees by the field and left her for an hour while he practiced with the scout squadron. When Tiz returned to the area, he saw Pari surrounded by three boys, taunting her and kicking dust on her. One boy, holding a rock, kept feinting as if he would throw it at her. With the speed of one trained to combat, Tiz pounced on the boys so fast they could not escape. He grabbed one boy by the nape of his neck and lifted him, and with his right hand, he grabbed the boy with the rock by his arm and lifted him. Then, as if he were swinging two feather dusters, he smashed the two boys together with such force he knocked the wind out of both of them. Pari cried, terrified by both the boys' action and the ferocity of Tiz's attack.

Men close by saw Tiz attack the boys and rushed to their assistance, including the father of one of the boys. By the time they reached the group, Tiz had placed the two boys on the ground and tended to Pari. The father of one of the boys screamed at Tiz, and the situation escalated until cooler heads prevailed and convinced the boys' father to bring charges against Tiz with the elders and let them adjudicate the affair. The next day, Tiz appeared before Fardad, the head elder of the Family, and his accuser presented evidence against Tiz. Pari also gave testimony and explained the events leading up to Tiz's actions. Fardad ruled that Tiz acted correctly in coming to the defense of Pari but warned Tiz that if he ever took physical action against any of the other children in the future, he would no longer be allowed to care for Pari. There was no subsequent event for two excellent reasons, Tiz would do anything to ensure he would be with Pari, and the children in the Family were terrified of displeasing Tiz.

At almost the same time that Navid arrived in their home's common area, Jahan also arrived for the morning meal, and they sat on their mats to eat. First, as he did every morning, Jahan prayed about the things God placed on his heart. "Almighty God, Creator of Heaven and Earth, your ways are far from our ways, as far as the east is from the west so far are your ways from our ways. We seek your guidance and will this day as the Council meets to discuss what you have revealed. Bless us and guide us, and bless this food to our bodies. Amen." Everyone used the freshly made bread to scoop the hot and savory stew from the pot set between them.

No one spoke, not having any idea what to say. Of course, Jahan talked to his wife about what they saw, and she shared it with the girls and Gul when she woke them, and the decisions to be made by the Council this morning weighed heavily on everyone's mind. Everyone internalized what this would mean to them and to the people they loved. There was nothing to discuss. The Council would meet and decide the fate of the Family.

With the meal finished, Jahan rose and, without a word, looked at Navid and nodded. Navid joined his father, and they walked together to the school, which also contained the Council meeting chamber. The other Council members were there: Kevan and Marzban, Rahim, Ram, and of course, Fardad. Sasan was missing, Jahan's younger brother. Over the years, Sasan became increasingly attracted to the Magi of the Court in Susa and spent more and more of his time there. He loved the political intrigue and the mystical religions and astrology and was more comfortable with the like-minded Magi of Susa. However, he fell away from the worship of Jehovah and hated his time in Persepolis. His relationship with his brother, Jahan, was strained for years. Sasan, jealous of Jahan's leadership role and relationship with their father, chose to go to Susa. But there was a quorum, and the Council would proceed without Sasan. They seated themselves on their mats and waited for Fardad to begin.

Fardad called the Council to order, not announcing the purpose of the meeting; it was evident to everyone present. Ram stood and spoke first. "I know we all saw something last night, but I don't think it's a good idea to jump too quickly to conclusions. Even if it is a sign, a sign of what … The Messiah? We have waited all these years, and now we have seen a new star to the west, and we immediately want to believe it is the long-awaited sign. So I recommend caution and patience. If it is the Messiah, and if God wants us to help Him, He will get a message to us. It's too soon; we need to wait and see what develops." With that, Ram sat down. It was the longest string of words they ever heard from Ram. He spent his whole life with horses and spoke to them readily, but communication with people was rare for him.

Rahim stood. "What we saw last night was no ordinary star, and you know that. Do I believe it is the sign of the Messiah's arrival? It is possible, but I agree with Ram that this is not the time for haste. We need several more sightings of the star, if that is what it is, to verify its fixed position, and we need to be in prayer for guidance to see what Jehovah would have us do. If it is the sign of the Messiah's arrival, are we going to Israel to help form His war Council or train His court and officer core? Or are we to stay right here and form a nucleus from which He can launch an assault against Persia? We don't know nearly enough about His plans or intentions to help Him. At most, I would recommend sending a small delegation to Israel to meet with Him to understand how He wants to use us."

Sage counsel; well done, Rahim, Navid thought—precisely what he would recommend. Now, when he stood in support of Rahim, he would appear obedient and deferential to his elder, not as if he feared an early total commitment. And with those thoughts buoying his spirits, he rose to speak, but as he did, Fardad raised his hand and motioned him to stay seated. Fardad had never silenced a Council member before. Every member had a right to rise and speak before Fardad weighed all arguments and spoke on an issue. He was about to protest when Fardad rose to speak.

"My friends and brothers, I apologize for not speaking first, but I thank Ram and Rahim for their counsel, and I weighed those same thoughts during the night. Early this morning, about an hour before dawn, when the night seems the longest and our thoughts are the darkest, a man appeared in my chamber. I grabbed my sword, but he held out his hands to show me that he was not armed, and he told me not to be afraid. 'Fear not,' he said, 'for I have been sent to you to explain the Star you have seen.'"

Oh no, oh no, thought Navid. *Anything but this. What possible argument could he use against an angel? Rahim's response had been perfect.* Ram and Rahim would have supported him, but an angel of the Lord. Navid shook his head in disbelief.

"'The Messiah has been born this night in Bethlehem in Judea, and you are to take your Family and go and worship[6] Him.' I had a thousand questions for him, but he disappeared. My heart hammered in my chest; I could not catch my breath. I must speak to him. There are so many things to decide. We needed answers, but he left. He came, and he left, and he told me all that we need to know."

Navid felt everything slipping away; his hopes for the future, Leyla, the Satrapy, military, and political leadership. The very existence of the Family was in jeopardy. He was furious, but he held his emotions in check. There would be no way to fight Fardad and his father now.

"We are to go, the entire Family. We are going to worship Him. Worship Him? We worship only God. As He states so often in Scripture, God is one, and we are to worship only Him, but this Angel from the Lord told me we are to go and worship. I cannot understand it or explain it. I also thought about whether to send a delegation or to travel with the Family. I have three concerns; if we send a delegation and Queen Musa finds out, she may punish those who have remained. Secondly, it is a long and dangerous trip, and we have a better chance of surviving if we all go. Lastly, and most importantly, this Family has waited hundreds of years for the coming of the Messiah; everyone has earned the right to see and worship him." With that, Fardad sat down.

Navid's worst fear had come true. The whole Family would go unless another council member objected to the plan. He knew he could not take the lead against this plan.

There was a long silence. No one stood to talk. Every Council member thought about how to respond to what Fardad had said? The wizened veteran of many wars and much training, Kevan stood to speak. "I am a simple man. I have known Fardad my whole life, and we have all conjectured how we would respond if the Messiah came. The Angel has said we are to go and worship. I don't see how we can send a delegation. Fardad is right; the Family must go. We are fortunate in one thing, the court is in Susa for the winter, and both the school and military training camps are closed until the end of winter. We will have, for the next few weeks, our greatest opportunity to leave without discovery. In the future, we will measure everything from today. The day of the Star is day zero, the day the world changed."

Fardad looked every man in the eye. "Day Zero. Kevan is right; this is the day the world changed. The decision for the Family to go must be unanimous. Do we follow the Lord and go?"

Navid's heart sank. It was over. No one would speak against the plan. They were blindly marching to their deaths, and only he could see it. All he could do now was fight with everything in him for the Family's survival. And that is what he would do.

Almost as one, every man stood and saluted Fardad by placing their right fists over their hearts. "We will go," they all said. Grandfather stood and embraced each one of them and said, "And so we shall."

CHAPTER 2

The Journey - Day 14

Navid loved this time of the morning, the usual quiet before first light, the smell and feel of the dew, the first stirring of the prey that survived the nocturnal hunters. But this morning was different.

Today they would depart. Navid did everything he could to gather enough support to forestall the departure. He did not want the Family to make this trip, but he failed. Even the Scouts, whom he led, were reluctant to join him in his efforts to sway the elders. No one understood that sending representatives was a far safer course than taking the whole Family to Israel. Now it was too late; the Family had packed food, their belongings were in wagons, tents made or repaired, weapons stockpiled, herds and flocks brought from their grazing grounds. In a few hours, the compound where he sat and had spent his life would be empty. As empty as his soul. Everything he ever hoped and dreamed ended today. He would not be Satrap of southeast Persia; he would not be the leader of the Magi; he would not become the military leader of Persia. He sat on the rooftop watching the sunrise, but he had no joy or hope today, only despair.

Navid heard someone climbing the ladder and turned to see Grandfather's head appear through the roof opening. Grandfather knew Navid would be here.

"You seem deep in thought," Grandfather said. "I know you are troubled by this trip. Can we talk?"

Fardad was fifty-eight years old, had grey hair, and had a slight stoop when he walked. He had a long beard, deep-set eyes, and dark leathered skin from constant exposure to the sun. He led the Magi Family, and his word was law. He was the kindest and wisest man Navid knew. Navid nodded yes, and Grandfather sat next to him.

"It's not fair, Grandfather. Why does everyone have to go?"

"You know why. The Council voted, including you, that the Family would travel to Israel to meet and worship the Messiah. We presented the decision to the Family, and everyone agreed. Navid, the Magi are—"

Navid blurted, "—an important part of the Persian Empire. When Queen Musa discovers the Magi have gone, she will be enraged. If she doesn't kill all of us, we will be a people without a country. We will never be allowed to return to Persia, and it's not fair."

Fardad's shoulders drooped. "Not fair? That is the boy I used to know who is speaking, not a man, not a Council member. *We* have not chosen the timing; God has. God is the Creator and Sustainer of all you see. From the beginning of time, He had a plan to redeem fallen mankind. The coming of the Messiah fulfills that plan, and God has called us to go and worship Him."

"Maybe my faith isn't as strong as your faith, Grandfather. I know who God is, but I just don't think we have to be part of His plan."

"We have not arbitrarily chosen to go. The angel of the Lord instructed us to go and to worship the Messiah. You were in the Council meeting, you heard the discussion, and you agreed on the decision. Why this vacillation?"

"In my heart, I know that we are about to destroy this Family. Nothing good can come from this trip. After we worship the Messiah, then what? What do we do then? We cannot return to Persia, and the Angel didn't reveal what would happen to us. Did He?"

Grandfather's face tightened. "You were part of the decision, and you know what the Angel said."

Navid looked at his feet. "I voted *aye* because I didn't want to disappoint you; I didn't want to disappoint Father, not because I truly supported this journey."

The roof was silent. Navid could hear the whisper of the wind; he could hear the sounds of preparation far below. He sat there with his head bowed, not wanting to see the disappointment in his grandfather's face. Navid felt a gentle hand on his shoulder, "Navid, do you think God loves you?"

This was not a question Navid expected. "I don't think God thinks about me very much. He's pretty busy with more important things. He let the most beautiful and faithful person I know be born with a congenital disability. No, I don't think God gives us a second thought."

"He has blessed you with loving parents. God has gifted you with strength and intelligence, and He has given your sister an unshakeable faith. Despite her disability, she sees and feels His love."

"Do I have loving parents and a loving family? Yes, and I am thankful for them. My intelligence I inherited from my parents and you. Plus, I have had the best teachers in all of Persia. As for my strength, I have worked endless hours to harden myself and build myself into the man I am today."

"God has kept you safe from harm; He has provided food and clothing. He has done everything for you."

"You give God credit for everything, Grandfather. The Family plants and harvests, and mother weaves, knits, and prepares animal skins for our clothing. I know who to thank for all these things, and it isn't God."

Grandfather continued, undaunted, "In His wisdom and omnipotence, God has decided the time is suitable for the Messiah to come. And He has chosen us, of all the people he could have chosen; He has chosen us. We are privileged to be called to go and worship his Chosen one."

"You act as if God has done us a huge favor. We will be running for our lives to escape Persia before the Immortals can find us. We will spend a few days worshipping the Messiah, and then all hope for a future ends for the Family. That is the fate we chose for the Family."

"Do you think God, having chosen us, will not provide a way for us to reach Israel? Do you think after our obedience to His command, He will abandon us?" Grandfather asked. "Navid, you must have faith. Now get up; this will be a long day, and you have much to do. We can talk again tonight."

Navid was furious. "Faith. I have faith in my sword and my bow. I have faith in the Scouts, who I will lead on this journey. I have faith that we will do everything in our power to get this Family safely to Israel. I love this Family and will do everything in my power to protect it. That's what I have faith in." With that, Navid descended the ladder and went to join his family for its last meal in Persepolis.

The two weeks of preparation were now complete. The Magi would be traveling with seven ox-drawn carts; three would carry the old and the young who could not complete the journey on horseback or camel. The other four carts would have tents, clothing, food, baking ovens, portable forge ovens, and weapons. The only people who would complete the journey on foot would be the shepherds, who would care for the families' herds of sheep, goats, horses, and cattle. They were leaving nothing behind; they would travel with everything they owned.

In the center of the formation, each day would be the women, the children, and the elderly. Kevan assigned every warrior to one of the protection forces. Navid and his twenty-five Scouts would lead the caravan. They were the vanguard.

Flanking the main body would be two groups of twenty men each. Adel would lead the right flank. Adel was thirty years old and a seasoned veteran, as were most of his men. Hosh, the elder statesman of the military team at fifty years of age, led the left flank. There were discussions concerning his age and his ability to endure the rigors of riding flank on a trip of 1,000 miles. In the end, Kevan decided to leave him in leadership. Still, he appointed a second in command, Jangi, to take over should the physical demands of the trip take a significant toll on Hosh.

Trailing the formation each day would be the rearguard led by Jahan himself. While they were still in Persia, their most significant concern was that Queen Musa might send a force to stop them from reaching the border. The flocks, herds, and shepherds would travel among the right and left flanks and the main body. Most of the shepherds, both men and women, had served in this capacity since birth. Helping them on the trip would be some older boys and girls. All of the herders had trained with the sling and were perfectly capable of helping to protect the animals. They would only be able to travel each day at the pace of the slowest group, and that would be the oxen and the grazing herds. On most days, they would cover ten miles. They may exceed this on some of the flatter sections, but in the mountains surrounding Persepolis and the deserts they would cross, the travelers would be fortunate to make five miles a day. They would also have to stop periodically to let the herds graze.

The first three weeks of the journey might very well be the most hazardous of the trip. The vanguard spent the past two weeks scouting the area to the Persian Gate, the pass they would use to cross the Zagros Mountains to get to the western plains of Persia. The passage through the mountains meant they must use the Persian Gate, located northwest of Persepolis. Using the Gate presented one of the greatest dangers of the trip. There were three main concerns—the Uxians, a small hill-tribe that lived near the pass and demanded a "toll" from anyone desiring to use the Gate, the possibility of snowstorms, and lastly, the concern that the Uxians would send word to Queen Musa of the passage of the Magi.

To overcome the first obstacle, Kevan met with Taghi, the elder of the Uxians, in a village near the pass. Kevan negotiated with Taghi for two days before reaching an agreement for the terms of passage. Naturally, the payment would be made in gold and amounted to almost three times the standard rate. The fee covered the toll for the Family and six Uxian warriors to accompany the Magi for the next two weeks since they were more familiar with the territory beyond the pass and could serve as guides. As Taghi knew, the Magi had been integral in mapping most of the Persian Empire. Therefore he knew the Magi didn't need guides. Selected among the six guides were two of Taghi's sons; the message to Taghi was clear that if he warned Queen Musa, the guides would die. It wasn't perfect, but it was the best they could do. Now, they hoped that Taghi liked his sons more than gold. A definite toss-up.

Navid did not know how they would keep the passage of the Magi Family from the attention of the Royal Court for the next three months, but their lives depended on doing just that. Navid loved his grandfather and knew him to be a wise man, but it was obvious his Grandfather had no idea how to hide the Family's movement through Persia. Every time Navid brought up the subject, Grandfather responded by telling Navid to have faith in God. Unbelievable. Grandfather had indelibly etched in Navid's mind the saying—"God has called us to go to the Messiah, so God will get us there, and nothing can stop us." Navid wasn't sure he could bear to hear it one more time.

Navid thought, *seriously, this is the answer? God will somehow make us invisible or something. God will perform a miracle. He will surround us with angels and fight for us. What? If He wants us to get through, He better send an army and a big one at that. We are not Israel; God has not chosen us. We are a bunch of Gentile Magi who have studied the Hebrew Scriptures for more than 750 years and have deluded ourselves that somehow we are to be a part of some mystical plan of God's.*

Navid couldn't believe only he could see this.

The Magi had one thing in their favor. Their Family was the only people left in what was once the capital of Persia, Persepolis. Alexander the Great destroyed the city more than 300 years ago, but he did not touch the Family compound because of its distance from Persepolis.

The Family chose the remote canyon location because of its solitude and security for the training camp and classrooms. This rural location suited them perfectly. The Court abandoned Persepolis; there was nothing left. The Court moved the summer capital to Estakhr, around fifteen miles to the north. Fortunately, the Court wintered in Susa, and therefore, the Family's movements would go unnoticed for some time. They chose the mountain road instead of the Royal Road to the west because the Queen would hear of the Family's movement much sooner if they took the Royal Road, whereas the mountain road through the Pass had almost no travel on it during the winter months. The only logical decision was to take the eastern route then go west through the Gate to reach the flatlands west of the mountains.

When Navid went down to the kitchen, the house was still dark, but he saw fresh bread and a stew pot on the hearth. The family would be too busy to sit down to a meal this morning, so Navid dipped some of the stew into a small bowl, broke off a piece of the bread, and went to his eating mat. There was also fresh goat cheese on a board by the mats, and he used his knife to cut off a piece and put it on his bread. They always prayed before eating, but Navid was mad at God this morning since He was sending the Family to its death, and Navid chose not to pray. *There, take that*, he thought. So he ate in silence, and as he finished, Tiz came down carrying Pari. Tiz gently set her on her mat and went and got food for both of them.

They were both dressed for traveling, as was Navid. The first section of the trip, through the mountains, would be bitterly cold. Pari wore a dark-blue heavy woolen robe that went to her ankles, and she wore deerskin boots lined with fox fur. She wore two beautiful gold necklaces, one with a large, deep-blue stone of Lapis Lazuli set in it, and it was Pari's prized possession, a gift from Tiz. No one knew where Tiz got the stone, but it was worth a small fortune. She never took it off. Pari also put on two wool scarves; her mother and Fahnik had each knit one. She would need them both to keep out the mountain winds blowing down from the north.

Tiz and Navid dressed alike. They both wore white, heavy-wool outer coats that reached their knees; the coats had a slit on each side that reached from knee to hip, so the coat would drape over their legs when mounted. They wore deerskin pants tucked into the top of their boots to protect them from the wind. Their outer garments were white to blend with the snow in the mountains. They wore silk shirts under their coats to keep in their body warmth. The silk also worked with the light chest protection made of woven reeds worn under their coats to protect them from arrows and swords. It wasn't a lot of security, but it was often adequate to keep a wound from being fatal. They also wore woolen scarfs, and their robes had hoods lined with fox fur. Like Pari, they wore deerskin boots lined with fox fur, along with deerskin mittens to protect their hands. The mittens were attached to a cord that ran through both sleeves. The cord kept the mittens from being lost if they needed to remove them quickly.

Their weapons stood next to the door; for the remainder of the trip, they would carry a six-inch hunting knife, a curved iron sword, and the shorter recurved bow, meant to be used from horseback. They carried small wicker shields, smaller than their standard combat shields, but would be adequate in a fight from horseback. In addition, they carried two quivers on their backs, one with arrows and the other with their javelins.

The javelin was their favorite weapon; it could be thrown or used to stab. They were all trained and skilled with every weapon.

Navid picked up his weapons and walked out the door. The air was cold but dry this morning, and the winds were down. This weather was a good omen for the first day of travel. Outside, he looked at the rock walls, forming this perfect canyon. The walls kept them safe and secure from bandits and armies for the past 500 years. He walked to the rock base and climbed to the parapet; the last guard force came down to prepare for the journey. He walked down the length of the parapet, looking at the small city his ancestors and he called home for all of their lives and felt a tug of homesickness, and they hadn't even left. He scanned the surrounding valley and mountains, searing the images into his memory, places where he learned to ride and hunt, streams he swum and fished. He remembered running through the wheat fields under the wall along with Utana and other childhood friends. Navid's eyes misted, and he shook his head, trying to shake away this feeling of loss. He didn't want to forget these images of the home that had sheltered him, grew him to manhood, and that he might never see again. He couldn't imagine feeling more conflicted than he did at that moment. He stood on the parapet and did a slow pirouette, taking in everything he could see.

Then, without hesitation, he descended the stairs and walked across the central square to the stables. Three of the Scouts were putting tack on their horses. They would each be taking a string of four horses; three would stay in the herd driven by the herdsmen each day. Navid saddled Anosh, his three-year-old black Arabian of fifteen hands, and his favorite. The horse's coat was jet-black, and he had beautiful conformation. He was not the most seasoned of Navid's mounts, but he had an instinct for hunting and combat and was the fastest horse in the remuda. Anosh was a gift from Ram, who selected him, especially for Navid. The horse was strong-spirited, and Ram wanted him taught, not broken. He knew he could trust Navid to bend the horse's will without breaking his spirit. It took great patience, but the big Arabian and Navid now thought and moved as one. In the hunt, he never used reigns— slight knee pressure was all that was required, and even that wasn't required often.

Anosh always knew how to put Navid in a perfect position and speed to deliver a killing blow when hunting. In combat, he was even more adept since the stakes were far higher. He used his great bulk to cause an opposing horse to stumble at just the right moment. This provided Navid the fraction of a second necessary to deliver a blow. Anosh's favorite move was to close with an opponent from Navid's off-hand and then, at the last moment, to leap to his left, hitting the oncoming horse flush in the nose and bringing Navid's sword or javelin to bear. The force of the blow delivered this way was enough to sever a man in two. The first time the horse did this, it happened so fast Navid had no idea what the horse had done. The force was so great he strained every tendon in his arm. The second time he was still almost as stunned, but he knew how to manage the blow. Finally, the third time Navid figured out that Anosh did it on purpose; one of them was a slow learner. The only downside to his uncanny ability was Navid could never ride him in combat exercises—he terrified the Scout platoon, and no one would oppose him.

Over the next thirty minutes, the rest of the platoon showed up, put the tack on their horses, and mounted. Every other man would carry a ram's horn used to signal the men in the company. In addition, there were general signals for oncoming weather or wind storms, friendly contact, unknown contact, and hostile contact. Navid led the Scouts out of the stables and formed them in ranks in the compound's central courtyard; Jahan and Kevan were there to greet them and give last-minute orders. As the Scouts rode up and sat tall, they saluted Jahan and Kevan. They were all young men, experienced in combat and hunting, but today marked the beginning of a journey unlike anything they had ever known. They would be moving through unfamiliar territories populated by people who may or may not want to be their friends, and the Scouts were responsible for the Family's safety.

On every face, there was tension and concern. Jahan read that tension in them and was glad of it; it would keep them sharp. They halted in front of Jahan, and he addressed them from horseback. "Each of you knows your job. You will ride in pairs in the front of the line of march, to the left side and right side of the main formation. You will ride in an arrowhead formation. In case of trouble, you need to give the Family as much warning time as possible. When attacked, you need to slow the enemy till the flanks can move up and help you. You are the vanguard, the safety of everyone in the Family is in your hands, and Kevan and I have absolute confidence in you. As you ride out today, look around and remember your home; it has served the Family well for more than 500 years. We have no idea if or when we will ever see our home again. God has called us. We are riding out today in absolute faith in God and His Word; our lives are in His hands, and we can't ask for any more than that. We go to meet the King of Kings whom Israel has waited for since Abraham[7]. This trip is a mission that each of us must decide to follow on our own; we will not force any man to go whose heart is not in it. If any feel they need to fall out and remain behind, now is the last opportunity you will have. Fall out now, and no one will think any the less of you for your decision." Jahan sat atop his horse and looked into the eyes of each man. In the back of the platoon, someone beat his javelin against his shield rhythmically. Another picked it up and then another until the platoon drummed their shields in a time-honored salute to their commander before combat. Jahan let it build into a thunderous sound, wanting the whole compound to hear them before he waved them to silence. He smiled at the Scouts, sat tall on his horse, saluted, and said, "Go with God." Navid signaled forward to the Scouts and led them out of the compound.

The first day, Navid rode point with his friend Utana riding behind him. He expected the first day to be easy; even though they climbed into the mountains, the grades were gentle. However, as they climbed, the trees thinned, and the main body of travelers slowed. About an hour before sunset, Navid pulled the vanguard back to the primary formation, and when all outriders were in, Kevan gave the assignments for perimeter watch. Those who weren't in the first watch went to find their families and talk about the first day's events. When the Scouts arrived, the women had fires going with cauldrons of meat stew and vegetable curries boiling; the women decided to serve all meals communally. Navid could smell the fresh bread baking and sweet yogurt rice. Navid felt as if he hadn't eaten in a month.

Navid found his mother and Gul baking bread, nearby, Tiz placed eating mats under a small fir tree, and Pari sat on her mat. Tiz told Navid that Fahnik had first watch with the herdsmen and would eat later. Jahan joined them, and they filled small pots from the larger communal cooking pots, taking care to complement the cooks, and then sat down to eat. Jahan gave thanks for good travels that day and for the food they were about to receive. Spirits were surprisingly high tonight, and they talked easily of the events of the day and what each of them felt as they said *goodbye* to their home.

Utana showed up to see how "they" were doing, and Navid could see the look of disappointment on his face when he noted that Fahnik was missing. "Utana, how kind of you to stop by to see if mother needed help," Navid said, barely keeping the sarcasm out of his voice. Utana blushed a bright shade of red and stuttered, "Asha, um I wanted to, um check on you…no, no, not check, I mean wanted to see, um."

"Utana," Navid continued, "what in the world has happened to you? You seem to have suddenly developed a speech impediment. Are you well?"

Asha came to the poor lad's rescue, "Oh for heaven's sake, Navid, could you please try not to act like the rear end of a donkey in front of our guest?" That brought a broad smile to Utana's face as he stuck his tongue out at Navid.

"Utana," said Asha, "Fahnik has first watch with the herdsmen tonight and will be in later."

Utana brightened and offered to take some bread out to her until she could get back for dinner.

"Boy," said Jahan, "I don't think the girl will starve to death in the matter of a few hours."

Asha cut off two slices of bread and slathered on goat cheese; she wrapped it in cloth and handed it to Utana. "Please ignore these two idiots, and thank you for being so considerate."

Utana took the package, gloating as he looked at Navid, and went out to find Fahnik. Mother merely glared at Jahan and Navid as they shook hands and congratulated themselves on their fine wit.

A short while later, Rahim rang the evening study bell, and the children of the Family gathered for their lessons in grammar, writing, mathematics, and history. Just because they were traveling didn't mean there would be a cessation in learning. Schooling would continue for the Magi children as it had for the past seven hundred years.

CHAPTER 3

Rahim

Scene 1 Northwest Of Persepolis - Day 14

"Good evening, children," Rahim greeted the children seated on the ground around him in the center of the camp. "During the day, I will be teaching the younger children who are in the wagon with me. In addition, we will hold abbreviated teaching sessions each day following the evening meal for those who have duties with the flocks. I know you will be tired from the day's journey. Therefore, our lessons will focus primarily on history. This trip is an opportunity for us to review the history recorded by our ancestors. These recorded events cover 750 years and explain why we are on this journey. The older children have heard this history several times, but this will be new for the younger children. For 2,000 years, the Patriarchs, Judges, Kings, and Prophets of Israel had received revelations and visions by God, visions of a Messiah who would come to save His people. We believe that He has now come, and as God has commanded us, we will go and worship Him.

Our lesson tonight starts with, Domara, a Magi in the court of the Assyrian king, Tiglath-Pileser III. Domara was the first of our family to recognize the truth of Jehovah, and he was..." Rahim paused because, in the front row of the children, eight-year-old Farida, the daughter of Marzban, stood with her hand held straight up above her head, waving wildly.

"Yes, Farida," Rahim said softly.

"Does that mean we're Jewish, teacher?" Farida asked with her eyes wide and staring in wonder.

Rahim smiled at her, replying, "No, of course not, Farida. We are the descendants of a long line of Chaldean magi, who have been taught the scriptures by Isaiah and Daniel, themselves, two of the most devoted prophets of Israel." Seeming satisfied, but with a bit of a mystified look on her face, Farida sat down.

Rahim continued, "Domara was the father..." And just then, standing like an exclamation point once again, Farida waved her tiny hand wildly.

"Yes, Farida?" he asked.

"I don't understand," she began. "Then why would Yusef say to the other boys that since we're going on this trip, we might as well be Jews?" She pirouetted and pointed directly at twelve-year-old Yusef, sitting with the older boys in the back of the group. Having proven her point, she harrumphed and sat down with a satisfied smile on her face.

Turning his head without moving his body, Rahim fixed on Yusef, but he did not smile this time. "Yusef, I want to talk to you after class tonight. I'm very interested in your views of this trip, and I'm sure they will be enlightening."

Continuing and relaxing his expression, Rahim began, "Domara, was in the inner circle of Tiglath-Pileser III, King of Assyria, and even though he was a Magi—"

"BAIL_dan–BAIL-dan–**BAIL_dan--BAIL-dan**" came from the back of the group.

Rahim fixed the back of the class with a fierce look, despite wanting to laugh at the little monsters. "You bloodthirsty little heathen, we'll get to Baildan in due time, but if I hear one more chant, I shall remove him from History for all time. It shall be as if he never lived."

The chant ended, with, of course, the boys in the back grinning wildly since they genuinely were blood-thirsty little heathen.

"**Domara**," Rahim tried again, "was the first of our ancestors to recognize that something was happening in Israel, that change was coming. He wasn't sure what or why, but he knew that something was happening in the nation of Israel and that it was significant. These events began approximately a hundred years before the birth of Domara. Two prophets, Elijah and Elisha, prophesied judgment against Israel. Then Jonah came to Nineveh, Domara's ancestors' birthplace, and told them God would destroy them if they did not repent and follow Him. Domara's grand-father met Jonah, and, like everyone else, he put on sackcloth and ashes and repented. Domara heard about a new prophet the year before this, but in Judah, not Israel, Isaiah. Isaiah was prophesying God's judgment on Israel and Judah.

"Whether Domara believed it or not didn't matter; what mattered was whether the Israelites believed it.

"Domara was a shrewd and calculating man. His intellect allowed him to ingratiate himself and carve out a niche for his family in the Persian Court. His objective was to survive political intrigue and change in Assyria. The priesthood, the primary function of the Magi, had a poor life expectancy, and priests rarely survived failed predictions. Therefore, Domara focused his family on two specific areas—education and warfare. They became experts in almost all disciplines, including astronomy, math-ematics, logic, and military history. In addition, they took their knowledge of military history and developed military tactics and training programs for Assyria's military leaders. They also developed unique units, such as the King's guard and special units trained in building and using siege engines. To survive frequent leadership changes, they remained as polit-ically neutral as possible.

"Domara's plan was simple. He had four sons, so he sent his oldest son, Meesha, to the court in Jerusalem under the guise of an emissary. His second-oldest son, Baildan, he sent, more or less, to Rezin, King of Syria. Baildan's mission was dangerous. He posed as the leader of a group of desert horsemen to infiltrate the Syrian military. Domara wanted to know if the Syrians and Ephraimites were allying to expand their territory. Or were they revolting from Assyria? Baildan was to gather information and report to Domara. He was still waiting for his first messages from Meesha when messages started coming back from Baildan—not all of them good. But why don't we let the Assyrian storyteller who was there tell us in his own words what happened?" Rahim seemed to change his personality entirely as he assumed the role of the Assyrian storyteller. He opened the scroll, handed down since the time of Domara; he lowered his voice and began the story...

Scene 2 Syria - 734 BC

Baildan was twenty-six years old and was the second oldest son of Domara. He had been a warrior since he was fifteen. He was deeply tanned with lines on his forehead and had dark eyes with thick eyebrows. He was five-foot-ten, heavily muscled from constant weapon training. He had a scar that ran from his hairline to his left cheek and an intense stare. It was difficult to explain what men felt when Baildan looked at them; it felt like he could see your very soul. If you were his friend Baildan's look could make you uncomfortable at times, but if you were his enemy, his countenance was terrifying.

Baildan looked at the cavalry's position in the order of march and grinned. The best thing about leading a cavalry unit— its position in camp. Chariots were usually in the center of the formation, but they were on the leading edge. Their position meant they had forage for their horses, access to clean water, and somewhat fresh air. Following them came the archers and slingers, the infantry, and last were the engineers and siege-works builders.

From a camp standpoint, the infantry occupied the least desirable position. Imagine an army of 200,000 men, plus another 20,000 camp followers and support personnel. They traveled in a front less than a quarter-mile in width, depending on terrain. The front could be much smaller in the hill country, compressing the rank into a line more than two miles long. Now imagine the infantry wading through the churned earth and the excrement of thousands of men and horses, and then making camp at the end of the day in the middle of that same filthy mess. Then compound the problem with being surrounded by hundreds of unwashed bodies, and you have a good picture of life in the infantry. Therefore, Cavalry was a simple choice. They roamed free all day, clear of the noise and dust and noxious odors, and they camped on the periphery of the great host at night. Almost six months ago, at the behest of his father, Domara, Baildan led a troupe of 100 men south from Assyria into Syria. His assignment was to monitor the activity of the Syrian army and report back to his father, hence to the great King, Tiglath-Pileser III.

Spying was a dangerous game. If King Rezin of Syria suspected for one moment that this unit belonged to the inner court of Assyria, the unit would meet an end that would not be pleasant. They passed themselves off as a troop of raiders coming out of the deserts south of Babylon, thieves who made a living by raiding caravans and small groups of nomads. Therefore, they came in from the east when they entered Syria and carried no equipment or clothing to identify them as Assyrian troops. They formed up in Damascus, in the spring, in time for King Rezin to begin his southern campaign. The army moved as a single unit as far as Karnaim, which sits on the Syrian border with Israel.

King Rezin split his forces into two equal parts, with half moving southeast, led by Rezin through Ammon, Moab, and Edom to subjugate those countries and make them vassals of Syria, not Assyria. The other half, to which Baildan was attached, would move south to link up with Ephraimite forces and King Pekah, king of Israel, in Shechem. The Syrians, going to Shechem, were led by Nabil, a field commander, second in command to King Rezin.

One of the things Baildan loved the most in a campaign was the constant change of environment. They came out of the deserts north of Karnaim, and this morning they woke in the fertile river valley just east of the Sea of Galilee. A slight mist came off the lake this morning, and the air was sweet with moisture and the smells of early wheat and barley. Insects and many species of migrating birds filled the air with a variety of sounds. The sun rose but was still slightly masked by the small hills to the east. The camp started to stir, but Baildan took a moment to sit on his sleeping mat and enjoy the sounds and smells of the morning. Of course, nothing goods lasts long.

"Shall I roust them, boss man?" came the gravelly voice of Baildan's second-in-command, Ashur. Ashur was slightly older than Baildan, and they had been together since his youth. He was taller than Baildan by a couple of inches and forty pounds heavier; his hands were large and calloused. Ashur's right arm and wrist were massive due to constant sword work and training. He was not only second-in-command but also responsible for sword training for the cavalry. With a grin, Baildan gave a slight sigh and looked over his shoulder at Ashur. "Roust 'em out, Ashur. We need to check the ford over the Jordan and report any problems to Nabil, the Syrian field commander."

Ashur walked down the line of sleeping mats to Eilbra, the young novice who would serve as signaler for this campaign. Ashur lightly kicked the young man's feet. "It's time to get 'em up and on the move."

The boy turned over and covered his head—wrong response.

Ashur then went to wake-up method number two, reaching down and grabbing the boy by the collar of his robe and the seat of his pants, lifting him three feet in the air, dropping him back to the ground. This method had the desired effect and would serve to reinforce method number one in the future.

Eilbra was instantly on his feet, not wanting to find out what method number three might be. He retrieved his ram horn from his bedding and blew the three short notes that signaled the start of the day, and he began the process of packing his gear and getting ready to move.

Baildan had a dedicated supply train and cooks, who rose before first light and prepared the morning meal. The smells set his saliva flowing, and he made his way over to the cooking area. The cooks prepared several fires, and pots of goat stew were simmering over the fires. Next to the fires was freshly prepared flatbread and pots of goat cheese. Baildan crossed his legs and sat next to one of the pots, and men joined him around the pot to share the morning meal. They would eat in haste this morning; everyone understood the urgent requirement to find and check the ford across the Jordan. The Sea of Galilee emptied into the Jordan River at the south end of the lake. The job of his troop was to find a safe route and a place for the army to ford. As they gathered around the fire, everyone greeted each other. They used flatbread to scoop the stew from the pot and the soft cheese from its clay jar. The men kidded each other, joyful as they welcomed the beginning of the day, the excellent weather, and the knowledge that they would not have to fight today. Their mood was professional but light.

The smallest man in Ashur's command, Mardokh, approached the fire and sat down, his hair and beard a mess, his eyes crusted with sleep. "You look like the south end of a camel heading north, and your breath smells like that south end," Ashur kidded him.

"I look like the magnificent fighting man that I am," said Mardokh. "As for the smell of my breath, I would say that your sense of smell has been tainted by smelling too many of those camel butts."

A low chuckle went around the fire but ended with the hard stare Ashur gave the men. "I can see we need extra sword work, looking at the weak arms of the ladies around this fire," growled Ashur.

Baildan grinned at him. "I agree on that sword work, brother, but it will have to wait until this evening; we have work to do this morning." Baildan looked at the men around the fires and noted that most had eaten and were beginning to rise and prepare to leave. Baildan saw Eilbra at the adjacent fire and called to him to sound assemble.

Eilbra stood and blew his ram's horn, and men now moved with speed and purpose, rolling up gear, stowing it in a matter of minutes, moving toward the corral. Each man had a string of three horses, and as the men reached the corral, they found their tack and their mounts for the day.

Baildan approached the corral and called for one of the grooms to bring him his favorite mare, Arbella. It would be a long day of riding, and she had the smoothest gait of any of the horses in his remuda. Her seat was like being on a swift dhow with a fair wind and smooth waters. Since the probability of the need to fight was low today, he didn't need one of his warhorses. Arbella would do nicely. The groom brought him a standard felt pad for her back, held in place by a surcingle around her barrel. The pad served two purposes—it protected the horses back and the rider's nethermost areas. The surcingle served two purposes—it held the pad in place and provided the rider a handhold should he need one to keep him in place. Next, he placed the bridle on the horse, and the horse's tack was complete.

Mounting was relatively easy since most of their horses were Barbs or Turkomans fourteen to fifteen hands tall. They were slim-legged and had great endurance. Arbella was a dappled gray, and he mounted her by grasping the surcingle and leaping onto her back. Eilbra sounded assemble, and the troop formed outside the corral. The troop of 100 men contained ten squads of ten men each. The squads provided several benefits. The small groups could perform complex maneuvers, impossible to achieve as a single large troop. The squads also offered the benefit of command continuity. Regardless of what happened to the upper command structure, the smaller unit could continue to function and make independent decisions. Baildan moved to the front of the troop and motioned the troop forward using a hand signal.

They rode in tight formation for about thirty minutes until they were some distance from camp, and Baildan called the troop to a halt. He scanned the back trail, and as usual, a single horseman was trailing them. A single rider trailed them every day and made no effort at concealment. Commander Nabil accepted their services (their horsemanship and weapon skills were too great to turn down), but that didn't mean he trusted Baildan. Nabil wanted them to know he was watching, and at the first sign of a problem, he would eliminate this desert troop.

The troop dismounted and formed a semicircle around Baildan. These men knew who they served, had absolute confidence in Baildan, and understood their mission. Baildan expected them to gather information from any source possible, from serving girls to assistant commanders; no source was unimportant.

At the beginning of each day, Baildan gathered them and gleaned information obtained the previous day. This conversation was not one for Syrian ears. "Anyone hear anything yesterday concerning King Rezin, Pekah, or their actual intent?" began Baildan. Rising from the third row of men was Jamal, of course, tall, with delicate features, long, soft black hair and beard, and piercing, almost-black eyes with long lashes. His family was one of the most powerful in Assyria; he carried himself with confidence and assurance. The ladies found him irresistible.

Baildan recognized him, "Ah, our itinerant lothario. I expected no less."

The men greeted the comment with laughter and good-natured jibes.

"Fair leader and master of men, can I help it if the gods have gifted me with all of the beauty? Do you think it doesn't break my heart to see all of you lesser men who struggle to find love and acceptance even in the darkest of rooms?" said Jamal. "It is not my fault, but I am obligated to use the gifts the gods blessed me, in the service of my master, burden that it may be."

"Oh for gosh sakes, just spit it out, Jamal. Did you find anything useful or not?" growled Ashur.

Jamal smiled at Ashur, "Always so impatient—as I was saying. Last evening, I spent some time with Rima, one of Nabil's serving girls, who expressed grave concern for my safety. According to Rima, though appreciative of our skills, Nabil is highly suspect of a group of desert raiders with such skillsets. He finds it hard to believe that we would have drilled in small unit tactics and precision formations. He is more used to the normal brand of desert-raider who rides fast, attacks first, thinks second, and retreats at the first sign of organized opposition. Let's say that Baildan has not convinced him that we are who we say we are." He bowed deeply, in a great show of mock humility, and slowly seated himself with the grace of a cobra.

In all seriousness now, Baildan thanked Jamal for his report. "Anyone else?" he asked. Standing in the front row was Samir, a captain of fifty, the same as Ashur and third in the command structure. He was the oldest member of the troop, with a calm and quiet demeanor and no outstanding features, except for the scars on his jaw and arms from swords that came just a little too close. He was a man who blended in seamlessly and with whom people felt comfortable, but he did have one small vice. He loved to gamble and, thankfully, was pretty good at it.

"Our Syrian friends held a small wrestling contest last night, and let me just begin by thanking my good friend Pera for assisting me in taking money from our Syrian hosts," Samir said. The only thing that exceeded Samir's love of gambling was Pera's love of wrestling. He was legendary among the Assyrians, and in Assyria, it would be almost impossible to find acceptable odds on him. Still, here in Syria, he and Samir would make a lot of money, at least for a while. Pera was an excellent wrestler, even though he was not very tall. His opponents soon found out his strength and speed more than made up for his lack of stature. He had large hands, and he could wring blood from a man's forearm. Baildan feared no man, but he would rather face a lion with a knife than Pera in the circle.

Samir continued, "Saif, one of Nabil's captains of 1,000, had a man wrestling last night on whom he gave two-to-one odds, and there were few takers. I took the opportunity to invite him in to share tea and bread and to discuss a possible contest between his man, Yusuf, and Pera. From the tea, we moved to a lovely wine I saved for just such an occasion. We came to terms at three-to-one. In sharing information on the current campaign, Saif casually mentioned that he believed a united Syria and Israel might not need the protection of vassalage to Assyria. It appears your father was correct, Baildan. This war is more likely an act of rebellion than merely defeating Judah and reuniting Israel as one nation. We need more confirmation before we reach that conclusion unequivocally, but I think it certainly has merit."

"Thank you," Baildan replied, "If there's nothing else to add, I suggest we proceed."

Every squad of ten was assigned responsibilities for the day. Dinkha's unit rode point. His group would precede the central column by about a half-mile; Ador's group would ride drag, following the central column by one-half mile; and Yadida and Madsa would ride left and right flanks, respectively. The morning was uneventful, with the heat of the day increasing as the morning wore on. All men wore loose-fitting linen robes or wraps as protection from the sun, which allowed their perspiration to evaporate to provide a cooling effect. They also wore a shawl, linen in summer, and wool in winter, to cover their faces in the case of a sandstorm. The shawls were generally white, but the wraps, extending to just above the knee, ranged from white to green, red, or blue with colored patterns or decorations of yellow. All the colors were dark or muted, and there was no sheen to the fabrics. In addition, they wore a wide sash or Kammar cinching their wraps. They used the Kammar to hold the sheaths for their swords and knives.

Riding point, Dinkha was the first to notice the temperature change, from the dry heat of the desert and the surrounding foothills to the added element of humidity, increasing the heat. Then, he noticed the slightly rank smell of rotting vegetation. Within the next half mile, he saw the low foliage of stunted trees and the low, weedy vegetation of typical marshlands appearing before them and extending from the shores of the Sea of

Galilee to the base of the hills to their east. Dinkha nodded to his signal-man, who blew one long and one short note. Dinkha's squad stopped in place, the men relaxed, waiting for Baildan to respond to the call. Within two minutes, Baildan reigned in his horse next to Dinkha. As he looked forward, he saw the issue and knew why Dinkha signaled. Marshland was nothing to be taken lightly, with snakes to spook horses, with tigers and wild boar, and worst of all, with quagmires that could suck down both horse and man in a matter of minutes.

Baildan sent a rider back to inform the unit to form into a narrow column and call in the flank riders. Till they were past the marsh, they could not deploy the flank riders. He sent another rider back to Nabil to inform him of the swamp and tell him he didn't see a way around. This compression of the front would slow the army considerably and extend the column for miles. With communication completed, the troop dismounted and cut down small saplings, eight or ten feet tall, to be used to mark the route through the marsh.

Everyone remounted, and each man took the coil of rope they carried and tied themselves into a human chain about 100 feet long. Using this method, they would ride abreast, but they could pull a man to safety if he began to sink. The cut saplings were passed to the men on the far right and left of the line to mark the area of safe passage, and they entered the marsh at a slow walk. Several of the horses were extremely nervous, eyes dilating, nostrils flaring, uncomfortable with the softness of the ground and the strange creatures slithering on the surface.

After about a quarter of a mile, they could see the end of the marsh about 200 yards ahead, and the men relaxed slightly. The footing was adequate so far and would support the army following them. But they relaxed too soon; Baildan could feel Arbella struggling to lift her front feet. The horse dropped her rump, transferring all of her weight onto her back legs. Without thinking, Baildan untied the rope from around his chest and looped it around the surcingle, and called to Dinkha, to whom he was tied, to do the same. Dinkha understood, tied off around his surcingle, and backed his horse. For a long minute, everything remained status quo as Dinkha's horse fought mightily to move back and Arbella's legs remained firmly trapped in the sucking mud. The force on the rope was sufficient to drag more of Arbella's weight onto her rear legs, and she almost seemed to sit down. With her hind legs compressed, she applied maximum force and straightened them shoving herself backward and extricating her front legs from the quicksand. She took a couple of quick hops using her rear legs and found herself on firm footing again, but she trembled mightily. Baildan slid back onto the riding pad and gently stroked her neck until she no longer quivered. He and three others dismounted and, using the cut saplings, walked forward, probing the ground to find the edges of the quagmire. They marked the perimeter of the swamp by tying red streamers to the stakes. The army following could see the quarantined area.

In a short while, they exited the marsh and could see the end of the Sea of Galilee to their right, where it emptied into the Jordan River. They rode up a flat rocky rise for the next mile and had an excellent view of the river as it wound south. The banks were thick with trees and brush. Still, within 200 feet on either side of the river, the vegetation disappeared into the dry high desert terrain. There were small fields of managed crops on the west side of the river, showing where the Israelis dug irrigation ditches from the river, bringing life to the fertile soil in the lush valley.

The closer to the river they came, the more signs of habitation increased. There were small groups of huts to shelter laborers during planting and harvesting seasons within the irrigated fields. Trees lined the river banks on both sides, with the poplars being the tallest. Mixed in were cinnabar, olive, eucalyptus, and pistachio. In the fields close to the river, black iris wildflowers in their magnificent purple grew by the thousands. It pained him to think of what those fields would look like after the army passed; once the thousands of marching feet destroyed the vegetation in the fields, the dirt would dry. The constant winds would allow the desert to claim this area, not only now but possibly for a long time into the future.

Baildan looked at the beauty and fertility in front of him, "Ashur, do you ever think about what happens to an area like this after we march through?"

Ashur replied, "My father was a farmer in an area just like this. One year the army marched through our lands; they ate everything we had and trampled the crops. We had nothing for two years; my brother and sister both starved to death, and I don't like to think about the things I ate just to survive. Yes, I think about those years every time we march through a place like this, and it always grieves me."

Baildan looked at the burly warrior in a new light. "I didn't know. I'm sorry, Ashur. I have seen what it looks like after we pass, but I never thought about the unintended death we leave in our wake," Baildan added.

Ashur sat taller on his horse, "That's why I fight, Baildan. The sooner we can subdue and bring peace to an area, the sooner their suffering will end. I know it seems strange that I fight to bring peace, but that's what I do."

Baildan nodded, and they rode on.

Once clear of the marsh, Baildan formed the troop into its standard scout formation, and he sent Dinkha and the point riders as close to the river as possible to search out a ford for the crossing. They hadn't gone more than three miles when Dinkha saw the first possibility. The river narrowed considerably, being no more than about seventy yards across, and the river was passing over a rock shelf that covered most of that distance. Just as they had crossed the marsh, he lined his ten riders abreast and linked them using a rope. They entered the river, with some of the horses going wide-eyed and beginning to sweat, not being used to the slick footing and flowing water that was gradually moving higher on their legs. Then, ten yards from the bank, the river shallowed to four feet. Their horses found footing on the rocky slope and climbed onto the shelf. The water stayed between two and three feet deep until they neared the other bank, where the rock shelf ended. The water scoured the mud's depth to four feet, almost approaching five feet until it reached the west bank—an easy successful mission.

Scene 3 Jordan River - 734 BC

It was the spring of the year, and many things happened every spring. Kings went off to war, the black iris bloomed in the Jordan River valley, new growth appeared on trees, and animals mated. That meant in the Jordan River; it was hippopotamus mating season. Springtime caused young hippo bulls to challenge old bulls for the leadership of bloats. This section of the Jordan was the territory of a 25-year-old, almost 4,000-pound bull and his bloat of 30 cows. Coming of age in the bloat was a 10-year-old bull of nearly 3,500 pounds who decided it was time to challenge for leadership.

The challenge had nothing to do with conscious thought. The young hippo was being driven mad by the hippo cows in heat and by his surging hormones. The youngster didn't like or dislike the old bull, and he didn't think about consequences. He knew only one thing, he wanted those cows, and the thing standing in his way was the old bull. The old hippo bull was standing in about three feet of water, pulling up grass from the water and masticating it.

The young bull approached from his right side, coming out of the deeper water with just his nostrils, eyes, and ears visible. He ponderously climbed the bank toward the old bull, and from about 20 feet away, he opened his jaws almost 180 degrees into what appeared a massive yawn and bellowed his challenge to the lead bull. It wasn't enough to defeat the old bull; the bloat had to see it. He needed to impress them and show them that he and he alone would fight for them and produce strong progeny. He bellowed again, a horrible deep-base roar, full of spittle and hate.

The old bull turned to meet him; this was not his first fight, and he had the scars to prove it. He opened his jaws, bellowed back with the full force of his lungs, and in so doing displayed the massive foot-long lower canines. The bulls would use their deadly teeth, primarily, to settle this battle.

The challenge, given and accepted, the two bulls charged each other with their jaws wide open. Their massive chests absorbed the impact of their combined four tons colliding, with the result that the young bull, who was still in the process of climbing the bank toward his elder, was pushed backward. The old hippo took quick advantage to lower his jaw slightly below the youngster's and deliver a cutting blow with his canines to his adversary's neck and lower jaw. The young bull was so enraged he barely felt the wound though it was bleeding heavily. He backed up another foot and charged again, their jaws met, still in the fully extended position, and it was a collision of canines and incisors as they fought to turn the other bull's head to the side to deliver a blow to the side of the neck. The bulls hammered each other, churning the river bank to a pulpy mess, and the water swirled red around them. Both bulls were becoming exhausted, and the ending was predictable, as the weight and experience of the old bull took their toll. Realizing he was running out of strength, his heart hammering in his chest, the young hippo backed up, slowly at first and then faster. The old bull continued to press the attack, then sensing it was over, he lifted his head from the water and bellowed in victory. The young bull took the opportunity to turn and flee upstream. The challenge now changed his life forever. He was isolated and alone, he could no longer stay in the territorial waters of the old bull, and he would not be welcome in a new bloat. He would live out his life in isolation until he either died without the protection of the bloat or until he grew strong enough to challenge for leadership of another bloat. For now, he was alone, hurt, and enraged, and his vision was red and blurred from the horrible exertion. He moved through the water with just his ears, nostrils, and eyes barely showing above the water when he noticed motion in front of him.

Scene 4 Baildan's Cavalry - 734 BC

At the south end of the line of men, in about four feet of water, rode Adjinah, a twenty-five-year-old warrior. Adjinah grew up in the same village as Dinkha, and they both served under Baildan for the past eight years. Adjinah's peripheral vision caught the swirl of motion in the water. He shouted, "Hippo," and with cat-like quickness, he pulled his left leg from the water and stood on the back of his horse. The man to his right, acting equally as quickly, pulled the rope that attached him to Adjinah. The rider had Adjinah sprawled face down over his horse's rump in seconds. The bank to their front was too steep to climb, so the remaining horsemen, acting almost as one, dropped the rope connecting them and turned and rode back up the rock shelf until they were back in about two feet of water.

Half the men pulled their bows and strung them, notching arrows. The other half pulled a javelin from their quivers. Although for the moment Adjinah was safe, his horse was not as fortunate. The enraged bull hit the horse without slowing. He raised his head from the water, fully extended his jaws, and brought them down on the horse's head. The long canines drove up the horse's windpipe as the mouth closed around his head, crushing the skull, and for good measure, the hippo twisted its head and snapped the horse's neck. Death was instantaneous. He then saw the men and horses on the shelf above him, and with unbelievable speed, climbed to their level, opened his mouth, and bellowed his challenge. The riders backed their horses and increased the interval between them to perform an enveloping attack. The riders with bows drew and released, filling the soft tissue of the hippo's nose and face with arrows. The hippo opened his jaws wide and bellowed in pain and rage, allowing the archers to place several arrows down his gullet into his throat, from which blood poured profusely. The hippo, sensing he was in trouble, charged the closest horse and hit it in the right shoulder, knocking it over, crushing the off leg of the rider beneath him. Both horse and man both screamed in pain.

The men with javelins drove their spears behind the hippo's front legs, searching for the heart and lungs. Again the bull bellowed in rage and pain, but this time the bellow contained a stream of bright-red blood. Then, as the jaws were open, another rider took the opportunity to charge directly at the bull and drive his javelin into the open maw. The colossal beast stood for a moment, shaking its head and swaying from side to side before its front legs buckled. The hippo gave a heaving, gurgling sigh and lay still in the bloody water.

The men still in the saddle raised their weapons and gave ululating cries of victory, celebrating that they still lived and would see another sunset. Unfortunately, the celebration was short-lived due to the cry of pain from the downed man and horse. Everyone dismounted, and to ensure the thrashing wounded horse caused no more damage, one of the men thrust a javelin into the horse's heart. The animal gave a few last spasms in death and then lay still. Everyone else surrounded the man and horse. Three men grabbed the surcingle around the horse's barrel and lifted it enough for the others to drag the screaming man from under the animal. This wound was not a simple break; the horse crushed his leg in several places below the knee. These were experienced warriors, very familiar with injuries, and it was evident that Barseen fought his last battle.

Baildan and the troop were in sight of the ford and saw the end of the battle. Baildan sent a rider back to fetch the supply wagon from the back of the formation; the wagon contained medical supplies and the troop's healer. Dinkha's men gently carried the wounded man across the ford and placed him under a poplar tree in the shade. Others were busy attaching ropes to the two dead horses and the hippo's legs and dragged them across the ford and up onto the bank. Nothing would go to waste from the hippo or the horses. The cooking team, also in the supply wagon, would rend the fat down to be used in lamps and then salt and cure the hams and shoulders of the hippo. The women would use the tendons, skin, and bones to make thread for sewing, shields, and tools or glue, respectively. They would use the horses for meat and glue.

Baildan waited on the supply wagon and rode with it across the ford. When they reached the far bank, it was too steep for the horses pulling it to gain traction, so several men dismounted and assisted the horse team by grasping the wagon wheels and helping to turn them; between men and horses, they were able to bring the wagon across the ford safely.

Baildan joined the healer as he examined Barseen, the wounded man, and after a quick examination, the healer looked at Baildan and shook his head. He then looked back at Barseen, took his hand, and told him the leg would have to come off at the knee. Even the strongest men blanched when informed they were about to lose part of their bodies permanently. Barseen asked the healer to lift him to see the leg; Baildan moved to his head and gently lifted him by the shoulders until he could see the crushed leg. A look of resignation came into Barseen's eyes, and he looked at the healer and shook his head in acquiescence.

Marona, the healer, went to the wagon, took his medical kit, and called his assistant. When traveling with the army, he always carried a gummy substance, a poppy flower product. He mixed it with tobacco in a pipe and gave it to Barseen to smoke. It didn't take long before it took effect, and Barseen was lying still, with his eyes closed. Marona's assistant gathered water from the river above the ford; he filtered it through clean cotton and boiled it over the fire. Once it reached boiling, he placed Marona's saw and knife in the boiling water. He then took some of the boiled water and, using a clean cotton pad and astringent soap, washed the crushed leg from the knee to the ankle. He then placed a sturdy board with a cotton pad under the leg, and Marona was ready to proceed. He would leave as much of the leg bone under the knee as he could. He began by taking his knife and making a circling cut below the level of the bone that he would amputate. Next, using his knife, he folded the skin back to a point above where he saw the bone; with the bone exposed, Marona used his saw to cut the bone, and he then used a small file to file smooth the bone. Finally, he folded the skin flap back over the bone and sewed the skin together, covering the bone. The process took him only minutes. He learned long ago that the faster he worked, the greater the patient's probability of survival. Baildan watched the procedure, and he went over to Marona, placed his hand on Marona's shoulder, and thanked him for his compassion, skill, and quick work.

As Baildan walked away from Marona, Ashur rode up, "What do you think, boss?"

Baildan knew what the question entailed, "This is as good a place as any to make camp. Not much of the army will have enough daylight left to ford tonight. So let's go ahead and move back upstream a little way to clear water, and then we'll leave early in the morning."

Baildan watched as Ashur gave orders to the commanders; then, he casually rode upstream along with the main body of men. Men formed the camp in the same groups of ten in which they rode. The cavalry placed their tents in a circle, with horses and support personnel in the center for protection. Central cook fires were already starting, and as soon as the cook wagons arrived, they would begin preparing the evening meal. Men were sorted into work parties by their commanders, setting up perimeter security and gathering wood. They sent out hunting parties to search for deer, antelope, and feral pigs. Pigs, especially, would be abundant since the Israelis wouldn't eat them, so the pots should be full tonight. Then before sunset, a rider came to the encampment requesting that Baildan join the other commanders in a meeting with Nabil, the commander of the armies in the west.

Scene 5 End of Day 14

"Children, I think this is as good a place as any to stop our lesson for tonight," said Rahim. "I have seen a few heads beginning to nod." There were a few groans from the older children, but it had been a long day of traveling, and almost everyone was ready for their sleeping mats.

CHAPTER 4

The Gate

Scene 1 Southeast Of the Persian Gate - Day 27

It took the Magi two weeks to reach the Persian Gate from Persepolis. The grades were not steep, but some of the narrow trails slowed their travel pace. Navid slept for just a few hours and knew by looking at the night sky that it was at least six hours before dawn. He was tired from the first two weeks of travel but was becoming trail-hardened like everyone. Tonight would be the first time he would be leading the Scouts into danger, and to make it worse, they would be moving and fighting in the dark. This is what the Scouts trained for, but that didn't make it any easier.

A rime of frost covered everything, and the temperature was still dropping, with a wind slightly more than a breeze coming from the north. Navid slid out from under his covers and did not put on his usual traveling clothes. The pants and coat he put on were fleece-lined, dark brown with a dappling of gray, as was the wool scarf covering his head. Navid wore a heavy reed vest, covered with water buffalo hide, which barely covered his chest and stomach. His war vest covered him from neck to groin. He gathered his war bow, which had a much heavier pull than his hunting bow, and his double quiver. The top quiver held his arrows, and the lower quiver his javelins. He laced a cord of wool between the arrow and javelin shafts to ensure they would not rattle on tonight's operation, and he put his long sword and knife in the sash, which held his coat closed.

Navid walked to the corral that held their horses and found Tiz and a few other Scouts already there. The rest of the Scouts arrived, along with ten of the best hunters from the flank teams. They would not be riding their regular mounts tonight. Instead, they were riding mountain-bred horses because of their strength, endurance, and agility.

The Magi didn't trust Taghi, the leader of the Uxians. He knew the Magi Family was traveling with their wealth -- gold, silver, livestock, and arms, and the temptation would be too great for Taghi.

Two days ago, using animal trails, Navid sent Scouts up both sides of the pass. They remained hidden and camouflaged until this evening. After dark, they slipped back into camp. As expected, Taghi placed parties of thirty men on both sides of the pass. The Uxians prepared boulder-and-log slides they intended to use. The avalanche created was designed to crush the Magi warriors and separate them into two parts when attempting to pass through the Gate today. So far, Taghi had acted as expected. Therefore, Navid's biggest concern was, "What had they not anticipated?"

When everyone arrived, Navid called them together to go over the mission one last time. "Utana and I will lead fifteen Scouts up the east side of the pass and will come in from above the Uxian ambush team. Tiz will guide the remaining Scouts and the flank team up the west side and come in from above the ambush team on that side. We know one thing: there are at least thirty men on each side of the pass, but we don't know if Taghi anticipated our moves, and there are others in place. We also don't know how they will react when we attack. For example, are they to release the landslide early if attacked? One of the dogs will accompany each of our teams to provide early enemy detection."

War dogs were not the same as hunting dogs. The two dogs selected—Arsha and Bendva—were both Mastiffs, bred from an ancient breed of Assyrian dogs trained for war. Both dogs were eight years old and were not only well trained but experienced in battle. They learned stealth, patience, and silent aggression, weighed more than 150 pounds, and were taller than a man when standing on their hind legs. The strength of their jaws was enough to crush a man's leg bones.

Arsha would accompany Navid's team, and Bendva would go with Tiz. They put leashes on the dogs; they needed their noses, and there was no need for them to range ahead of the riders. There were no questions, so every man did a last-minute check of another man. This inspection ensured no loose equipment gave away their position and that everyone was properly armed and equipped with climbing ropes. Inspection completed, they rode out of camp.

It was approximately five miles to the base of the Persian Gate. Taghi's village lay between the Scouts and the gate. The Scouts skirted the village to avoid detection and contact. The village itself was not the problem. The problem would be the herds of goats and sheep pastured around the village. Shepherds and dogs would accompany the herds, being awake and vigilant, watching for predators. The Scouts returning from the Gate this evening noted the locations of the sheep pens. The pens should be easy to avoid, but the shepherd and his dogs were less predictable.

Scene 2 Uxian Shepherds

In the Uxian shepherd camp, Alibai rose quietly from her sleeping mat and thought about her brother, who would be on the far side of the sheep pen making his evening rounds by now. Her watch wouldn't start for another five hours, so she stood and, staying crouched over, moved into the low scrub surrounding the area. It was about a half-mile to the hill that she and Zard, her betrothed, chose as a meeting place. She made the trip so many times she didn't need much light to find the trail. She moved with the grace and quiet stealth of one born to the outdoors. She was born a shepherdess of the Uxians and would die a shepherdess. Her life was one of caring for the herd, overseeing the grazing, moving the flock when forage was low, leading them to water (or carrying water to them) when they were thirsty, protecting them from wild animals, having fought both bears and lions with her sling. She monitored the ewes as they gave birth, helped them through difficult ones, and—on rare occasions—opened a mother's womb and removed the lamb.

Alibai was a young woman, comfortable outdoors, confident and secure in her abilities. She was going to meet Zard, a young man about three years older than her to whom her parents pledged her. Fortunately, she was also in love with Zard.

His flock was about two miles from their meeting place. The hill they chose lay between the flocks of the young couple. They met secretly to avoid embarrassing their parents. They were betrothed but still could not be alone together.

Thankfully, notwithstanding the clandestine meetings, unlike some other young men, Zard was respectful and didn't let their meeting go beyond the boundaries of the tribe's decorum. They met, held each other, and talked of the future, but that is all they did and would never think of going beyond that.

Zard arrived first and was seated on the flat rock near the hill's apex, where they usually sat. Alibai climbed and sat next to him. He wrapped them both in the blanket he brought. She put her head on his shoulder and luxuriated in his strength, warmth, and tenderness. She loved these first moments together. She yearned for the time when this would be their regular evening routine. They put their heads together and talked of their days and their future together. They knew that these few stolen hours would end all too soon.

Scene 3 Arsha

Navid was riding in the lead when suddenly Arsha lay down and wagged his tail. A hunting dog would bay when it picked up the scent of game; a war dog will not. Navid raised his right arm. Everyone behind him dismounted. Navid signaled that he and Utana would go forward to investigate. Fortunately, the breeze tonight was in their face, and Arsha gave them ample distance to respond before getting too close to what lay ahead.

Using hand signals, Navid indicated that he would circle the hill to the right, and Utana would go left, staying crouched low and even crawling when necessary. They would spiral their way to the top until they found the source of the dog's anxiety. About halfway up the hill, Navid saw the outline of two people huddled closely together and whispering. He was too far away to hear distinctly but based on the pitch, it sounded like a man and a woman—not good. He knew that Utana would also hear them if he hadn't already. Navid continued to move until he was slightly behind the couple. He climbed within touching distance, directly behind them. When Navid looked to his right, there was Utana. Navid never heard a sound.

Scene 4 Zard

It wasn't anything he heard or saw, but the hair on the back of Zard's neck was standing up. It was a feeling, and he knew better than to ignore his feelings. What he sensed was the presence of either predator or man. If a predator, he knew that he and Alibai could deal with them. If a man, it could be one of their tribe, which, while embarrassing, would merely lead to an awkward discussion. If not of their tribe, that left in all likelihood only the Magi, who camped just west of the pass tonight. He knew about the Magi and their Scouts and would not like to meet them in the dark.

Zard continued to talk in low, quiet tones to Alibai, but very gently, he squeezed her arm, and when she looked up, he raised his eyebrows and rolled his eyes to the right. Then, again, moving very slowly, he moved his hand to the hilt of his long knife, tucked into the belt of his robe. Zard drew it from its sheath as Alibai did the same, unfortunately, or in this case, fortunately, neither knife cleared the sheath before Zard felt the sharp point of a knife in the center of his back and heard a low voice whispering to them …

Scene 5 Fight for the Gate

Navid wasn't big on killing women or children; it was something he would not do. He was no assassin, but this posed a horrible predicament, and the safety of their tribe might depend on the decisions he made in the next few minutes. "Don't make a sound, and please take your hands off your knives," said Navid. He reached up, grasped the blanket draped over the two people and pulled it over their heads, and let it drop to the ground behind them. "Now, with two fingers of your left hand, pull your knives and toss them down the hill, then your slings and stones, and lastly, take your feet and push your shepherd staffs down the hill. Navid didn't have to ask who they were. A look and a whiff were all he needed to figure out that they were shepherds. "We have a problem," Navid continued, "I can't let you raise the alarm. You know Taghi is setting a trap for us tomorrow. My men and I are going to block that plan. I imagine you are both due to begin a watch in your camp very soon. If you don't return, they will notify your family, and a search will begin.

"The safest thing I can do is kill you both, make it look like an animal attack, and count on the fact I will be able to accomplish my mission before anyone knows better. OR—you can give me your word that you won't tell anyone of our presence, and you will live, and your brothers or sisters back with the herd will live. It is your choice—life or death."

Zard seemed barely able to speak. "Why would you trust us?"

Navid asked, "Are you both honorable? Can I trust your word, and will you swear by your god?"

"Yes," replied Zard, "we are honorable, and we will swear by our god, Zahäg," which they both then did.

"Good," said Navid, "show me your amulets." They both produced poorly carved wooden figures hung on a leather thong around their necks. The amulet was the bust of a man with a snake growing out of each shoulder, Zahäg. "I accept your word. Go ahead and retrieve your staffs and weapons and go back to your herds. But, just for safety, I'm going to have a man follow each of you back, and if there is any sign of betrayal, if anyone attempts to leave the herd, he will kill you and everyone with you. Trust me, you will never see him or hear him, but he'll be there, and if you are lying to me, he will not only kill you and those with you tonight but your entire flock. Are we clear?"

They could barely speak. The horror showed in the couples' faces. They both replied, "You have our word." They each picked up their staff and weapons and returned to their herds.

As Navid and Utana were walking back to the men, Utana asked, "Was that wise? It would have been safer to kill them; now, we will be two men short to watch them. Utana could not see Navid's smile in the dark.

"We will not be short; none of us is staying. I trust their word, but even if I didn't, they have seen what we can do. They are both highly trained, and we came to within feet of them without their having seen or heard us. There is no way they'll take a chance on us 'not' being there; the risk is too significant."

They arrived back where they left the men, and Navid signaled everyone to move out. They had eliminated the threat or danger, and there was no need for conversation. The Scouts had absolute trust in their leaders.

Tiz was on the opposite side of the valley from Navid. Tiz's route did not contain any sheep pens. Has able to move to the base of the Gate without detection. He and his team would follow an old animal trail that lay about a half-mile from the Gate. The trail should allow his team to move into position above the Uxians at their ambush site. The trail was wide enough to ride about a third of the way up the mountain before the trail narrowed and became steeper. Tiz and his team dismounted, and they formed a tight circle around Tiz. He told them, "We should be safe enough on this trail, but tonight is not the time to take any chances. We know where the ambush site is, but what we don't know is how the Uxian troops dispersed after our Scouts returned to camp." Tiz called out five of the men. "You will continue up the trail, but move slowly. I will send Bendva with you; since we are downwind of anyone above us, the dog should give you more than enough warning if anyone is there. The rest of us will make our way through the rock and scrub to the west. If anyone is on the trail, stop where you are, and give us a single sheep bleat."

Tiz and his men moved off to the right to parallel the trail. The going was slow because they moved noiselessly through the low scrub. Tiz signaled his team to move a little more to their right to increase their distance from the trail. Then they continued to climb. The terrain was becoming more obstructed as they went. They traversed bolder falls. In addition, there were sections of rock face which they could free climb; all of this in the near dark with falling temperature. After almost forty-five minutes of climbing, a single bleat, imitating a sheep, came from the trail to their left and slightly above them. They climbed almost thirty more minutes after they heard the sheep bleat, and Tiz believed they were now above the position of the Uxians on the trail.

Tiz signaled his men to form into a tight group. The men formed a half-circle around him, and he whispered instructions. "Farva, you will take seven men with you." Tiz pointed to the seven men. "I will take the rest with me. Farva will remain on this side of the trail when we reach it, and I will cross over to the other side. Descend until you have identified the location of the ambush teams; if they are well trained, they will be on both sides of the trail. Do not move until you are certain that you have identified all of the Uxian positions. My team will do the same.

When you are ready, begin the attack, and we will follow your lead. Swift and silent is the work tonight. When you are in position, remove your bows, javelins, swords, and scabbards; this is knife work."

There were no questions, so they continued on the rock shelf until they reached the trail. Farva stopped, and Tiz and his group silently crossed the path. Once across, both teams descended until they sensed the first presence of people to their front. Both teams stopped and, using all of their senses, located the positions below them. They all stood as still as the rocks surrounding them. They heard the sound of silent war, leather against a rock, the scrape of a pebble, the smell of garlic, body odor, sweat, or a puff of condensed breath. Both teams identified, to the best of their ability, the men below them. Where there was an unusual gap between positions, they assumed another person to be in that position.

Tiz dreaded what was about to happen. He trained for war, fought, and killed, but it never got any easier. The killing tonight was the worst of all, close up, a man's breath in your face, darkness covering the movement of hands and feet, fear, bowels releasing, desperation, men clawing for eyes, ripping at your mouth, your ears, anything available. There could be no hesitation; you got in close and killed fast. Once your man was down, you looked to help someone else or sought overlooked enemies. He bowed his head and prayed to God to protect his men and give them a quick and merciful victory.

Tiz and his men noiselessly placed their unnecessary weapons on the ground and pulled their short knives. Tiz's stomach was knotting, and he could taste the sour bile he struggled to keep down. Then he saw motion below them, and his men launched themselves at their assigned targets. Tiz took the man at the farthest position, but he would not surprise the man. The Scout in front of Tiz leaped at his target and hit him with a brutal forearm to the head. The enemy's head snapped back, and that was the last Tiz saw. His focus was on his target, who turned and pulled his knife.

Tiz did not hesitate; he feinted left with his knife hand, or what would have been his knife hand if he were right-handed, but unfortunately for the man to his front, he was not right-handed. The man used his left hand to push what he believed to be Tiz's knife arm up and to his right. Tiz grabbed the sleeve of the man's left arm and continued to pull him in the direction he was moving. The movement was so swift the man's back was to Tiz before he could stop himself, and with the speed of a striking snake, Tiz's knife came in from behind, entering just below the man's left jaw, moving upward into the brain, killing him instantly. The man's legs collapsed as if they had no bones, and he lay at Tiz's feet. There was no time for thought.

Tiz checked each of the positions and saw a large man, not one of his, trying to get to the trail to escape. Tiz leaped onto a small boulder to his right, skipped across two others, and was on the man before he could reach the trail, slamming into the man's back, knocking him to the ground. The big man was quick for his size and rolled to face Tiz, now lying next to him. The big man attempted to bring his knife up from under him, going for Tiz's stomach. Tiz dropped his knife from his left hand to his right and clamped his left hand onto the man's wrist before he could strike. The big man did the same, securing Tiz's right wrist in his left hand. Chest to chest, butting with their heads, biting at any body parts that came near, the two men struggled soundlessly. Thrashing wildly with their legs, they tried to clamp the other man or to roll on top. This kind of fight never lasted long. The exertion required was tremendous, like being in an all-out sprint for more than ten minutes. Even with adrenalin, it can't go on for long. Then all of a sudden, it was over. Tiz felt the man's hand go slack on his knife arm, and his knife found the man's exposed stomach, which was hardly necessary since the man was already quite dead.

Tiz never saw the boulder one of his men brought down on the man's head; he was so focused on the fight. The rock squashed the man's head like a ripe melon. As his heart slowed, Tiz noticed the blood and brain matter all over his face. He rolled onto his hands and knees and retched up the contents of his stomach. Tiz took one of the scarves from his head, scrubbed furiously at the wet mess on his face, beard, and hair, and then stood. His boulder-wielding savior stood before him looking for any wounds Tiz might have before looking up at Tiz and sheepishly pointing at a place on his beard, making a flicking motion with his finger. Tiz used the scarf to clean away the last of the residue from his face. "Thank you, Frya. That was a close one, but maybe next time, a slightly smaller boulder or a little less force."

"No problem, Tiz. I'll search a little more carefully next time for a more suitable tool," Frya replied.

"Um, point well taken, my friend. You mash away with whatever you find handy. I'd rather face the cleanup and live to fight another day. All right, gentlemen, let's finish this mission, back to the trail, and put Bendva in front. We'll stay to the trail and make sure we're in position above the ambush before first light."

Navid's team avoided the Uxian flocks and made good time on the smaller horses. They were able to ride closer to the ambush site because of the terrain on their side. Navid and his men dismounted, put their dog, Arsha, in the lead but still on a short leash. They proceeded up an old animal trail toward the location above the ambush site. The trail was rocky and difficult to follow, but Arsha had no problem and led them upward. Navid and his men were supremely fit. Navid was confident in his men's ability to complete the climb and be ready to fight.

However, the dropping temperature and the almost absolute darkness around them added an extra strain as men fought to maintain their balance and stealth. The men were breathing hard as they hit some of the more difficult ascents on the trail. The Uxians on this side of the gate did not bother to set up an ambush site. *The question is, why not,* thought Navid? It was now an hour before dawn. They were almost at the location above the ambush site when Arsha lay down and wagged her tail. Everyone stopped moving and dropped to one knee as they drew their fighting knives. "Well, it looks like the old boy leading this bunch isn't quite as dumb and careless as I hoped." Navid whispered to Utana, "You're one of our best climbers; pick someone you trust and get above the position. We need to know what we're up against."

Utana picked Hugav, who was small and wiry and an excellent climber. Hugav was around twenty-three, Utana thought. When he wasn't teaching or training, Hugav was in these very mountains climbing and hunting. Both men shed all their weapons, unnecessary gear, and their thick outer coats. They kept their fighting knives. They would be moving fast and exerting much energy, so Utana wasn't overly concerned about the dropping temperature. They moved left of the trail and forward until they reached the sheer rock face that would take them above the Uxians. They tied a length of rope to each other, and Utana moved forward to take the lead.

Hugav placed a hand on his arm and whispered, "You're good, but I'm better, plus my lighter weight will give us some advantage if we run into loose shale."

Utana didn't argue; he stepped back and let Hugav take the lead. In the first part of the climb, they found good foot and handholds, and in some cases, small fissures in which they could jam their hands or feet. When they were about thirty feet from their objective, Hugav could feel nothing but smooth rock above him. His heart sank with the thought of having to go back to find another path up to the ledge. There was just enough light for Hugav to see a small rock protrusion about a foot above and four feet to the right of his current position. A light bead of perspiration formed on his brow as he stared at the small rock; it was a blind jump. It was too dark to see anything above or below, but he knew time was running out. Fortunately, Hugav had a good foothold.

Crouching slightly, he created as much tension as possible in his left thigh, and then he pushed off with all of his strength as he stretched his right arm as high as possible. His right hand hit the smooth rock face, and he slid down. His hand searched for anything to grasp. He continued to slide until suddenly his wrist scraped over the rock protrusion, and his fingers grabbed it with every bit of strength he had remaining. He took a deep breath and tried to slow his breathing. He couldn't stay here long; his grip would eventually give way. He searched directly above him and saw nothing. Fighting to remain calm, he moved his left hand to the rock hold, and grasping it with his left, he let go with his right hand. Using his right hand, he searched the rock face for anything that would give him a purchase—nothing.

Using his remaining strength, he pulled himself up with his left arm, and again using his right hand, he searched the rock face above him and to his right. There it was, a small fissure into which he jammed the fingers of his right hand, just as the strength in his left hand gave out. He hung for a second, then pulled himself up with his right arm and felt for the fissure above with his left hand and found that the crack was widening slightly. He jammed his left hand into the crevice, pulled up, searched above with his right hand, and found the fissure again. He continued this method for another six feet, with the fissure ever-widening, and at last, he found purchase with his right foot on a small protrusion from the rock face. He rested for a minute before looking up and saw that the fissure not only continued to the shelf he was seeking but also widened almost into a chimney. Hugav took a moment to thank God for not leaving or forsaking him on the rock face. He did not believe in luck; he believed in providence. God was with him tonight.

When Hugav recovered, he continued his journey up the cleft until he reached a point where he could get both his hands and feet into the fissure. This position allowed him to move to the rock shelf he sought. It was about three feet wide, and to his great relief, followed the cliff's face around and above the Uxians. He searched and was able to find a sizeable boulder. He removed the rope from around his shoulder and waist, tied it off on the boulder, and gave two tugs. He saw the tension on the rope, indicating Utana was climbing.

Hugav saw Utana's head. He reached down, grabbed Utana by his robe, and pulled him up and over the edge. Utana lay there for a moment recovering his breath, peering back over the edge and down the cliff face. He looked back at Hugav in sheer amazement and said, "I'm glad it was too dark for me to see how you got up here; that rock face is sheer." Hugav shrugged his shoulders, "That's why I led. Sometimes you can't see the way; you have to believe it is there."

Utana nodded silently and followed as Hugav led them around the ledge to the area above the Uxians. They both peered cautiously over the edge, moving in the smallest increments possible. The two men lay perfectly motionless, watching for any break in a pattern, noise, or sign of movement. Suddenly, there was just the slightest break in the clouds. Below them were two men, an early warning team in place on a shelf above the ambush team. Utana knew the time was now. They tied two ropes to the closest boulders they could find. No instructions were necessary; both men knew how to kill silently. Then, almost as one, they threw themselves over the edge and repelled, without breaking, straight down. Hugav had the man on the left and Utana the man on the right.

Hugav's man sensed something at the last minute and turned, but he was too late. Both Hugav and Utana grabbed tightly to the rope the instant their hamstrings made contact with the men's shoulders. They clamped their legs around the men's heads and twisted their bodies as hard as they could to the right. You could hear the Uxians' necks snap. Hugav and Utana kept their legs clamped firmly around each man's head and lowered them to the ground.

Utana took a second to examine the shelf they were on and confirmed that there had only been the two men. Then, lying flat, he stealthily moved to the edge of the shelf. About thirty feet below him was the ambush site. There were stacks of logs and boulders that stretched about fifty feet along the cliff face. The shelf below was deep, and the Uxian attacking force was against the cliff wall to avoid detection. As Utana watched, he heard faint movement on the trail leading up to the shelf he was on.

Utana saw Arsha pad onto the ledge, followed by Navid and the Scouts. Navid quickly assessed the area and saw the two dead men. The climbing ropes of Hugav and Utana hung from the cliff. Utana backed away from the edge and stood. He grasped Navid's forearm, a gesture Navid returned in kind, and the two men embraced.

"Well done Utana", said Navid. "What's the situation with the Uxian force below us?"

"The Uxians have their backs to the wall," replied Utana, "and we can't get a headcount. We can see the logs and boulders they have assembled for the attack. But we cannot assess their strength."

Navid thought for several minutes. "We still have time before we begin the attack. Assign watches to monitor activity. Let's see if we can gather more intelligence on their strength and position. Set lookouts, Utana, and have the other men get some sleep." Utana did as instructed, and they waited for the time to begin their attack. Navid advised the men that the attack would commence before first light when the sky started to turn a lighter gray.

As the time approached, Utana woke Navid and gave him an update on the activity. They counted five men, who checked the deadfall periodically, and ten, who had relieved themselves. "My guess," Utana said, "the force is between fifteen and twenty men. Based on the noise we can hear, the Uxians are spread equally over the length of the rock shelf, and there doesn't appear to be a concentration anywhere."

Navid thought for a minute before gathering everyone around him and whispering, "We have just a few minutes before we begin. We will stay with the original plan. Space yourselves evenly along the length of this ledge. It's about a thirty-foot drop to the shelf below us. We must rope down, but it needs to look more like a controlled fall than a rappel. We must land between the Uxians and the deadfall. Make certain none of the Uxians reach the release levers. Kill them all and kill them quickly. I will position myself in the center and serve as last defense, should anyone break through our lines."

He didn't need to explain the decision not to take prisoners. Still, it was his decision and responsibility, his and his alone, and they needed to hear him say it. That formality over, they moved to the cliff edge and anchored their rappelling lines. Everyone was tied off. They held the rope in front of them with their dominant hand and looped it behind their backs. They bent their knees slightly and simultaneously launched themselves out and fell. When they reached the bottom, they applied pressure on the rope with both hands breaking their fall.

At the same time, on the other side of the gorge, Tiz's men were also in launch position. They leaned out over the cliff face, knees bent, waiting for the first sound of battle from across the gorge. To save their strength, they tried to relax as they waited. Then they heard the meaty sound of javelins penetrating flesh and men's screams. Because of their long wait and the difference in reaction times, their launch from the wall was ragged.

Tiz was in the very center of the men he led. He braked with only his left hand when he reached the shelf below. He held a javelin in his right hand, ready to throw. Tiz saw a man in front of him. He threw his weight forward onto his left foot and released the javelin. It entered the center of the man's chest and severed his spinal column. The man dropped, dead before he hit the ground.

Tiz searched for another target, but his men had engaged everyone. He backed up five steps and made himself the second line of defense. He would stop anyone from reaching the deadfall. He kept his eyes straight ahead and relied on his peripheral vision to detect movement on the left or right.

He heard a man yell and looked to his right in time to see a small man leap over one of the Magi who had a nasty-looking leg wound. Everyone always assumed it was the big men you had to be most concerned about, but they were wrong. Speed and strength are a deadly combination. He could tell from the short man's bulk that he would not be an easy kill. Tiz released the arrow on his bow, but the small man dropped to one knee and threw his shield up, deflecting the arrow. At this range, the force of the arrow almost knocked him backward. The two seconds it took him to recover his balance and rise to his feet was all Tiz needed to draw his sword and swing his shield from his back to his left arm.

Tiz ran straight ahead and closed with the little man, using his momentum to throw his weight behind his shield. He hit the man at a dead run. The man set his feet and leaned forward into Tiz; regardless, Tiz drove him back three feet. Tiz raised his sword and brought it down in a powerful overhead arc. The little man raised his sword to deflect the blow. There was too much force. The sword dented the right side of his helmet. Close work was no time for finesse. Tiz used both his shield and his sword as weapons, reigning blows with both. The little man was weaving side to side from the blow to his head. Tiz pressed him unmercifully. He thrust his shield forward, pushing the man's shield back against his chest. Instead of pulling his shield back, Tiz hooked the man's shield. Pivoting his weight onto his left foot, he tore the man's shield away. Tiz completed his turn, dropped, and lunged up with his sword. The sword's point entered at the base of the man's throat and continued upward through the man's jaw and into his brain.

Tiz stood and scanned the line of his men in both directions, looking for any breakthroughs, but there were none. There was a long line of enemy, dead and wounded, and Tiz had one man down with a leg wound. Tiz's hands trembled as the adrenalin from the battle subsided. He looked at the last man he had killed, and he wanted to walk away. To leave all the killing behind, but he had men to lead, and they needed him.

Navid was not quite as fortunate as Tiz. Standing before him when he landed were two men talking and who, unfortunately, had excellent reflexes. Both men reached for their swords just as Navid landed.

Navid did not go for his javelin. Instead, sliding his shield from his back to his left arm, he drew his sword. Neither man had a shield, which provided him a slight advantage. The men separated and circled him. Navid did not think—hundreds of hours of training and muscle memory kicked in. His brain told him the man circling to his right was the most dangerous. He pivoted backward on his right foot. Navid positioned both feet and was now between the men and the deadfall, where he wanted to be.

Like Tiz, Navid used his shield and sword as offensive weapons, hammering his shield up at the man's head. The man blocked with his sword. Navid reversed the motion, bringing the shield down on the man's right foot, breaking the bones and causing him to stagger to his right. The man was off-balance. Navid swept his sword sideways, catching the man in his left side just under his vest, opening a deep cut. Navid pulled back on the sword while continuing to cut and slit open kidney and bowels. The man was down and out of the fight.

Navid squared off with the other man. The man's eyes were open wide. He panted for breath and trembled. This man was a farmer, not a warrior. Navid hesitated for a moment, despite the instructions he gave his men. Navid raised his sword, suddenly the man's eyes opened wide, and his mouth formed in a silent scream. The farmer pitched forward with a javelin sticking out of his back. Behind the dead man was Aref, one of the younger men in the group. He was almost beautiful with a soft light brown beard and skin that had not weathered to leather yet.

"Many thanks," Navid said, but Aref merely looked down and barely whispered, "It is no less than you would have done for me." Navid stuck out his right hand; Aref grasped his right forearm with his right hand, just as Navid did in return. Aref looked his leader in the eye, and they both nodded. Nothing more needed to be said. Navid surveyed where they stood and could see that all of his men were still standing. Two men received minor leg wounds but nothing that would keep them out of the next fight. "Check the Uxians," Navid commanded, "and provide a merciful death to any still living." Based on the amount of blood he saw pooling around the downed men, he didn't expect that too many were still alive.

With that said, he turned and walked over to the man he had wounded. The man was on his back, gasping for breath and grimacing with the effort of just breathing. Navid placed the tip of his weapon above the man's heart. The man looked into Navid's eyes and nodded his head in gratitude, thankful for the mercy stroke he was to receive. The man then looked to the east and lifted his hand toward Navid, palm out, signaling Navid to wait for a second. The man looked back toward the east and was rewarded with the sight of the first streaks of light as the faint grayness of the sky gave way to the dawning morning. He watched as sunlight crept up the mountain face, seeping first through mountain passes and fissures lower down on the mountain. The man then reached into his jerkin and pulled out an image of the sun god, whom he worshiped, and with the amulet, firmly in his grasp, he looked up at Navid and nodded his head. Navid leaned all his weight onto the shaft of his weapon and saw the light leave the man's eyes as the pumping of his lifeblood ceased.

Navid could hear the movement of horses and wagons below him as the Family drew nearer. He prepared the signal light they brought along for this purpose—a small oil lamp with a shiny steel backdrop. Lifting the cover reflected the light in one direction. Navid waited until he could see shadowy figures coming through the pass and then lifted the lamp's front cover three times. The signal the Scouts controlled both sides of the Gate.

The same signal came back to him, acknowledging they had received the message. At the head of the troops preceding everyone into the pass was Kevan, the leader of the Military School. Navid could not see him but knew he would be there. Then would follow Fardad and the women, children, and herds of animals; lastly would come the rear guard, led by his father, Jahan. Now the waiting game began.

Jahan saw the lantern flashes too and now knew two things: Navid and Tiz had successfully removed the avalanche teams, and Jahan knew the location of the avalanche site. Knowing they were safe from the avalanche was the most critical piece of news. Knowing the position of the avalanche gave him an advantage against the Uxians; Jahan knew when the Uxians would attack. The certainty of an attack was confirmed when Taghi failed to send his sons and the other guides to the Magi camp that morning.

The Magi caravan moved forward. Jahan and the rear guard stopped just below Navid and Tiz's position. Jahan watched the caravan and was relieved when he knew they were well past the potential avalanche. Jahan pulled his bow and strung an arrow, and so did the rest of his men. The attack would come any minute now. An Uxian ram's horn blew right on time, signaling the Uxian avalanche teams to trigger the avalanche. Simultaneously, the Uxian horsemen launched their attack, expecting to trap the Magi against the deadfall. But, of course, there was no deadfall.

Now, the Gate became the enemy of the Uxians, forcing them to attack a narrow front against the best archers in Persia. Methodically, the Magi walked their arrows from the front of the enemy charge to the rear; corpses littered the ground between the two forces. The Uxians in the back could not move forward, and the Magi continued to rain down arrows.

Suddenly, Jahan raised a hand, and the Magi horsemen turned as one and raced off toward the leading Magi group. The rear of the Uxian column picked their way through the tangle of fallen men and horses. Taghi led the Uxians in pursuit of the fleeing Magi.

Navid and Tiz positioned men at each avalanche lever and watched below as Jahan and his men cleared the avalanche site. When they were clear, Navid had one of his men blow two short notes on his Ram's horn. Jahan and his men rode another 100 feet, then stopped and turned, waiting on the Uxians. They didn't have long to wait before Taghi, and the rest of the Uxians entered the kill zone.

Navid watched from above; when Taghi's men were under the avalanche site, he and Tiz released the deadfall. The logs and boulders rolled down the mountain, gaining speed as they went. Everything in the path of the avalanche started to move. The roar of the falling detritus blocked out all other sounds, covering the Uxian screams of terror. The dust cloud created by the avalanche mercifully obscured the sight of the dying men and horses. Jahan and his men held their position until the great cloud of dust began to clear. There in front of them were Taghi and twenty men who rode clear of the avalanche. And just behind them were the body parts of men and animals sticking out from the wall of logs and rocks that buried them.

Jahan and his men walked their horses forward. Still in shock at the significant loss of friends behind them, Taghi and his men looked at the Magi coming toward them. They dismounted and dropped their weapons at their feet. Jahan stopped his horse before Taghi and looked down at him.

Jahan asked, "Was your greed worth it"?

Taghi looked up but did not answer. Jahan had his men collect the Uxian weapons. They remounted and turned to rejoin the caravan. Jahan looked at Taghi and the men with him. Most of these men were farmers and shepherds and were here only because of Taghi's greed. More deaths today would be meaningless. The Magi were safe. Jahan said, "We have every right to kill you for your actions here today, but we will not. You may still have men alive under this rubble. I would suggest you get busy searching." With that, Jahan turned his horse and left.

Navid and Tiz led their men down the mountain to their horses. They followed the game trail past the ambush site. The path led down to the central column. Navid sought out his father, who, upon seeing him, smothered him in one of his great bear hugs until Navid's vision blurred. Thankfully his father released him, and Navid stood for a minute trying to regain his senses. Jahan placed both hands on his son's shoulders and said the one thing that Navid always wanted to hear, "You did well today. You and Tiz saved the Family from destruction. I couldn't be more proud of you."

At that moment, Navid was perfectly at peace; his father's love and respect were the two most essential things in the world to him. For the first time in his life, he understood just how deeply he needed his father's affirmation. When Navid recovered enough to speak, he said humbly, "You should have seen the men with me today; they were magnificent. We eliminated the Uxian force on both sides of the Gate, and we suffered only three minor wounds. It was my decision not to take prisoners, Father. I pray it was the right decision."

Jahan knew how difficult that decision was. He nodded and said, "You made the right decision for the safety of your men and the Family, and there was nothing else you could have done. "Come," he said, "let's find something to eat; it has been a long morning already."

"Father, before we eat, I need to talk to you and Grandfather."

Jahan watched his son for a moment and looked into his eyes. He nodded, "You wait here; I will bring your grandfather."

Jahan returned a short while later with Fardad. The three men sat on small boulders nearby, and the two older men waited for Navid to begin.

Navid took a moment to look back at Taghi and his men as they searched the rock pile for survivors. Then he looked up at the cliff face and recalled the fierce battle. His eyes began to mist, and he turned and looked at his father and grandfather. "I have been a fool," he began, "I have done everything I could to stop this journey. All I could think about was everything I was going to lose—Leyla, the Satrapy, power, and glory. I am so ashamed. When I watched our people fight today, I saw a united people. They want to complete this journey and find the Messiah. Please forgive me. I have acted like a child and a fool. I will do everything in my power to serve this Family and to ensure our success."

"Do you still think we will fail?" Grandfather asked.

"Do I still believe Queen Musa will send the Immortals? Yes, I do. I pray that it will be too late by the time she finds out, and we will be outside Persia. But do I think we will fail? No, the Angel of the Lord called us for a reason, and we cannot fail."

Grandfather walked over and hugged Navid, "You have become the man I always knew you would be. I love you." The two men stood there hugging each other as tears ran down their faces.

The three men walked back to camp and sought out Tiz, and the four of them found the cook wagon. Anticipating the needs of the warriors, the cooks had warm bread and goat cheese ready. It was the best meal Navid could remember—the best ever.

For the rest of the day, the Family rode on and cleared the pass. They found a small valley that would be perfect for the evening camp. No one felt much like talking that night. People ate their evening meal in silence. Rahim announced to the children there would be no class tonight. Families prayed, hugged each other, talked, and went to their sleeping mats. For the first time, the scope of what lay in front of them was clear—a long fight, a fight not all of them would survive. To those of great faith, the coming journey was one they knew they must endure. It was God's will. But others questioned the wisdom of this trip; seeds of dissent were growing.

CHAPTER 5

Meesha

Scene 1 Southwest Of the Persian Gate - Day 28

Pari was awake before the dawn. Because of her disability, she exerted herself less physically and often awoke early. She lay thinking of yesterday's events, the fear and tension of everyone before entering the Gate. Would Navid and Tiz be successful in capturing the Uxian ambush site? How large would the Uxian force be? Would Jahan be successful in leading the Uxians into the trap? How many men would die? She prayed from the time she woke yesterday that God would keep them safe. She knew He called them and would provide the means to get to Israel.

As she lay there, the first rays of dawn lightened the sky. There was a light fog this morning that would burn off as the sun rose. A few low clouds obscured the mountain tops. From her sleeping pallet, she could see the scars on the side of the mountain left by yesterday's avalanche. She tried to imagine the horror the Uxians felt as they saw and heard the falling rocks. They knew that death was inexorably coming, and there was no escape. What a horrible last few moments they must have had. She thought of those men and the mothers, wives, and children they left behind, and tears came to her eyes.

Asha was up by now, ready to start her day. She saw Pari sitting on her sleeping mat, tears falling silently down her cheeks. Pari's love and empathy for everyone made it difficult for her to see the bad in anyone.

Asha walked over and sat beside her. "You're thinking about yesterday, aren't you? Would you like to talk about it?"

Pari looked at her mother and was silent for a moment as she formulated her thoughts. "At first, the only thing I could think about was our Family. I prayed all morning for safety for the men who stood between the Uxians and us. God heard and answered my prayers. Then this morning, I thought about the Uxian wives and daughters who offered up prayers yesterday. Prayers to idols, to hunks of wood, who could neither hear nor intervene. Their futility and hopelessness overwhelmed me. Their husbands, fathers, and sons would not be coming home. What a horrible waste; what a useless sacrifice. They trusted their leader, Taghi, who proved to be greedy and false. His evil killed them all. My heart breaks for them, mother."

Asha stroked her daughter's hair and held her close. "You are more precious to me than I can ever tell you. Your love and your sweet spirit for God and His creation put me to shame. I don't know what I would do if I didn't have your eyes through which I could see the world as God intended it to be."

As Asha finished speaking, Tiz came through the tent flaps. When he saw Asha and Pari sitting together, he offered to come back in a little while. Asha raised her hand and waved him in. "It's time to start cooking. I'll join the women to help get things going while you help Pari get ready." Asha did not think twice anymore about the strange union between Tiz and Pari. When she looked into Tiz's eyes as he gazed at Pari, she knew one thing—her daughter was safe. Tiz was not a boy. He was a man and a warrior who chose to care for her daughter. But he was more than that. He would defend Pari with his life. No harm could ever come to her daughter as long as Tiz lived. Tiz loved Pari, and Asha knew it.

"You look sad this morning," Tiz said as he looked at Pari's tear-streaked face. "You're thinking of yesterday, aren't you?"

Pari tilted her head and looked at Tiz. "Yesterday, yes, and about the trip ahead of us. Queen Musa and King Phraates aren't just going to let us go. Before this trip is over, there will be more fighting and more bloodshed."

Tiz remained thoughtful for a moment. "Regardless of how much we were willing to admit to ourselves and others, I think we all knew that this would be a costly trip. There are enemies behind, and in front, and wilderness and desert to cross. There is no way through this gauntlet without bloodshed. Why did the Messiah choose to come at this exact time? Hundreds of years, we waited for a sign. It could have come to our children or our children's children, but it did not. It came to us. Could we dishonor all those who preceded us, who waited and watched, who studied the Scriptures and taught generation after generation that Messiah was coming? Could we ignore the sign and the angel of the Lord? No, it was a simple choice. God chose this time, and He chose us. I would gladly give my life to ensure we complete this journey. The Family must make it to Israel."

Pari sat there in shock, thinking about quiet, contemplative Tiz. That was by far the longest speech she ever heard him give. What else was stored up in there?

"Tiz, that was the most eloquent statement I have heard from anyone about why we are going and the dangers we face. Thank you for opening your heart to me."

Tiz turned slightly red, picked up Pari, and began their day.

Tiz helped Pari dress and then carried her to the eating mats under a tree. The rest of the family was already there, except for Asha and Gul. The two women were approaching, laden with the morning meal. Tiz put Pari down on her mat, just as Asha and Gul set the goat in a spicy yogurt sauce between everyone, along with rice, bread, and cheese. The aroma was overwhelming.

As he did every morning, Fardad prayed for the day and thanked God for His mercy and bounty. The meal passed almost in silence. The men who fought yesterday were trying not to think of the shocked looks on the faces of the men they killed. Everyone at the meal was trying to give the warriors the time they needed to deal with that horrible trauma. They finished eating, wished each other a good day, and moved off to their assigned duties. Tiz lifted Pari and began to carry her to the family's wagon, but Pari stopped him. "Take me to Rahim's wagon. I will help him teach the young ones today, and I have some questions on Scripture, which he and I can discuss later."

Tiz changed direction, carried her down the line to Rahim's wagon, and placed her in the back. "I'll be back later to get you. Enjoy your time with the children and Rahim." He smiled at her and left to join the other Scouts, who were riding out.

Rahim talked to three of the children who had already arrived. He heard Tiz and turned to see that Pari had joined him in the wagon. "Good morning, little one. To what do I owe this great pleasure?"

"I thought you might like help with the children this morning, and I was missing you and them."

"Ah, I can understand your missing the children, but me an old man?"

"Of course, I miss you when I haven't seen you for a while, but…"

"BUT, I knew it. You have ulterior motives. 'But'… what?"

"As I was saying, but after the children leave, I have some Scripture I want to discuss with you. Some things have been troubling me."

Rahim looked suddenly serious. "It's about the Messiah, isn't it?"

"You always could read me," Pari said, "but how could you have possibly known that?"

"It's been on my mind ever since we saw the star, and knowing how much you love the Scriptures, I knew it would be on your mind too. So we'll talk after the children leave."

Just then, the last three children arrived, one of whom was Delara. She was five years old, with huge black eyes, an expressive face, and boundless energy. It was difficult for her to be in the wagon for even a few hours. Just as Delara climbed into the wagon, she saw Pari, and her face lit up in a huge smile.

Delara hopped down from the wagon and ran around in an ever-expanding circle. After about a minute, she stopped, picked something up, and raced back to the wagon. As she climbed back into the wagon, she began talking even before she finished getting in, "Pari,Pari,Pari,lookatthisIgotitforyouisn'titbeautifulIthinkit'sthemostbeautifulrockIhaveeverseenWowyoulookbeautifultodayDidyouhearthatbignoiseandseethatbigdirtcloudyesterdayitwasreallyreallyscaryMydad…"

"Delara," Pari interrupted, laughing, "take a breath; slow down. You have plenty of time to tell us all about yesterday."

Delara said, "Mom tells me that all the time. She says I talk way too fast."

And too much, thought Pari.

Rahim looked around at the children, "Now that Delara is here, we can get started with the morning lessons, but before we begin, who would like to tell me about what they saw and heard yesterday, and how it made you feel?"

Rahim was a wise man. He knew it would be no use even attempting to start the morning lessons until they dealt with what the children saw yesterday. These were not just students; they were children. They each saw something different and heard various perspectives from their family. As each spoke, Rahim noted the expressions and body language they conveyed. This information helped him know how to deal with them individually.

Pari studied Rahim as each child spoke and marveled at this wonderful man. Rahim had been her teacher all her life. Once discussions of yesterday were over, they began their regular morning reading, writing, and mathematics lessons. Rahim was patient with each child, understanding that each had different strengths and weaknesses. What was unique about Rahim is he focused more on each of their strengths than on their weaknesses. The morning passed swiftly, and it was soon time for the noonday meal. Rahim dismissed the children, who hopped down and knew exactly where to find their mothers in the procession of wagons and people.

Rahim turned his attention to a wrapped package next to him. He opened it to reveal bread, cheese, and grapes, more than enough for two people. "I knew after yesterday that you would want to talk. So I gathered enough food for both of us."

Pari was not surprised, and she bowed her head and folded her hands as Rahim gave thanks for God's protection and His bounty. They ate and talked casually of family, the trip, and even of Tiz. They finished eating, and Rahim wrapped anything left in the skin and placed it in the box from which he took it. Dusting the last of the crumbs from his fingers, he looked at Pari, "Now, what is troubling you about the Messiah we are going to meet?"

Pari nodded and began haltingly, "I don't know which Messiah we are going to meet. That's what is troubling me. Isaiah prophesies a virgin who will bear a child, and He will be named Immanuel—God with us[8]. So it seems we are going to meet a baby. Next, Isaiah says He will establish a government, and there will be peace and justice from that time and forever.[9] So it seems we are going to meet the King and ruler of this world. Then Isaiah says, He is despised and rejected by men...acquainted with grief...He is wounded, bruised, and chastised for us, and with His stripes, we are healed...and in the end, He dies and bears the sin of many[10]. So who is this Messiah, Rahim?"

"Ah, I wondered when you would ask. I'm just surprised it has taken you this long."

"I thought of it before, but it wasn't pressing and urgent until now. Is this the forever King who is bringing peace, or is He coming to die for our sins?"

Rahim bowed his head and was silent for several minutes. Then, raising his head, he looked into Pari's eyes and said, "I think the answer is YES. Isaiah's prophecies range across hundreds, if not thousands, of years. He sees the destruction of nations; God destroys some in Isaiah's lifetime, some happen during the two-hundred-year period after his death, and some will happen in the final Day of the Lord. He sees the Messiah as King and ruler over the earth and as a suffering servant. How can the ruling King precede the suffering servant? I think it would be impossible. Are these events sequential or separated by hundreds of years? There is no way for us to know at this point. We will not know until we meet Him. So, patience, little one. God will reveal all in due time."

"How did I know you would say that?" Pari sighed. "It's so hard to wait, Rahim. I so long for the King to rule and reign over this fallen, evil world."

"Be careful what you wish for, little one. Isaiah says the suffering servant is coming to save us from our sins. That sounds like a far greater victory than a military victory, which forces people to serve Him who hate Him. So have patience; the Messiah will be all that you hoped and wished for and more. And while you are waiting, you can teach the beginning lesson on Meesha tonight. I am tired, and the children would love a break from this droning old man."

Rahim smiled and winked at her, and Pari knew he had said all he intended to say on this subject.

Pari and Tiz finished eating the evening meal. Pari asked Tiz to take her to the area they cleared for the evening's classroom, and Tiz found a box to use as a seat for Pari, piled cushions on it, and placed Pari on the pillows. He then sat next to her on the grass. Pari loved this arrangement. She could see all the children, and Tiz dealt with any misbehavior. The children in the clearing were seated in a semicircle around Pari. Some faces were bright with anticipation since Pari was teaching. Other children were too exhausted from days spent herding sheep, goats, and horses. Pari looked at the children closely to judge how long she thought she could keep them interested and awake.

Pari looked at Tiz, who clapped his hands loudly two times. The children began to calm down and focus on Pari. Rahim approached with the Assyrian scroll, from which Pari would teach tonight, but Pari shook her head no and declined the scroll. She had read it so many times, she knew it by heart. Pari let her vision travel from one side of the group to the other as she spoke. "As you all know, during this journey, we will be teaching the history of the Magi. This history will help you understand why we are on this journey. Last time, Rahim introduced Baildan—"

And so the chant began—"Baildan, Baildan, BAILDAN, BAILDAN." Tiz slowly rose to his full height without moving his upper body and stared at the boys seated in the back. A deathly quiet came over the clearing. Just as slowly, Tiz sat back down.

"As I was saying," Pari continued without even a break in her ever-present smile, "it is time for the Assyrian storyteller to tell you the story of Meesha."

Like Rahim, she lowered the timbre of her voice and began the story.

Scene 2 Jerusalem - 734 BC

Baildan, the younger son of Domara, led an Assyrian cavalry troop of one hundred men that had joined the Syrian army. The army was marching south to ally with the Israelites of the northern tribes in Shechem, Israel. Syria and Israel had formed a coalition to attack Judah and other territories east of the Jordan River. At the same time, Domara's elder son Meesha was in Jerusalem, serving as Assyria's ambassador to the court.

Meesha was thirty-two years old, tall, thin, with light brown and gentle eyes, and he moved with the grace of a dancer. He was married to Hano, and they had one son, Zaia. Hano was five years younger than Meesha, and there were two things she loved, Meesha and Zaia. She was tall for an Assyrian woman, more closely resembling an Ethiopian than an Assyrian. Hano was taller than her husband. She had dark skin and finely chiseled features. Her face was thin with high cheekbones. Hers was a beauty unmatched in all of Jerusalem, if not Assyria. Hano loved two things, and her love was a beautiful thing to see when directed at those two. Hano also loved all who loved and supported Meesha and Zaia. However, if you were not one of those who loved and supported Meesha and Zaia, then you were Hano's mortal enemy.

Zaia was ten years old and tall for his age, resembling his mother more than his father, with her same dark skin and coal-black eyes, but he was gentle, thoughtful, and a lover of knowledge, like his father.

The family finished its morning meal, and Zaia asked his father, "Are you going to court this morning?"

Meesha smiled at his son. "Yes, King Ahaz is returning from Lachish this morning, and I'm sure he'll be holding court. Why? Would you like to come?"

Zaia smiled, "May I? Father, why is Ahaz king when his father Jotham still lives?"

"Of course, I think it is important that you come. As to why Ahaz is king, his father is not well and cannot perform the king's duties. Also, there is a strong faction of counselors who do not like the lack of religious freedom under Jotham, and they are free to worship other gods under Ahaz. I have also heard King Ahaz may be ready to ask for our help with his current military situation. With Syria and Ephraim allying on the northern border of Judah, the King is certain he will not be able to stand against their joint force without the help of Assyria. Go and get your robe. We will get to the palace before the King arrives."

As they stood, they were startled by a knock on the door. Guests at the house were rare since they were not Jews, but it was unheard of this early in the morning. Hano went to the door and opened it but did not see anyone until she looked down. Standing before her was the shortest Israeli man she had ever seen. He was barely five feet tall, but his long salt-and-pepper beard and bushy eyebrows told her this was no child. He had a slightly bulbous nose and large ears, and it was all she could do to keep from laughing at this little troll of a man. "Good morning, Hano," the little man greeted her. "I am Adin. Is Meesha here?"

By now, Meesha had made it to the door, and peering over Hano's shoulder, he greeted his friend, "Good morning, Adin. My apologies, Hano; this is Adin, a disciple of Isaiah. He has been instrumental in teaching me Israel's history and beliefs about their God YAHWEH and the Law God has given them. Come in, come in, Adin. Can we offer you something to eat or drink?"

Hano backed into the room, but Adin did not follow. "Thank you for the offer, Meesha, but you know the Law forbids me to enter the home of a Gentile. I came to tell you that Isaiah is going out to the highway by the fuller's field to meet King Ahaz when he returns from Lachish. I have some idea what is about to happen, and I'm sure you will want to hear."

Meesha knew the Jewish law and was embarrassed, "Forgive me, Adin. I do know your Law, and I respect it. So why would Isaiah confront the king on the highway? Why not just go to court, as is normal?"

"Simple," replied Adin. "God spoke to him during the night and told him to take his son, Shear-jashub, and deliver a message to Ahaz on the highway by the fuller's field."[11]

"I would love to go with you. Is it all right if Zaia comes with us? He is going to court with me today. Also, why did God want Isaiah to take his son with him today?"

"Of course Zaia can go with us, and the reason for Shear-jashub is because his name is part of the prophecy. Isaiah delivers a message of hope and God's protection to Ahaz, or he can reject the worship of God and face the consequences. The name Shear-jashub means, 'the remnant is converted.' To reject God is to bring judgment on Judah, and after the judgment, a small group will remain who will believe and worship the Lord. So Ahaz has a choice."

To Meesha's mind, this was not the political answer he wanted to hear, but this was the time to listen and learn, not to offer an opinion. "Let us get our robes," replied Meesha, "and we will join you."

The men left the house, and it was quiet on the street where they lived. Many people joined as they got closer to the highway north of the aqueduct leading to the fuller's field.

Meesha saw a group of four men walking together. One of the men saw Adin's robes and prayer shawl and approached them. The man addressed Adin, "Rabi, word has spread through the city that Isaiah will meet King Ahaz. Can you tell us the prophecy he will deliver?"

Adin smiled at the man and nodded at the men with him. "Word has come to the prophet that Ephraim and Syria have combined their armies to defeat Judah and place a new king on the throne. I believe Isaiah will reveal a prophecy to King Ahaz concerning what the Lord has shown him about this potential war."

Ahead they saw the crowd growing, filling both sides of the highway. In the center of the road, Meesha saw Isaiah, five feet and seven inches tall, with dark hair and a full bead. His features were commonplace, with dark eyes, dark bronze skin, bushy eyebrows, and a nose with just a slight ridge and hook. Coming down the King's Highway from the other direction, he saw King Ahaz, accompanied by his nine-year-old son, Hezekiah. The king's honor guard of thirty Mighty Men surrounded the king and his son.

Adin turned to Meesha and suggested, "It may be a good idea for you and Zaia to stay on the outside of the crowd. I have a bad feeling, and I don't want you in the middle of the crowd if Isaiah mentions Assyria." This was an excellent suggestion to which Meesha readily agreed since he was in his formal white robe and conical hat.

When the honor guard reached Isaiah and his son, they halted, and the King came forward to speak with Isaiah. Ahaz dismounted, not wanting to disrespect the prophet in front of so large a crowd.

"Prophet, what is so important that you must stop me in the middle of the road?" Ahaz wore his riding clothes, but they were the same dark purple as his royal robe. His beard was bronze and neatly trimmed. He had piercing, deep-set brown eyes that shifted constantly. It wasn't easy to know to whom he was talking. He always looked at the crowd, seeking either threats or affirmation. He was an expert at playing to the public.

Isaiah stepped closer to the King but spoke loud enough to carry to the crowd. "Of what are you afraid? What do you fear? The two kings gathered against you, Rezin of Syria, and this pretender of a king, Pekah, the son of Remaliah, are all smoke and no fire. They desire to destroy you and put Tabeel of Syria as king over Judah. This will not stand. It will not come to pass. I tell you now that within sixty-five years, Ephraim will be broken; it will no longer even be a people. This is the truth, but God will take the kingdom from you if you do not believe. If you doubt what I am saying, then ask for a sign from the Lord your God. The sign may be in the depth or the height above."

Ahaz looked at the crowd trying to gauge their reaction to Isaiah's words. He knew they were just as terrified of the combined armies of Syria and Ephraim as he was, and he needed a response that was not a response. So, with a voice as silky as oil on water, Ahaz extended his arms, turned his palms up, and shrugged his shoulders. "I will not ask, nor will I test the Lord!"

Isaiah glared at the King, stood straight, and pointed his finger at him, "O house of David! Is it a small thing for you to weary men, but will you weary my God also? Therefore, the Lord Himself will give you a sign: Behold; the virgin shall conceive and bear a Son, and shall call His name Immanuel. Curds and honey He shall eat, that He may know to refuse the evil and choose the good. For before the Child shall know to refuse the evil and choose the good, the land that you dread will be forsaken by both her kings. The Lord will bring the king of Assyria upon you and your people and your father's house—days that have not come since the day that Ephraim departed from Judah."[12]

When Isaiah mentioned Assyria, all eyes turned to look at Meesha, who instinctively stood in front of Zaia to shield him from the crowd. But when he finished speaking, Isaiah turned his back on the king and walked away, defusing the situation.

Adin turned to Meesha and said, "It's time to leave," Meesha nodded. The three of them walked toward the palace, where the king would be holding court in a little while.

Meesha gave Adin a troubled look and asked, "I'm not sure I understand everything the prophet just said, all that stuff about signs and virgins and Assyria's role."

Adin smiled back at him. "If it's any comfort to you, I'm not sure any of us understood all of it. Isaiah told him clearly that God would fight for Judah only if Ahaz put away the worship of foreign gods and foreign alliances and turned his heart to God. That is what God has always demanded of His people. But Ahaz has no intention of putting aside his other gods, nor will he rely on God to fight for Judah. So the king evaded Isaiah's offer to give him a sign from God. The sign was a trap, and King Ahaz knew it. If God gave him a sign, he must obey God. The part about the virgin gets a little cloudy, but it is a future event, and before it occurs, Assyria will destroy both Syria and Ephraim and bring judgment on Judah. That part is as sure as God's Holiness."

Meesha nodded but remained quiet for the rest of the walk as he contemplated the things Adin had just told him. It was a short walk to the palace, and when they reached it, Adin looked at him with sadness. "It will be difficult for you to know which master to serve. Your king has sent you here for a moment like this. Judah is in your power. Will you listen to Isaiah, or will you serve Assyria?"

Meesha thought for a moment before answering, "I am the representative of the King of Assyria, I will present King Ahaz with all of the facts, and King Ahaz must choose a course for Judah. Thank you for all you have done for me today. I have listened to everything Isaiah and you said."

Meesha and Zaia turned and entered the palace and went to the court, where king Ahaz would soon appear. They didn't have long to wait. The king and his counselors entered the chamber, and it was apparent from his red-faced scowl that King Ahaz was furious.

He sat on his dais and began venting, "Who does he think he is? The prophet confronted me in the middle of the highway with half of the city present. He addressed me like a pagan dog. If it weren't for my fear of the people, I would drag him in and remove his eyes and tongue, and then let's see him prophesy." Ahaz saw Meesha standing there and yelled, "Well, what do you have to say? Don't stand there like a gaping fool."

Meesha was stunned by the ferocity of Ahaz's words and expression and knew that this was a time for calmer heads. "Great king, I heard the words of the prophet, and two things were clear to me. First, the might of the combined armies of Syria and Ephraim would be extremely difficult and costly for Judah to deal with alone, and the people seem to agree with your position on seeking an alliance. But, second, if the prophet is right, Assyria will successfully conquer both Syria and Ephraim, ridding you of an imminent threat on your border. As to his statement concerning Assyria taking military action against Judah, that is in your control. You need only ask other nations who are subjects of King Tiglath-Pileser III. They will tell you that when they deal honestly with Assyria and pay their annual tribute, their kings are left to govern their countries as they see fit."

Ahaz leaned back in his throne and stared fixedly at Meesha. "My, what a generous offer—Assyria will raise a massive army, come against both Syria and Ephraim, and do it all for the love of poor little Judah."

Meesha smiled at the king. "Oh, I must have left off the part where you send all the gold in Jerusalem to King Tiglath-Pileser III as an incentive and a sign of goodwill.[13] I will need an inventory from you by the end of the day of the tribute you will be sending, and I will include it with my message to the King of Kings. Then, if you need nothing further from me, I will leave and draft our agreement, which you may sign later today." Saying so, Meesha turned and left the chamber.

Zaia followed his father. As they walked, he looked up at his father. "Father, what will you do now, and why did you decide to help Judah?"

Meesha looked down at his son and knew this was a valuable teaching moment. "We both heard Isaiah and his prophecy today. He prophesied that Ahaz was not to seek assistance from Assyria and that if he did, God would take the kingdom from him. Yes, Syria and Ephraim will fall to Assyria, but Judah may also suffer. My responsibility was to lay the proposal before Ahaz, but he freely chose his path. We have little experience with this God of Israel, but this will be an excellent test of the prophecy of Isaiah. If the prophecy is true, Assyria benefits. If it is not true, we lose nothing. I have been studying the Scriptures with Isaiah's disciples. I know the marvelous things they claim God did for Israel, but it seems like ancient history. Now all of a sudden new prophets are arising. First, it was Elijah, Elisha, and Jonah, and now it's Isaiah, Amos, and Hosea. Isaiah has already prophesied judgment on both Ephraim and Judah, although we do not know what this judgment will look like and when it will happen. I feel it's coming, and Assyria will play a key role in executing it. We stand in a unique place in history, Zaia. I think we will see something unfold that the world has never seen before. If we are fortunate, we will both live to see it. As to the second part of your question, I will go home and draft an agreement between Assyria and Judah for Ahaz to sign. After that, I need to talk to Eliya to prepare him for the trip to Assyria." As he finished speaking, they arrived home, and Hano greeted Meesha and Zaia.

"You two are home early. What happened in the meeting between Isaiah and Ahaz," she asked as she wrapped her arms around her husband.

"I'll give you all the details later," Meesha whispered to her as he kissed her lightly on the cheek, at which Zaia grimaced. "Right now, I have to draft an agreement between Assyria and Judah. Hano, could you find Eliya? He has a long journey in front of him." Hano left to find Eliya as Meesha sat to draft the agreement.

By the time he finished the first draft, Hano had returned with Eliya, an Assyrian who came with Meesha on his assignment to Judah. Eliya was five feet, ten inches tall, and had wavy black hair and a shortly cropped black beard. He was well-muscled and had trained in the military schools of Assyria. He served as the family bodyguard, manservant, and anything else the family needed.

"Ah, my friend, good to see you. I have work for you." Meesha looked fondly at his old friend. Eliya, a man of few words, stood patiently looking at him.

"I am drafting an agreement between Assyria and Judah, which I need you to carry to my father, Domara. Baildan is with the Syrians at their base in Shechem, and he needs to know that this message is going to Domara. Baildan must return with his men to Assyria as soon as possible. I don't need to tell you how dangerous this is, but there is no choice."

Eliya stood for a moment, thinking, before he said, "I know two men, Judeans. Both have seen military service, and they are trustworthy. I will take them with me. I will get racing camels from Ahmed, who has a good stable and will deal fairly with me. Draft a copy of the agreement for one of the Judeans to carry if something happens to me. Enclose a promise of a healthy payment in gold to be paid to them by your father. They will need an incentive to carry on without me. We can be ready to go by this evening." Having said what he needed to say, Eliya left to prepare for the journey.

Meesha finished the agreement's final draft and had Zaia take it to Ahaz's clerk for the king's signature. Zaia returned a short time later with the signed document. Meesha looked over the tribute inventory. He leaned back in his chair and whistled. Ahaz had stripped the temple of all of its gold and bronze and imposed a tax on every citizen. He knew the Assyrian king would be more than pleased with the tribute. He sealed the documents, including a separate letter to his father. He placed the original documents in a leather pouch for Eliya and the copies in a matching pouch for the Judeans. Shortly after the evening meal, Eliya arrived with the camels and Ali and Samuel, the two Judeans, dressed for war. Each man had bows and arrows strapped to their saddles, carried swords, daggers, and javelins. The two Judeans even had a bag of stones and slings tied to their waistbands. Meesha went out to greet them, carrying the two pouches. Eliya dismounted and took the pouches from Meesha, putting the original inside his robe, securing it with a sash around his chest. He gave the pouch with the copy to Samuel, who secured his the same way. Meesha gripped Eliya by both arms and pulled him close. "We have been through much together, old friend, but this is a journey I wish you didn't have to take. I could send you east, and it would take a few extra days to reach Assyria. This route would be safer, but then there would be no one to warn Baildan. I don't see an option."

Eliya's face softened as he stared back at his old friend, and with warmth, he replied, "I too have thought through the options, and there are none. We will ride through the night to avoid as many contacts as possible, and we will meet Baildan by the morning. The greatest difficulty will be getting around the pickets and the outriders of the Syrians. Once we're past them, we should make good time. We will make it to Nimrud in six days if all goes well. So do not be concerned about us; rather, pity the poor fool who decides to get in our way."

With his last sentence, he put on his war face. Eliya was a serious man who would kill anyone who stood in his way. Having said all he needed to say, he mounted, nodded down at his friend, and turned his camel toward the valley gate.

Eliya led the way with Ali following and Samuel bringing up the rear. Each man had two camels, with the extra camels tied to each man's saddle. They would need the additional camels to exceed the 100-miles-per-day goal, which Eliya set.

Once clear of Jerusalem, they kept a steady pace descending the mountain toward the Jordan River to the east. They would take the river's valley as far north as possible to avoid the mountains between Jerusalem and Shechem, and they would turn back west just past Mt. Gerizim. Finally, they would take the valley between Mt. Gerizim and Mt. Ebal to get to Shechem. The good thing about the Jordan River valley was it would save them time. The downside was it was a significant farming area with small cities, villages, and shepherds with their dogs. There would be no way to avoid unwanted attention.

They rode steadily but at a careful pace descending out of the mountains. Shortly after sunset, Eliya could smell the dense air of the valley, full of rotting vegetation, animals, and the unmistakable odor of the river itself. From behind, he heard Ali whispering to Samuel, "Nothing better than the smell of cow manure, I always say."

Samuel replied drily, "That's because it reminds you of your wife." The two were working to stifle their laughter until Eliya turned and looked at them. The laughter died. A good road used to transport goods to market ran north-south in the valley. Eliya would have been more comfortable traveling off-road, but the time savings of the road was too tempting. He wasn't concerned about meeting elements of the army this far east, but he didn't like advertising their presence to anyone. Once on the road, he called "Hut, hut" to his camel and the increase in speed was immediate. Behind him, he heard Samuel and Ali also calling to their camels. They rode at this pace through the early evening.

There was enough moonlight to see the newly plowed fields; there was the pungent odor of freshly turned dirt, and in some areas, they could see the first shoots of wheat and barley. Close to the river, the vineyards stood on the hills above them, and they were beginning to bud. It would be a beautiful place to see in the daylight, but they had more pressing business right now. The men passed several villages and one city, Archelais.

A few people were still out, but the men rode fast and didn't provide an opportunity for conversation. However, they got a few hard stares. They rode for about three hours before Eliya called for a rest. They were in a small wooded valley surrounded by a marsh, and it seemed like a quiet area to rest the camels and have a small evening meal. They did not start a fire, not wishing to draw attention to themselves. Instead, they ate goat cheese and bread and drank wine diluted with water. They were relaxing for a minute after eating when Samuel leaned forward and whispered, "We have company."

Neither Eliya nor Ali looked around, but as they strained to hear, they heard men moving in the woods around them. In a well-coordinated move, five men walked from the woods and surrounded them. A large, very filthy man with an unbelievably ripe odor stepped forward, clearly, their leader, "Gentlemen, what brings you to our little valley so late at night?"

Eliya rose, along with Samuel and Ali. The three men stood back to back, with Eliya facing the leader. Eliya knew there were bands of brigands who preyed on caravans traveling through the valley, and unfortunately, they had decided to make camp in the middle of their lair. These men were murderers and outcasts, and their intention was clear.

"We are on the king's business," replied Eliya calmly and evenly. "We carry nothing of value and are of no interest to you."

The big man smiled back, but there was no warmth in his eyes. "Oh, you would be surprised at the things that interest us, like those six beautiful camels for one. Also, we would certainly like to see the things you carry for the king. That would certainly interest us."

Eliya decided that talking was over and drew his sword faster than the eye could follow. He took two steps toward the big man, who was still drawing his sword. He raised his sword above his head on his first step, and on his second step, he stamped down, transferring all his weight to his front foot as his sword flashed downward. The blade caught the big man on his right shoulder and sliced through his clavicle; it descended through ribs and lungs to his navel. The big man stood there for a minute, his organs spilling out, his mind gone blank from the shock of the blow. He stood there without making a sound looking at Eliya before falling like a felled tree at Eliya's feet. Without hesitating, Eliya turned to the man to the left of the leader and advanced on him. He could see from the fear in the man's eyes that this wouldn't take long, and it didn't. Eliya turned in time to see Ali and Samuel finishing the other three men.

"Is everyone all right?" Eliya called to them.

Ali was beside himself, filled with adrenalin from the quick action. "Oh sure, now he speaks; now he speaks. How about a little heads up next time? We need a signal like you whistle or say something like 'lion' or something. I mean, we're standing here thinking negotiations are ongoing, and the next thing we hear is steel coming out of its sheath. Huh? A little heads up, you know, just a little signal, you know—'Hey, guys, I'm going to start killing people,' just something."

Without changing expression Eliya, repeated, "Is everyone all right?"

Ali, dumbfounded, said, "Yeah, we're good. I'm just saying we need some signals."

"Then let's mount up. We still have a lot of ground to cover. Oh, and forget the signal; next time, remember, I don't negotiate."

Eliya turned and walked to his camel. Ali grinned at Samuel, "He don't negotiate. That would have been good to know."

They continued up through the valley for the rest of the night without incident. They passed shepherds periodically, but usually in the distance, a few of their dogs raising alarms. The riders were moving so swiftly the shepherds did not have time to call out to them. The riders passed the city of Phasaelis, perched up in the foothills. Next, they reached Coreae, which was at the branch of the Jabbok River, the road forked here. One fork continued north, up the valley, and the other turned west toward Shechem. The riders turned onto the west fork. Eliya turned in his saddle and spoke to the two men behind him, "As we near Shechem, we may encounter Syrian/Israeli patrols or even Judean patrols who are monitoring the Syrians. It could get a little crowded and a little messy. To avoid as many people as possible, we'll continue on the road for a few more miles, and then we'll ride off-road the rest of the way. The last Meesha knew Baildan provided cavalry support for the army on the right flank, which means we will have to circle to the north of the Syrian army to reach him. We will ride north around Shechem since most of the patrols will be to the south. We will also raise less suspicion riding toward Baildan by coming from the north."

For the rest of the night, they worked their way through the foothills of Mt. Ebal. They saw a few small patrols to the south, but they would stop and kneel the camels until the patrol passed and then resume. They were on the northwest side of Shechem just before dawn, and now came the tricky part. In this massive group, they had to find Baildan.

The army itself was easy to find. Before daybreak, in the valley south of Shechem, cooking fires dotted the landscape. The fires gave them a clear picture of the perimeter of the camp. Baildan should be on the southwest corner of the army since his cavalry unit would be used primarily as scouts. The sun was peeking over the mountains to their east as they neared Baildan's location. They were to the west of the army, trying to keep as much distance as possible between themselves and the patrols when Samuel spoke. "I see horse corrals about a mile ahead. That should be Baildan."

The three men stopped and conferred. Eliya began, "I have an idea. The three of us riding into the camp seems like a bad idea. Let Baildan come to us. Undoubtedly, the army will send out morning patrols. All we have to do is to wait for him to come to us. We'll continue riding south of his position, and we should be in a good spot to intercept him. As a precaution, Samuel, you will drop back a mile behind us in case there is trouble. You are not to wait to see what happens. In that case, you are to leave immediately and make your way to Nimrud to deliver your package to Meesha's father, Domara."

Then, Eliya leaned out of the saddle toward Samuel and shook his hand, "Good luck, my friend. Travel safely."

Eliya and Ali continued riding south, and Samuel stayed where he was until they separated themselves, and then all three men rode south. They didn't have long to wait. About an hour later, they saw a large horse patrol heading almost toward Eliya's position. Eliya stopped near a small rock outcrop, which provided him some cover, and Samuel rode into a deep gulley to stay out of sight.

Eliya waited until the patrol was about 100 yards from him before riding out from behind the outcrop. Baildan's outriders drew their bows and trained them on the two men. Three men broke off from the patrol and advanced toward them until the two groups were about twenty feet apart. The leader, with a weapon balanced across his knees, began, "I don't believe I have seen you before. Who are you, and who do you serve?"

Eliya said humbly, "We serve a man named Meesha, and we seek Baildan. We come in peace."

Baildan looked around and decided to be cautious. "I am Baildan, but I don't know a Meesha. Who is this man you serve?"

Eliya raised his left hand, reached into his robe with his right hand, extracted the leather pouch, and tossed it to Baildan. Baildan opened the pouch and saw the two documents, a legal agreement and a letter to his father. Their wax seals had the mark of his brother's signet ring and bore his brothers' signature.

Baildan put both documents back in the pouch and tossed them to Eliya. "Well, this should be an interesting story."

Eliya smiled at Baildan. "I have heard much about you from your brother. He has sent me to warn you that I am carrying a document to Tiglath-Pileser in which King Ahaz requests an alliance with Assyria against Syria and Ephraim. It most surely will mean war, and your brother requests that you return to Assyria at your earliest convenience. Therefore, as soon I have delivered my message to you, I am to ride to Nimrud to deliver these documents to your father."

Baildan sat for a moment in stunned silence, listening to the wind whispering through the rock formations around them, "You may tell my father we are marching against the Judean army gathered to the south. There is no way to extract my men before the battle, but in the chaos afterward, we will turn north and ride for Assyria."

However, Baildan became suddenly concerned and, looking around, spotted what he feared he would find. Sitting on a slight rise to their north was a single horseman, Nabil's spy, who shadowed them daily since they had joined the army. He most certainly would report this encounter to the commander, and Eliya and Ali would stand no chance of escape. He was calculating in his mind the probability that he could cut the spy off before he reached the camp, but the odds seemed long. He looked back at the spy again, but instead of seeing the man, he saw only the man's horse standing there with an empty saddle pad. A few minutes later, a man on a camel topped the rise, twirling a sling above his head.

Baildan turned and looked at Eliya, who grinned back. "I hope that wasn't a friend of yours. The gentleman on the camel is Samuel, who I suppose surmised that the horseman on that rise was not a friend, and I can only hope that he surmised correctly. The man may be only uncon- scious, but it's equally possible he is...well, you know."

Baildan grinned back at him, "You may thank Samuel for me; he surmised correctly and ask him to please dispatch the man for me."

With this, Eliya looked up at Samuel and made a slicing gesture with his right hand across his throat. Eliya watched as Samuel drew his sword. Eliya turned to Baildan and said, "I believe you can consider your problem properly dispatched. We will leave you now and dispose of the body. We will take the horse with us so it doesn't go wandering back into camp. Once we have cleaned things up, we will head to Assyria."

Baildan looked at him with gratitude. "I know the risk you took coming here, and I want to thank you. We would have been in a terrible position without your warning. Be safe on your journey." Baildan reached out and embraced Eliya, kissing him on both cheeks. Eliya nodded to him, and he and Ali rode toward Samuel.

Scene 3 Magi Camp - End of Day 28

"Children, that is more than enough for one night. We will continue again tomorrow," Pari said as she yawned. A few of the children began the Baildan chant, at which Tiz rose, and the chant ceased.

"Off to sleep, children; tomorrow is another long day," Tiz said in his gentle voice, and he picked up Pari and carried her to her tent.

CHAPTER 6

Leyla

Scene 1 South Zagros Mountains - Day 38

Once they left the Gate, they began a slow descent toward the Persian Gulf. It had taken them ten days to reach tonight's camp.

Navid watched as his sister finished teaching and followed Tiz as he carried Pari to their tent. Pari had taught tonight since they were studying Scripture, and it was her favorite subject. When he helped set up the tent this evening, Navid had been careful to place his sleeping mat next to the tent flap. Navid entered the tent, greeted everyone, performed a convincing fake yawn, and knelt by his mat to pray. His mind was so cluttered, prayer was impossible, but he earnestly prayed that the trip he would make tonight would be successful. He felt like a fool, sneaking off in the middle of the night. He was too embarrassed to talk to his father about taking Leyla with them on the journey, and he certainly could not ask her father, Baraz, for permission. Baraz was a Satrap, and Navid was not sure how much he could trust him. He would sneak into Baraz's compound, tell Leyla the truth about the Magi and their journey, and ask her to come with him. There was no question she would want to come. He would let her decide whether to tell her father. He didn't look forward to confronting Baraz, but he would do anything to have Leyla.

Having finished his prayers, he lay down, covered himself with his robe, and closed his eyes. Then he waited while his mind worked endlessly on what he would say, how he would act and react, trying to consider all actions and possible reactions. He lay there long enough to ensure everyone's breathing seemed slow and deep, rolled off his mat, gathered his weapons, and snuck out of the tent. He made his way to the corral, found Anosh, and put his tack on him.

"Took you long enough. I was about ready to go back to sleep."

Navid jumped and turned at the same time. "Utana," he whispered with as much force as possible, "You scared me worse than a tiger. What are you doing out here?"

"Oh, you mean why am I standing here in the corral waiting for you to show up?" He whispered back, "That part is easy. We are now as close as we will get to the compound of Baraz, and there is no way you are leaving without Leyla."

"Utana, you need to go back to your tent. Things could go wrong, and you don't want to have any part in it if they do."

"Navid, we have been best friends since birth. This past year you have talked of little else than your betrothed. Leyla is so beautiful. She has eyes like a doe, her voice is like a murmuring brook, the body of a goddess," Utana whispered as he minced about batting his eyes, at which Navid punched him in the shoulder, sending Utana into a fit of giggling.

"Shut up, you idiot," Navid said, "or this trip will be over before it starts. AND you're not going."

This time in all earnestness, Utana looked at his friend with compassion. "I'm going, whether you like it or not. You're not leaving here without Leyla. I know how much she means to you, and I understand the risk." Utana grabbed his horse's mane and swung himself onto the horse, "You coming or not?"

"I guess we're both fools, but at least, whatever happens, I'll have you with me, and there is no one I would rather be with."

Navid looked at his friend, shook his head, and swung onto Anosh's back. The two men turned their horses north and rode in silence toward the compound of Baraz. As they neared the perimeter of the Family's camp, a horseman appeared from behind a stand of trees, and there was just enough light to see his outline.

"Halt! What's your business?" a voice said firmly.

"Aref, is that you?" Navid queried. He knew that Aref had perimeter duty this evening.

"Navid? What are you doing out here?"

"Father wanted Utana and me to scout ahead," Navid lied smoothly.

"Makes sense," Aref nodded. "You be careful out there."

"You too, Aref. Stay alert. We'll see you later." Navid and Utana put their heels to their horses and broke into a steady lope. They could travel at this pace for a long time. They turned west for a few miles as Navid searched for the trail that would lead them to Baraz's compound, and after about an hour of riding, he found the path and turned northeast. The compound wasn't far, probably a few hours—just enough time to collect Leyla and make it back to the Family encampment before sunrise.

As they rode, Navid thought back on the times he had visited Baraz over the past years. Baraz was a few years younger than Jahan, portly with a round face and deep-set eyes. He had amassed much wealth mining iron ore to supply the ever-growing need for weapons by the Persian army. The ore also found its way to the Romans and others, but money was money after all. Father had first met Baraz while acquiring military supplies five years ago. Leyla, twelve at the time, had been with her father. Leyla didn't look twelve. She was physically mature and well-schooled. Baraz's wife had died three years before of a consumptive disease, and he had not remarried. His sister, Omid, who lived with them, stepped in and took responsibility for the young girl. Baraz had several concubines, but Leyla was his only child and his only love. She was schooled in language and arts by Omid. Baraz's Satrapy was vast, covering southeast Persia. He took Leyla with him whenever he traveled through his Satrapy, teaching her the art of negotiation, management, and leadership. He had even schooled her in the use of the sword, bow, and spear. Hers was not the education of most young girls. Baraz was grooming her to be the next Satrap of this region. Jahan was impressed by the young girl, and two years later, Navid traveled with him when he visited Baraz. Navid was fifteen when he first met Leyla and was stricken by her beauty, grace, and self-assurance. She was not like anyone he had ever met. She was certainly unlike the girls of the Magi Family.

She was only two or three inches shorter than Navid, with thick, black hair falling to the middle of her back. The time outdoors, traveling with her father, caused her to be deeply tanned. She had deep-set hazel eyes, a slim nose, full lips, and though she was only fourteen, she had already developed significant womanly features. Navid and Leyla were accompanied everywhere by Omid, and for the first few hours, Navid could barely speak.

Finally, Leyla teased him about being shy, and he relaxed. After that first meeting, Navid and Jahan returned three or four times a year. When he was seventeen, the fathers knew these two were meant to be together and arranged their marriage. Navid remembered it like it was yesterday. The fathers held a feast to announce the engagement. Many of the Magi traveled to the event, and all of the headmen, from the Satrapy and their wives, were there. The feast lasted for three days, drinking and eating, eating and drinking, games and contests, wrestling, archery, javelin, sling, and even races. How much everyone had wagered on the competitions was impossible to estimate. It was loud, it was joyful, and it had been the highlight of his life. The crowd lifted the chairs on which he and Leyla sat and put them on their shoulders. They paraded them around the compound. Navid remembered the joy in Leyla's eyes as she laughed and smiled at him as the people carried them. Now he was on his way to claim his betrothed. Carrying her away in the middle of the night was not the way he had planned them to begin their life together, but this is the way it had to be. He knew Leyla would agree, and grandfather could marry them tomorrow.

When they got closer to Baraz's compound, the terrain steepened. Utana was the first to see the outline of the wall and parapet breaking the skyline and gave Navid a soft whistle. They slowed their mounts as Navid searched for a small ravine, which he knew was ahead. He saw the familiar gnarled tree at the entrance to the hollow and signaled for Utana to halt. Both riders dismounted.

"Utana," Navid whispered, "you stay here with the horses. I know an old tree that grows close to the wall, and I can climb it and get in. If I am not back in a short while, you are to take the horses back to camp and tell Jahan what has happened."

Utana nodded, and Navid crouched as he moved toward the wall. It helped that he was a hunter and a warrior; stealth was a skill he knew well. It did not matter how alert the guards were. They would never see or hear him. He found the tree just where he remembered, but there was one small problem. The tree had been hit by lightning recently and was broken well below the height of the wall.

Undaunted, Navid continued his search as he moved along the base of the wall. Periodically, he heard guards moving on the parapet above him, but no one saw or heard him. Navid continued around the wall for another twenty minutes. He was wasting valuable time. He needed to find a way up quickly. He continued another twenty feet and found a creeping vine that climbed the wall. The central stalk of the vine was substantial and should hold him. How he was going to get Leyla back down the vine was another issue. He removed his weapons, except for his dagger, and laid them at the base of the wall. Speed and silence would be the key from this point. He grasped the vine and climbed, leaves making slight sounds as they broke under his weight, but there was no helping that. He ascended to the top of the parapet and cautiously raised his head over the lip. If there was a guard here, he was lost. There was no one in his view, but he still did not move. He saw movements to his right and left on the opposite side of the compound, two men. Baraz must be reasonably secure; he had a minimal guard, and they were facing outward. Navid pulled himself over the wall, recognized where he was, and, staying as low as possible, moved to the first stairway he found. He descended and was now in deep shadows.

Keeping against the wall, he entered the hallway that led to Leyla's room. He found the door to her room and as quietly as possible he opened the big door. In the darkness, Navid could barely see her bed on the other side of the room. He moved beside the bed and saw the sleeping form lying there. Slowly, he reached down and placed his hand over her mouth.

Leyla's eyes flew open in bewilderment and terror. "Leyla, Leyla; it's Navid," he whispered, "don't be afraid. I'm going to remove my hand. Please don't make a sound."

Leyla lay there utterly confused. "Navid, have you lost your mind? What are you doing here, in my bedroom, no less?"

Navid shushed her holding two fingers up to his lips. "Leyla, it's a long, long story, and we haven't much time."

Leyla sat up, holding her bedclothes around her. "Get a brand from the fire and light one of the candles."

Navid found a brand in the hearth, which was barely burning, and lit a candle next to the bed.

Leyla patted the bed next to her, indicating for Navid to sit. "This better be good," she whispered angrily. "Father will be furious when he finds you here."

Navid hesitated and then began, "I'm going to tell you as short a version of this story as possible. I'm just going to need you to trust me. There are things about our Magi Family that you don't know. That no one knows, and I'm about to put my whole Family in jeopardy with the things I'm about to tell you." He paused, thought for a minute, and began. "We are who you think we are— military leaders, trainers, educators, astronomers—we are all those things. BUT what you don't know is we are followers of Jehovah, the God of Israel. We believe their history is true. We believe their prophets are accurate, and we have witnessed it over the past 700 years. We believe their written Scriptures are the inerrant Word of God and that in those Scriptures, it tells us a Messiah will come to bring peace to the world. The Messiah's coming is indicated by a star or heavenly light shining over Him, and we have seen this star shining over Israel. We have watched the night sky and have waited for 500 years, and now He has come. His arrival was further confirmed to us by an angel who visited Fardad. Therefore..."

"Therefore," she hissed at him, "therefore, what? What are you rambling on about, Jews and Jehovah, Messiah, stars, and angels? What is all this? Why are you here with this crazy story?"

"Therefore," Navid continued, "The Magi Family has left our home in Persepolis and is making the journey to Israel to find the Messiah, God's chosen King over the world. We may be gone for as many as two years, and I will take you with us. I cannot imagine living life without you, and I know neither one of us wants to wait two years."

Leyla forced herself to calm down and think. "You're serious, aren't you?"

"Yes, the Family is camped about fifty miles from here tonight."

"Navid, let's slow down and think. Queen Musa is going to find out about this and kill you all. Even if she doesn't reach you before you leave Persia, your lives will be over. You will never be able to return to Persia. Where will you go? What will you do when this Messiah you are chasing turns out to be smoke? No, Navid, you are here now, and you are safe. My father will welcome you gladly; he has no son. All of this can be yours one day. Wealth! Power! Me!" As she said this last, she let the bedcover she held around her drop back to the bed. Her arms and legs were bare, and she had on a thin, almost transparent shift. She looked magnificent and used it to her advantage.

Navid rose, never taking his eyes off her. "Leyla, I cannot abandon the Family or the Messiah. He is here. Isaiah's prophecies have never been wrong, not even once. It's Him; He's here. You must want to be a part of being one of the first to meet Him. I have to go, Leyla," he pleaded, the heartache and conflict apparent in his voice and face.

Unfazed by anything he said, she continued calmly, "Navid, father has raised me all my life to be Satrap when he is gone. So you and I can rule together in a few years. Just think, becoming a Satrap, not just a little nobody in some nothing school training others who will rise to power and prestige. You can be somebody."

Shocked more by her look of disdain than her words, Navid repeated, "I will not abandon this mission and this journey. It is at the very core of who I am as a man."

"You whiny little weasel," she hissed at him, "I'm offering you everything. Everything any man could want, and you keep sniveling about the Family, about this mythical Messiah. What did I ever see in you? My father was a fool thinking that you were a real man. So I'm giving you one last chance to change your mind and stay."

Navid backed up, shocked at what he saw. This Leyla was not a Leyla he had ever seen before. The hatred and intensity in her face and eyes were truly ugly. "Leyla, I cannot stay. I love you. Please come with me, and everything will be just as I have told you. Please."

A madness seemed to come over her, and she opened her mouth and screamed. Navid was aghast but still moved quickly. He jumped forward and clamped his hand over her mouth. She struggled, scratching and biting him. He stood frozen, hoping that no one had heard. He thought through all his options. He pleaded with her to stop, but she became all the more violent, pounding his chest and face and kicking his legs. Out of options, he did the only thing he could think of—holding her mouth with his left hand, he removed his right hand and hit her with a sharp blow just behind her left ear. The effect was immediate, she became dead weight, and he gently lowered her to the bed. *I guess this means the wedding is off,* he thought to himself. *I've got two options: tie her up and take her with me, or tie her up and leave her.* Leaving her placed the Family in jeopardy, but kidnapping her was something he just couldn't do. There was a third option, and that was something he couldn't even contemplate. He took the bedsheets and wrapped her up like a mummy. Using a shawl that was hanging on the wall, he tied a gag around her mouth. He was sick to the point of nausea. What had he done? He was a complete fool.

Standing here wasn't going to do him any good. He knew a back door out of the compound. That was his safest and fastest route. He made his way through the grounds, found the door, unbarred it, and was out and against the wall again. He moved around the wall, discovered his weapons, and hurried to the ravine where he had left Utana. He spotted the old tree and entered the ravine, but it was empty. For once, Utana had listened to him. It had taken him too long, and Utana was riding, with both horses, back to the camp. The last place he wanted to be when the sun came up was anywhere near this compound. So he did the only thing he could do, following the trail on which they had come, he ran. He ran as if his life depended on it. He had run two miles without slowing when he saw a man standing in the road with two horses. "Utana, thank heavens; for once, you didn't listen to me. We've got big trouble."

Looking behind Navid, he queried, "Where's Leyla?"

"Long story," Navid said, shaking his head, "I'll tell you as we ride." With that, both men threw themselves on their horse's backs and rode at a canter for the Family compound. Both horses were fit and rested, and they never slowed their pace the rest of the night. As they rode, Navid told Utana the whole ugly story.

Utana whistled as Navid finished the story. "I hate to say it, but option three was the safest one for the Family. Brother, you are going to be in serious trouble with the Council. Your actions have put everything and everyone at risk, and I'm not sure you picked the right option."

"I picked the only option I could live with."

With that said, they rode in silence back to camp, arriving about an hour before sunrise. Some women were leaving their tents, going to the communal cooking area when Navid and Utana rode into the corral. They removed the tack from their horses, rubbed them down with straw, and gave them food and water. The horses cared for, Navid turned toward his tent, and Utana turned to go with him. Navid put his hand on his friend's chest and shook his head no. "This is something I have to face alone, Utana. Go to your tent. I'm going to keep your name out of this."

Utana was about to protest, but when he saw the look on Navid's face, he shook his hand and turned toward his tent.

Navid hesitated outside his tent, gave up, grasped the tent cover, and crept into the tent. He could have skipped the stealth. Everyone was wide awake and sitting on their sleeping mats, and as he entered, every eye turned toward him.

"Where is Leyla?" Fardad asked.

Navid was amazed. "How did you know?"

Jahan interjected, "When Pari woke early and found your sleeping mat empty, we all knew where you had gone. Well, where is she?"

Navid hung his head, and tears streamed down his face. "She didn't come," he sobbed. Fahnik rose from her mat and hugged Navid. He stood there for a moment, composing himself before he related the story in detail. While he spoke, Fahnik never left his side; she stood there with her arm around her brother's shoulder. She stood there and wept as he relayed the hate and rejection he had faced from the one woman he truly loved.

Jahan rose, walked to him, and clasped him by the shoulder. "No use dwelling on your decision. Now we must decide how we proceed," he said. "You stay here and compose yourself; I'll call the Council together. Come to the meeting tent when you are ready." Jahan left the tent.

A short time later, Fardad arose and said, "If you're ready, Navid, I'll walk with you to the Council." Navid nodded, and the two of them left the tent. It was a short distance to the tent of meeting, but it seemed like several miles. Navid was mentally exhausted and could barely form a coherent thought.

They entered the tent. The rest of the Council was already there, and Jahan rose instead of Fardad to open the meeting. "This will be a short meeting. We need to begin traveling very shortly." Jahan took a deep breath and began, "Navid left the camp last night and went to the compound of Baraz, whom you all know. His intention was noble and honorable. He intended to get Leyla, whom you all know, to marry her and bring her with us. He explained everything about the Magi, our belief in Jehovah and the Messiah, and the reason for the trip we are undertaking. Unfortunately, things did not go well. She became furious, forcing Navid to knock her out and tie her up. In a few hours, someone will find her, and Baraz will send a rider to Susa to tell the Queen. It will be a trip of some 300 miles and would take their best rider at least six days, maybe even seven, depending on the weather in the mountains, to reach Susa, and another day for them to get organized. But I think it's obvious that it is now a race to reach Babylon."

Marzban jumped up, spittle flying as he shouted, "You idiot, you complete fool. What have you done? You have killed us all. My wife, my children, everything I have you have put in jeopardy. I move that Navid be removed from the Council and expelled from the camp. He has lost the right to lead, and he should no longer be a part of the Family."

Fardad glared at Marzban, and Ram rose to speak. He addressed the group in a much calmer voice, "We have all known Navid his entire life. He has always dedicated himself to serving the needs of the Family. We know him to be a man of honor. We were with him at his betrothal feast. We know Leyla. Who could have imagined such a rejection? We all knew what would happen when Queen Musa found out we were leaving; it was just a matter of time. This event has shortened the timeline. I don't like the position we're in any better than anyone else, but I can certainly understand what Navid has done."

Fardad looked at the other Council members, "Does anyone have anything else they would like to say before we vote?"

No one moved or spoke.

"I will leave it up to the Council, but Jahan and I will not vote," Fardad said. "So all those in favor of expelling Navid, please stand."

Marzban leaped to his feet. He was the only one standing. He looked down at his father, who was still sitting. "Father, he betrayed us," he pleaded.

Kevan looked up at his son and shook his head, "We don't abandon each other when things get difficult. I love you, and I love Navid, and we will all need each other now more than ever. We will travel fast and long these coming days to put as much distance as we can between us and our pursuers, but if the Immortals come, we will make them sorry they ever left Susa."

Deflated, Marzban sat down and hung his head.

Jahan closed the meeting, "We will need to push everyone today, but this is not the time to panic our people. They do not need to know the reason for our haste, and it is something we would have done anyway now that we are out of the mountains. Do we all agree?" They all stood and left except for Navid and Marzban. Marzban still sat there, too deflated to move.

Navid walked over to Marzban and sat facing him, "Marzban, I think you are perfectly justified in your feelings. I have let everyone down and have exposed us to a horrible danger. I didn't mean to, but that doesn't mean anything at this point. I don't need a Council vote. If you still want me to leave, I will."

Marzban looked up, shook his head, and said softly, "No, actually, I should thank you. That is the first time my father has ever said he loved me, and he's right. We don't abandon each other. I know you; you would fight to the death for any one of us. There is no way you could have foreknown the outcome, or you would never have gone. We'll run, but if we have to fight, we'll stand back to back and fight to the end." Marzban reached out, and they clasped forearms.

Navid stood and left the Council tent. He returned to his tent, grabbed his weapons, and headed for the corral. It was time to ride.

Scene 2 Compound of Baraz

Baraz sat down for breakfast; Omid was already there. Smiling, he said, "Where is Leyla? It's unusual for her to be late. Do you think we should check on her?"

Omid, knowing how Baraz liked to start the day with his daughter, smiled back. "I'll just peek in on her to make sure she's okay."

A few minutes later, he heard Omid scream and ran to his daughter's bedroom. Lying on the bed, trussed up like a hog for the market, was his daughter. He ran to the bed, took off the gag, and unrolled her from the bedclothes. She leaped out of bed, "I'll kill him," she said in absolute fury.

"Kill whom?" her father said in astonishment. "What in the world has happened? Who did this? Did they violate you?"

"Who? Who? Navid is who," she screamed, "and I swear when I get my hands on him, he'll regret the day he was born."

Now her father was indeed in shock, "Navid? What are you saying? Have you lost your mind? Navid? You better start at the beginning on this one. You're making no sense."

So she did start at the beginning, telling a story that still made no sense, about Jews, and a Messiah, and the Magi Family's hidden beliefs, and about a 1,000-mile trip to do something. It was a jumbled mess by the time she finished trying to piece together the events and conversation of the previous evening.

Baraz called for his steward, who came immediately. Half the compound seemed to be crammed into the hallway outside Leyla's room, having heard her screaming and shouting.

"Yes, master," the steward mumbled, bowing low.

"Find two fast riders and send them south. Leyla believes the Magi Family camped about fifty miles to the south, and if so, I need to know, and I need to know fast."

His steward backed out of the room, still bowing, and then turned and raced down the hall looking for two of the household guard. As he neared the end of the hall, he saw two men he knew, Hamed and Javad. "Just the two men I need," the steward said. "Baraz needs two men to ride south about fifty miles to look for a large group of travelers who we believe to be the Magi Family. Trust me; if you're not back in six hours, don't bother coming back at all. Now go."

The two men needed no further encouragement or instruction. They ran for the stable, threw their tack on two horses, and rode south. After less than three hours, they found a large site where the grass had been disturbed, but no one was there. "What do you think?" Hamed growled; he had a voice like a black bear. "Should we ride back and tell them we found the campsite?"

Javad looked at him as if he were an addled child and mimicked a two-year-old's sing-song voice. "I think we should go back; ya, let's go back," and then growled back at Hamed, "Of course we're not going back, you cretin. We're going to follow this trail and find out who camped here last night. So go back? What a moron!"

Hamed shrugged and shook his head, and the two men turned northwest following the trail of the Magi. After a little less than two hours, they topped a rise and could see the rear guard of the travelers. Both men stopped their horses and looked closely at the men below. There were over thirty well-mounted and well-armed men, and these were professional soldiers, not just some knock-off caravan guards. With the Magi identified, Javad turned his horse and headed back to the Compound. The two men rode at a trot and reached the compound in the late afternoon. They hurried in and found the steward, who led them to Baraz.

Baraz looked at the two weary men and demanded, "Well, are you going to stand there like mutes, or are you going to tell me something?"

Hamed hung back, trembling before the powerful man, but Javad stepped forward and reported, "We followed the trail northwest for about two hours, and we ran into the rear guard of the travelers. There were over thirty well-armed professional soldiers in the rear guard. They are the Magi."

Baraz turned to his steward, "Get these men something to eat and some of my best wine; they have earned it. Then find the fastest rider you can and bring him to my study." Baraz left the three men, called in his clerk, and dictated a message for Queen Musa. She needed to know that the Magi were attempting to leave Persia. He included all the pertinent facts, the things that Navid had told Leyla, the report he had received from

Javad, and closed by offering any aid that he could—knowing, of course, that she certainly would not need his help.

As he finished the message, the steward arrived with the rider. Baraz took the note from the clerk. He sealed it with wax, marked it with his signet, and handed it to the rider. "It's too late to start tonight, at first light ride without stopping to the Capital. Place this directly into the hands of the Queen. Give this to no one else, only to the Queen." The rider left, and Baraz leaned back on his cushion, smiling with great pleasure. *Undoubtedly the Queen would be delighted with him and would want to reward a servant as faithful as him,* he thought.

Scene 3 Magi March - Day 39

Jahan sat his horse and saw the two figures on the hill. They watched the Magi for a few moments and then turned their horses and headed back east. Undoubtedly scouts from Baraz. That was good news. Baraz was not taking any chances; he had sent riders to confirm the Magi's identity before sending word to the Queen. That bought them an extra travel day, which might be enough.

CHAPTER 7

The Match

Scene 1 Magi Camp - End of Day 39

The Magi traveled with little rest; Jahan pushed everyone. He announced that they needed to speed up now that they were out of the foothills. Everyone understood, and they traveled late into the evening that day. Everyone was exhausted, and Rahim decided not to hold school that evening. They journeyed long again the next day, but Jahan, seeing the strain the oxen were under, called a halt before sunset. They set up the camp and prepared dinner. Rahim came to Jahan and told him that he did not want to miss teaching the children two days in a row, and Jahan agreed. Jahan blew his signal horn, and the children all proceeded to the area they had marked out as the evening's classroom.

The children dragged in, looking like exhausted rabble. They sat down in the clearing with the older boys in the back, as usual. Rahim stood and watched the children gather. He knew the lesson better be exciting, or he would lose them. So he jumped up on the box they had brought him as a platform, looked out over the children, and shouted at the top of his lungs, **"BAILDAN!!"** At this, the boys in the back row leaped to their feet, jumped up and down, ululating and chanting—**WAR! WAR! WAR! WAR!** The parents standing near looked into the clearing, then at each other, grinning and shaking their heads. The boys were blood-thirsty little heathens, but they were their blood-thirsty little heathens.

Scene 2 Shechem in Israel - 734 BC

Baildan watched as Eliya and his two companions faded into the distance on their trip north to Nimrud. Baildan scouted south, looking for the main body of the Judean army or any signs of recent activity. It was a beautiful spring day, with a light wind, and the sun brought pleasant, gentle warmth to the men. The breeze was from the west, coming off the Mediterranean Sea, bringing the smells of the cultivated fields of the Sharon Valley. Baildan watched as hawks circled on the weak air currents looking for prey. White storks filled the sky, making their annual migration north. As he watched the birds, he thought what a tactical advantage it would be to see the battlefield from their vantage. He also thought what a marvel, the things and places they saw, the inner drive that caused them to axiomatically find the same nesting and breeding ground year after year. Who could have designed such a fantastic creature? He almost forgot their mission entirely as he relaxed on the gently moving horse and contemplated his life and the world around him.

"What you thinking, boss?" The husky voice of Ashur brought him out of his reverie.

"I was just thinking how peaceful the silence was," Baildan replied in a pleasant tone as he turned and smiled at Ashur.

"I get it." Ashur blushed. "You was thinking how pleasant it was until I started yammering."

Baildan shook his head and laughed. "No, actually, I was thinking how fortunate I am to be spending the day on my favorite horse, enjoying this marvelous day with men who mean everything to me."

"Hah," Ashur snorted, "this smelly lot. I'd as soon spend the day with a camel herd and my three wives. The smell and the nagging would remind me perfectly of this lot." Ashur said it loud enough for the men in front to hear, knowing they loved his good-natured ribbing.

A voice came from the front, "I didn't know camels could nag." The retort brought a roar from the men around them, including Baildan.

They rode through the foothills and reached a small river just before noon. The river was not in flood, and the crossing was easy. The river was north of Bethel, which was the southernmost city in Ephraim. Once across the river, Baildan split his men into five groups and spread them out in half-mile increments to scout a broader front but still maintain contact. They continued south for another half hour when the center group, led by Jamal, stopped and raised a signal flag.

The other groups joined Jamal's squad. Jamal was on a slight rise, and in the distance, they could see the city of Mizpah, the northernmost town in Judah. Sitting just north of the city was the army of Judah. There were more than 150,000 men in the camp, Baildan estimated, based on the size of the area they were occupying. King Ahaz must have called up most of the men of war in Judah. He was going to risk it all in a single deciding confrontation with Syria and Ephraim. Baildan was surprised they hadn't run into a screening force and decided not to push his luck. He signaled for the squad leaders to join him.

Baildan looked at his leaders, "Time to head back. It's difficult to imagine we haven't been seen this near to their camp. If the Judeans have seen us, they may signal to a blocking force. If we encounter their cavalry, and they don't have a significant numbers advantage, we fight. Otherwise, we run.

Baildan signaled to the men; they rode north toward their camp. It was as Baildan feared. There was a cavalry force of their size between them and the river. Baildan shouted to his riders, "They should have brought more men. Let's see if we can discourage them."

They rode at the Judeans, and at the last minute, they wheeled as one man to their right, turning just their upper bodies to the left, loosing off a stream of arrows into the opposing horsemen. Their bows had a much greater range than the Judeans', and the answering shots fell short. Reaching the end of the Judean force, Baildan's men wheeled back along the Judean front and loosed again. By now, they had killed or wounded more than a fourth of the Judean riders or horses. Men were down, and riderless horses were panicked and rearing in the mass of men. It was chaos.

Taking advantage of the chaos, Baildan rode straight at the Judeans, loosing arrows at an unbelievable rate. The Judeans had seen enough, and they bolted toward the east, leaving dead and wounded in their wake.

Baildan rode into the river at a gallop. The shallow water splashed everywhere around the men, soaking them before they exited the river. Clear of the river and riding at a gallop again, one of the men called out, "Ashur, you look like a drowned goat," at which hysterical laughter broke out. Baildan was not surprised; this frequently occurred after a violent action. Men would laugh, cry, shake or completely withdraw. Then they would check themselves for wounds and look around to see if any of their friends were missing or needed help. They were fortunate; no one was missing, but more than one man looked down and saw blood running down an arm or leg, where an arrow had grazed them. These men would usually grow quiet for a moment, contemplating what could have happened. Then someone would ride over to them, bandage the wound, and the two men would catch back up with the troop.

Baildan said nothing after the action. He slowed to a trot and held the gait until early afternoon when their camp came into view. Reaching the camp, they rode into the open corral and turned their horses over to the grooms. Baildan walked to his tent, where Karim, his aide, greeted him. Baildan had captured Karim in a raid five years ago and kept him as a groom and horse handler. He was a small man with a wiry beard, pale complexion, and unusual green eyes. He was a terrible groom, but he proved to be intelligent and resourceful. In every army, some men know how to get around the system and produce results regardless of obstacles. Karim was such a man. Baildan had recognized his attributes early and had made him his aide and armor-bearer.

"I knew you would be hungry," Karim almost whispered in his soft voice. "I have some things ready for you. Nabil's clerk was by a little earlier, and he and King Pekah want to see you as soon as you return. But it can wait until after you have eaten. I have also prepared your armor for tomorrow, and I understand there will be a wrestling contest tonight between Pera and the Ephraimite champion Zichri. Now eat."

Baildan did as instructed; he folded his legs, sat on a cushion by his sleeping mat, and dug into the warm bread, spreading soft cheese on it. Then, he looked at Karim, "What do you know of this Zichri?"

Karim frowned. "Nothing good. They say the man has no soul, no compassion, no joy, and many companions but no friends. They say he is huge, a descendant of the giants who used to live here, and that he is fearless and does not feel pain. But then you know how people tend to exaggerate."

Baildan continued to eat, but concern showed on his face. Then he gestured toward the tent flap and commanded, "Go get Samir. He and I need to talk about this match."

In a short while, Karim returned with Samir.

"Baildan, Karim says you want to talk about tonight's match," Samir said, smiling at his friend.

"I don't like what Karim has told me about this Zichri. Have you seen him or watched him wrestle? What do you know of him?"

Samir was no longer smiling; he turned serious. "I met him when we arranged the match. He is large, but nothing Pera can't handle. He's a cold fish, doesn't speak; he stares at you with this blank look. I think it's some kind of intimidation nonsense. I can tell you one thing; I'm getting unbelievable odds from these Ephraimite yokels. We're going to make a killing on this match."

"I don't like it," Baildan said flatly, "the odds you're getting should have told you something. They may be yokels, but these Israelites are clever men with money. They wouldn't be betting on this match unless they know something you don't know."

"It's a wrestling match," Samir persisted, "not a sword fight. So the worst thing that happens is Zichri beats Pera. Pera's a little bruised, and I'm out some money. But if we back out now, we look like cowards and are a laughing stock."

Baildan thought about it before continuing. "All right, go on with the match, but you make sure you arrange ahead of time that if we throw in the towel, the match is over."

"Done, boss," Samir replied, smiling once again. "You'll see, Pera will destroy their little giant and send him home crying like a baby." Samir slipped out of the tent before Baildan could have a change of heart.

After eating, Baildan went to the command tent, where he knew he would find the King and Nabil. Four behemoth guards with spears crossed were at the tent flap, barring entrance. They recognized Baildan, came to attention and raised their spears. Baildan nodded at them and entered the massive tent. A large table occupied the center of the room. A map of Israel drawn on sheepskin was on the table. King Pekah of Ephraim and Nabil, the Syrian field commander, sat at the table.

When Nabil turned toward Baildan, his mouth smiled, but his eyes did not. "Ah, if it isn't the little scout. It's about time you reported," he said. King Pekah didn't bother to look at Baildan; his rank was too low for the King to be bothered.

Baildan bowed deeply and did not allow Nabil to bait him. He replied smoothly and confidently, "Great King Pekah, Commander Nabil, it pleases me to tell you that we have found the Judeans." Baildan walked over to the map and pointed to a spot between Mizpah and Bethel. "It appears King Ahaz is willing to risk everything in a single large battle, and winner takes all. There are at least 200,000 warriors in the camp, 2,000 archers and an equal number of slingers, 700 or 800 chariots, and the rest swordsmen armed with long spears. The Judeans have a small cavalry whose main purpose is scouting. We encountered about 100 of their cavalry at a river north of Bethel on our return and managed to route them without a great degree of difficulty."

Now he had King Pekah's attention, who looked at Nabil and raised his eyebrows. Nabil continued with his same degrading tone, "Are you asking us to believe the entire Judean army is at Mizpah? You want us to believe that Ahaz is so stupid; he's holding nothing in reserve. Is that what you're telling us? Oh," he said, narrowing his eyes, "and while we are talking, where is my man, Yana?"

Baildan kept his face stoic and said, "Commander, I am but a lowly scout. I am not asking you to believe anything. I'm merely reporting what I have seen. I apologize if I misstated the Judean intent, and I'm sure the Judean's strategy would be far beyond me. I apologize for my conjecture. And about this, Yana, did you say? I'm afraid I do not know him."

"Yana, yes, you know him," fumed Nabil. "He is the liaison I sent to work with you. Unfortunately, he did not report back in this afternoon."

Baildan looked confused and then slapped his forehead, "There has been a rider shadowing us in the distance since we got here. Is that Yana?"

"You know very well that is Yana. Where is he?"

"Commander," Baildan lied smoothly, "we did see the man early this morning, but after we crossed the river north of Bethel, we did not see him again. Maybe he was unseated when his horse shied crossing the river. Maybe he ran into the Judean cavalry troop we encountered. Maybe a wild animal spooked his horse, which threw him. I'm sure I could speculate all day on where Yana might be, but the truth of the matter is I just don't know." Baildan raised both hands waist high, held them palms up, and shrugged in the universal sign of bewilderment.

Nabil glared at him, not believing him but also not having any proof. "I will find him," he said vehemently.

"Excellent," said Baildan, smiling. "And when you do, you can introduce us, and from now on, he can ride with us instead of skulking along behind." Baildan turned to leave when the King spoke.

"I understand we are to have a wrestling match tonight, our champion Zichri and one of your men."

Baildan stopped dead, the hair on the back of his neck rising. "Great king, we are indeed matching our best wrestler Pera with this Zichri. It should be an entertaining match."

"I don't know that entertaining is the word I would use. Amusing if you are an Israelite, terrifying if you are some desert tribesman," King Pekah said haughtily.

Baildan really, really wanted to pull his sword and kill these two fops, but he restrained himself. "I'm sure Pera will do his best," he said, bowing as he backed his way out of the tent.

Baildan felt like he needed a bath; just being in the presence of those two made him feel dirty. He arrived back at the camp as the men were sitting down to the evening meal. Baildan found a large mat with Samir and Pera on it and sat with them. He saw Ashur coming and waved for him to join them. Tomorrow would be an exhausting battle, so the cooks had made extra of everything. The men would load up on rice and bread tonight to increase their endurance. They also ate roasted lamb, goat stew, and yogurt with dates and prunes. The men would eat well tonight, and they would need it tomorrow.

They also drank copious amounts of the wine cut with water to hydrate. In battle, dehydration was also your enemy. Men died from thirst because the exertion leached the water from your body. Baildan looked around at his men with satisfaction and affection. These were professionals. They understood what was coming and how to prepare. Many in the army would get dead drunk tonight out of fear for tomorrow. His men drank water with just enough wine in it to make it palatable. When they finished eating tonight, they would tend to their armor and their weapons. All of them would be fighting with iron weapons and iron armor, including their iron helmets. The only exception was Baildan's bronze sword. He had carried it for as long as he could remember. When he was young, Domara had taken him to see an old metalsmith in Nineveh, who had made weapons for the king and his court. The man was a wizard in metallurgy and had found a combination of copper, tin, and arsenic that produced the hardness and durability desired in a sword. The real artistry was in the mold itself. He created a mold and poured the liquefied metal into the mold to make a bronze sword. Iron weapons were made by heating an iron bar until the metal was malleable and then hammering it into shape. Therefore, the mold allowed the designer to create details you could not duplicate in an iron sword. Baildan had loved the sword from the minute he had seen and held it. It had a dark-gold color when it was new, but as it had aged and oxidized, it now had some greenish tones in it. His men often referred to him as the Green Warrior.

Baildan looked over at Pera as he ate and broached the subject, "Have you seen this Zichri you're fighting tonight?"

Pera nodded. "I've seen him, and I saw him wrestle last night. He's tremendously strong, and he relies on his strength instead of technique. It won't be easy, but I can beat him with speed and technique. One of the biggest problems is his mass. I don't think I can even get my hand around his forearm. I have to work on his legs, get him off balance, and put him on his back. If I can get him down, I can beat him."

"They say he has no soul, no compassion," Baildan continued with genuine concern in his voice, "if this guy is as big as they say, he could be truly dangerous. So if I think things are going bad, and you are in danger, I'm stopping the match. Is everyone clear on that?"

Pera and Samir looked at each other and nodded. Samir tried to lighten the mood, "It's a wrestling match, Baildan; there are rules. You're worried about nothing, and Pera will be fine."

"Are we clear?" Baildan repeated with greater emphasis.

"We're clear, boss, we're clear. If things look dangerous for Pera, I'll be the first one to throw in the towel," Samir said contritely.

The men finished eating and sat with each other, talking about the upcoming match and tomorrow's battle. As the sun descended, fading behind the mountains, Samir and Pera rose and headed for the arena.

Without a word, everyone stood and followed them. The Assyrians could tell by the noise they were close. There was a natural amphitheater in the center of the camp, where the ground sloped down on all sides, and there was a large flat area in the center. They had ringed the area with torches poles which cast everything in flickering yellow light with long shadows. The seating area was filling fast; no one wanted to miss this fight.

Baildan found a spot large enough for all of his men, but no one sat. They stood, waiting for the match to begin. Samir and Pera continued down to the flat and stood outside a large circle marked in the dirt. Samir had a small bucket and a towel with him. Pera stripped down to a wrestling thong, which provided enough cover to ensure modesty and prevent his opponent from crippling him by grabbing his groin. Samir took the towel, dipped it in the sheep fat in the bucket, and rubbed the fat on Pera liberally. Zichri was large and had large hands. Samir wanted to make sure that he could not simply grab and hold Pera, and the grease would partially offset the size difference.

As Samir finished rubbing down Pera, there was a ripple in the crowd, and then the cheering and the chants began as Zichri descended into the arena. He had already stripped down to a wrestling thong, knowing that the sight of him would rile up the crowd and provide an incentive for any reluctant bettors to put down their money. It certainly had the desired effect on the Assyrians, who stood gaping at him. He wasn't just a big man. The Assyrians had seen and defeated plenty of big men in combat; no, Zichri was indeed a descendant of the giants who used to live in this area. Seven feet tall, with shoulders the width of a span of oxen. The man carried no fat. Every muscle on his body was large and stood out in marked clarity. Baildan looked down at Pera; Baildan was ready to call this off. Pera looked like a child next to the giant.

Pera looked at the man descending into the arena, and his conviction and resolve hardened. He was big, but Pera knew he could beat him. Pera wasn't arrogant, but he was confident in his abilities and the plan he had developed. Pera was more concerned with Samir and Baildan's reactions. He turned, looked up, and found Baildan in the crowd. Baildan looked at him and shook his head no. Pera turned to Samir, "You need to go talk to Baildan. He wants to stop the match, but this crowd will tear us to pieces if he tries. They're drunk, and their blood is up. There's no stopping now. Tell him I can take this guy, and if not, I'll keep a safe distance until he wears out. Baildan cannot stop the match."

Samir bounded up the slope and yelled in Baildan's ear, "I know. It doesn't look good. Pera knows too, but he says, and he's right, that if we try to stop the match, this drunken mob will tear us to pieces."

Baildan looked down at Pera, who looked back and shook his head yes. Baildan looked at Samir and nodded his head. "All right," he shouted back, "he wrestles, but he keeps his distance from this guy. Whatever this Zichri is, he sure isn't human."

As Samir descended back to the wrestling circle, Baildan looked over at the King and Nabil. Nabil was staring back with a look of smug contempt. He had led them into this trap and knew there was no way they could extricate themselves. Baildan made himself a promise, he would take great pleasure when he led the Assyrian army against this pompous pig, and Nabil would never leave the battlefield alive.

By now, Zichri and his attendants had reached the circle. The King rose and held up his hands, at which a hush fell over the chaotic assembly.

"Gentlemen, for your entertainment, we offer you a contest of will and skill tonight. In one corner we have…" (He stopped and looked down at his aide, who whispered something to him) "Yes, we have the little man from the desert, Pera, of some nomadic sheepherder tribe or another." This derisive comment brought a roar from the crowd of Syrians and Israelis. "And in this corner," the King continued, "we have the mighty Zichri, Lion of Ephraim. The King's champion. The slayer of men and the creator of widows. A man among men and the ultimate warrior. He has no fear, and he feels no pain. I give you the mighty **ZICHRI**."

The crowd erupted, and Zichri strode to the center of the circle with both hands held high above his head. The two wrestlers and their seconds approached the center of the ring, where the referee, a subordinate of Nabil, met them. "Just a friendly match. You both know the rules. The loser is the first man to fall three times. To be counted as a fall, the man's back must touch the ground, or his opponent must throw him out of the ring. Any punching must be below the neck, with no biting or gouging. Any violations, and I will stop the match, and that man automatically loses. Any questions?" Neither man spoke. Their eyes had been locked on each other the whole time, each man trying to assess and intimidate the other. The referee and the seconds left the ring, and the two men circled each other. Zichri's tactics became obvious early. He would make a rush, punch at Pera's chest, and try to use his upper body weight and strength to either knock Pera over or push him out of the ring.

Pera had expected this attack. Fortunately, his shorter height and massive lower body now proved to be an advantage. Once Pera gauged the timing of the big man and could anticipate when Zichri would charge, Pera would drop low and deliver a stunning blow to the man's thighs and knees with a fist, forearm, or even a sweeping leg kick. They continued to move, circle, and lunge for what seemed like an eternity, with Pera never taking his eyes off the giant. Zichri was beginning to sweat, and his breathing had increased. Good signs, Pera knew, and he circled even faster.

Zichri lunged again, and Pera was ready. He dropped low, spun, so his back was to Zichri, and lashed out a backward leg kick to Zichri's knee. The giant lost his balance and crashed to his back. You could have heard a gnat flying. The Ephraimites were stunned. It wasn't a win, Pera knew, but it was the first step. His resolve was even firmer; patience was the key. He did not celebrate or rejoice. He merely took his wrestling stance as the big man got to his feet, but this time with a slight limp.

Pera circled again, but Zichri was learning. Instead of rushing and lunging, he closed the distance between himself and Pera to stay in tight and keep the little man off his legs. Pera would step back, and Zichri would follow. Zichri tried several times to get a good grip on Pera's forearms to throw him, but the grease made this problematic. Zichri continued to move forward, and Pera continued to retreat. They were close to the circle's edge when Zichri hit Pera with a forearm to his chest. The blow lifted him off his feet and sent him out of the ring. The crowd erupted; Zichri was back in the match.

One fall each. Now endurance would begin to tell. They had been wrestling for more than an hour, pushing, gripping, moving, mass against mass, every muscle straining. Pera looked at Zichri. The veins in his neck throbbed, his chest heaved, fighting for breath, and his thighs and shins were bloodied and bruised. Pera decided it was time for a strategy change. He had been circling to his right all night and had become too predictable, which is just what he intended. Pera circled right, then changed direction to the left, move, change, lunge, move, change, lunge. He could see the frustration on Zichri's face, the first emotion he had seen. Two more quick changes and Pera went in fast, delivering a forearm to the massive thigh. Pera threw himself flat and swept the big man's feet out from under him. It sounded like a tree falling as Zichri's feet went up in the air, and he landed on his back, with his head hitting the ground.

Again stunned silence; they had never seen anyone stand up to the massive warrior for more than a few minutes. Recognition dawned on a few of the Ephraimites. They recognized the tremendous skill and ability of the little man, who stood erect in the dirt ring. There were even a few chants of "Pera," as the bolder expressed their appreciation for what they were seeing. But one look from the King, and those chants stopped.

This time, Zichri was much slower getting up and had a pronounced limp. Pera stared at Zichri's face, and he didn't see concern or confusion. Zichri radiated pure hatred. Pera knew he needed to end this quickly before Zichri lost control. Pera circled again, left, right, left, but Zichri moved forward, trying to close with him. Again, Zichri made a quick lunge, and with all the hatred and malice he possessed, he landed a stunning right hook to Pera's temple. The little man staggered backward, stunned, and Zichri followed. Two more blows to the head, and Pera fell flat on his face.

Baildan and the Assyrians were furious. They yelled at the referee to end the match, but he just stood there, motionless, looking at Nabil.

Baildan charged toward the ring, but before he could get there, the giant stood over Pera and delivered a crushing blow to the back of his neck as he lay on the ground, then simply walked out of the ring. Baildan and Samir rushed over to Pera, but they were too late. The last blow had broken Pera's neck and killed him instantly. Samir glared at the giant, and his hand dropped to the hilt of his sword. Baildan put his hand on Samir's forearm and shook his head no. Baildan walked over and stood in front of Zichri, who still showed no emotion. Baildan said coldly, "This is not over. This is not the time or place, but there will come a time, and then I will come for you. Your death will not be quick. I will make you suffer and cry for mercy, but there will be no mercy."

The Ephraimite had won, but there was no cheering. There was no honor in what they had just seen. Pera was the better man in everyone's eyes, and they had just witnessed a cowardly act by the man who was supposedly the champion of Ephraim. There would be no celebration tonight. Baildan and Samir lifted Pera and carried him. Several Ephraimites came forward from the front row and wordlessly lifted Pera above their heads and carried him from the arena. It was the funeral procession of a fallen hero.

Everyone in attendance knew who the true hero was tonight. They brought Pera back to the cavalry camp, and several men gathered logs and brush for a funeral pyre. The Assyrians gathered around the pyre with Pera lying on top, and Baildan put a torch to the wood. The wood was dry, caught quickly, and burned fast. Soon, the fire consumed Pera's body, but not one man left or took their eyes off their fallen comrade. They seared every emotion and every sight into their minds. They never wanted to forget this moment. Like Baildan, his men knew they would be back, and when they came, they would extract a terrible price for the murder committed this night.

Scene 3 Magi Camp

Rahim looked around the clearing and saw little heads nodding, "That's enough for tonight, children; we will take up the story of Baildan again tomorrow."

The older boys in the back jumped up and began shouting, "**NO!! NO!!**" and of course, they were bouncing up and down and ululating as they cried.

Jahan, who had been standing nearby, walked into the clearing, stood in front of Rahim, and shouted, "Anyone who is not in their tent sleeping in five minutes will feel my big boot on his backside."

Jahan's threat sent boys scurrying in every direction, and they flew to their tents.

CHAPTER 8

War!

Scene 1 Magi Camp - Day 44

Navid woke early the following day. He was exhausted, but not because of the long rides of the past five days. His mind was in turmoil. He ran over and over again the confrontation with Leyla. How could he have misjudged her so badly? He was a fool. He had only seen the things he wanted to see. Her father had trained her early on in the skills and subtleties necessary to be a Satrap and have political success. She thought of little else. She talked of little else. Navid had just assumed that she focused on those things because it was her current life. After they married, he had thought that she would blend into the Family and be content, knowing that Navid would one day lead the Magi. What more could a woman want than to be the wife of such a man. He had asked her not only to give up her current life but to join him in an expedition, which in all likelihood would end poorly. What would he be? Head of the Magi, with no home and no nation to serve? A promising future, he thought in hindsight. But continuing to brood on his loss was not doing himself or anyone else any good.

Navid needed to refocus, and he needed to do it now. The Family was well aware of what had happened between him and Leyla. The Council had kept it quiet the first few days, then decided it was best to let people know. Navid had a few awkward conversations after the announcement, but the Family was empathetic and supported him for the most part. He was glad to have it behind him so he could get on with his life. He arose and got dressed. The camp was stirring, and the cooks were heading toward the cooking fires. He left the tent and stood watching as the first rays of light peeked over the mountains to the east. The light fractured off the ice caps at the higher levels, and the diffused light shone in a rainbow of colors. The sky was clear and gave a hint of the day to come. The days were warming now that the Magi were out of the foothills. They were nearing the Persian Gulf, and there was the faint smell of saltwater in the distance. Navid stood looking at the mountains, memorizing every detail, not knowing if he would ever see them again. The women had started the cooking fires, and Navid wandered over to where they had gathered. The smell of fresh, hot bread was more than he could resist, and he reached to take one of the flat loaves when a wooden spoon whacked the back of his hand. He turned and saw Ava standing there, grinning at him, with a wooden spoon in her hand. "Hey, who did that?" he said grumpily, even though he was not hurt, just offended.

Ava was the only daughter of Hosh, the leader of the left flank. Hosh's wife had been barren for years, and Ava had been born to them when Hosh was thirty-four. She was now sixteen, not what you would call beautiful, but very attractive. Ava had beautiful eyes and a complexion like dark honey, her nose was small and straight, and she was…womanly. She was one of the most considerate and compassionate people in the whole Family. If a child was crying, Ava was there to wipe the nose, kiss the knee scrape, or hug a frightened child. If one of the elderly was dying, Ava sat with them, whispered to them, and helped them on their passage to see God. It was Ava who stood up for those being taunted or abused. She was a bully's worst nightmare, grabbing them and marching them to their parents, where she disclosed the full deeds of the miscreant. She was the friend that everyone wanted and needed. If you were her friend, she showed up. She stood beside you, was honest with you, and defended you. If anyone threatened you, she was a lioness, ready to protect. Navid had known Ava his whole life. How had he not seen her before? She stood there grinning and smiling at him, her hair up in a scarf and flour on her face and robe, and at that moment, she looked beautiful to him.

"You'll eat when everyone else eats, mighty commander," she said, and she laughed as she looked up at him.

Oh, Navid thought, *I forgot; she was kind of short too.* "Ow, that hurt," Navid whined as if Ava had injured him.

"Ooh, do you want me to kiss your boo-boo?" Ava baby talked back to him as if he were a three-year-old child.

Navid blushed, looked down, and then chuckled. Ava always had that effect on you, and she was merry, and being with her just made you feel good.

"Tell you what, since you are injured. You go sit with your family, and when everything is ready, I'll bring it to you."

Navid looked at her, still chuckling to himself, and did as instructed. That was another thing Navid had noticed. People always did what Ava told them to do. He walked over to where his family was sitting and joined them.

"I saw you talking to Ava," Navid's mother said with a sly look on her face. "Did you figure out she's not a child anymore?"

Navid was stunned. His mother was the wisest person he knew, next to his grandfather, but how could she have known that from a conversation she hadn't even heard?

"She hit me with a spoon," Navid said, jutting his chin out as if offended, "and I was remonstrating her."

"Didn't look like a whole lot of 'remonstrating' going on to me," Asha replied as she peered at him through slit eyes. Asha stopped speaking as Ava approached, carrying a pot of stew, fresh bread, and cheese.

"Morning, everyone," Ava said and grinned at them as she put the food down in between them. "My family is already eating. I will join you," she said as if it was something she did every day. She plopped down next to Navid, patted him on the knee, and baby talked again, "How's that boo-boo?"

Navid looked over at her and began laughing. *What is going on*, he thought.

Fardad grinned at Ava, smiling, "Perhaps you would like to lead us in prayer, Ava?"

Ava's whole countenance changed as she became serious, "I would love to, Fardad. Heavenly Father, creator, sustainer, and redeemer, thank you for calling us, for giving us the privilege to see You. At the end of this journey, we will come face to face with the Messiah. Who are we that you would glorify us in such a way? Thank you, and thank you for this day and for this food we are about to receive. Keep us safe today and make us holy. Amen."

It seemed to him one of the most beautiful prayers he had ever heard. "Thank you, Ava. That was beautiful," Navid said, turning and looking into her eyes. Now it was her turn to blush.

Asha chuckled and shook her head.

Jahan looked at the three of them, bewildered. He leaned over and whispered to his wife, "Am I missing something here?"

"You are such a baboon," she whispered back and slapped him playfully on the back of the head.

When they finished eating, Jahan looked at Navid and Fardad. "I have called for a quick Council meeting." Fardad and Navid acknowledged and stood to leave. Navid looked down at Ava, "Will I see you tonight?"

Ava blushed and said, "Of course; you know where to find me." She also stood, and the three of them left.

Jahan again looked at Asha, "What is going on?"

"It looks like one of you finally grew a brain," she said as she too left.

Jahan looked down at Fahnik, Pari, and Tiz and demanded, "What is happening here?"

The three of them looked at each other and shrugged; they had no idea what Jahan meant.

Jahan looked at the three of them and shook his head. "Imbeciles," he muttered as he walked to the Council tent. When he got there, the rest of the Council was there.

"Good morning," Jahan began somberly to the assembled Council, "we have a problem. Based on our rate of travel, even at the accelerated rate of the past few days, we could not get out of Persia before the Immortals cut us off. We need a new route of travel. They will expect us to continue northwest, staying on the east side of the Tigris River. After we pass the tip of the Persian Gulf, we will turn and ford the Euphrates near Ur. Then continue our journey on the west side of the Euphrates. We will be almost impossible to find if we follow this route."

There was silence for a few minutes while everyone considered this proposal. Kevan stood and faced the Council, "I agree with one thing: we cannot outrun the Immortals on our current route. The single biggest problem with the western route is it is not well known to us, but we know one thing: the oxen will not pull the wagons in the soft soil and sand, plus the heat will be too much for them. We'll also stand a fairly high chance of bumping into some of the desert tribes on that route."

Kevan sat down, and Fardad stood, "Does anyone have anything to add to Kevan's concerns? West, we face the unknown, and following the Tigris will almost certainly bring us into conflict with the Immortals. I agree with Jahan. We must cross the Euphrates and hope we reach it before the spring flood. We will unload the wagons and take only the things the camels can carry. The oxen will serve us one last time by becoming beef jerky." This last comment brought a look of horror to Ram's face. "Sorry, old friend," Fardad said, patting his shoulder. "We will need the additional meat to survive the desert." Ram shook his head in grim affirmation. He knew what to do.

Jahan stood. "If there is no disagreement, that is the plan. Let's get the people moving. We have another long day in front of us." The Council stood and began leaving the tent. Jahan called out to Navid, "Wait up a minute. What was all the nonsense this morning? What got into you and your mother?"

Thinking back on Ava at breakfast, Navid grinned as he replied innocently, "I have no idea what you are talking about." He turned and headed toward the corral.

"Another imbecile," Jahan grumbled as he too headed for the corral.

They traveled long again that day, but thankfully things were uneventful. Ava joined them for the evening meal; she and Navid talked and laughed through the meal. Fahnik and Pari loved having a new female companion, and both girls adored Ava. Asha continued to look at the young couple in happy recognition that Navid's life was about to get much better.

Jahan followed Asha back toward the cooking area, where she would help to clean up. "Asha, what's with all the giggling and laughing, and Ava showing up to eat with us again."

Asha looked at him like he was a child, "You can be such a bonehead sometimes. You can track a goat on a rocky crag, but you are impervious to the obvious signs right in front of you. Navid has found someone."

"Ava? Ava? But she's—she's not—Ava? Wow. I didn't see that one coming—Ava. Well, I guess I better talk to Hosh tonight." He continued to shake his head and mumble to himself as he walked to the clearing where Rahim would be teaching tonight.

The children rushed to the clearing after the evening meal and now sat with eager, expectant faces. Tonight was unusual. The adults had joined the children. They loved the story of Baildan, and many of the men were chanting along with the older boys. As Rahim neared the clearing, he could hear the chants beginning to increase and grow louder. "Baildan, Baildan, Baildan, Baildan." The boys were jumping and ululating in an ecstatic frenzy by the time Rahim reached his platform.

Rahim raised his hands to silence the children (both large and small), and they stopped, eager for the story to begin. Rahim opened the ancient Assyrian scroll and read…

Scene 2 Shechem Israel - 734 BC

Baildan rose early, unable to sleep, replaying the horrible death of Pera last night, and beginning to think about the battle to come. Baildan could hear the grinding of metal coming from outside Karim's tent and knew; Karim could not sleep either. There he sat, with his foot spinning the wheel as he put an edge on Baildan's weapons, not just his sword but his javelins, fighting knife, and even his arrowheads. When Karim finished honing, he would go over every arrow in Baildan's quiver to ensure tight fletchings. Karim knew how to prepare for war.

Any detail could mean life or death. Karim would carry extra arrows for Baildan, javelins, and a replacement shield and sword. His job as armor-bearer was to place himself directly behind Baildan when they fought dismounted. Karim's responsibility was to ensure Baildan always had the proper weapon at hand. He also carried water. In a long battle, water is as crucial as a weapon. Baildan watched Karim work, picked up the sword, which Karim had already sharpened, and admired the quality. The sword had blood grooves, which had nothing to do with blood. The grooves give the sword the strength of a thicker blade without adding extra weight. The oiled blade shone in the light from the campfire, and he admired the unusual green tarnish. It was a beautiful weapon, but today it had an ugly purpose. He would take many human lives with this sword today. It was war, and even though he held no animosity for their enemy, that would not matter when a man stood in front of him with the intent of taking his life or the life of one of his men. He would kill. He would not enjoy it; he would do it nonetheless.

Baildan sat there with Karim for a while, neither man speaking, both thinking of the day to come and wondering who would return to camp tonight. More men emerged from their tents, unable to sleep, and they too prepared their weapons for the day to come. Baildan watched the sky to the east, waiting for the first faint light of morning. He loved to see the sky begin to lighten, even before the sun rose before any rays were visible. The sun is saying, "Here I am, but not just yet." In this light, he could see the form of things, but not the things themselves. In his mind, he could see the structure of the battle, the two masses of men formed up against each other. The light would bring clarity to the image in his mind. Then he would know where and how to attack the enemy.

Baildan sat there for a while longer until he smelled the food cooking for the morning meal. He wandered toward the cooking fires and sat with his leaders on one of the eating mats. They nodded to one another, no one feeling much like talking. Ashur was in armor, letting his body adjust to the feel and weight. Samir sat with his head down, still grieving over the loss of Pera, his best friend. Samir looked up at Baildan, his voice filled with sorrow, "I will fight for Pera today." He patted the hilt of the sword he was carrying. Baildan recognized the scabbard, and it was Pera's.

"Pera would like that," Baildan replied with conviction. "He always loved a good battle. It will be hard not seeing the two of you standing side by side."

"I fight alone today."

"No one fights alone today. Your brothers will surround you. Today, we have each other, and that is all we have and all that matters. We stand and fight as one. We live or die together. No mercy." At that, Ashur nodded in agreement and patted Samir's shoulder.

Baildan looked around him at the gathered men. They ate large quantities of food. Many of them were not hungry, but they ate regardless. They knew they would need all the energy they could pack in. These were knowledgeable men going to war, and they knew what to do. When they had finished eating, Baildan had Ashur assemble the men up so he could address them. He stood looking at them, fully armed and armored, steel helmets shining in the morning sun. He was filled with humility, thinking that these warriors trusted him enough to lead them into battle. "Before us today are the Judeans. They want to kill you. They want to take your life and leave you bleeding in the dirt. Not all of you will see the end of this day. We are facing a well-trained disciplined army fighting on their soil, defending their homes and families. They will be determined; they will be fierce. Unfortunately for them, they have never seen warriors like you. You are smarter, faster, stronger, and you are the best-trained fighting men in this battle. You are a terror, a horrible visage that will leave those who live with eternal nightmares. Look at the man to your left and your right. That is your world today; nothing else matters. You will protect each other. You will not grow weak, and you will not tire. As the day wears on, the Judeans will grow hungry. They will grow thirsty. They will faint with weariness. You will not; Judean blood will cover you from head to foot. You will be the very image that has always haunted their nightmares. You will look in their eyes, at their fear, as they realize death is coming for them. They will see Hades' yawning mouth as they look into your eyes. You are death."

Baildan looked at each of them and saw their grips tighten on their weapons. "Today, when the battle is over, and they are defeated, there will be a route, and the Syrians and Ephraimites will chase after them, seeking to destroy them and to pillage their cities. You will not follow. Instead, you will listen for the signal to assemble. At the end of today, we have other business. Am I clear?"

As one man, they pounded the butts of their long spears into the ground in acknowledgment of the command.

"All right, we have work to do."

They all turned and went to the corral, where the grooms had put the tack on their horses. Baildan led them south again toward Bethel. They knew where they were going this time, and it didn't take them long to reach the river. They topped a rise, and the river became visible. On the other side of the river, there was a blocking force of approximately 10,000 infantry, archers, and cavalry. Their only purpose was to buy time for the main force, located north of Mizpah, and make the river crossing as miserable as possible for the Ephraimites and Syrians. It was what Baildan had expected to see. He turned in the saddle and waved Ashur up, "Ride back and tell Nabil and Pekah what we have found. We will stay here and wait for the main body."

As the morning wore on, the heat increased; there were no clouds and no breeze. This fight would be hot dirty work. Baildan and his men dismounted to save the horses' strength for later. They looked north and south as they sat on the knoll, keeping an eye on the Judeans and watching for the coming army. Long before they saw the approaching army, they saw its cloud. Two hundred thousand men, plus horses, wagons, and chariots, kicked up a lot of dirt. It looked like a massive sand storm sweeping down from the north. Then, still long before they could see them, they heard them. They listened to the sound of the army's feet, the squeaking of wheels, the thud of horses, mules, and camels. It was like a moving grist mill, grinding and destroying everything in its path, leaving a broad stretch of bare dirt in its wake. Local starvation and disease killed almost as many after a significant military engagement as did the battles themselves.

Baildan sat and watched the monster approaching, and when they were near enough, he led the men down to their position on the right flank. It was one thing watching the giant dust cloud approaching, and it was another thing immersing yourself in it. He and his men covered their faces with headscarves to keep out the dust. They saw the army top the knoll on which they had spent the morning.

The army's front spanned almost half a mile as they approached the river. The 10,000 Judeans in front of them could not match the breadth of the Ephraimites. So they concentrated on the shallowest section of the river crossing. The Ephraimites, now in the vanguard, stopped about 100 yards from the river and sent 2,000 archers and shield-bearers forward. They would be the first to cross. Each archer had a shield-bearer, who covered and protected him. Ram horns sounded once they were in place, and the lead elements moved methodically into the river. When the Ephraimites were in the river, the Judean archers shot. The Judeans had set up range markers to increase their accuracy. Regardless of the shield-bearers, Ephraimite archers dropped up and down the crossing. It wasn't long before the stream ran red, and bodies in the river slowed those still coming.

Many of the Ephraimite archers were now across the river and returning fire. The black-shafted arrows commingling as they sluiced through the air in both directions looked like black rain. The hiss of their flight was audible above the din of the battle. Another horn sounded, and it was time for Baildan's troop. The scout unit joined the main cavalry on the right flank, and along with the cavalry on the left flank, they forded the river. Baildan's unit rode at a gallop toward the left flank of the Judeans. Their counterparts on the left flank attacked the Judean right flank. The cavalry added their firepower to the infantry archers, and the mass of arrows targeting the Judeans grew exponentially. It was a blood bath. The Judeans sent out their cavalry to meet them.

Both sides used their lances as the two groups of cavalry met with shocking speed. A man on a big roan charged Baildan. He carried a large scimitar, and his screaming distorted his face into a mask of rage. At the last moment, Baildan raised his spear point, striking the man squarely in the center of his chest. Their converging force was so great the spear point went through his armor and exited his back. The scream ended as his mouth formed a surprised O. The hatred in the man's eyes turned to shock and disbelief as he pitched off his horse. The momentum tore the spear from Baildan's hand, and he pulled a javelin from his quiver.

Another rider rode at a diagonal toward in front of Baildan. Using his knees, Baildan clamped his horse's barrel, rose, and hurled the javelin. It hit the man just under his helmet, entering the side of his neck. Baildan turned to look for another threat. He faced a large rider on a plow horse. No time for another javelin, he drew his sword and blocked the bigger man's overhand swing with his shield. The closest target he could see was the man's leg, and with his sword engaged with Baildan's shield, Baildan swung under his guard, opening a deep wound on the man's leg. Baildan backed off for a moment; their horses circled each other.

You could tell this was neither horse's first battle. They knew what they were doing without leg or rein pressure. They closed again, and this time the Judean made a lunge, which Baildan blocked. Baildan's horse charged forward and caused the other horse to stumble. The big man lost his balance and hung on to keep his seat. But Baildan brought his sword in a sweeping flat arc, which caught his shield arm on the triceps, cutting through his armor, slicing to the bone. Blood was now running freely from the leg and arm wounds. The man was beginning to weaken. His left arm hung loosely at his side. He backed his horse up, hung his head in shame and pain, unable to look at Baildan, and turned and left the field of battle. Baildan did not pursue. There was no one to his front for the moment, but a group of three men converged on Samir. Baildan rode into them, staggering one of the horses. He used his javelin as a stabbing tool and drove it in under the man's armor into his stomach and kidney. The man screamed, grabbed the wound, and fell from his horse, who then proceeded in its terror to stamp him into a bloody pulp.

Samir engaged with the third rider. Baildan stowed the javelin, pulled the bow from his back, and loosed an arrow over Samir's shoulder that went in through the man's left eye and exited through the back of his head. Samir, shocked, turned and yelled at him, "Hey, you nearly took my ear off." Baildan grinned at him and saluted. "You're welcome," he shouted as he turned and went back into the fight. The fighting lasted another twenty minutes before the Judean cavalry blew their trumpets and retreated from the field, with Ephraimite cavalry pursuing them and continuing the slaughter. The blood lust of the Ephraimites and their hatred of the Judeans were now very evident.

Baildan turned and found Eilbra. He raised his right hand and twirled it in a circle above his head. Eilbra took his trumpet and blew three sharp blasts, signaling everyone to assemble. Within minutes, the troop had formed in front of Baildan, and after taking a quick look around, the squad leaders reported to Ashur and Samir, who summarized the reports for Baildan.

Ashur frowned. "I have one significant wound, arrow in his shoulder, three with minor wounds, but can still fight, and two dead."

Samir followed, "I have two significant wounds, one a belly wound, that I think will prove fatal, the other a sword cut that also broke the clavicle, four minor wounds, and three dead."

That was a heavy bill for such a short encounter. They had been in the lead and took the brunt of the enemy charge.

"Send the severely wounded back to the physicians, patch up the minor wounds, and follow me," Baildan said and led the troops back to the army's main body, which had finished mopping up the infantry that had met them at the ford.

The Judeans were fleeing back to Mizpah. They had accomplished their mission and had slowed the Ephraimite advance. The cavalry took up their assigned position on the right flank. The Assyrian armor-bearers were there, and they replaced expended arrows, javelins, and spears. The army ground forward again. Topping the rise over which the Judeans had fled, they saw the main body formed up against them. The might of Judah stood there. King Ahaz had combined his armies for one deciding battle. A look at their breadth and depth told Baildan they were facing well over 200,000 men, just as he had told Nabil. The Judeans had chosen the ground well. It was not a perfectly flat plain, hampering the Ephraimite chariots. The Judeans were on a slight rise, and the Ephraimites would be fighting uphill. The battle was going to be a horrible carnage, regardless of who won.

The Ephraimite army advanced down the hill and paused in the valley. Again trumpets sounded, and archers and slingers moved to the front as they closed with the enemy. Just as in the earlier battle, arrows flew from both sides. The difference this time was the volume of arrows. The total number of archers combined meant three to five thousand arrows in the air at any time. It was the Black Death. Men and animals died. Ephraimite archers continued to advance, firing as they went. The hiss of the arrows, the screams of wounded men and animals, served to heighten every sense. The cavalry wheeled to the right, moving out of range of the Judean archers. Baildan's men waited, hands sweating, mouths dry, fear churning their stomachs, waiting for the next phase of the battle to begin.

They didn't have long to wait. The archers opened their lines, trumpets sounded, and the chariots began their charge into the Judean center. The uneven terrain restricted the chariots and funneled them into the narrowed target areas. That was also the signal for the cavalry to begin to harass the flanks, as both the east and west cavalry units raced along the Judean flanks, filling the air with arrows. The arrows served their purpose. The flanks moved inward to avoid the fire, bunching the enemy toward the center. When the cavalry reached the end of the enemy column, they wheeled back the way they had come, continuing their fire. This pattern continued for two more passes; each pass compressed the Judeans more. The Judeans sent out their cavalry to meet the Ephraimite cavalry to provide some relief for their infantry. The Judeans were woefully few, and the Ephraimites destroyed them quickly. Ephraimite horns blew again, and bile rose in Baildan's throat as he looked at the mass of Judean infantry they were about to charge. The Assyrians rode into the flank of the Judean infantry. For a few minutes, they fought as mounted cavalry, using the weight of their horses and their height as an advantage. Unfortunately, the one advantage a dismounted enemy has is his ability to attack the horse's underside. When the Judeans figured this out, horses screamed and died.

Baildan waved to Eilbra, who blew his trumpet and ordered the dismount. As one, the troop leaped from their horses and fought as infantry. They swatted the horses and sent them out of the battle. Some of the horses, crazed from the smell of blood and the cacophony of the fight, stayed. These horses ran wild, striking out with hooves at friend and foe alike. The men fought in pairs primarily to offset the numeric advantage of the Judeans. The Assyrians fought back to back or with one man attacking with the sword or Javelin, and the man behind him used a long spear. The spearman struck at the same target, lunging either over his partner's front shoulder or under his shield at the man facing them. The two-man attack was the most effective and almost indefensible. They waded into the press, and the Judeans turned from the front to face them. Now Judeans became men, individuals, some with long beards, others closely cropped, well-armed and armored, some with converted farm implements. When a man turned to meet them, in a fraction of a second, their mind processed an unbelievable amount of information-- size, weight, weaponry, right or left-handed, nimble or ponderous, good fighting stance, or relatively untrained. They didn't think about it; the mind just processed the information, and they reacted.

The first man Baildan faced was large and ponderous, with a decent sword and sturdy shield. He wanted to use his bulk to hammer Baildan with his shield, knock him off balance and finish him as he fell. Not happening, Baildan quickly sidestepped and severed the man's hamstring, and as he fell, Baildan stepped in and thrust to his neck. Next was an older man, a man who didn't belong on this battlefield. Baildan blocked the scythe the man was using as a weapon and struck him on his unprotected head with the pommel of his sword. He was out of the fight. Baildan could not bring himself to kill an unarmed man.

On and on, the battle went. Each of Baildan's men would step out of the front line for a brief rest when they had a chance. By now, their armor bearers had found them on the battlefield and would hand them a water-skin, check them for wounds, bind up the bleeders, and replace any broken weapons, and then the warrior would step back into the melee again. They fought on through the late morning and the early afternoon, and still, there were men in front of them wanting to kill them. Baildan lost track of everything. All he could think of was how tired his arm was—Baildan's tongue clove to the roof of his mouth. The stench of blood and released bowels was nauseating.

The blood was everywhere. It had created blood mud, in which the men fought and slipped; blood covered their sword arm to the elbow. The blood had formed into sticky brown glue, which bonded their hand to their sword hilt. The blood formed a crust on their faces and in their beards. Human flesh, torn from living bodies, mingled with the blood. The blood of every man they had killed or wounded clung to them, stuck to them, and had congealed into a dark brown cloying substance, which clothed them. The blood identified Baildan as a killer to every man he met. Baildan could see the fear in the eyes of the Judeans when they looked at his horrible and terrifying visage.

There was a gap in front of Baildan, and he stepped out of the line. Karim was there to meet him, and he took the water skin from him and drank greedily. Karim assessed his equipment and replaced his sword with an iron one. He also exchanged his shield and filled his quiver with javelins. Baildan took a few moments to walk up and down the line to assess how the troop was doing. They were still fighting, but they were beginning to weary. He picked up a long spear he found lying on the ground and moved in behind men he saw struggling with their current adversary. He would land a telling blow, and they would finish the man. They would turn to see who had helped and would nod their thanks and then turn and keep fighting. The noise of battle, the screams, the pleas for mercy were becoming increasingly louder as the front of the Ephraimites, and Syrians ground their way deeper and deeper into the Judean army. The shadows on the battlefield grew longer as the sun continued its journey westward, oblivious of the men struggling and dying on the field far below it. The Judeans couldn't last much longer. The Assyrians would all die of exhaustion if something didn't change soon. And then it happened, slowly at first: Judeans breaking engagement and moving toward the rear. Then larger groups began moving together, backing away, still facing their enemy, before turning and running south. In the end, it was a route, but the killing wasn't over.

The Ephraimites pursued the fleeing Judeans, killing every man they could catch. Then the Ephraimite archers and slingers went to work, filling the air with arrows, which found easy targets in the backs of the fleeing Judeans. It had turned from a battle into a slaughter. The Ephraimites didn't want to defeat the Judeans; they wanted to destroy them. Baildan had never seen anything like this, and it sickened him. Baildan's men also stood in shock, watching the Ephraimites stream by in their frenzy to pursue. There was no doubt in anyone's mind that they would chase the Judeans to the gates of Jerusalem.

Baildan was walking off the battlefield when a hand reached up and grabbed his calf. He drew his sword, ready to strike, and the man on the ground held up his hand palm out to stay the blow. Baildan recognized the man; he had fought him just a little while ago. The man lay dying, his wounds grave, he signaled for Baildan to lean down, and Baildan knelt next to him. The man began speaking in Hebrew, thinking Baildan was an Ephraimite. Baildan held up his hand and replied in Aramaic, "I am not an Israelite." Despite his pain, the man smiled and started again, but this time in Aramaic, "My name is Tola," the man wheezed through a voice too parched to speak. Baildan signaled for Karim, who came over with the water skin and gave the man a drink. "Help me," the man said, his voice louder but still weak.

Thinking that the man desired a mercy stroke, Baildan pulled his knife, but he shook his head no. "My wife," he continued, "and my son. They are in Mizpah. Once the Ephraimites have breached the walls, the rape and slaughter will be terrible. They hate us more than anything in the world. I have gold. My wife is young and beautiful and will need protection. Please, please help her." He told Baildan how to find his house and begged again, "Please help."

Baildan shook his head no, "This is not something I can do. My men and I have a long ride in front of us tonight. I cannot help you."

In his final moments, the man's strength became almost superhuman. He gripped Baildan's arm tightly, "Please do this. The gold will be yours, my wife will be yours, and my God will bless you. Please save my son. Swear to me you will do this."

Baildan looked into the dying man's eyes, and for a reason he did not understand, replied, "All right. You have fought well today. I swear I will attempt to save your wife and son, but I may already be too late."

The man nodded his head in thanks toward Baildan. Then his stare turned glassy. He had gone to meet his God. Baildan nodded at Eilbra, who signaled, and the men formed in ranks in front of Baildan, whose heart broke at the sight of them. The Judeans had wounded many of them. They stood there; some shook, some cried, some laughed. The stress of combat affected each man differently. Some sat on the ground, their exhaustion so great their legs would no longer support them. Baildan called for a report, the squad leaders, or their replacements, reported to Ashur and Samir. Thankfully, his two commanders had survived the battle. Ashur and Samir both reported. They had lost twenty-five men between the morning action and today's battle. There were six men too injured to move, four had significant wounds but could still ride, and the rest were nicked up but could still fight.

He looked at the two captains and said what they knew he would say, "We have no choice; we either leave now, or we will be trapped here in Ephraim. We will have to ride much of the night. There will be food back at camp; Karim has organized everything there, and our support wagons are already on the way north. The men will have to eat on horseback tonight. I will not be going with you. I have something to do in Mizpah, and then I will catch up with you."

The two men looked at each other and knew this had something to do with the Judean who had just died. No use arguing. Ashur spoke up, "Samir will lead the men north, and I will go with you. No way am I letting you ride into that chaos alone." Baildan agreed and gripped Ashur's hand in thanks.

The grooms had rounded up the horses from the battlefield and had brought up replacements for any wounded or missing horses. The able men mounted, and the grooms handed up the more severely wounded men to the riders, who sat behind them and supported them until they could reach the wagons. The troop turned north, and Baildan and Ashur headed toward Mizpah.

The Ephraimite army was there and battering the gates, just as Tola knew they would be. With no defenders left in the city to slow them, they would be through very quickly. Baildan led, using his horse to push men aside as he made his way toward the gate. The Ephraimites glared up at him. They were eager to get at the women and gold and didn't like being pushed aside. Baildan ignored them and continued to go forward. As they neared the gate, there was a mighty cracking sound as the blocking bar gave way. The Ephraimite army surged forward, eager to be at the booty, but the men against the gate, which was not open yet, were crushed to death. Finally, the weight of the mass behind them pushed the gate open.

Baildan kicked his horse hard. The horse reared and lunged forward, crushing more men as he bolted through the opening with Ashur close behind. The two men were through the gate. Baildan rode past the city square, past two more buildings, then turned to his right and saw a large home on the left, just as Tola had described it to him. No time to knock.

Baildan rode at the door, rearing his horse; his hooves and weight shattered the two large doors when the horse descended. Baildan jumped from his horse and threw his reigns to Ashur. He raced into the house and saw a young woman standing at the back wall. She held a boy, about twelve, in front of her with a knife to his throat.

The woman screamed at him in sheer terror, "I will kill us both before I let you filthy Ephraimites touch either one of us."

Baildan stopped dead in his tracks and held up his hand. Speaking Aramaic, he replied, "We don't have much time. There is a wild mob of those Ephraimites just behind us. Listen to me if you want to live. I am Assyrian, which is why I do not speak Hebrew. You're husband Tola made me swear to him before he died that I would come for you and save you and your son."

"Why should I believe you?" she yelled in Aramaic, still wild-eyed and terrified.

Baildan stopped for a second and looked at himself, covered from head to foot in Judean blood. He wondered what he must look like to this poor, frightened woman. Still holding up his hands, he advanced toward her, speaking slowly and softly, "I am Baildan, the son of Domara, and my home is in Nineveh. I came here as a spy for the king of Assyria, and I am returning to Assyria tonight. Your husband begged me to take you, your son, and your gold. I must leave for Assyria now. You must decide. If you want to live, come with me; otherwise, stay here and die, or even worse."

The woman still trembled, and her eyes darted around the room as if she were looking for help. She looked at him pleadingly, "Will you truly save us?"

"On my father's life," Baildan swore.

She rushed to the opposite wall and pushed one of the blocks. Baildan stared in amazement as a door opened to a shallow room filled with chests. The woman entered, grabbed two bags out of one of the chests, and closed the wall again. "They will never find this door. We will return for the rest one day."

"Put on your husband's clothes," Baildan demanded, "we'll never get out of the city with you dressed like that."

She hurried from the room and came back in her husband's robe and headscarf, it wasn't much of a disguise, but it would have to do. The three of them rushed from the room.

Baildan grabbed the boy and threw him up behind Ashur. "Hold on tight," he commanded the boy. "Things will be a little bumpy until we are clear of the city." He raced to his horse, grabbed its mane, and swung himself up. The woman needed no instruction, and she grabbed Baildan's tunic and jumped up behind him. Baildan was impressed. He turned his horse toward the road they had come in, which was filling with soldiers when the woman grabbed his arm.

"No," she shouted in his ear, "This way." She pointed toward a side street, "there is a back gate we can use."

Baildan and Ashur turned their horses in the direction she indicated and found the gate, which unfortunately had also been found by a few Ephraimite warriors.

The group's leader, a filthy, unkempt man with no blood on him, sneered up at them, "Well, and what do we have here?" he said, reaching for the bridle to Baildan's horse. He never heard the answer to his question because Ashur's javelin caught him squarely in the center of the chest. These were shirkers, not fighting men, and the rest of the small group bolted off down one of the alleys, looking for easier pickings.

Baildan saw three primary groups once they exited Mizpah, one intent on chasing the Judeans to the gates of Jerusalem. Another group was intent on sacking and pillaging Mizpah, and a third group—the worst. The camp followers, mostly women, were spread over the battlefield, stripping the dead of anything valuable and mutilating and killing any Judeans left alive. These were scavengers no different than hyenas or wild dogs. It was a gruesome sight, human vultures, the Ephraimite women's hatred of the Judeans seemed to match that of their men folks'. None of these groups gave them a second look. Both men dug their heels into their horses, and they rode at a gallop, seeking to catch up with their comrades. As they passed the site they had fought most of the day, Baildan glanced down. There lay the older man, whom he had knocked out, his throat was slashed, and the scavengers had mutilated him. The sight sickened him. When they reached the stream north of Bethel, Baildan and Ashur both jumped down and scrubbed themselves until they had washed off most of the blood. Baildan didn't feel clean, but it was the best he could do. His clothing soaked, he walked back to his horse and mounted. "Sorry," he said, turning his head, "you're going to get a little damp."

"Believe me," she said coldly, "I'd rather be wet than continue looking at the Judean gore covering your face."

Baildan did not respond. He could certainly understand how she felt. They rode steadily for another hour. They passed a farm field that the marching army had destroyed, and a man knelt in the center of the field. He hugged two young children; his wife lay on the ground next to them, unmoving, and the three still living wept. Baildan turned and looked at Ashur; he too was looking at the macabre scene, and tears were running down his face.

They rode on and topping a rise saw their troop riding ahead, slowed by the wagons and the wounded.

Karim saw them in the distance, and by the time they caught up, he had food prepared for them, flatbread filled with goat meat and cheese, which he carried in his saddlebags. He distributed the food to the four of them. The two men ate ravenously, not having eaten since morning, and when they finished, Karim was ready with more. He passed a wineskin between them, and the flooding warmth of the alcohol was welcome. Sated for the moment, Baildan quit chewing, looked at Karim, and said, "Where are my manners, Karim? This is, um, come to think of it; I don't know your names."

The woman behind him looked at Karim and smiled, "Thank you for the food and wine. We appreciate your kindness. My name is Rachael, and this is my son Benjamin."

"I am Karim, Baildan's servant," he replied, smiling back. "Anything you need, you only have to ask me, and I will get it for you. I look forward to getting to know you better."

They rode steadily through the evening and early night until they reached a point north of Samaria. Baildan halted them there for the night. If he hadn't, men would have started falling out of the saddle.

Karim assembled Baildan's tent, and Baildan led Rachael and Benjamin into it. Karim had made up a pallet for Benjamin on one side of the tent, which he went to and was asleep almost immediately. Rachael walked over to the other side of the tent and saw two pallets lying side by side. Without hesitation, she let her robes slip to the ground and moved toward one of the mats.

Baildan wasn't easily shocked, nor was he often at a loss for words, but right now, he was both. The woman standing before him was the most beautiful woman he had ever seen. Long black hair, a long neck, thin waist, and full hips, he could only imagine the view from the front. He turned his back and stammered, "There has been some misunderstanding. Why don't you put your robe back on and move your pallet over by your son." He heard her robes rustling, and after a moment, he turned around, and she was facing him.

"I assumed you would want to be thanked properly for your efforts on our behalf," she said coldly.

"I know what you assumed," Baildan said just as coldly. "But you assumed wrong. I have never taken a woman against her wishes and never will. There is no joy in such an act, and I'll have no part of it."

She hung her head and said more warmly, "I am young, and I am still learning the ways of men. My husband kept me very sheltered, and I apologize if I have offended you."

Baildan also softened and smiled at her. "I am not offended. You are a beautiful woman; any man would be thrilled at the thought of being with you. But not here, and not like this. We have a long journey in front of us. Who knows, we may learn to become fond of each other. Now pick up your pallet and join your son."

Scene 3 Magi Camp

Rahim, the storyteller, looked out over his audience. The very young could barely keep their eyes open, and even the older ones were losing interest now that the story of the battle was over. "Children, I think we have had enough for one evening. In summary, Baildan did make it back to Assyria. The Ephraimites did chase the Judeans to the gates of Jerusalem, and Zichri, the wrestler who killed Pera, caught up with the chariot bearing the leadership of Judah. Zichri killed the king's son Maaseiah, the officer in charge of the palace, and even Elkanah, the second in command. Scripture says 120,000 Judeans died on the battlefield that day; the Second Book of Chronicles tells us they died because they 'had forsaken the Lord.'[14] King Ahaz could have avoided this great loss if he had listened to the Word of God sent to him through the prophet Isaiah. Now off to bed. I will see you all tomorrow."

With that, the children and their exhausted parents dragged themselves off to find their sleeping mats.

CHAPTER 9

Sasan

Scene 1 Compound of Baraz - Day 39

Mirza rose early and prepared everything he needed for the eight-or-nine-day ride he faced. Baraz had been clear. Mirza would ride to Susa and deliver the message he carried directly to Queen Musa. He didn't need to know any more than that. Mirza had picked two horses, and the grooms should have them ready. He dressed warmly in a thick robe with fleece lining, heavy fleece pants, riding boots, and a headscarf. Mirza was a small man, thin and wiry with ropy solid muscles. He was Mongolian, and the horse was an extension of himself. He loved the feel of the mass under him, the animal's strength, power, and nobility. Mirza looked forward to the journey; he would be doing what he loved best. He reached the corral, but instead of two horses, there were four. Mirza looked at the groom, "What are you doing? I gave specific instructions last night. I only need two horses." The groom looked at him, then looked over Mirza's shoulder and nodded in that direction. Mirza turned and looked, striding purposefully toward him was Leyla, the daughter of Baraz, and she too was dressed in heavy riding clothes.

"Well," she said with great authority, "are you ready to go?"

"My lady," Mirza stammered, "no one told me you would be going. I will be riding fast, and the roads are dangerous, and I am concerned for your safety." He bowed.

"I can keep myself safe; that is not something that concerns you. Your job is to guide, and I'll do the thinking."

"My lady," Mirza pleaded, "may I at least go to your father before we start to ensure I have authority to take you."

With that, Leyla stepped in close to him and was mere inches from his face. She glared at him and poked him in the chest with her finger. "I'll decide what authority you need. You can mount that horse now, or you can leave the compound forever; your choice."

"Let's ride, my lady," Mirza said, resignation in his voice. "We have a long day in front of us."

Mirza rode at a steady lope and held to it without variation. Leyla was a far better rider than he expected. She kept up and never complained or asked to stop, but this was just day one, and there were 300 miles to go.

Ever since her confrontation with Navid, Leyla's anger had grown, and it was still simmering. First, his stupid demand that she leave Persia with him, all to see some goat herder running around in some pasture in Israel, and then he had hit her. **HIT-HER. Bound** her. When she caught up with him, she would kill him slowly. Hitting her was a huge mistake. Leyla saw little of the countryside that morning; she was so focused on her hatred. Head down, she followed Mirza, trusting that he knew the way.

They stopped periodically to eat, water, feed the horses and change mounts. Leyla took the time to look around her; they were in a sloping valley, and as she looked to the northwest, she could see they would be ascending into a snow-covered pass later today. It was cold and dry in the valley but bearable for this time of year. The area they were in had so little vegetation it smelled of nothing but dust. Small boulders surrounded the trail they were following, and periodically she could see scrub pine, but very few. To be a live tree in this valley was a testament to the tree's irrepressible will to live.

Leyla also took a moment to examine her traveling companion more closely, small in stature, thin but with a well-cropped beard, and curly black hair that hung almost to his shoulders. His hands were tough and calloused from hard work and riding, and he was a natural extension of his horse, which is why the steward chose him. They had already covered a lot of ground, and she knew they would cover many more miles today.

Mirza studied Leyla whenever she looked away or down to eat. Leyla was a beautiful woman and had no business on these mountains trails with him. But he had to admit one thing; she could ride. The two horses she rode were magnificent animals, Arabians. They were fine-boned, nearly white, with speed and endurance. They cost a fortune. The kind of horses Mirza knew he would never ride, but that didn't stop him from dreaming. They still had more miles to cover today. "If you are ready, Leyla, we need to go."

They climbed toward the pass, and the snow changed from a mere dusting to an inch and then to six inches. The horses could handle this depth without much trouble. The biggest issue was they couldn't see the small rocks under the snow. If a horse broke a leg, their lives could be at risk. Mirza did not slow the pace.

He signaled to Leyla to ride up beside him. "We have to clear this pass before nightfall, the wind will be strong, and we'll freeze to death if we have to spend the night in the pass," he explained. "It slopes down steeply on the other side, and we should be able to find decent cover not too far from the summit."

Leyla looked at him, thankful that he knew the trail so well. "Your call. You lead; I'll follow."

They reached the summit an hour later, and as he had predicted, the wind was howling through the pass. The sun was dropping, and the temperature was falling fast. Leyla pulled her robe closer around her, burying her face to the nose in the soft fur, leaving just a slit for her eyes. She looked at the trail leading down. It was steep, which was to their advantage. They descended and found shelter behind a formation of large boulders. They took care of the horses first, removed their tack, rubbed them down, then fed and watered them. Then they sat on their sleeping pads. The thin pads provided scant comfort on this ground, but it was better than nothing. Mirza unpacked dried meats, cheese, and bread he had packed for the trail. He was starving. Leyla was so tired she could barely stay awake to eat. "You must eat, my lady. Your body must have the energy to replenish what you lost today and to strengthen you for tomorrow," he said to her compassionately.

Leyla looked at him; she may have underestimated him. She took the food from him and smiled. "Thank you, Mirza. You are right, and I'll be too weak to ride tomorrow if I don't get some food in me." Still smiling, she reached behind into her pack and brought out dried figs and dates. She handed Mirza some. "You aren't the only one who remembered to pack."

Mirza grinned and nodded in thanks.

When they finished eating, Leyla lay down on her mat, but Mirza stood, shifting from foot to foot, extremely uncomfortable. "Well?" Leyla looked at him quizzically.

"My lady, even though we are out of the pass, it will be bitterly cold tonight. We will both be much warmer if we share a blanket. I...I know I should not be saying this, but I don't want you to be cold," he stammered. Mirza looked down, not wanting to make eye contact with Leyla.

Leyla laughed inwardly. She felt very safe sharing a blanket with him. Her father would torture him if he even thought of touching her. She looked at him, "You are correct. We will be much more comfortable with our combined body heat. Bring your sleeping pad over here." He brought his pad over, covered them both with a blanket, and then turned with his back toward her.

Mirza woke before dawn. His eyes flew open in terror. There was an arm draped over him, and Leyla was puffing air lightly into his ear as she slept. He needed to get up, he had drunk a lot of water last night, but he continued to lie there in agony, afraid to wake up the young woman. Cautiously, Mirza wormed his way from under her arm. He rolled onto his back and gently took the cuff of her sleeve, and lifted her arm as he squirmed the rest of the way off his mat. Once free, he jumped up and ran around to the other side of the rock.

Leyla lay there chuckling to herself. She had been awake the whole time and enjoyed watching Mirza trying to extricate himself. A minute later, Mirza came back around the rock, and Leyla burst out laughing. He turned crimson and glared at her. "You were awake the whole time, weren't you? I almost died of agony lying there."

Leyla continued to laugh as she went around the rock and answered the call of nature. When she came back, Mirza was feeding the horses.

Finished, he came back, took food from his pouch, and shared it with her. Mirza smiled and nodded at her, acknowledging the humor in her little trick.

He then put the tack on both horses and swung himself onto his horse. Leyla followed suit, grabbing the surcingle and swinging herself up—when suddenly the surcingle slipped, and she found herself sitting in the dust next to the horse. She sat there in shock as Mirza howled in glee, "You might want to tighten that up just a little before you mount next time."

She was about to explode at him but then decided that turnaround was fair play and merely nodded. She jumped up, tightened the surcingle, and swung onto the horse. The three events seemed indistinguishable they happened so fast. Mirza grinned, pleased with himself and equally delighted with his traveling companion. There may be more to this girl than just being a rich man's daughter.

He turned his horse, headed back to the trail, and put his heels to the horse. Leyla was close behind, and the day followed the same pattern as the day before. The terrain changed little as they rode, stark and barren. The sun was brighter today, and there was a light breeze in the valley. She warmed as the day wore on, but Leyla covered her head with her scarf, keeping just a small slit for her eyes. This shawl protected her from the glare of the snow.

They stopped by a small group of boulders close to the trail again that evening. They cared first for the horses and then sat down to eat, sharing food from each other's food pouches. The conversation was much freer this evening, despite the gap in their status. Mirza hesitated before asking, "My lady, I know it is no concern of mine, but what happened? Why are you here?"

Leyla hesitated before answering. There was no way Mirza should be addressing her with such familiarity, but for some reason, whether it was just the isolation or that she was comfortable with him, whatever the reason she decided to reply. "You're right, Mirza. It would be best if you hadn't asked, but since you did, I'll tell you," and she recounted the story of Navid, their relationship, and what had happened two nights ago. It was funny that she found that talking about it had released some anger as the story unfolded. She was able to tell the tale with relatively stable emotions.

Mirza looked back, stunned. She had talked to him—spoke to him like a friend. He gazed at her with admiration. "He's chasing a star? Is he looking for some religious guru? Did he choose that over you? The man is a fool, good riddance. I'm glad we're riding to tell the queen of this betrayal."

For some reason, Leyla blushed. His warmth and affirmation seemed important to her. She was amazed at her reaction.

Leyla looked at Mirza. "You know something of me, but I know nothing about you. Tell me about yourself, Mirza."

"There's not much to tell, my lady. Eight years ago, when I was twelve, my parents and I were traveling through these mountains. We had come from an area far to the north and fled a Khan offended by my father. Some local raiders attacked us, and they killed my parents and all of our traveling companions. I had fallen off my horse and had a bloody head wound. The raiders thought I was dead. A few days later, your father found me and took me with him. He saved my life, and I have been with him ever since. Your father discovered my riding skills. In my tribe, they put children on a horse shortly before they could walk. I was an excellent rider, and I was small and light, making me a perfect courier."

Then Leyla spoke, "It's late, and I'm exhausted; will you keep me warm?"

"If my lady wishes. It was wonderful to be warm last night, and no doubt we rode better today because of the rest." So as they had the night before, they moved their pallets together, covered with a robe, and slept back to back. Mirza forced himself to relax. Her nearness was intoxicating. Fortunately, he was exhausted and fell asleep quickly, avoiding wasted thoughts and desires.

The same pattern of riding, resting, eating, and sharing a blanket repeated itself each day, with the two becoming more comfortable together. As they neared Susa, the terrain changed.

Susa lay in the lower foothills of the Zagros Mountains between the Karkheh and Dez Rivers. It was on the eastern edge of the Fertile Crescent, and as they descended toward Susa, the vegetation changed, with the frequency of trees increasing—alder, oak, beech, and Juniper trees. Leyla could smell the junipers, and it was a pleasant change from the sterility and the dust of the western range of the Zagros Mountains. Also filling the air was the fragrance of her favorite flower, the Dionysia, which grew in every rock crevice, and fields of saffron crocus filled some of the meadows. The crocus was not only beautiful in its pale purple, but fragrant and edible. Leyla could feel her spirits lifting as the cold decreased and the trail became less rocky.

They camped the last night about thirty miles from Susa. For their evening meal, Mirza found enough wood to make a fire, something he could not easily do in the eastern mountains, and with his sling, he had been able to kill two plump angora rabbits. Leyla enjoyed the warm juicy meat and the last remnant of their cheese and bread, topped off by the dregs in their wineskin. It was the most delicious feast she could ever remember. Sated, she leaned back against a boulder and stared at Mirza.

He was pleased with Leyla's satisfied look. "Now, that was a great dinner," he said, grinning at her. Then he became more somber. "What happens after tomorrow? Do we head back home?"

Leyla considered for a moment, hesitant in her reply, "I don't know. I don't think I can take that ride again any time soon. We may stay in Susa for a while. I know some people in the city, and they will house us for as long as we need. We'll report to the Queen and King, and then we'll just wait and see what happens."

Mirza's stomach churned, and his palms were sweaty when he thought about the change that was about to take place. He wished they could keep riding. It had been one of the happiest times in his life. Once in Susa, their status would separate them as surely as a stone wall. Mirza would walk slightly behind her. He would not look at her, and he most certainly would not address her unless she addressed him first. Their conversation would consist of her giving him a command and him nodding in obeisance. He had been a fool letting himself get too close to her.

Leyla got up and placed her sleeping mat next to the fire, and Mirza put his on the opposite side of the fire. Neither of them said a word; neither had to. Leyla had been having the same thoughts as Mirza and knew that tomorrow, they must each take up the roles into which life had placed them. Best to start tonight.

Scene 2 Susa - Day 47

Leyla and Mirza rose with the sun, as they had every day, and descended toward Susa. By mid-morning, Leyla could see the Karkheh River flowing to the west of Susa. Trees and brush grew thick along the banks of the river. Leyla could also see the city, sitting on a mound in the center of the plains around it. The palace of Darius sat on a hill and was visible even from this distance. The sight never failed to take her breath away. Here was the seat of power, ultimate power—the ability to control the lives of thousands of people. Queen Musa or King Phraates could either choose to elevate you to a seat of power or take your life on a whim. There was no one to question their authority. She and Mirza rode toward the palace, where her friend Safa lived. Safa's father was a lower official in the court.

Mirza and Leyla stabled their horses. Leyla affectionately hugged both of her horses and thanked them for carrying her so far. The two then walked up to the palace and entered through the King's Gate. Leyla knew the way to her friend's apartment, and Mirza followed, a respectable distance behind.

When they arrived, Leyla knocked on the ornate door, using the large brass knocker. The family's steward, a hefty eunuch, answered the door. "Miss Leyla," he greeted her, with no expression or change in tone. "We were not expecting you. Let me go and get the lady, Safa."

They entered the apartment, and Mirza stood there gaping. He had never seen anything so beautiful. Hangings and tapestries on the wall, flowers in vases placed everywhere, a stone table for large dinners stood prominently next to a window overlooking a magnificent garden. They had arranged couches draped in colorful silk around the room. It overwhelmed his senses. The steward had no sooner left than skipping across the room came Safa, a year or two younger than Leyla, obviously idolizing her older friend. She barreled into Leyla, almost knocking her down, and then hugged her tightly.

"It's good to see you too," Leyla gasped as she extricated herself from the hug.

Safa giggled and then gaped. Leyla, I'm thrilled you are here, but where is your family?" she inquired as she looked around the room.

"I am alone," Leyla said, realizing for the first time how awkward this was going to be to explain. "There is an emergency, and Mirza," she said, nodding toward the rider, "came to guide and protect me."

"Your father sent you on an eight-day ride, through the mountains in the middle of winter, with just this man," she said incredulously, her eyes narrowing.

Oh well, time to come clean, "Well, not exactly. Father sent Mirza as a messenger to the Queen. He has a sealed packet for her," which Mirza confirmed by removing it from his tunic and showing it to the unbelieving girl. "I decided the message was too important to entrust to just one person. What if he had an accident on the way? The message would never have gotten here, and we would have never known. So, I decided I must also come. Plus, I am a first-hand witness to the information contained in that letter. What if the Queen didn't believe the messenger, or what if she had questions? No, no far better that I came also," Leyla lied convincingly.

Safa nodded, beginning to understand the situation partially, "Your father has no idea you're here. Have you lost your mind? He's going to kill you when he gets his hands on you."

Leyla held firm. "None of that matters. What matters is I have a message for the Queen and have to see her as soon as possible. The first thing I need is a bath and something to wear. I can't see her looking and smelling like a shepherd."

At this, Safa nodded in agreement and clapped her hands. The steward appeared as if by magic. Safa commanded, "Have someone draw a bath for Leyla and lay out my best clothes for her to wear. When you have finished that, take Leyla's rider to the servant quarters."

Safa dismissed Mirza; he wasn't surprised. Bowing, he handed the leather pouch with the letters to Leyla. The entire time Safa had spoken, she had never looked at him. Even a pet dog would have gotten more attention. He was a tool, nothing more. Ride, fight, take a message, clean my horse; his feelings and emotions were of no concern to these people. He was a work animal like their ox or donkey; his status was lower than a favorite horse or dog. He now realized how much he would suffer, having tasted a different life, even if just for a few days. He had never grieved his status or condition before. He had never known anything other.

Leyla looked at him briefly as she took the packet from him, and she saw the look of hurt and confusion in his eyes, and her heart went out to him. "You did a good job on the trail, Mirza. My father will certainly show you his gratitude when we return." She knew it wasn't much, but it was all she could say to console him.

Again, he bowed deeply, "You are too kind, my lady. I was only doing my job."

Having arranged everything for Leyla, the steward returned and snapped his fingers at Mirza, indicating that he should follow him. The two men left the room, and Safa led Leyla to the bath. It was a massive bath carved out of a single boulder, and two attendants were standing in the water waiting for her. Leyla stripped off the riding clothes she had been wearing for the past eight days and stepped into the bath. Safa then began talking nonstop during her bath, telling her every bit of court gossip she could think of, but never touching on the incestuous relationship between Queen Musa and King Phraates. The walls had ears in this palace, and if you valued your life, there were some subjects about which you never spoke.

The hot water almost put Leyla to sleep, but she fought the urge to luxuriate and climbed out of the tub. The two attendants then dried her, gave her a warm robe, sat her down, and worked on her hair. It must be an absolute rat's nest by now, she thought. They oiled and brushed her hair, and it was absolute heaven. Hair and makeup completed, they brought out a beautiful dress with vertical panels of deep red and green. The dress was full and flared beautifully around her legs. A red sash completed the dress. They placed necklaces and bracelets on her and put a deep green turban on her head. Safa looked at her in wide-eyed wonder, "Why don't I ever look that good in that dress?" she simpered.

Leyla laughed and said, "I'm sure you look every bit as beautiful; you just can't see yourself." Safa then called for the steward, who came in and bowed to the two women. "Please take Leyla to see the Queen. She has a matter of extreme urgency."

Leyla grabbed the pouch and followed the steward out of the room. He made several turns before Leyla said, "Wait a minute; this isn't the way to the Throne Hall. Where are we going?"

The steward turned, and without expression or inflection, spoke. "My lady has been absent from the palace, and things have changed. No one goes directly to the queen. You go to the chief counselor, he reviews your request, and then you both go to see the queen."

"But you don't understand," Leyla continued raising her voice slightly, "This is an emergency."

"Yes, I fully understand," he intoned, "and that is why I am taking you to the chief counselor. It is the only way you will ever get to see the queen. You must trust me in this."

Leyla nodded reluctantly and followed the steward as he continued to walk. They came to a set of double doors. The steward knocked, and one of the palace eunuchs answered the door, ushered them into the room, and led them to an inner study.

The most handsome man she had ever seen was seated in the study. He was of medium height, light-brown complexion, a slight hook to his nose, long black curly hair, and eyes that seemed to change color, depending on the light from black to dark green. He had long slim hands, the hands of a leader, not a warrior. She could see why he was the chief counselor.

The steward stopped in front of the man's desk and bowed low, indicating to Leyla that she should do the same, which she did. "Lord Counselor Sasan, may I introduce Lady Leyla, the daughter of Satrap Baraz." The steward droned in his usual flat voice.

Sasan rose, and Leyla noted his long white robe, the robe of a Magi. Her heart caught in her throat. Surely it couldn't be.

He bowed to Leyla and indicated that she should sit, which she did.

Sasan looked at the young woman. "My lady, we are blessed to have you with us, but you are a long way from your Satrap." He looked around as if something was missing. "Where is your father? I know your mother has passed away, but I cannot imagine your father not being with you. What brings you all this way?"

Leyla hesitated and then began, "It is a long story, Grand Counselor, but the sum of it is I bear an important dispatch, which my father has instructed me to place into the Queen's hands. Coincidentally, I know a young man named Navid who has an uncle named Sasan. Are you familiar with Navid?

Sasan brightened. "So you know my nephew, the son of my brother Jahan. That truly is a coincidence, but I am not surprised. Your Satrap is not far from Persepolis." He held out his hand. "You may give me the dispatch."

Leyla paused, terrified at the thought of giving the message to the Uncle of Navid, and then said almost apologetically, "My father instructed me that it is for the Queen's eyes only."

Sasan looked at her, trying to judge her mettle. "You are new to this court, and therefore I will be patient with you. You do not understand. I take nothing before the Queen that I have not thoroughly reviewed, for which you may be extremely grateful. More than one person has not left that chamber alive because they delivered the wrong message or the person delivered it the wrong way." He held out his hand again. "The dispatch, please."

Leyla hesitated again, but she handed over the pouch when she saw the look on Sasan's face. Sasan sat, opened the pouch, and read. When he finished, he threw back his head and let out a barking laugh, "No wonder you didn't want to hand this over. You rode all this way to tell the Queen that the Magi are defecting. Then you end up delivering it to the Uncle of Navid, the son of the leader of the Magi, Jahan. Well, Satrap Leyla, what do you think is going to happen now?"

Leyla sat, eyes wide, frozen in terror. Tears were streaming down her face. What had she done? She would never leave this palace alive. She couldn't speak.

Sasan let the drama play out for a while, enjoying watching Leyla as her mind worked through every awful possibility, and then he spoke, "I'll tell you what is going to happen, Satrap Leyla; we are going to take this dispatch to the Queen. I will praise you for your loyalty and courage, and I will ask the Queen to give you great rewards. You have delivered to me everything I have wanted. I will ask the Queen to give me a company of the Immortals, whom you and I will accompany. I will ask her to allow me to pardon all but the leadership of the Magi. I will banish Fardad and Jahan from Persia and allow you to punish Navid. I will tell her that I will take leadership of the Magi, and we will move the school from Persepolis to Susa, where I can monitor them and continue my duties as Chief Counselor. That is precisely what we are going to do, Leyla. AND that is exactly what is going to happen."

Then Sasan stood and indicated that Leyla should follow him.

Leyla saw him move and saw him wave, but nothing was working. She sat there traumatized by the events and the reprieve, and she could barely think, much less stand. Shaking his head, Sasan came around his desk, gently took her by both arms, and stood her on her feet. She wobbled for a moment until her senses returned, and without a word, Sasan led the way to the Throne Hall.

Sasan stood at his full height, shoulders back as he marched into the Hall. The Steward announced Sasan when he entered, and Sasan approached the throne and knelt with his head to the floor, which Leyla mimicked. Sasan waited for the Queen to tell him to rise, which she did, and he and Leyla stood.

Sasan addressed the Queen in a loud tone, "Great Queen, I have a dispatch for you from Satrap Baraz, which was delivered to me by his daughter. Leyla rode alone through the mountains to deliver the message, a heroic act in the service of her Queen."

The Queen's steward approached, and Sasan handed him the dispatch. The steward knelt and gave the message to the Queen.

She tossed the message aside and looked at Sasan, "Am I going to have to wait all day, or are you going to tell me what has caused the Satrap such anxiety?"

"Most assuredly, Great Queen," and Sasan did, outlining the betrayal of the Magi leadership. The coercion Fardad and Jahan must have used to force the Family to make the trip and the need to banish Jahan and Fardad from Persia. He outlined Navid's brutal treatment of Leyla when she tried to stop the Magi journey, and Sasan asked for justice for Leyla. He then requested that a company of the Immortals pursue the Magi and bring them back. Sasan would lead the Immortals, and Leyla would accompany him. Sasan would offer the Family immunity if they returned to Susa, where he would assume the Family's leadership. If they refuse the offer, the Immortals will destroy everyone and everything.

The Queen jumped to her feet, her face crimson in her anger. "I will pardon no one," she shouted. "We will kill every last one of them. There will be no immunity and no mercy. I will impale them all, and their bodies will line the Royal Road for all to see what happens to traitors."

Sasan dropped to his knees with his forehead to the floor again, then raised his head just enough to speak, "Great Queen, forgive me; you should destroy those who have betrayed you. The dispatch tells of the God Yahweh, whom they worship. Fardad and his predecessors used this mythical God to frighten and control the people. This religion is a cult of a long-dead God; there are even no images of Him. He is powerless. You should impale the leaders, but the people are too valuable. These are the men who have trained the Persian leadership and military for centuries. They have been loyal to Persia. They fought the Babylonians, the Greeks, and the Romans. If you must punish someone, so be it, but do not lose this valuable asset. Once free of Fardad, I can indoctrinate them to the traditional gods of Persia. Great Queen, I think only of what is best for Persia."

The Queen motioned for him to rise, which he did. She eyed him narrowly and said, "Very well; we do need the Magi trainers, but we will impale Fardad, his wife, children, grandchildren, and their wives and families—outside the Palace Gates. They will serve as a reminder of what happens to those who betray me. And as a personal favor to me, you shall oversee the impalements. As for Leyla, she will receive the greatest reward possible. When you return, she will become my Lady in Waiting."

With that, the Queen waved her hand at them and dismissed them.

Sasan and Leyla left the throne room. A row of benches was outside the Hall, and Sasan sat down, not trusting that his legs would hold him. Leyla stood looking at him, trying to process everything she had just heard. What had she done? Leyla had wanted to punish Navid for his insolence, and now his family was to be impaled outside the Palace Gates. As her reward, she was to become Lady in Waiting to the Queen. She didn't even know what a Lady in Waiting was.

Sasan looked up at Leyla, shaking his head, "We both got what we want. I will be the leader of the Magi Family. For your reward, the Queen will impale Navid, and you become the Queen's Lady in Waiting." Sasan held his head in his hands, horror-struck at what he had just done, "We have paid a horrible price for our success. I must murder my father, mother, brother, two nieces, and a nephew, and you will be locked in the palace, you will remain a virgin, and you will serve the Queen night and day. Congratulations."

It all sank in. Leyla turned and retched up everything in her stomach. Her head was spinning. In her rashness, she had managed to destroy her own life and happiness. *Yes, indeed. Congratulations.*

After a while, Sasan rose. "You will meet me in my quarters two days from now, prepared for travel. I will organize the Immortals and the baggage train. Prepare yourself for an arduous journey. Knowing my brother, he will make himself very hard to find."

Leyla turned to leave, then stopped, "What shat I do about Mirza?"

"Who?"

"I'm sorry, Mirza is the rider who accompanied me to Susa, and I promised him I would reward him for his service. He is fabulous with animals; could he help with horse management for the Immortals?"

Sasan couldn't believe she was thinking about some stable hand at a time like this. He shrugged and thought, well, maybe at least one person should get something good out of this mess. "The horse manager is getting too old for this trip. I will tell him he is staying behind. You may tell Mirza he is now the livestock manager for the Immortals."

Leyla expressed her appreciation, turned, and left. Two days and she had a lot to do.

CHAPTER 10

The Iron Army

Scene 1 Magi Route - Day 46

Navid rode in the lead with Utana, as he usually did. The countryside was becoming greener and vegetation more plentiful as they reached the northern end of the Persian Gulf. The smell of the salt air was prevalent. He longed to see the Gulf and hoped they would find some fishermen; fresh fish would be a welcome dietary change. The sun warmed the Scouts, but the breeze off the water made them comfortable; the morning was beautiful.

Navid contemplated the last few days and their slow movement northwest. They were making better time without the wagons, and oxen were not slowing them down, but with each mile, his anxiety grew. Navid knew the Immortals could intersect their route soon. The sooner they forded the Euphrates, the better. Their probability of escaping detection in the wilderness west of the river grew exponentially.

"You're quiet this morning, brother," Utana said, noting Navid's distant stare.

Navid smiled at his friend. "You know me too well. I'm getting eye strain looking for the Immortals, and I'm starting to see them under every rock."

Utana nodded. "We're all nervous the closer we get to Babylon, but some are better at hiding it than others."

They rode in silence for the rest of the morning. Both lost in their thoughts.

"I heard that Jahan talked to Hosh," Utana said, raising one eyebrow as he spoke.

Navid blushed. "True. I think he wanted to wait, but with the constant danger, he thought a wedding might lift everyone's spirits. We are to have a double wedding."

Now it was Utana's turn to blush. "Fahnik is too good for me, and I'm terrified I will disappoint her. I can barely eat any more just thinking about her."

Navid laughed. "That was a small ox you ate for breakfast. It didn't look like your appetite was too affected."

Utana looked offended. "That's exactly my point; normally, I could eat a large ox."

Both men laughed. It felt good to think about something other than the force bearing down on them. By midafternoon, they changed direction westerly and saw the Gulf to their left.

Navid spied a small village with several fishing dhows beached on the sand. He and Utana kicked their horses into a trot, and the Scouts did the same. Nearing the village, they saw a group of fishermen standing by their boats. The two men rode up, and the villagers eyed them suspiciously. Navid and Utana raised their right hands, indicating they came in peace.

Navid noticed one man in the front of the group, clearly the village headman. Navid addressed him, "Greetings, we pray that you are doing well."

The headman looked at Navid. "We do well. We fished all morning and came in early because our boats were full."

Navid smiled. "This could be a good day for both of us. We have a large group following who would certainly love to have fresh fish tonight instead of goat or lamb."

He led Navid over to a large number of baskets, all filled with fish. Navid was amazed at the quantity and variety. There were pink-eared emperors, a small fish, but excellent eating. There was angelfish, with their bright-red fins, bream, big-eyed and grey, with some of them at least ten pounds. There were also snappers with their yellow nose, tail, and fins, and trevally with their gold spots. The headman and villagers were smiling. "The gods have blessed us both this day."

"How much can you sell us?" Navid asked.

"All of it," the headman said eagerly, rubbing his hands together. He and Navid haggled for a short time and finally agreed on a price for the fish. Navid told him he would send someone to get the fish shortly. Then, he signaled to one of the Scouts to handle the job. Navid thanked the headman and led the Scouts back onto the trail. They traveled until early evening. They had now turned west and were heading for the Euphrates, which they should reach tomorrow.

Navid signaled to the Scouts, and Utana blew the horn, signaling for the Family to stop for the day. The riders repeated the signal until everyone had heard it, including the group riding drag. Navid and his men approached the main camp, where people were in the process of setting up camp and lighting cooking fires. The Family was highly proficient at this by now.

Navid and his men rode their horses to the remuda. The grooms collected their horses, rubbing them down, and fed and watered them. Navid found Asha, Gul, and Fahnik erecting their tent, and he helped them. Finished, Asha and Gul joined the other women to prepare the evening meal. Before long, the smell of grilling fish permeated the air. Everyone gravitated toward the cooking area. The new and welcome aromas drew them. Thankfully, it didn't take fish long to grill. Navid selected a large bream, big enough to feed the family. Fahnik collected bread, cheese, and fruit, and she and Navid set up a blanket for the family. Ava, Hosh, and his wife also joined them, as did Utana and his parents.

Fardad gave thanks as usual, but tonight was special, "Jehovah, maker of heaven and earth, we give you thanks for this day, for safe travels and good weather. We praise Your name, and we bow our will to Your will. Father, tonight we gather to plan the weddings of Ava and Navid and Fahnik and Utana. We thank you for these young people, and we dedicate them to you. Guide us as we prepare for the future and as we travel to meet the long-awaited Messiah." Amen resounded around the blanket, and the meal began. The fish was the finest any of them could remember.

The oil from the fish coated their hands and faces, and their dry skin was thankful for the balm.

Asha was the first to speak. "Dara," (Utana's father), "and Hosh. I know it seems as if we are rushing, but I suggest we hold the wedding ceremony and feast tomorrow night. We can have the ceremony before we cross the Euphrates, and it will take everyone's mind off the trip. It will also allow the young couples some time together before we begin traveling again since the crossing could take us several days."

Dana and Hosh both looked at their wives and nodded. Hosh said, "I don't want to speak for Dana, but as for us, we are fine with tomorrow. I don't think Ava could wait much longer anyway," he said, looking at his daughter. Ava blushed bright red and looked at her hands as if she had never seen them before.

Dana said, "Mehr and I agree. Fahnik and Utana have waited long enough. Anyhow, Mehr can't wait to have a daughter in our family," he said, smiling at his wife, who pinched his leg.

Asha was glowing as she looked at the two young couples. "We have watched these children grow since birth. They are the future of the Magi. I couldn't imagine two better matches. None of us know what God has in store for us, but we know one thing, He will get our Family to Jerusalem. After that, everything is in His hands. We have faith that He has a plan for us after we reach the Messiah. He has not revealed it yet, but I have faith that He will. As He told His people, He tells me now, 'fear not for I am with you.' The wedding tomorrow is just what the Family needs. Everyone talked all day of what dishes they would make, of what they would wear, and of how they would dance until dawn."

Navid grinned, looking at Ava, "Dancing until dawn is not what I had in mind," at which Jahan cuffed him lightly on the chest with the back of his hand—sending him flying off his cushion. Ava looked in shock at Navid lying in the dust as he sat up grinning, looked at his father, and said, "Still not dancing," at which the group broke into laughter. They spent the rest of the meal discussing the details of tomorrow night's festival. It was a night of peace and joy, old friends sharing old stories, all with bright hope for the future. It was an evening they all desperately needed.

Pari interrupted the reverie. "I hate to be the spoilsport, but I must go. Rahim is about to begin teaching, and I promised him I would be there."

Tiz rose, picked up Pari, and carried her to the clearing where Rahim would be teaching. The children had assembled with the older boys jumping and ululating in anticipation of another of their favorite stories. Rahim suddenly appeared in the clearing and stood on his teaching platform. Firelight was behind him, illuminating him. He was dressed head to foot as an Assyrian warrior, wearing an iron helmet, iron shield, iron greaves protecting his arms, hobnail boots and iron greaves protecting his shins, and carrying a long spear. The eyes of the young children in front were open wide, and their jaws hung down in awe and terror. The older boys in the back went into a frenzy. Rahim raised his shield and his spear and shouted, "**The Iron Army**." A hush settled over the clearing. Rahim, as usual, unrolled the ancient scroll and read…

Scene 2 South Of Nimrud - 734 BC

Baildan and the remainder of his troop were south of Nimrud. They were almost home. Three more men had died from their wounds; every loss tore at Baildan's heart. Thankfully it had been an uneventful journey from Shechem in Israel, and everyone was excited that night as they made camp. Baildan sat at the evening meal with Rachael and Benjamin; joining them was Ashur and Samir. Everyone was in a good mood, even Rachael, but Samir continued silent and downcast. He had been unable to recover from the death of Pera at the hands of Zichri.

Baildan looked at his old friend. "Samir, look at me. There is nothing you could have done. Pera died doing what he loved, and there is nothing any of us could have done to stop him from wrestling. It would be best if you moved on. Pera, would not have wanted to see you sulking about."

Samir looked at Baildan, sighed, and then smiled. "You're right, I know, but every time I remember the deadly cold eyes of Zichri as he took Pera's life, it sends me into a fury. I'll not be happy until I stand over the dead body of that man, with his blood on my sword."

"I'm sorry to disappoint you, but you will not be the one standing over that dead body; I will. I will not lose another man to that monster. I promised him a long, painful death, and believe me, that is what he will have." Samir looked into Baildan's eyes and knew there was nothing else to be said. Once Baildan had decided, it was irreversible; he nodded his head in grim satisfaction.

"Well, now that we have finished with all the cheerful talk, can we talk of something more pleasant? We will be in Nimrud tomorrow. Tell me what it is like," Rachael, whom Baildan had rescued, asked in earnestness.

Baildan's face lit up. "The city sits on a mound, with steep hills on all sides. It is opulent and magnificent. Within its gates is the wealth of the King's empire. A wall five miles long surrounds the inner city. King Ashumasirpal II founded the city 100 years ago and built the first palace. Tiglath-Pileser III has added massive sculptures at all the palace entrances, depicting man gods.

"What is a 'man god'?" asked Rachael.

"Men with the body of a lion or a bull and even some with wings. They depict the power and the invulnerability of Assyria. He has added gardens and carvings of our history and battles.

"All of the battles? That must take up a lot of space," said Rachael.

Well, actually, the king saves space by only depicting the ones we win. The King has filled the city with food, material, and slaves from every corner of the empire. It's a little noisy and smelly for my taste, but the King keeps the ugliness far from the palace. I will show you everything when we get there. There are two palaces: the southwest palace, which the king no longer uses, and the much larger northwest palace. The king has a separate Governor's Palace, used for local administration since the king does not bother himself with minor local matters."

"So first Assyria conquers and subjugates a kingdom, and then strips them of their wealth and people. A city built on the blood of others," Rachael said with a sad look.

Baildan considered the young woman for a moment. "It has always been so, Rachael. Look at the history of Israel. The Israelites came out of Egypt with nothing but what they could carry in carts. They owned no lands or cities. Then before you know it, Joshua marches them into the land of the Canaanites and takes the land from them, including all their cities. He slaughters every man, woman, and child who will not flee. Even your own Jerusalem was the possession of the Jebusites until King David took it from them. There is nothing else. Assyria is the mightiest empire the world has ever known. We are not cruel to those who serve willingly, but there is no mercy for those who resist. It is the way of things. The power of the raging river as it races to the sea does not consider the damage done by the trees and boulders it carries along. That is its nature. So too is the nature of Assyria. We are like that river."

Ashur looked at the young woman. "You need fear no longer, Rachael. You are with Baildan, and he will let no harm come to you or Benjamin. You are safe with him."

"You are sweet," Rachael said softly. "Thank you, Ashur."

The meal was over, and everyone retired to their tent. Once inside, Rachael asked the question that was really on her mind, "When we arrive in Nimrud, what will become of Benjamin and me?"

Baildan was pensive for a moment as he gathered his thoughts. He walked to Rachael and placed his hands on her shoulders. He lifted her chin and looked into her eyes. "I suppose this isn't very romantic, nor is it the way things should be, but we haven't much time. Once we arrive in Nimrud, I expect to see the great King readying the army for a campaign against Philistia, Syria, and Ephraim. It will be a long campaign, and I could be gone for more than a year. I have grown very fond of you on this trip. You are an honest, sweet woman, and Benjamin and I have already begun to form a relationship. If you would, I will take you as my wife. I know you haven't known me long, but the safest thing for you is to be my wife and for Benjamin to be my son."

Rachael looked at him and then put her arms gently around him and reached up and kissed him. "We are now one flesh; where you go, there I will go. Your people will be my people, and I will keep and devote myself only to you."

Baildan held her close and kissed her gently and passionately, filling himself with her smell and softness. Pulling back, he replied, "We are now one flesh. I will guide and protect you; no man will ever harm you while

I live. Benjamin is now my son, and I will train him and guide him into the ways of manhood and will defend him to the death."

Benjamin was standing there in stunned silence. Rachael turned to him and said soothingly, "Baildan is now your father. You owe him your loyalty and allegiance, and you will honor him as if he were Tola and obey him in all things."

Benjamin smiled broadly and looked at Baildan. "Gladly, Mother, I will bring Baildan glory and honor. So help me, God."

Baildan smiled back at the young man. "Go to bed, Benjamin; tomorrow will be a long day."

The young man went to the opposite side of the tent, separated by a hanging rug. Baildan took Rachael by the hand and led her to his sleeping mat.

Baildan awoke at first light and looked over at his sleeping bride. He shook her gently, and she looked at him groggily. "I hate to wake you, my love, but we need to discuss Benjamin. In a few days, the army will march and could be gone a year or more. If I leave him in Nimrud, I am concerned he will not get the training he needs during one of the most formative periods of his life. I would like to take him with me as my aid, so I can train him in the skills he will need in the future."

Rachael shook herself awake and sat up. She put her hand on Baildan's chest, whispering so Benjamin would not hear, "My lord, this is your country and your people. I do not know the ways or customs, and I know I cannot give Benjamin the guidance or training he will need. I will miss him terribly, but you must do what you think is best. If he goes, you must promise one thing. You must keep him safe."

Baildan nodded. "That is why he will not be my armor-bearer. He will remain with the support personnel in the rear when we are fighting and be perfectly safe. There will be no one we face that can defeat this army. I will tell Benjamin during the morning meal."

Rachael woke Benjamin while Baildan dressed and left the tent. Baildan sought out the tent of Mardokh, the smallest man in his command

and the fastest rider. Mardokh was standing outside his tent and was breaking it down. Baildan strode up to him and placed his hand on Mardokh's shoulder. "Leave that; I'll have someone else bring your equipment. Take two of the fastest horses and ride to Nimrud. Find Domara, my father, and let him know we will be there by nightfall. Tell him I'm bringing my wife and son, and I would like a wedding feast prepared for all my men. Tonight, we will celebrate."

Mardokh grinned at Baildan, knowing there is always a reward for the bearer of good news. "Congratulations, commander. I will ride like the wind, and everything will be ready by the time you arrive."

Without another word, Mardokh ran to the supply area, grabbed bread, cheese, and a skin of water, and ran to the corrals. Before Baildan could even blink, Mardokh was riding at full gallop out of the camp. Baildan shook his head; those poor horses were in for a tough day.

The men were up, and everyone was breaking camp, preparing to leave. Baildan wandered over to the cooking fires and took food for himself, Rachael, and Benjamin. He saw Ashur and Samir and sat with them. Two other men joined them, and then Rachael and Benjamin.

Without preamble, Baildan looked around and announced, "I have taken Rachael as my wife and Benjamin as my son."

Ashur looked pleased, "Congratulations, boss. I'm sure I speak for everyone when I say you couldn't have made a better choice." Everyone nodded in agreement and offered their congratulations.

Baildan continued, "I have decided to take Benjamin with me as my aide on the coming campaign. Ashur, you will be responsible for his arms training. Samir, you will train him in horsemanship and tactics."

Benjamin's face lit up, "I'm going with you? Thank you, Baildan, thank you. I was afraid I would be left behind."

Baildan looked at him seriously, "After these two train you," he said, pointing at Ashur and Samir, "you may not be so thankful. Their job is to turn you into a warrior, and it is not easy or pleasant, but it is necessary."

Benjamin turned to stare wide-eyed at his two new trainers, who were both leering at him. There was suddenly a lump in the pit of his stomach.

Ashur turned to Rachael. "Do not fear, my lady. No harm will come to him while we live. He will leave you as a boy, but he will come home a man."

Everyone finished eating, packed up, found their horses, and began the day's march. The land they were riding through was rocky and barren. Rachael wondered how men from such a place could have become so powerful. There was little sign of natural resources as she looked around. By midafternoon, she saw a rise in the distance, with light shimmering off water and buildings. As they drew nearer to the city, the image clarified. They climbed a slight ridge, which obscured the view momentarily, and when they reached the summit, she was looking down at the city of Nimrud and the largest army she had ever seen. She could see them and hear them. It was a continuous roar as men trained at arms in the valley south of the city. Then, Rachael saw the main roads that led to the town. The roads leading into the city, as far as the eye could see, were filled with caravans, caravans of pack animals and wagons bearing cedar from Lebanon, iron ore, and other metals from Persia, flocks, herds of horses, camels, grains, cloth, and every other resource imaginable from every corner of their vast empire.

Baildan rode up next to her, "It's a bit much to take in at first, but you will get used to it. Also, much of this will die down after the army leaves."

"What river is that which flows around the city?" Rachael asked.

"That is no river. The king had a channel dug from the mountains to the west to bring water to the city, primarily to water his new gardens," Baildan said.

Rachael shook her head in amazement and laughed. "I see I have much to learn."

As they approached, the city rose above them, the town on a promontory at least two hundred feet above the valley floor. Baildan instructed Ashur to have the men set up camp just outside the city, and he, Rachael, and Benjamin continued over a bridge, across the canal, through the south gate, into the city. As they rode past a botanical garden, Benjamin's mouth hung open. The botanists had filled the garden with flowers, unlike anything he had ever seen. The Assyrians had also filled the garden with songbirds of every color.

Next, the riders rode past a zoo. There were animals from every corner of the empire; Benjamin didn't know the names of half the animals he saw. He was in total awe of this city. A short distance later, Baildan stopped in front of a large two-story home, and a groom came running from the side of the house to take their horses.

"Is this where you live?" asked Benjamin. "Not even in Jerusalem have I seen a house like this, except for the king's."

"This is my father's house. He is the second most powerful man in Assyria. With that power comes great wealth," Baildan said as he led Rachael and Benjamin into the house. Standing in the portico waiting for them was his father, Domara, and his mother, Khannah. Tall and stately, Domara was forty-six years old, with the first hints of grey beginning to show in his hair. He looked every bit the statesman, except for the scar from his ear to his chin. He had not always been a statesman. Khannah was also tall for an Assyrian woman, with a few lines beginning to grace her brows, but her beauty was still there. With deep black hair and olive-colored eyes, she was trim, exceptionally well-groomed, and well-dressed.

Domara stepped forward and hugged Baildan. "Welcome home, son; we're thankful that you were successful and unharmed."

Baildan returned his father's hug. "I'm glad to be home, father. The battle in Judah was terrible, and I lost a fourth of my men. I'll tell you about it later."

Turning, Domara looked at Rachael and Benjamin and said, "And this must be your new bride and son." He stepped forward and hugged them each. "We are thrilled to have you in our family and are anxious to hear all about you both."

"Baildan has told us much about you and Khannah, and I look forward to getting to know you both. If it were not for your son, Benjamin and I would be lying dead in Mizpah instead of standing here with you. We have much for which to be thankful."

Domara looked at the newlyweds, "Thanks to Mardokh, we had ample time to prepare everything for tonight. It will be an evening of great joy and celebration. Baildan, I have already sent a servant to your camp to notify your men. We have everything set in the courtyard and will begin in two hours."

Khannah spoke for the first time, far more reserved and formal than her husband. She nodded at Rachael and Benjamin. "Rachael, you best come with me if we are to get you cleaned and dressed before the banquet. Benjamin will go with Baildan, and the servants will make them both presentable by the time of the feast."

Domara smiled, "Mother has spoken, so let it be, everyone."

Rachael left with Khannah, and Domara turned to Baildan. "So tell me, how did you meet Rachael? This must be a fascinating story."

Baildan blushed slightly and bowed to his father. "It is a long story, father. I will tell you everything during the banquet tonight. Right now, Benjamin and I need to bathe and dress."

Domara nodded in agreement, and they proceeded to the men's quarters.

Cleaned and dressed, Baildan entered the courtyard. Most of the guests had already arrived. In addition to Baildan's men, Domara had invited numerous court officials and several close friends. Baildan moved efficiently around the courtyard, greeting everyone and thanking them for coming. The wine was flowing, and servants offered a wide variety of sweets and fruits on trays. The mood was festive. Baildan and Benjamin seated themselves at the head table, and the guests sat in small groups on elaborate cushions around the courtyard. The guests were getting hungry but waited patiently for the bride and her new mother-in-law. They didn't have long to wait. Coming in through the north entrance was Rachael, followed by Khannah.

Baildan stared in amazement. Gone was the dirty, travel-stained little Jewish girl; an Assyrian woman of great beauty replaced her. She had a long dress of various shades of green, covered by a robe cut in a V from the waist to her ankles that opened in the front to reveal her dress. There was a gold sash around her waist and a deep red turban on her head. Her hair had been oiled and hung down her back. Beautiful didn't come close to what Baildan saw before him. What he saw was a woman who was more than equal to any princess in Persia. She stood tall, filled with a confidence he had not seen in her before. Even her walk changed; she seemed to glide into the room. Baildan looked around the room at his men; they were awe-struck.

Rachael saw Baildan and Benjamin seated at the head table, and both rose as she walked into the room. She was as amazed as Baildan had been. Gone was the shabby-looking desert raider; before her was a prince of Assyria. His servants had neatly trimmed and oiled his hair and beard. Baildan wore a silk purple jacket woven with patterns of gold. His turban was also gold to match the patterns in his jacket, and he wore bloused pantaloons. Standing next to him was not the boy she had fled with from Israel, but a young man, who was the mirror image of his new father. As she looked at them, her heart melted. God had been gracious to her.

She approached the table and sat between her husband and son. Domara sat next to Baildan, and Khannah sat next to her husband.

Domara clapped his hands, and food came in from every corner of the room. The servants carried in whole goats and lambs on spits. There were cuts of beef, golden-yellow saffron rice, rich curries of chickpeas and other vegetables, and of course, mounds of fresh flatbread. Everyone ate greedily, but none more so than Baildan's troops, who had traveled hundreds of miles on camp rations. They were famished, and food disappeared rapidly, only to be replaced by servants carrying still more of everything. The wine continued to flow, and as people became more 'relaxed,' the volume of conversations increased, as did laughter and good-natured jibes. The noise level had reached the point where one had to lean in and speak loudly to hear one another.

Domara leaned in toward Baildan. "You promised me a story."

Baildan bowed to his father and began the story. Telling him of the battle at Mizpah, the dying request of Tola (leaving out the part that he was the one who had killed Tola), the rescue of Rachael and her son, and the trip home.

Domara spoke loudly, "Well done, Baildan. You honored a noble enemy's last wish; that was honorable. One look at Rachael, and it's obvious how you fell in love; she is beautiful and intelligent. I will explain it all to your mother later."

The eating and drinking continued late into the evening, and then the dancing began with a troupe of dancers from Ethiopia dressed in tribal dress and a steady rhythm on the drums.

The Ethiopians were tall and beautiful, both men and women over six feet tall. They moved, swayed, leaped, and everyone sat transfixed at the detailed choreography and the flawlessness of their movements. The drums beat faster, and the dancers moved more quickly; it was inconceivable they could keep that pace for so long. These were unique athletes. The dance ended, but not the entertainment. Next came the fire eaters and magicians, who made everything disappear, including some of the guests. There were jugglers and every other form of entertainment known to Nimrud.

The last entertainment was the wrestlers. Two men came out, both of them tall and well-muscled; one of the men bore a scar from his left shoulder to almost his navel. Baildan searched the guests to find Samir and saw him staring fixedly at one of the wrestlers. Watching the wrestlers may be just what he needs, Baildan thought. The contest began but didn't take long. The man with the scar was like lightning, and his hands were enormous. When he gripped the other man's forearm, you could see the man wincing in pain. After the third fall, Samir shot out of his seat and went over to the victor.

Baildan witnessed a short conversation, after which Samir slapped the man on the back. Turning, Samir looked over at Baildan and was smiling from ear to ear. Baildan smiled back, knowing Samir had not forgotten Pera but had moved on.

Even with the entertainment finished, many guests continued to eat and drink, especially Baildan's men. Baildan knew—come morning—he would find many of them passed out where they sat. Let them, he thought. They were celebrating life. They had faced death and come home. They were releasing the tension of their clandestine assignment, the horrible battles they had fought, and the quick trip home. They were alive, and that was enough for tonight.

Baildan leaned toward his father. "We are going to retire, father. I want to thank you. The feast was magnificent, and how you put all of this together in a few short hours is beyond me."

Domara smiled at his son. "You do not become a counselor to the king by not knowing how to get things done quickly, and of course, I used all of the power of my office to make things happen," he said as he tapped his signet ring, the official seal of his power. "The King has summoned us to attend him first thing in the morning. Rise early; I want all the details on Ephraim and Syria before we meet with the King."

Both men rose, as did their wives and Benjamin, and the wedding party retired for the evening, leaving their guests to enjoy themselves for as long as they liked.

Baildan rose early, as instructed, and met with his father in his study. Domara's servant had already made a large pot of tea, and Domara was sitting and enjoying his first cup. The servant poured for Baildan and then left them alone. Domara looked at his son with genuine affection. "I think we will need all of the tea we can hold after last night's celebration."

Baildan nodded and then stopped, trying to keep the room from spinning. "Couldn't the audience with the King have been just a little later?"

Domara looked serious as he spoke. "The great king does not organize his day around mere men. He speaks, and we obey. Now tell me what you know, and I will tell you what I have learned from your brother Meesha."

Baildan organized his thoughts, then said, "We joined the coalition in Syria and marched with the Syrians into northern Israel. King Rezin of Syria split his forces, taking a portion east of the Jordan River to sweep south and consolidate those territories. I was under the command of a Syrian named Nabil, whom I intend to kill. We met up with the Ephraimites in Shechem in northern Israel. Gathering information was not easy at first, but we slowly put together a picture. The two king's battle plan was not a mission of subjugation and territory control. King Pekah of Ephraim and King Rezin of Syria had approached King Ahaz of Judea, requesting that he join them in a coalition against Assyria. When Ahaz refused, they sought to force the issue by taking Jerusalem. They had with them a Syrian official, whom they referred to as the 'son of Tabeel.' I never met him, but they intended to install him as king over Judah.

There were rumors the Philistines had joined this coalition and were marching against Judean cities in the west. I do not know if they are part of a coalition or whether they are merely opportunistic. Either way, they are not friends of Assyria.

We met the main body of the Judean army just north of Mizpah, and it was a slaughter. The Ephraimites were not just after territory, and you could tell they truly hated the Judeans. Once they had routed the Judean army, it was a blood bath. There were no captives. I have already told you what happened after the battle, and that's all I know."

Domara considered for a moment. "That fits with what I have learned from Meesha. In response to the threat, King Ahaz paid a large sum of money to enlist our help against his enemies. That is what is in the official correspondence to Tiglath-Pileser. What is not in that correspondence is the private letter I received from Meesha. There is an internal conflict between the religious leadership and Ahaz, specifically between him and a prophet named Isaiah. He publicly warned the king not to seek Assyrian help. He told him their God would fight for them if they would ask Him. He told Ahaz that if he turned to Assyria for help, Assyria would be the downfall of Judah. It appears the man has been prophesying against both Judah and Ephraim ever since King Uzziah died[15]. He's telling the people that their God, Jehovah, will judge them for following other gods. He says that Israel will be destroyed, but not Judah. Judah is to be punished but not destroyed. From the tone of the letter, I believe that this Isaiah has even convinced your brother. I intend to share your information with the great king, but not the things of Meesha's letter. We'll just stick to the facts."

The two men shook their heads in agreement, and Domara led them to the Throne Room. The king was there when they arrived, standing next to a large table covered with a map. Both men fell to their knees at an appointed spot with their foreheads pressed to the stone floor. There was a brief pause before the king commanded, "Rise." He then signed them to approach.

The map on the table showed a route from Nimrud to the Mediterranean Sea, and there was an X on the map at a location north of Sidon. The course continued south through Tyre, swung inland through

Dor, and culminated at the southern tip of Philistia. The king watched both men's expressions as they studied the map.

Without preamble, the king asked, "What information does Baildan bring us from the Ephraimites and Syrians?"

The king's tone was commanding, authoritarian. A man used to control; he did not tolerate weakness, deceit, or pandering. He had a commanding presence, dressed in his royal robes, scepter in hand. He had large eyes, a slightly flattened nose with a downward turn, and plaited hair and beard. On a whim, he could reward you or terminate you. He was master of all he saw.

Domara bowed to the king and recounted the information he had received from Baildan.

"That is consistent with the information received from Meesha," the king said. Then he pointed at Baildan, "I see you have questions about the map. Speak."

Baildan barely hesitated and then looked the king in the eye. "It appears from the map that the thrust of the campaign is to control the coastal sea trade. It is Ephraim and Syria that are in revolt, and I do not understand why we are not attacking them directly."

The king did not smile. "We are attacking along the coast because that is my choice. Your observation is accurate; first, we will isolate Ephraim and Syria from coastal trade and protect our backs. In the next campaigns, we will destroy Israel and then Syria. This map is the first phase of the campaign, not the entire campaign. I have heard good things of you, Baildan. I have decided you will command the cavalry on this campaign: 1,000 horsemen. I have added a company of light horse to the cavalry, made up mostly of Medes. They are skilled riders and excellent scouts."

Baildan bowed. "You honor me greatly, my King; the cavalry will serve you well. Our horses will grind your enemies into the dust from which they sprang."

The king looked intently at Baildan. "We leave in five days. You don't have much time to organize and train your unit, and you may start now."

With that, they were dismissed and exited the Throne Room.

Scene 3 The Campaign - Philistia 734 BC

For the past four days, Baildan had worked constantly. He had selected the leaders of one hundred, and they had practiced every maneuver many times. Most of his men were seasoned cavalrymen, and the rest were learning fast. The least seasoned of the riders was a large, well-muscled man with a scar on his chest in Samir's company. When Baildan had inquired whether the man was fit for the cavalry, Samir had merely grinned and stated that he was a cavalryman born and bred, no doubt.

With the training exercises for the day completed, Baildan and Benjamin returned to his father's home. Both went to the bath, dressed, and joined the family in the courtyard for the evening meal.

Domara smiled at them both. Baildan looked the picture of health, a warrior ready for battle. Benjamin, on the other hand, could barely hold his head up. Ashur and Samir had worked him hard; he winced from bruises or muscle fatigue. It made Domara think of his training at that age. "Productive day, Baildan?"

"I would like to have had more training time, but the men are ready, and we can practice formations on the march."

They ate for a while, chatting about each of their days. Rachael paid particular attention to Benjamin, cooing over him like a mother bird.

Baildan feigned sternness and commanded, "Leave the boy alone. You'll make him soft."

Rachael was about to become angry until she saw the smile in Baildan's eyes. Instead, she merely punched him in the stomach, "There that should harden you."

Khannah eyed Baildan and Rachael; she was concerned about the Jews' effect on her sons. First, Meesha and this prophet in Jerusalem, and now Baildan being married to a Judean woman; she said with no apparent emotion, "Do not forget we are going to the temple of Assur tonight. We are making sacrifices for a successful campaign and safety."

Baildan glanced at his wife, whose expression had not changed, and then at his mother, "Of course, Mother, you, Father, and I will go right after our meal."

Khannah arched her eyebrows and looked at Rachael, "Oh, are you not joining us, my dear?"

Baildan was about to intercede when Rachael spoke up, "Mother, I do not mean to offend, but neither Benjamin nor I can enter the temple of a foreign god. We are Israelites of the tribe of Judah. Jehovah is a jealous God, and His Word commands that we worship Him alone. As a young girl, I promised that I would always worship only Him, and it is a promise that I must keep. The same is true of Benjamin."

"What would you do if your husband commanded you to attend him tonight?" Khannah pressed, not wanting to give in easily.

Baildan did not wait this time. "Her husband did not command, nor will he ever command her to worship Assur. Whom they will worship is a matter only Rachael and Benjamin can decide.

"But..." Khannah started.

"But nothing," countered Domara in a soothing tone. "Baildan is no longer a boy. He is a man and the head of his new home, and if this is his decision, neither of us will interfere."

Baildan looked at his father quizzically, "What new home?"

"Did I fail to mention that I bought the house next to us yesterday for you and Rachael? It was an oversight, I'm sure. It is our wedding gift to you, and I have also staffed it with servants. We didn't want Rachael to feel like a dependent of ours while you are gone. She now has a home of her own, which she is to manage in your absence, and we are right next door for company or advice whenever she chooses."

Rachael had tears running down her face as she rose and knelt next to Domara and Khannah and hugged them each. "Your generosity has touched me deeply, and I cannot begin to express what your gift means to me. I had my own home in Mizpah, which I managed. My husband Tola traveled much, and the house brought me peace and purpose. I will make sure that this home brings Baildan great honor."

Khannah's heart melted as she looked at the young woman, and she softened, "We are glad this means so much to you. We'll have great fun next week shopping for furnishings with Domara's money. And don't worry about going with us tonight. I think it is only right that you should keep the promises you have made to this Jehovah, and I hope that He has power in Assyria."

Baildan had difficulty sleeping; it wasn't the new surroundings. It was the thought of leaving Rachael. He looked at the woman next to him and realized how empty his life had been without her. He understood marriage, duty, responsibility, but this feeling of joy, peace, and longing had never been centered in one person before. He rose and dressed and then went downstairs. The house was dark and quiet, but he could see light coming from one of the rooms. He looked around and found a heavy candlestick, then snuck toward the light. He reached the doorway, paused just out of sight of the entry, and then sprang into the room with the candlestick raised.

Karim smiled at him, holding up both hands, "I surrender."

Once he was over the shock, Baildan laughed at his servant. "What are you doing here at this time of the night, and however did you know I was here? I didn't find out I owned a house until last night."

Karim pointed at the room around him, and Baildan saw neat piles of everything he would need for the campaign, his armor, weapons, tent, all the way down to his undergarments. "The obvious answer is someone has to pack. The second question, 'How did I know you were here,' is simple. My job is to know everything. That's why you have me."

Baildan laughed at his old friend. "Then, I better leave you to it; we have a long journey in front of us." Baildan left the room and walked out onto one of the patios. The city was quiet, except for the roars of the nocturnal hunters coming from the zoo. Baildan looked out over the city, the marvel of the known world. Tiglath-Pileser was the greatest king Assyria had ever known. Baildan looked at the city's south wall and saw the glow of fires on the other side of the wall. The army was up and getting ready for the day. He heard the patter of bare feet behind him and turned. Rachael was there, wearing just her sleeping silks. She walked into the moonlight, and he knew he had never seen anyone so beautiful in his life. His heart ached at the thought of leaving her. She came and nestled against him, and he put both arms around her. The smell of her perfume was intoxicating. He could stand here like this for the rest of his life and be perfectly content.

"Did I wake you?" he whispered into her ear.

"No. Like yourself, I have dreaded this day. The thought of being without you is a physical torment. I have tried not to show how much I need you, but you are my life. I can barely breathe at the thought of you marching out of here in a few hours. Please promise me you will keep yourself safe, that you will not throw yourself into the thick of the battle. Promise me."

Baildan pleaded. "Do not ask this of me, my love. I am a warrior of Assyria and the leader of the Heavy Cavalry. We will smash into the foe on horseback and then dismount and fight as infantry. I cannot lead men from the rear; they must see a lion in front of them. They must have confidence that I am leading them, and that I am committed to the battle. I cannot lead any other way."

She stepped back and looked up at him. "I knew that would be your answer, and anything else would have been a lie. You are Baildan, the terror of Assyria. So the only thing I can ask of you is to do your job well. Kill them all. Let your love for me fill you with strength and fortitude. Kill every man who wants to take your life. Then come home to me."

He had never known such pride. What a woman! A feeling of grim determination came over him, and he almost growled, "Rest assured, my love, I will kill them all. That is a promise I can keep. Nothing and no man shall ever keep me from you."

As they stood on the patio holding each other, the first glimmer of light peeked over the city wall. Baildan heard footsteps coming again, and Benjamin walked out onto the balcony. Seeing his mother in her sleeping silks, he turned around and faced the other direction, "Forgive me, Mother, I didn't mean to interrupt."

Baildan looked at the young man; he was fully dressed and ready to ride. "Are you packed?" Baildan inquired.

Benjamin, still facing away, replied, "No need. When Karim finished packing you, he packed me before I ever got up. He is worth his weight in gold."

Baildan looked down at Rachael, "It appears it is time for me to take my leave. Rest assured, my love, your son and I will return safely. Pray to your God for us; He must honor one who loves Him so much. I will send messages back as often as I can."

He hugged her one last time, and then he and Benjamin strode from the room.

By the time he reached the camp, Baildan's captains had the men mounted. The whole army was up and forming into the line of march. Baildan rode to the head of the formation and found King Tiglath-Pileser along with his commanders. The army would march in the same formation in which it would fight, moving in phalanxes, ten men wide and twenty men deep. The phalanx marched and fought as a single man and knew only one direction: straight ahead. These were not part-time soldiers, gathered for a few months and then going home to their farm. These were full-time professionals dedicated to the art of war year-round. The world had never seen such an army before. The infantry carried long spears, swords, daggers, and shields. Every infantryman wore the same uniform—an iron helmet, armor, greaves and shin guards, and heavy leather hobnailed boots. This army was nothing like that fielded by Ephraim and Syria; they were well-organized, well-trained, and disciplined. Units of 10, 100, and 1,000 comprised the command structure.

Every leader knew the battle plan and did not worry about command breakdowns due to death or disability. The army was also efficiently supplied; they would live off the land in certain areas, but they did not rely on that. Every vassal state provided them with trains of pack animals carrying food, weapons, and war materials. They also supplied replacement horses, camels, mules, donkeys, and men.

This army did not have to stop a campaign because of winter; they could fight year-round. Behind the infantry came the archers, with their new composite bows. The bow's range was greater than any of their enemies'. The slingers, chariots, siege engines, and mobile missile platforms followed the archers.

The sight of more than 300,000 men assembled for war took even Baildan's breath away. He rode up to the king, dismounted, and bowed his head to the ground.

Baildan rose and addressed his king, "Great King, the cavalry is ready to ride, and I understand the route. We are to ride southwest to Mari, where we will cross the Euphrates. From there, we will continue west across the northern tip of the Syro–Arabian desert to a point on the Mediterranean Sea just north of Sidon."

The King looked down on Baildan from the horse-drawn throne on which he rode. Tiglath-Pileser III was a fighting king, not just a figure-head. He would ride on his throne when they marched and switch to a four-man chariot when they fought. He nodded, "Your main job after we cross the Euphrates will be to find water in the desert. This army will perish without water."

"Great King, I have several men in the light cavalry from Tadmor to the west of Mari. They have lived their whole lives in this desert and know all of the oases and wells. They are also excellent at finding new watering holes. They will not let us down, and this army will have water."

Without changing expression, the king said, "See that they do." With that, the King dismissed Baildan.

It took the army ten days to reach Mari and another ten days to cross the Euphrates. Baildan left the heavy cavalry at Mari under the command of Ashur and rode with the light cavalry as they scouted the desert. Their first job was to find all known wells and oases and ensure they had water. Their second job was to find any new water sources. Baildan left his armor in Mari, as did Benjamin; a metal helmet was the last thing you needed in the desert. They dressed as the local tribesmen, with loose-fitting white scarves covering their heads and faces.

The sand in some places was pretty packed, and the footing wasn't difficult for the horses. In other areas, the sand was soft, their rate of travel was slower, and the horses tired faster, the horses sometimes sinking up to their fetlocks. The light cavalry rested in the afternoons when the sun was at its zenith. In the shade of his horse's shadow, Baildan sat and watched the heat shimmering off the sand. The heatwaves and glare caused the air to distort and shimmy, having an unsettling effect on people who had not seen it before, like Benjamin.

Baildan looked over at his son. "Well, what do you think of the desert so far?"

Benjamin didn't hesitate. "The scope is vast; I wasn't expecting that. It seems as if this sand will never end. The heat must equal the fires of

Gehenna. When I look at the riders from Tadmor, I wonder how they could live in this place. Then I wonder who would have established a city in the middle of the desert."

Baildan smiled at him. "The desert has made the Bedouin a breed apart. They are not like other men. They are indefatigable and fierce warriors who can go without water longer than any other human I have known. Watch them closely and learn everything you can."

They traveled for three days, finding all known watering spots and verifying their water was at expected levels. In addition, they found two more oases and a well that some unknown group had dug.

They scouted for two more days before returning to the camp at Mari. Baildan left the riders and rode to the tent of the king. He dismounted and approached the tent, but the king's guards barred his way. Baildan chastised himself for forgetting his garb. He unwrapped the scarf from his head and face. The guards recognized him and snapped their spears upright, allowing him to pass. Baildan was met at the entrance to the tent by the king's counselor, who went into the tent to announce Baildan and request permission for him to enter. Even from outside the tent, Baildan could hear the stentorian voice of the king command, "Enter."

Baildan entered the tent and knelt at the king's feet, his head touching the massive rug covering the tent's floor.

The king commanded, "Rise," and Baildan stood, waiting for permission to speak.

Tiglath-Pileser frowned, "You set a bad example for your men dressed as a desert raider. Put on your armor; then, return."

Baildan was shocked by the remonstrance, but apologized to the king, left, and returned looking like a proper Assyrian military commander.

"Speak," the king commanded without preamble.

"Great King, our gods have blessed us. We have seen all of the known watering sites, and there is abundant water in them. We also found three more sites with large quantities of water. The army should be able to make the passage with minimal loss of men and animals." Baildan did not promise there would be no losses. Some men could not bear the heat of the desert and would be overcome, water or no water. These were expected and acceptable losses.

The King stared at him dispassionately for a moment. "Well done. We will march tomorrow; pick a line through the watering sites that will take us on a straight route to the coast."

Baildan bowed to the king and backed out of the tent.

The army did make it successfully through the desert, arriving at the Mediterranean just north of Tripolis. The city officials knew they could not face the Assyrians in open battle, but they felt safe behind their thick walls. The king sent his supreme commander to the city's gates to demand their surrender. But the city officials derided the commander and refused to submit, a bad decision.

The king brought up the archers and slingers; Baildan's men dismounted and joined this group. They marched within range of the wall, and the archers went to work clearing the rampart of enemy soldiers. Even as they were firing, infantry phalanxes moved forward with carts and shovels and built a dirt rampart against the city wall. When the rampart was high enough, the siege engines were rolled up, along with mobile firing platforms filled with archers and slingers who continued to fire from the elevated platforms. The siege engines used an upward-pointing digging tool on a long arm to break up the rock of the outer wall. There were five siege engines located close to each other, and they hammered incessantly at the wall. Slowly but surely, the rock lost the battle against the machines. One month after they started the attack on the wall, sections above the digging site crumbled.

The siege commander approached Baildan. "The wall will fall by the morning. Are your men prepared to enter the city?"

"The men are ready. Truthfully, they'll welcome the change after all this waiting."

The commander eyed him coldly. "The change will not be as pleasant as they hope, I am sure. As soon as the breach is adequate, we will pull the siege towers back, and you and your men, along with the infantry, may attack."

Baildan nodded to the commander and then walked to the cavalry's camp. He found Benjamin and Ashur engaged in sword training. Benjamin thrust at Ashur and the big man stepped inside the thrust then hit Benjamin with his shield, sending the boy flying. The boy was learning fast, and you could see the muscle mass he was gaining from all of the work.

Ashur looked down at the boy sitting in the dirt, his nose bleeding, and growled, "What did you forget?"

Benjamin looked up and sighed. "I reached instead of using my feet to get close, forgetting that your shield is an offensive weapon."

"Get up; we'll go again," Ashur commanded.

"Let's pause the training," Baildan interceded. "I need you to gather all the captains. It looks like we attack tomorrow."

Ashur had Eilbra signal the captains to gather. It took a few minutes, but the ten captains arraigned themselves in front of Baildan.

"They will complete the breach tonight," Baildan said. "We will join the infantry in attacking the breach tomorrow. We will assemble behind the first phalanx. Remind the men; we are the Assyrian army, not a band of rabble. We will maintain our ranks and our discipline. Also, we are not to kill the city leadership. The king wants them all alive. When we have overcome the defenders, the king will enter the city and decide the survivors' fate. All men will remain in formation until the king makes that decision. Make sure the men are clear. We will assemble before first light." The captains were dismissed and returned to their commands and relayed Baildan's orders to the men.

Baildan was up early, as always before a battle, nervous energy, fear, concern for his men—they all were there, the enemies of sleep. And as always, Karim was up preparing his armor and weapons. Baildan's green sword glimmered in the firelight; it was honed and ready for battle. He dressed, putting on his full armor and hobnailed boots. Lastly, he strapped on his sword and placed the helmet on his head. Like the infantry, he and his men would also carry a long, iron-tipped spear, their primary weapon.

Out of the corner of his eye, Baildan saw Benjamin approaching, fully armored and armed. Baildan looked at him and raised both eyebrows. "Where do you think you are going, young man?"

Benjamin stiffened and said, "I'm going with you. Ashur has said my skills are as good as many of the men, and I'm ready to fight."

The boy had just turned thirteen, and while large for his age, he would be no match for a more mature warrior. "Not yet, Son. You are developing well, but this is not the time. I'll let you know when you are ready. I expect this to be a quick sharp attack; even Karim will not be attending me."

Benjamin hesitated briefly before saying, "Yes, Father." He returned to his tent and removed the armor.

Baildan heard the rumble as the men removed the siege engines. His captains assembled the men, and Baildan led them as they marched behind the first phalanx. The first phalanx, 'the forlorn hope,' stood tall with pride. They were to be first through the wall. On either side of the infantry were the archers. They knew that lined up on the other side of that break were the enemy archers. The Assyrian archers would lay down as much covering fire as possible to thin the enemy ranks.

Assyrian trumpets sounded, and the first phalanx began a steady march over the rubble. Assyrian arrows flew, and as the first phalanx reached the apex of the wreckage, the arrows of the Tripolis archers filled the air. The infantry, wielding their large shields, marched into the arrow storm. No hesitation. Forward, ever forward. If a man dropped, as some did, the man behind him stepped up and took his place. They were an unstoppable machine grinding ahead without hesitation.

That was training, discipline, and bravery.

The first phalanx was through the breach, and Baildan's men were right on their heels. Once past the wall, the rubble sloped and widened. The enemy was flanking the first phalanx, and Baildan made a quick decision. He looked at Ashur and pointed to the right. He split his command with 500 men attacking to the right and 500 following him on the left.

The Tripolis were good warriors and fought to protect their families and city, but they were no match for the heavily armored Assyrians wielding iron weapons. Men stepped in front of Baildan, screaming their hate, and Baildan killed without thought or hesitation.

Once engaged, all fear was gone. Baildan moved steadily forward, parry, thrust, hammer with shield, stomp on feet and legs with his boots, everything was a weapon, and he used them all. Just as in Israel, enemy blood soon covered him from head to foot. He was thankful for the boots he wore; they gave him purchase in the bloody dirt. The Tripolis were slipping in the mire; the Assyrians were not. They pressed forward, and more infantry followed from behind. Soon, the Assyrians flanked the Tripolis and destroyed their army. At first, a few and then more threw down their arms, and then it was over. The killing ceased, and the Assyrian army stood at attention as if they were on a parade ground.

The city officials opened the gates, and the king's cart entered the city with Tiglath-Pileser sitting on his throne. The king called for the city officials to come forward, and ten men came forward. These were the senior and wealthiest men of the city, all with long grey beards. The king pointed at them, and his executioners came forward, grabbed the men, stripped them naked, and dragged them outside the gates of the city. They erected ten poles, approximately ten feet high with sharpened ends. The executioners placed the poles in holes in the ground, with five poles on either side of the gate. The executioners sat the men on the pointed poles, and screams of pain filled the air. The men's weight would force the pole ever deeper into their bodies, and they would die, eventually, of internal injuries and bleeding, but it would not be quick.

Having dealt with the leadership, the king turned to his waiting army and commanded, "Sack and destroy the city."

Now all discipline broke down. Men ran from house to house, looking for anything of value to steal. They raped and killed till no one was left, then they torched the city.

The army sat outside the walls of the city for a full day as the city burned. After the fire burned out, 200,000 men took the city apart, stone by stone, until there was nothing left but a pile of rubble. The king had carefully planned all of this. He would prefer to leave behind live people and resources to supply his empire. But examples were necessary. He had made Tripolis an example. Word of what had happened here would spread, and hopefully, other cities would capitulate and not resist.

The army left Tripolis and marched down the coast. They came to Sidon, a coastal city, and as planned, word of what had happened to Tripolis had preceded them. The city gates were open when they arrived, and the city officials came out to greet them. The King rode up, greeted the officials, selected two of them for deportation to Nimrud, and left two trusted Assyrian administrators in their place. This was his policy for all cities that capitulated.

When they moved south and came to Tyre, the king of Tyre came out, greeted the Assyrian king, and kissed his feet in submission. The Assyrians continued south into Philistia. One sight of the Iron Army and the entirety of Philistia submitted, but now the king's policy changed. The Philistines were too remote, and the king decided to ensure their future loyalty by deporting most of the current leadership and skilled artisans. The king replaced them with people from other remote parts of the empire. A large deportation team with thousands of captives had been following the army for just this purpose. Deportations occurred in Gezer, Ekron, Gath, and Raphia, though Gath was slightly different.

When they approached Gath, their king, Hanunu, shut the gates and sent warriors to the wall. Tiglath-Pileser sent forward the archers, slinger, and mobile missile platforms and built a siege mound. During the night, King Hanunu escaped out a back gate and fled to Egypt. The warriors were no longer on the wall in the morning, and city officials came out of the gate. The king came forward and met with them before he impaled them. There must be a severe example made whenever there was any resistance. The king conscripted the Gath army into the Assyrian army, replacing all the administrators with Assyrians, and again skilled craft people were deported. The campaign had been almost bloodless but had taken them most of the year. Philistia, as a nation, was no more. The army marched north, where they would spend the winter in Sidon. The port there made it easy to supply the army by sea. They stayed there through the winter, rested, and resupplied. The first phase of their campaign was complete and successful.

Scene 4 The Campaign Israel - 733/732 BC

Baildan sat at the morning meal with his men. He enjoyed the early-morning sun warming him and the smell of newly plowed fields in the farmlands surrounding the army. Winter was over, and they would be on the move again soon.

Baildan looked at Benjamin, who would be fourteen soon. The change in him was dramatic. His back, shoulders, and forearms had packed on muscle from bow, sword, and javelin training. Ashur trained Benjamin to fight with either hand, and he was equally adept with both. His legs—thighs and calves—were cords of muscle. He also sported the beginning of his first beard, not much of one yet, but it was beginning. Baildan knew he could not keep him out of combat for more than another year. He was developing too fast.

"Ashur," Baildan inquired, "how is your young pupil developing?"

Ashur growled, "He's not worthless, but he has a long way to go."

Samir grinned, "He sits a horse like a camel herder, but I must say, at least he hasn't fallen off for several days."

Benjamin rose from the mat without a word, walked to a weapons rack near them, and returned with two training swords. He threw one to Ashur, who caught it with one hand, "Why don't we show Baildan what I have learned, old man, if you're not too tired?"

"Old man, old man. It looks like it's time for a new lesson," Ashur growled, but this time the growl was a little louder.

Ashur rose, and the man and boy faced off.

Baildan was amazed. Benjamin's development was far more advanced than he had expected. The young man parried everything Ashur was throwing at him. He was much faster than the older, larger man, and he used it to his advantage.

After several minutes, Benjamin feinted left, then reversed and hit Ashur with a stunning blow to his kidney. Ashur winced. He negated the boy's speed by constantly moving forward and pressing the boy.

Benjamin thrust; Ashur sidestepped, used his left hand to slap the boy's hand downward and hit him a stunning blow to the top of the head with the pommel of his sword. Benjamin dropped like a puppet without strings and sat stunned in the dust.

"Old man," Ashur grumbled and sat back on the mat.

Baildan walked over to Benjamin, who was beginning to regain his senses and extended his right arm. Benjamin looked up, took the offered hand, and let Baildan help him to his feet. Benjamin shook his head, trying to clear the cobwebs.

"I'm sure you have rethought the 'old man' comment by now."

Benjamin grinned over at Ashur, "My apologies, Ashur. I humbly beg your forgiveness."

Baildan leaned over and whispered in his ear, "Had that been a real fight, I'm not sure he would have been able to deliver that blow after you had laid open his kidney. He knows it too, so no more 'old man' digs. I need Ashur to be confident."

Benjamin hung his head, "Yes, Father, I should have thought of that. I have much to learn about leading men."

Baildan ruffled the young man's hair. "You're learning."

As he finished speaking, a messenger ran up, "Commander Baildan, the king has called for you."

Without hesitation, Baildan walked toward the command tent. This was not a request.

Baildan entered the tent of the king and made his obeisance.

The king commanded, "Rise. It's time to march, Baildan. We have doubled the size of this army over the winter. I have decided to use a two-pronged attack. You will accompany me on the western attack. The new cavalry unit that has arrived will go with the Supreme Commander and attack to the east, subduing the Israeli land to the east of the Jordan in Gilead. Send out your scouts."

Baildan bowed and backed out of the room. He arrived back at the cavalry area and had, Eilbra, the signal-caller he used in Judah, signal assemble. The troop broke camp. Anything they did not need for the day went on the supply wagons. They were in enemy territory; every man was fully armored and armed, bows strapped on their horses, quivers and shield slung over their backs, carrying long lances with iron tips. A formidable force rode out of Sidon, moving southeast toward Ijon, the first city they would take.

They reached Ijon by early afternoon, and the city gates were closed. It was apparent to Baildan from the number of warriors on the wall that Israel had reinforced the city and intended to make a stand in their northern territory. Baildan sent a rider back to the king and had his men make camp. An hour later, the king's representative rode through the camp straight to Ijon's main gate and called for the city leader. The prince of the city did not come out but called down from the wall.

After a brief period, the representative rode back to the cavalry camp and met with Baildan.

Baildan knew this man was third-in-command of the army and asked, "Commander, how may I serve you?"

The commander smiled wickedly, "They will not surrender. The army will arrive tonight. I want you to harass the ramparts and begin to eliminate their archers." The commander then turned his horse's head and rode back in the direction of Sidon.

Baildan called for his captains, explained the plan, had Eilbra signal, and led his men toward the wall. The first few passes along the wall would be for ranging. Baildan rode toward the wall, and when they were within range of the Assyrian bows, he turned his troops so they would ride parallel to the wall. Because of their height advantage, some Israeli bows matched the Assyrian range, but most did not. Baildan had the cavalry dismount and spread out shoulder to shoulder parallel to the wall. Every other man would cover the man next to him with his shield. Baildan now had five hundred archers pouring a steady stream of arrows into the parapet. When a man ran out of arrows, he became the shield man, and his partner began to fire. The supply train had come up and was resupplying men as soon as their quivers were empty. They continued this for an hour, and the rate of return fire dwindled significantly. Baildan moved his men forward fifty feet at a time, not only continuing to thin the enemies on the parapet but also allowing the arrow storm to search blindly behind the wall for other targets. It was darkening as the main army arrived. Baildan had his men withdraw from the wall.

The king did not wait for the morning but sent working crews forward to build the siege engines' ramp. They would work in shifts through the night.

In the morning, the city prince looked out from the rampart at the army ranged in front of him. He shook his head, descended, and opened the gates to the city. As usual, the prince was executed and displayed at the entrance to the city, but they spared the city. The army was ready to move on, and the deportation teams took over. As they had in Philistia the year before, the king intended to leave Israel a population aligned and oriented to Assyria. When he finished, Israel would no longer be a people.

Finished at Ijon, the army ground its way south, with this pattern repeating itself at Abel-beth-maacah and Hazor. They defeated both cities after minor resistance. The king split his forces here and sent the Supreme Commander south to cross the Jordan at Beth-shan and invade Gilead. Tiglath-Pileser took the other half of the army, including Baildan's cavalry unit, west to subdue the northern regions of Israel. They came next to Kedesh and Janoah. Kedesh put up minor resistance, but Janoah capitulated without resistance. It was late in the year before the army turned south and came to the king's prize target, Megiddo.

Megiddo controlled the pass at the Wadi Ara defile through the Carmel Ridge and overlooked Israel's most fertile agricultural area, the Jezreel valley. He who controlled Megiddo controlled the north.

The city was built on a slight rise and had the thickest walls of any city they had faced. Israel had centered its northern army here, and Baildan knew this would be a long siege. Soon after arriving, the siege walls rose, but this time at a much slower rate. The defenders had higher walls, which served as a better defense against arrows. Also, because they had built it on a mound, it negated the Assyrian bow-range advantage. After a month, the banks were high enough to bring the siege engines forward. Baildan felt as if they were finally getting somewhere.

The waiting was always the time Baildan hated the most, despite the fact the cavalry was free to roam the countryside looking for enemy movement and hunting for game. The waiting time was the hardest.

During their daily rides in the valley west of the camp, his men encountered a large thicket with plentiful wild pigs and game signs. He surrounded the thicket with 100 men, who advanced simultaneously toward the thicket center, driving any game before them. As the circle tightened, the game tried to escape. It became a slaughter. They killed deer, rabbits, wild pigs, goats, sheep, a lion, and a couple of water buffalo. It wasn't enough for the whole army, but the cavalry would eat well today. In short order, they hung the animals from trees and bled and skinned them. They started cooking fires all around the camp's clearing. The men gorged themselves, satisfied for at least today. Baildan was smart enough to reserve a good quantity of prime cuts for the king. Pleasing the monarch was always a good idea.

The siege engine work against the wall continued for another ten days and then stopped one morning. Confused, Baildan approached the royal tent to inquire about the stoppage. There before the king was a group of Israelites on their knees. The king commanded them to rise, and an older man in a beautiful robe stepped forward carrying a basket. A guard barred his way, and the man stopped. He laid the basket on the rug in front of him and began, "I am Hoshea, and these men with me are the leaders of Israel. We have brought the king a present." He bent down and lifted the lid on the basket. Inside was a human head. "This," Hoshea resumed, "is the head of King Pekah, who plotted with King Rezin of Syria to revolt against you, **my king**. We have taken his life, and outside we have animals laden with gold, silver, and bronze equal to the one and a half times the tribute King Pekah owed the king this past year. We are here to pledge our loyalty to you and to beg you to cease your campaign against Israel."

The king leaned back in his throne chair and contemplated the man before him. "Are you a man of Samaria, and do you lead these men?"

"I am, and I do, king of kings," Hoshea said.

The king spoke loudly for all to hear, "I accept your fealty and your tribute. From this day forward, you shall be King of Israel. I have resettled your lands to the north and in Gilead with foreigners from every corner of the empire. I will do the same here in Megiddo; I will leave a garrison here, and this city will serve as my administrative center for Philistia and Israel. Please go to the city and announce this treaty to the Israelites there, and we will end our siege."

Hoshea bowed to the king, backed out of the tent with his delegation, and walked to Megiddo. The king followed, and so did Baildan.

Hoshea stopped at the gate to the city, opened up the basket, and held up for all to see the head of Pekah. "I am Hoshea," he yelled, "Many of you know me. This is the head of Pekah, who sought to lead us in revolt against our rightful king. I am now King of Israel; you are to lay down your arms and open the gates. This war is over."

There was a long silence, and then the gates opened. The military commander led a delegation; accompanying him was the giant Zichri—the man who had killed Pera. Baildan had sworn to kill Zichri. Without hesitation, Baildan walked up to the King Tiglath-Pileser, bowed, and requested permission to speak. His request was allowed.

"Great king, standing in the gate is the Israeli warrior Zichri, the champion of their army. He is the giant standing next to the commander. He is the man who killed Pera in cold blood in Shechem, who insulted you, my King, and I have sworn to kill him. I request permission to meet Zichri in single combat."

The king looked down at Baildan, "I have sworn a peace treaty and have ended this war. How could I permit such a thing?"

Baildan thought quickly, "This would not be an extension of the war. These armies have waited for months to get at each other, and I know they will be pleased with such a contest. This contest would be a personal challenge, which Zichri may accept or not. Single combat is the ancient way to resolve issues of national superiority."

"Presumptuous, Baildan," the king retorted, "who says that I would select you to represent Assyria? The man is a giant; you are no match for him."

Baildan replied without hesitation, "I will kill him, Great King, and as surety, I pledge the life of my son Benjamin. If I fail you, you may also end his life."

The king nodded grimly, "So be it, Baildan. Go make your challenge."

Baildan walked toward the delegation from the city and stopped. He spoke loudly enough for the Assyrians and the men on the walls to hear. "My name is Baildan, the champion of Assyria. The war is over, but I propose that Zichri," he said, pointing at the giant, "meet me in personal combat tonight to settle the question of who has the best warriors. If he is not afraid to fight me."

The Israelites laughed as they viewed the alarming size difference between the two men. The Israelites also knew Zichri, and the number of men he had killed in battle was legendary.

Zichri stepped forward until he was directly in front of Baildan and towering over him. "This will be your last night on earth, Assyrian; go and pray to your gods and prepare yourself for death," the big man yelled loud enough for all to hear.

Baildan stepped closer and said just loudly enough for Zichri to hear, "This is for Pera. I promised you a long, slow death, and that is what I will give you tonight."

Baildan turned and strode back to the cavalry camp. By the time he arrived, the camp was abuzz. News of the challenge spread fast, along with the news he had pledged the life of Benjamin to get the king's approval for the match.

Samir was the first to approach him, "Baildan, have no fear, you will kill this monster. The men and I are going to bet everything we have on you tonight. You will avenge Pera and make us all rich." He smiled, looking at his commander.

The next to approach him was Benjamin. A lump formed in the pit of Baildan's stomach. Benjamin merely grinned up at him, "Father, what a great honor. You promised to deliver me safely to mother when this campaign is over, and I know with certainty that you will win because you would never break a promise to her." Benjamin was now fifteen and no longer a boy. Baildan looked at the bearded, well-muscled man in front of him.

"You are right, Benjamin; I would never break a promise to your mother. Like your King David, I will slay my giant tonight. That is a promise," he said, grasping the young man by the shoulders and then embracing him.

In a small valley close to the city, they arrayed the armies of Israel and Assyria. The troops were on opposite sides of the valley. The noise of the combined forces was almost deafening as they made bets and encouraged the combatants. The sun set, and torches were lit all around the clearing. Servants brought the king's throne to the edge of the clearing from which he would have an unobstructed view. The king signaled for the contest to begin.

The giant Zichri came out in full armor from the Israelite multitude, and every Israeli warrior chanted his name. Then Baildan strode out of the Assyrian lines, dressed in a loincloth and carrying only his sword and fighting knife. In the torchlight, he looked every bit a primeval warrior, a throwback to some ancient time. A hush fell over both sides as everyone stared at Baildan. He had oiled his body, and every muscle and sinew showed in rippling cords from his neck to his feet. He looked like a god of war.

The giant Zichri stared at him for a moment and realized Baildan was challenging his honor. He threw down his sword and spear and stripped off his armor until he too stood before the combined forces in just his loincloth. He picked up his sword and fighting knife, yelled across the arena, "So be it," and advanced toward Baildan.

The armor-less fight was what Baildan had hoped for, his speed against the giant's power. The lion against the bull. He had watched Pera and knew how to attack. Moving, ever-moving, in, out, left-right, sword, and knife flashing, parry, thrust, block, Baildan moved ever faster, his hands and weapons a blur. A hush fell over the Israelites; they had never seen anything like this before. Each man had nicked the other by now, but nothing significant. The big man was beginning to tire, just as Baildan had expected. Baildan moved even faster, and his strokes were starting to take a toll. Deep cuts now appeared on the giant's forearm and upper arms, on his back and thighs, and he was bleeding freely. Baildan never slowed; he showed no signs of tiring. New cuts appeared with almost every stroke. The more the giant bled, the more he slowed.

Zichri's eyes showed fear for the first time; Baildan's face radiated sheer determination. Then, the chants from the Assyrians began: "Baildan, Bail-dan, **Bail-dan**." Baildan darted left then right, saw the giant's exposed leg, and used his sword to sever the hamstring of his left leg. The big man was now standing on one leg and was immobile, but he still had two good arms. Baildan knew this was no time to get careless. He circled the big man, who could not turn, and using both knife and sword, severed the tendons of both shoulders. The weapons dropped from Zichri's hands, both arms unresponsive and useless. Baildan did not stop; he made shallow cuts on every inch of the big man's body until Zichri toppled over and lay groaning in the dust.

"Finish it, **finish it**," the giant yelled, almost pleaded.

Baildan stepped back and, turning as he spoke, yelled to both armies, "He will lay there in the blood and the dirt. No man will help him, and he will lie and think about how he failed his God and the torment awaiting him in the life hereafter. I will kill any man who kills him or seeks to aid him."

It was over. The king motioned for Baildan to approach. Baildan came forward and knelt before the king, covered in sweat and blood, still holding his weapons. He placed both weapons on the ground in front of him and pressed his forehead against the earth. The king stood up, "Hail, Baildan," he proclaimed, which rang across the valley, "Champion of Assyria and commander of 10,000 from this day forward." He motioned. His attendants led out the most beautiful white Arabian Baildan had ever seen, followed by a large white mule with a basket tied to each side. "My gift to Baildan for serving his king faithfully and upholding the pride of Assyria. A horse from my own stable and the weight of Zichri in gold. Hail, Baildan."

The Assyrian army began chanting, "Bail-dan," again.

Baildan picked up his weapons and strode to the middle of the valley. He turned and held up the sword and knife above his head to salute the Assyrian army, and the cheering became frenzied.

Samir came out of the crowd, crossed the valley, and placed a stool at the head of Zichri so he and Zichri could see each other. Samir looked at the giant; he did not pity this man. "I told you I would watch you die, and I'm going to sit right here until you do. I want to see the light go out in your eyes when the end comes. You killed a great man in the most cowardly way possible. I can only hope you are in severe pain."

Zichri barely had the strength left to plead, "Kill me."

Samir did not speak; he only smiled. The monster in front of him would never hear another human voice. Samir sat there throughout the night, keeping guard and waiting for the end to come. As the sun came up, the light left Zichri's eyes. Samir smiled, stood, and walked back to camp.

Scene 5 The Campaign - Syria 732 BC

The east army finished conquering and deporting the Israelites in Gilead, and both armies spent the winter in Sidon again.

It seemed like déjà vu, the same early-morning meal, the sun heralding the coming of spring as it warmed him, and Samir and Ashur eating with Benjamin and Baildan. Benjamin would turn sixteen soon, and while age-wise, it might have been premature to call him a man, in every other aspect, he certainly was. He towered over Samir and Ashur, his beard had filled out, and he wore his hair and beard plaited—the same as older warriors did. When Benjamin was unaware, Baildan watched him at horse drills and arms training. He was a picture of the perfect warrior. His physical skills were impressive, but his mental skills were even better. He was always one step ahead of his opponent; he anticipated every angle of attack and every possible move. Baildan wasn't sure he had ever seen any warrior this developed at sixteen; he knew he certainly hadn't been.

"Ashur," Baildan inquired, "how is your young pupil developing?" the same question he had asked a year earlier.

This time, the answer was quite different, "I'm not sure I have anything more to teach him, Baildan. I have seen few like him in all of my years."

Benjamin blushed and intervened, "Ashur is far too kind. I know he holds back at times. He allows me to do well to encourage me."

Ashur growled, "I have never held back one day in training. Your training means the difference between life and death. My job is to prepare you for combat, and I did not accomplish that by ever holding back. Your humility does you credit, Benjamin, but your skills strain Samir and me to hold our own. We have more bruises than bullied children."

Samir winced as he said, "He unseated me yesterday, with a training lance. I may not be able to sit for a week."

Baildan looked at Benjamin, who was sitting and smiling at his two mentors. Baildan knew that Benjamin considered these men his family and that he loved them both. "We have a problem, Benjamin. I promised your mother I would keep you out of combat, but looking at you now, I don't think that is fair to you."

Benjamin nodded in agreement, "You promised Mother you would keep the boy she sent with you safe and that you would bring him safely home. I am no longer the boy who left Assyria, and you have fulfilled your promise of safety by equipping me to excel in combat. I know combat is unpredictable, but I am ready to fight in this campaign, Father. I need to fight in this campaign."

Baildan nodded. "You will ride with me, and you will have my back in battle. I will fight in the forefront, and you will be my spearman. Is that understood? I will be in the forefront?"

"Yes, commander," Benjamin affirmed, "you will be in the forefront."

Just then, a messenger ran up and announced that the king had called for Baildan.

Baildan thought; this all seems eerily familiar, and he stepped into the king's tent.

Without preamble, the king began, "Baildan, it's time to end this campaign. We have one objective left, the subjugation of Syria. We will swing north when we leave Sidon and work our way south through Syria to Damascus. Take your scouts and find the enemy. I want this finished."

Baildan bowed to his king and left. No clarification was needed. When he reached the cavalry camp, he had Eilbra signal assemble.

Baildan and the cavalry rode north along the coast, skirting Mount Lebanon, and then turned east. Just as he was about to turn south, to sweep down through Syria, his scouts came back with reports. Two different scouts recounted the same story, which they had heard from two different caravans. Both men reported that Queen Samsi of Arabia had an army in the Jabal Abu Rujmayn Mountain Range's foothills near Mount Saquurri. The queen had allied with Syria and was waiting in ambush for the Assyrians. If Baildan's scouts had not discovered the queen's presence, the Assyrians would have found themselves facing the Syrian army, with an enemy at their back. The results could have been disastrous. Baildan selected one of the scouts to deliver this information to Tiglath-Pileser, who followed them with the now-combined armies. The cavalry made camp, and several days later, the king and the army arrived.

The army arrived late in the day, and as soon as they had erected the king's tent, Tiglath-Pileser summoned Baildan.

Baildan entered the king's tent, made obeisance, and stood, waiting for the king to speak.

"Well done, Baildan; again, you have served me well. What are we to do with this rebellious Arab queen?"

It sounded like a question if you didn't know the king. Fortunately, Baildan knew the correct answer, "She is in rebellion against her rightful king, with this upstart Rezin, king of Syria. We will do to her whatever my king wishes, and please allow me to be the one to face her in battle."

The king almost smiled, almost. "Let it be as you have said. You will accompany the Supreme Commander with 150,000 men, and I will take the rest of the army south through Syria. There are hundreds of walled cities between here and Damascus, and I will destroy them all. When you have finished with the queen's army, bring her to me, alive. No one is to kill her." The king nodded at his steward, who called the next supplicant forward. That meant the king had dismissed Baildan, and he backed out of the tent.

When he arrived at his tent, he summoned his commanders. He was now a Field Commander over 10,000 and had ten commanders reporting to him. He had promoted Ashur as the commander of the cavalry. He had a commander for the archers/slingers, one for the charioteers, one for siege engines and fortifications, and six commanders for light and heavy infantry. It was a significant change in responsibility, but Baildan still rode with the cavalry and thought of himself as a cavalryman.

The commanders assembled, and Baildan relayed the king's commands. "We will seek out Queen Samsi tonight and bring her to battle tomorrow. I need scouts out now; they will ride all night until they find that Arabian army. I want to begin the attack tomorrow at first light. We will be one of fifteen units under the Supreme Commander. There is one critical command from the king. We are not to kill Queen Samsi; we are to capture her. Make sure that instruction goes to every man. Are there any questions?"

There were no questions, and Baildan dismissed the men. When he smelled the cooking fires, he began to salivate and headed to where the men gathered to eat. There is one thing that requires no training in the army: when and where to eat. Baildan saw Benjamin with Samir and Ashur; they already had a stew pot, cheese, and bread in front of them. He sat with them, and Mardokh, the little warrior, also joined them.

"We hear you are going to take this lummox into battle," Mardokh said, grinning, jabbing a thumb in the direction of Benjamin.

Baildan squinted at Mardokh, not sure how to take the barb, "Why? You don't think he's ready?"

Mardokh looked thoughtful for a moment. "Oh, we all thought it was a diversion. When the Arabs take one look at this baby, they'll start laughing, making it easier for us to kill them." Mardokh then roared at his joke.

Benjamin extracted a cube of goat from the stew and threw it. The cube stuck firmly to Mardokh's forehead with a splat, "That is a proper diversion," laughed Benjamin. "Now that is funny." Everyone was laughing by now.

Mardokh wiped his eyes and grew serious, "Truthfully, boss, he's been ready. We just wondered how long it would take you to see the change in him."

Baildan looked at Benjamin, "I know he is ready. You men know the dangers we face in battle. What we see in front of us we can control. It is what we don't see that kills us, an arrow from 100 yards away, a spear thrust from the side. It is chaos in battle. We have been gone for more than two years, and I cannot go home and face Rachael without Benjamin."

Everyone ate silently for a while before Benjamin spoke. "Father, I know you are worried. You brought me out here, a boy, and turned me into a warrior. You did not force it on me. I am now a man and have chosen this life. I love the camp and talking with men like these," he said, pointing at the men with him. "I love the training. I know the better I prepare, the better are my chances of survival. I know all this, and I choose to be here and to face the Arabian warriors tomorrow. I will protect the man on my left and the man on my right. That will be my whole world tomorrow. This is what I choose."

Looking at Benjamin with pride, Baildan leaned over, and he and Benjamin grasped each other's forearm and looked each other in the eye. "So be it. I'll be the man at your side tomorrow," said Baildan.

Mardokh looked at the two men and said warmly, "I'll be the man on your other side."

Sometime during the second watch, Karim entered Baildan's tent and shook the commander awake, "One of the riders has returned, and he has found the camp of Queen Samsi."

Baildan sat up, wiping the sleep from his eyes. "Go and tell the Supreme Commander, we need to move now," Baildan called for an aide, and he sent messages to his commanders to assemble all units.

Within minutes, men were up and moving, breaking down tents, putting on armor, sharpening weapons. The cooks started fires, and the men completed hundreds of other tasks. When the men were ready to travel, they hustled over to the cooking fires for a hurried meal. They ate standing up. Horns sounded the Supreme Commander's call to move, and every man sprinted to the corrals. Commanders assembled their units in the proper line of march. The chariots were in the forefront, and the army was ready to move. The sun had not broken the horizon, but the first grey light of morning was adequate to see. Baildan had Eilbra, still his signal-caller after all these years, signal move out. The cavalry rode out at a trot. They would range several miles in front, looking for any sign of Queen Samir.

They saw several Arabian outriders racing back to the north by late morning, taking the message to the Queen that the Assyrians were on the way. Her army came out of the hills before the Assyrians arrived, and Queen Samsi arrayed them across the valley, where she could use her chariots and cavalry more effectively.

Baildan gathered information from his cavalry and put together a picture of the enemy array and strength, which he relayed to the Supreme Commander. The queen had a force of roughly 170,000 to 200,000 men. She had a significant chariot core of at least 1,000 chariots and a cavalry of 2,000 men, made up of horses and camels. It was the camel core that intrigued Baildan; he had not fought against them before. Baildan was concerned by the height advantage the camel gave its rider but had no idea how effective they were in combat. He signaled for Ashur to join him.

"The camels concern me," Baildan yelled over the noise surrounding them. "I want you to pick 200 men and focus on that camel core. As much as I hate to, I think the best solution is to ignore the riders and take down the camels; they are lightly armored."

Ashur saluted and rode out to find two good captains to assign to the camel task.

The Supreme Commander and the army arrived. They arrayed in battle formation. Assyrian horns sounded, and the chariots began their slow trot forward, eliciting a similar response from the Arabian chariots. The Assyrians had their new, heavier four-man chariots in the front of the formation. These chariots carried two archers, a shield man, and a driver. The Arabs advancing toward them had lighter two-horse, two-man chariots, faster and more mobile, but half the firepower. Running behind the chariots were the archers and slingers. A natural defile protected the Arabian formation's left flank, so Baildan would put the full force of the cavalry against the right flank, which is where Queen Samsi had arrayed her cavalry.

Baildan put the cavalry into a trot, keeping pace with the chariots, and he watched the infantry as they marched in perfect formation toward the Arabians. The Iron Army, the sight of it, never failed to move Baildan. He looked at the Arabian infantry shuffling forward in small groups in their lighter armor, and Baildan pitied them. They had no chance against the machine that was coming at them.

Baildan signaled to Benjamin, who rode up beside him and kept pace. Baildan leaned toward Benjamin and shouted, "That's your spot; stick with me the best you can, but when the fighting starts, you must protect yourself first. Keep your eyes moving at all times, assess every potential threat to both you and me, and respond as you feel necessary."

Benjamin's countenance had changed completely, his helmet covered part of his face, his eyes were slitted, and he was almost snarling. This was his war face. Baildan had never seen it before. Every man had one; it was almost uncontrollable. Some men were wild-eyed, some mumbled, some screamed, some pounded their shields, working themselves into a frenzy; there were many war faces, but every man had one. On the other side of Benjamin was Mardokh, who was wild-eyed, screaming and pounding his shield. Baildan was thankful Benjamin was between them. Baildan also had on his war face; a look of grim determination and intense focus. Baildan pushed everything from his mind except the battle in front of him. He did not scream or yell. His cold stare told his enemy there was no hope.

The cavalry was now at a gallop as they closed with the Arabians. Every man had his long lance pointed forward, and there was a resounding crash as the two formations met. Lances unseated men on both sides, and lances broke from jarring impacts. The bleeding and the screaming had started. Benjamin had survived the first contact; he had neatly blocked a lance and then drove his lance through the man's chest. In his peripheral vision, Baildan saw the battle against the camel core; it looked completely different. The Assyrians had bows instead of lances, which would have been ineffective, and they were filling the animals with arrows. Baildan hated it. The camel core was almost defenseless against the attack. The heavier horses and armor of the Assyrians were proving just as effective against the Arabian horse cavalry.

The Arabian horses and riders were magnificent but not well suited for battle against heavy cavalry. The cavalry battle was over quickly. Baildan's men had their bows out and were pouring fire into the Arabian flank. The Arabians moved away from the arrow storm and were compressing inward, bunching up in the center. Baildan signaled the next phase of the attack. The cavalry formed into a V and drove into the center of the enemy flank. The cavalrymen were using lances as stabbing and throwing weapons, and their horses were trampling men underfoot. When they had driven the wedge as far as they could go, Baildan signaled dismount, and the men became heavy infantry. Baildan was in the thick of the fight as usual, with Benjamin at his back. Benjamin was using his long lance, stabbing over and under Baildan's shield. They were wreaking havoc in the enemy center.

One man after another appeared in front of Baildan, tall, short, fat, thin, muscular, and wiry; they all came, one by one, and they all died. A tall, blood-covered warrior approached; the man had a long beard. He snarled at Baildan and attacked. Baildan blocked his overhand swing and thrust when a stone from a slinger came out of nowhere and struck his helmet. Chaos. Baildan's sword fell from his hand; he stood there stunned and defenseless. The Arab facing him saw the opportunity and raised his sword; the blade flashed down, but astonishingly Baildan was not there.

As the Arab had raised his sword, Benjamin grabbed Baildan by the shoulder and hurled him backward with tremendous force. The stunned

Arab recovered quickly and now found himself facing young Benjamin. The tall Arab grinned at Benjamin, but the grin didn't last long. Benjamin attacked in absolute fury, blows reigning down on the Arab from every direction. The fight ended when the Arab lunged forward. Benjamin side-stepped and neatly cut off the man's sword hand at the wrist. Benjamin followed this with a neat upward stroke that almost severed the man's head from his body. Baildan sat in the dirt watching. What he saw astounded him. He had seen a berserker once; it had taken five men to kill him. The berserker had appeared almost supernatural he had fought with such fury. That was nothing compared to what he saw now. The battle had transformed Benjamin—one man, two men at a time; it did not matter. Benjamin was so ferocious men near him from both sides backed up and watched. Benjamin did not notice; he continued to press forward. Then it happened, men began to run from Benjamin, at first just a few, then a few more, and then the rout was on. Panic is an interesting thing; it's contagious. One minute you are fighting, and the next minute you see a few people running toward the rear. Then you begin to worry, am I going to be left behind? So you start running, and the next thing you know, everyone is running, and the rout is on.

Benjamin followed the fleeing Arabs, but Baildan quickly got up off the ground and yelled, "Benjamin, enough."

Benjamin whirled and faced Baildan and the other Assyrians, still grimacing and still in a fury.

"Benjamin, it is over. Benjamin, sheath your sword," Baildan commanded.

At that moment, all of his training kicked in, and he recognized the voice of his father. It was as if he were returning from some distant land after years of absence. His face softened, and he looked around. Between him and Baildan was a mass of dead bodies. He looked at his father, "Did I do this?"

"Yes, you did," replied Baildan softly, "you saved many lives today. I have never seen anything like this before."

Benjamin fell to his knees and retched. When his stomach was empty, men ran over to him and gently lifted him to his feet. Benjamin looked around wild-eyed, still confused at what had happened. He was terrified because he couldn't remember killing all these men.

Baildan walked over to him and put his arm around the young man's bloody shoulders; they walked a little distance from the other Assyrians. Baildan turned Benjamin to face him. "Look at me, Benjamin. I am going to tell you what I think happened. I have studied military history all my life. In the Israelite records are stories of other men like you. Samson killed 1,000 men with the jawbone of a donkey. Your King David had two mighty men, Josheb-basshebath, who killed 800 men with a spear, and Abishai, who killed 300 men with a spear. I always thought they were exaggerated stories, but what I saw today has changed my mind. The Israelite stories said the Spirit of your God came on them, and they performed these super-human acts. I think that is what I have seen today. I want you to leave here now, find Karim, who will take your armor, wash you, and then go to your tent and pray to your God. If it is He who strengthens you and gives you these powers, you must thank Him and seek His guidance."

Benjamin walked toward the camp; as he did, the Assyrian army parted, and everyone stared in silence at the young warrior who strode between them. Some men wanted to kneel, thinking that one of the gods had come to life. Nothing else could explain what they had just seen. Men would tell this story for generations to come.

Queen Samsi had been defeated but not captured, so Baildan sent fifty men in pursuit of her to bring her back to King Tiglath-Pileser. Within three days, Baildan's riders found the queen hiding in a small village and took her to King Tiglath-Pileser. Surprisingly, the king did not execute her. He believed she was the least troublesome of his options and allowed her to continue as Queen of Arabia. The Supreme Commander turned the army southeast. They would sweep down the eastern side of Syria, defeating field fortifications and cities as they went, and join the main body again at Damascus. They spent the spring and most of the summer subduing the entire country of Syria and deporting most people. There were few battles, word of the ferocity of this army preceded it, and most of the field forces they encountered surrendered.

Many of the Syrians sought to join the Assyrian army and were gladly accepted. The ranks swelled as they continued south. The Assyrians reached Damascus in mid-summer, and the army of Tiglath-Pileser was there. The king had already started building siege mounds against the wall, and within days the forty-foot-tall siege engines were rolled against the wall and began the work of breaching. The walls of Damascus were thick, and the siege engines hammered away day and night for the next month. Summer was ending when they breached the walls.

The army poured through the wall, and King Tiglath-Pileser saw what Baildan had seen against the Arabians—Benjamin, in action. The king was astounded as the bodies piled up around the young warrior, and men started to run in terror from him. The battle was over very quickly. The army found King Rezin and the man Baildan was most interested in, Supreme Commander Nabil, and dragged them before the king. The latter summarily executed them in his usual grisly fashion.

After the executioner impaled Nabil, Baildan walked up and stood there staring at him. "Remember me?"

Nabil stared down but was unable to answer in his pain-filled fog.

"This is for Pera. Zichri is already dead," Baildan said. "I have fulfilled my promise to Pera."

The Assyrians subdued and destroyed the Syro-Ephraimite coalition. It had been a long and bloody three years.

After the battle, Baildan and Benjamin were bathing when a runner from the king summoned them. The men finished cleaning up, put on fresh clothes, and went to the king's tent. They entered, made the usual obeisance, and waited for the king to speak.

"Rise," the king commanded. "I have heard of your leadership against the Arabians, Baildan, and of the mighty acts of Benjamin in that battle. Today, I saw the young man fight with my own eyes; I have never seen another warrior like him. Baildan, you may ask of me anything, and I will grant it."

Baildan thought carefully and looked at Benjamin before replying, "Great king, you do me too much honor. I want only one thing, my king, and that is to serve you. If you granted me land outside of Nineveh, I would start a school. The school will serve my king and the rest of the nobility throughout the empire. We will teach astronomy, astrology, military tactics, mathematics, administration, and personal combat. We will also

train the king's guard and groom them into an elite fighting force. I will
select the best men throughout the empire to staff the school. I would ask
that the king grant the school the right to function in perpetuity so that
no following king could overturn what you establish."

The king looked at Baildan and smiled for the first time that Baildan
could ever remember. "Granted. I will draft the command today. You and
Benjamin may select a small force and leave for Nimrud today. By the time
you are ready to leave, I will have the decree drafted, and you may take a
copy of it with you."

Baildan thanked the king, and he and Benjamin backed out of
the tent.

Once outside, Benjamin looked at Baildan quizzically, "A school?"

Baildan nodded. "A school. Kings come and go. Tiglath-Pileser is
aging and may not live much longer. The right he has granted us today is
invaluable and lasting. We will separate ourselves from all of the political
intrigues of Nimrud. I know the perfect piece of land outside Nineveh,
where we can build an enclave in a protected canyon. We, and the teachers
we select, will all move there with our families. We will mold the future
leadership of the empire by training the nobility, and in so doing will be
able to gather information from every area."

Benjamin nodded in understanding. "Sounds great, as long as I get to
do the personal combat training," he said as he grinned.

Baildan selected a force of 100 men and left Ashur in charge of the
cavalry. He received the decree from the king and rode north. He had
been away from home long enough. They rode long and fast and reached
Nimrud in two weeks. Baildan and Benjamin rode to their new home and
ran into the house. They found Rachael in the garden, tending her plants.

Rachael heard the rushing footsteps and was startled. She nearly
fainted when Baildan and Benjamin burst through the open arch into the
garden, but she recovered quickly, raced to Baildan, and threw herself into
his arms. He held her, and her feet didn't touch the ground. They kissed
deeply; the long years of yearning and waiting were over. After a while,
Baildan stepped back and held her at arm's length, drinking in her beauty,
absorbing her essence into his soul. Rachael remembered the second man
and was bewildered for a moment as she looked at him. When he grinned

at her, she realized it was Benjamin, and she jumped into his arms, kissing his cheeks and neck.

Rachael stepped back, still looking at her son. "Where is the boy I sent off to war three years ago? This is no boy."

Baildan looked sheepishly at Rachael, "You have no idea. It is a long story, and I will tell you all about it after we eat. Speaking of which, tell the servants to start preparing a small feast and have someone fetch Domara and Khannah. I have much to tell everyone."

A short while later, the family gathered, and they sat down to a copious feast.

After three years of field rations, Baildan and Benjamin could not get enough to eat. And they gorged themselves.

Sated for the moment, Baildan leaned back and looked at his family. He recounted the last three years, the territories, the people, the battles, Benjamin's training, and he got to the Syrian campaign with regret. "You are not going to like this," he said, looking pleadingly at Rachael, "Benjamin fought against the Arabians in Syria."

Rachael jumped up and fumed at him, "You promised me. You promised me you would keep him safe. You promised."

Palms forward, he waved Rachael down, "I know, I know, but look at him. That is not the boy who left Assyria three years ago. Ashur and Samir could no longer train him. He had become too proficient, and he has packed on fifty pounds of muscle over this time. Benjamin pled with me, and I could not deny him the opportunity."

Benjamin spoke up, "It's the truth, Mother. It was my choice, and I begged for the opportunity to go into battle. I am a man now, and only I can choose what is best for me."

Rachael looked at her son, shook her head, relented, and sat back down.

Baildan continued, "As it turns out, it was the right decision. Benjamin was at my back, and we were attacking as a unit against the Arabians. A slinger hurled a stone, which hit me in the helmet, stunning me momentarily. Benjamin grabbed my armor and hurled me backward with one hand. Then, he stepped up and took my place in the front line. I saw something I had never seen before, a man possessed by force so great he was invincible.

"Benjamin waded into the enemy, killing two or three men at a time. He must have killed fifty men in a matter of minutes. He was so fierce the Assyrians and the Arabs stepped back and watched him. Then the men in front of him broke and ran away, and before I could comprehend what was happening, the whole Arabian army began to run away. After the battle, I remembered events similar to this in Israeli military history. Mighty men had killed hundreds in a single battle, and Samson killed 1,000 men with the jawbone of a donkey. Rachael's God, Jehovah, fights for Benjamin; it is the only explanation. What I saw was not humanly possible.

"Then it happened again when we breached the walls of Damascus and fought the Syrians. This time the king himself saw Benjamin fight. Tiglath-Pileser called us in after the battle and offered Benjamin and me a reward for our bravery. I asked him to establish a school in perpetuity in Nineveh, and he agreed."

Baildan picked up the decree lying next to him and handed it to Domara.

Domara read the decree and was astonished, "What in the world made you think of starting a school?"

"I will not be able to continue to fight forever, and training new leaders and military commanders seemed a perfect fit for our family. But the real reason I have given the king was that we would teach the young men of the royal house and nobility throughout the empire. The king views this as a personal benefit. The real beneficiary is our family. This school allows us to gather information from every corner of the empire. It also allows us to build relationships with men who may someday decide that Assyria's time to rule is over."

"Brilliant, Baildan, brilliant! I wish I had thought of doing this years ago. When will you start building?"

"I want to build in that canyon to the north of Nineveh, do you remember the one? As for when, it certainly will not be tonight," he said as he took Rachael's hand, "and most likely it will not be tomorrow either." Saying so, he looked lovingly at his wife.

Rachael punched him in the arm playfully; she had blushed a deep red.

Baildan is right, she thought, *two days from now would be just fine.*

Scene 6 Magi Camp - Day 46

This lesson was the longest Rahim had ever taught, but he knew if he had tried to stop before the end of the three campaigns, the older boys would have rebelled. Despite its length, every eye was open as the children watched him in rapt attention.

"That is enough for tonight," said Rahim, "and there will be no class tomorrow. You will all be at the wedding." This announcement brought a wild cheer from the children and the adults alike. They all knew and loved the four young people who would be getting married tomorrow, and after a month of exhausting travel, everyone was ready for a celebration.

"The next lesson we have will be on the battle against Judah when Hezekiah is king. Now, off to sleep, everyone."

CHAPTER 11

Ur

Scene 1 Magi Journey - Day 47

Navid and Utana led the Scouts as they advanced on Ur, the ancient birthplace of Abraham. The Scouts held their typical formation today as they moved north, but Navid and Utana rode at a trot all morning. They were thirty miles north of the main body and had not seen signs of Ur. Navid had expected to see the city by now and was confused. Grandfather had always said it was fairly close to the Persian Gulf.

Nature called, and the two men stopped in a small cluster of trees near the river Euphrates. Navid carried a trowel for such occasions. He dug a shallow hole, which he would fill when he finished. But what he found surprised him. In the bit he'd dug up, there were mollusk shells and even a few fish bones. Navid was not a biologist, but he knew these were not from freshwater creatures. These were from saltwater, and the Euphrates in flood stage could not have deposited them.

With business completed, Navid joined Utana. "Utana, I'm not sure, but I think I know the reason we have not found Ur. When I dug a hole, I found the remains of saltwater fish and mollusks. I believe this area used to be part of the Persian Gulf. I have never scouted this area, but I remember Fardad telling me Ur was pretty close to the Gulf. Something has changed; it's as if the Gulf has receded. Is that possible?"

Utana replied, scratching his head, "You are way past my area of expertise, but based on the signs you found, I can't think of another explanation. How much has it receded is the question."

Navid knew Utana didn't care how much the Gulf had receded. Navid and Utana were to be married tonight when they stopped at Ur, but they would not reach Ur today. It didn't matter to the young men where Ur was. The only thing that mattered was the fact they would not arrive there today. "Utana, I know what you're thinking; I am also concerned," Navid replied. "I think our weddings will still happen tonight. The people are excited to have something to celebrate and have been preparing for days. I know everyone will be disappointed we did not reach Ur, but they will not postpone the celebration."

"I hope you are right, brother," Utana said, sulking. "I don't want Fahnik to be disappointed."

"I'm sure you don't want Fahnik to be disappointed," Navid said, grinning at his friend, "but I think I'm looking at the one who is disappointed."

Utana blushed. "Navid, I don't think I can wait another day or two. I want the marriage to take place tonight. We have waited for years, and I haven't been able to think of anything else once we set the date."

"I haven't waited as long as you," Navid said, nodding in agreement, "but I don't think Ava or I could stand postponing the wedding."

Utana hesitated for a moment and then proceeded cautiously, "Speaking of the wedding... did Jahan give you any advice about tonight? Ah, well, I mean, what to expect? How to act? You know what I mean. My father Dara is a shy man, and whenever I brought up the subject of the marriage night, he would say, 'Ask your mother.' Fat chance I'm going to ask Mom for advice concerning the wedding night?"

Navid turned severe, "Surely you don't intend to violate my sister tonight."

Utana was horrified. "Oh no, no-no, Navid. I'm so sorry I asked. I...I... didn't want Fahnik to be disappointed tonight, and that's all I meant."

Navid broke out laughing, "Knowing my sister. She'll kill you if you don't consummate your union tonight. Yes, Jahan did give me advice. Be patient. Don't rush; let your wife take the lead. Talk for a while, don't run into the tent, and jump onto your sleeping mat. Talk about each other's expectations and concerns. You will be married to each other for the rest of your lives. It would be best if you learned to talk about intimate things. Be honest about what you know and don't know. Tell her to speak to you before, during, and after you make love. Without communication, you will not know how to please each other. The first night is critical in setting the tone for your marriage. Your wife must know that you care about her as a person. She must know that her feelings and concerns are important to you. You become one flesh tonight. You are responsible for loving, caring for, and protecting Fahnik for the rest of your lives. She must know she can rely on you. Her trust will deepen over time with experience, but it starts tonight."

Utana breathed a sigh of relief. "Thank you, Navid. Jahan's advice is what I wanted to hear. I can do all those things. I feel much better. Jahan is a wise man, and I know I can trust his counsel. I wish my father weren't so shy. I would have loved for him to give me this same advice."

They continued north for a few more miles and decided they weren't going to find Ur tonight. They turned their horses south to rejoin the rest of the Scouts. When they neared the position of the Scouts, they heard a ram's horn blowing danger. The signal indicated someone was in trouble. Both men kicked their horses into a run; they laid their heads on their horse's necks and rode straight toward the unknown. They rode around a clump of trees, and there to their right was a cluster of men. Navid and Utana raced up to them and pulled back on their reigns at the last minute, causing both horses to squat on their hind legs and skid to a halt.

Esmail, one of the older Scouts at thirty-five, rode up. "We have a problem, Navid. Habib and I were riding by that thicket," he said, pointing at a cluster of weeds and reeds, "and a lion attacked Habib's horse."

Navid saw Habib standing at his horse's head, trying to soothe the animal. His horse was trembling and sweating. Navid saw two long gashes on either side of the horse's rump, and blood ran down the horse's legs. "Is Habib injured?"

"No," replied Esmail, "but the lion is. When the lion attacked, I pulled my bow, but I did not have a good kill shot. I put an arrow into the lion's right shoulder, and it went deep but based on the blood trail, I didn't hit the lung."

Great, thought Navid. *It's my wedding day, and now this.* "We can't leave a wounded lion. The people and flocks will pass this way tomorrow, and that beast will have to kill the easiest prey it can find, which will either be a sheep, goat, or child. We can't take that kind of chance." Navid looked at the men around him. "Shields and javelins," he yelled.

The men hobbled their horses and put their bows and quivers on the ground. Taking just their shields and javelins, they spread out and entered the thicket. Navid couldn't think of anything more dangerous than a wounded lion in a thicket. In a few moments, one of the men called out, "Blood trail." That man now became the center of the formation and was responsible for guiding everyone. They pressed deeper into the thicket. Everyone was nervous and was moving as soundlessly as possible. The guide stopped suddenly and pointed with his javelin at a spot in front of him. Navid and Utana circled to the right of the location. Two men on the left side of the guide circled to the left of the location. The five men compressed their half-circle. Suddenly, the lion leaped away from them, trying to escape. One of the men on the left had a fleeting shot and threw his javelin. The weapon struck the lion in the rump, and it sank deep, but the lion made its escape. It was trying to run, but it was laboring. The time for caution was over. Everyone took after the lion at a dead run. The Scouts chased him for a minute, and the thrashing to the front suddenly stopped.

Navid held up his javelin and yelled, "Halt. He's finished running; he's making a stand. He knows he can't win, but he would like to take one of us with him. He is fifteen yards in front of us. Form a circle; we cannot let him escape again. The Scouts circled the lion and then cautiously moved forward. When they were fifteen feet away, the lion leaped at Utana. Utana hurled his Javelin and threw up his shield. At the same time, Navid threw and sank his javelin deep behind the lion's left shoulder. The man to Utana's left threw his Javelin down the lion's open mouth. The lion hit Utana full force and drove him to the ground. Navid leaped onto the beast's back and sank his hunting knife to the hilt in the lion's neck vertebrae.

"Utana," Navid screamed, "are you okay?"

From somewhere under the lion, Navid heard, "Hrmph... shdpt...Hp."

The Scouts ran over, and six of them lifted the lion off Utana. He lay there, unspeaking, his eyes wide. He grimaced and focused his eyes on Navid. "This wasn't the best idea you had today!"

Navid knelt next to his friend and examined him, "Are you wounded? Did he claw you?"

Utana shook his head gingerly. "No, he was dead when he hit me, but I think he may have broken my shield arm."

Navid removed Utana's shield, which elicited a yelp of pain from him. He gently probed Utana's left forearm. "There is not a complete break, but based on the swelling already, it may have a crack in it."

As soon as they heard the word "crack," two Scouts searched to find straight sticks they could use for a splint. They found three, took their hunting knives, and shaved them smooth. Navid took the wood from them, placed it on Utana's forearm, and bound it tightly with one of Utana's scarves.

Navid helped Utana to his feet and patted him gently on the back. "Sorry, old friend; it looks like you're going to be a little banged up for the wedding tonight. The good news is you're going to be there."

Navid helped Utana mount, and the Scouts headed back to camp.

Ava had joined Fahnik today as she tended the flocks of sheep and goats. They had to keep them moving to keep pace with the camels and horses, but they had to let them stop, rest, and graze periodically, or animals would die. It was a delicate balance, knowing when to move them along and when to let them stop. Ava was too nervous to ride today, and that is why she was walking with Fahnik. That and the fact she wanted to talk about the wedding tonight.

"Do you have your dress ready for tonight?" Ava inquired.

"Mother finished making it two days ago, but she won't let me see it. I guess it's some old Magi tradition," Fahnik said, smiling at her friend.

"I know; same with my mom. I'm dying to see it. What if it doesn't fit?" Ava pouted.

"I know your mother," Fahnik said as she laughed. "It will fit. She's the best seamstress in the Family. Are you nervous about tonight? Did your mother give you any advice?"

"Yes, she said don't spill anything on the dress."

At this, they both laughed.

"You know what I mean. I mean, did your mother give you advice about the wedding night?"

Ava blushed. "Yes, she gave me advice, but I'm not sure I understand what she is trying to tell me. She seemed to be talking less about tonight and more about other stuff."

"Like what?" asked Fahnik.

Ava thought for a minute. "She said men are tough and confident on the outside, but inside they have doubts and fears. Mother said men need to know we respect and trust them, that it's essential to give them affirmation of the things they do right. If they often hear the things we respect and revere about them, they will learn to avoid the things we don't praise. She said positive affirmation is more important than criticism or nagging. Focus on the positive, not the negative. But about tonight specifically, I'm in the dark."

"I think your mother's advice is terrific; I'm going to follow it. Thank you so much for sharing. About 'tonight,' my mother did give me some advice. She said to take the lead, to make sure Utana knows I want him physically. She said that I should not be afraid to touch him and hold him. She also said I should talk to him and tell him what he does that gives me pleasure and the things that are not as pleasing. She said the more we talk, the better our physical relation will be."

Ava was blushing bright red. She was stunned into silence.

Fahnik laughed; well, actually, she laughed a lot. "I'm sorry, Ava, I didn't mean to embarrass you. My mother was more frank and descriptive, and I decided to give you only the essentials."

Ava had recovered from her initial shock. "No need to apologize, Fahnik. That advice is what I needed to hear. I think I was shocked because my mind was filling in the blanks as you talked. I know what your mother meant. Do you believe we are going to be sisters after tonight?"

"I feel as if we have always been sisters," Fahnik replied as she reached out and held Ava's hand. "We have known each other our whole lives, and you are my best friend."

Ava squeezed Fahnik's hand. "You are my best friend. Tonight, you will become my sister. Tonight, I will marry your brother, and he and I will become one flesh. Before tonight we merely felt like sisters."

The two women walked on in silence, still holding hands.

The Family stopped for the night and set up camp as Navid and Utana rode in with the Scouts. They turned their horses over to the grooms, and Navid went to find Jahan.

In the middle of the camp, Jahan and Fardad were erecting the family tent.

"Father," called Navid, "we have two problems; first, as you can see, we are not in Ur. Second, Utana broke his arm. Well, he didn't exactly break his arm; the lion broke his arm when it landed on him."

"The part about Ur, that much I can see," replied Jahan. "The big question is—where is it? The part about Utana and a lion, what are you talking about?"

Navid recounted the story of the lion hunt, and Jahan shook his head. "You did the right thing. You couldn't leave a wounded lion out there. Is Utana all right?"

"Fortunately, Utana killed the lion before it hit him. He got his shield up, but the force of the lion landing on him cracked the bone in his forearm. It is not a complete break and should heal fine. He's a little bruised and shook up, but he's fine.

"About Ur, Utana and I stopped about twenty miles north of our location. I dug a hole and found saltwater mollusk shells and fish bones. It appears the Gulf is receding."

Grandfather interjected, "I have never been to Ur. When I told every-one it was close to the Gulf, I was repeating what I had heard my grand-father say."

"Well, it's not close to the Gulf anymore," replied Navid. "What does that mean for tonight? Will we hold the weddings?"

Jahan said without hesitation, "The weddings go on as planned. Everyone is prepared and excited. There is no reason to postpone. It would have been nice if we were in Ur because you and Utana would have been able to spend three or four uninterrupted days with your new wives, and you will still be able to when we reach Ur. You are merely delaying your honeymoons for a few days. Why did you ask? You didn't think we would postpone the wedding, did you?"

Navid was about to respond when he noticed a new rounded tent sitting next to the family tent. "Whose tent is that Navid inquired? I have never seen a design like that before."

"It's your grandfather's and my wedding gift to you. Dara built one just like it for Utana. It's a design I saw in a caravan that had come from the Far East years ago. I think they called it a yurt or something." Then Jahan turned and led Navid inside. "It's a simple construction," he said as he pointed up. "It starts with that ring you see in the center up there. You dig holes around the perimeter, insert your poles, and bend them to fit in that ring. When you have inserted all the tent poles, the tent frame is complete. After that, you pull four animal skins over the frame, secure them together, and you have your tent. Easy to put up, and easy to take down and store."

"Father, what a marvelous gift! Ava will be thrilled. I never expected this; I can't tell you how much it means to me," he said as he stepped forward and hugged his father.

Embarrassed, Jahan stepped back. "Well, I did it for the rest of the family as much as for you. I figured none of us would get any sleep for the next month if you didn't have a separate tent."

Now, it was Navid's turn to be embarrassed. "Well, regardless of motive, it's a marvelous gift."

They left the tent, and Asha saw them and came over. "You two need to hurry. Clean up and get dressed. The food is ready, and everyone is anxious to begin." Asha hurried to the family tent to dress Fahnik. Asha wasn't sure who was more nervous, her daughter or her.

Scene 2 The Wedding

Navid's family walked together to the area that everyone had cleared for the celebration. Navid had dressed in green silk with a matching turban, and he had oiled his face and beard. He looked like a prince of Persia—incredibly handsome.

But Fahnik was magnificent.

Fahnik's hair had been braided and hung down her back. She wore a multicolored red, yellow and green fabric dress, and she had an outer wrap colored deep red. Pari and Tiz had picked wildflowers, which they braided into a crown, which matched Fahnik's outfit perfectly.

They had set up a low table, with cushions behind it at one end of the clearing. Utana, Ava, and their parents were sitting at the table, and Navid's family and Tiz joined them. Navid sat next to Ava and Fahnik sat next to Utana.

Navid looked at Ava. Her face shone; she was so happy. Her dress was snow white with a light lavender robe. Tiz and Pari had also woven a garland of flowers for her hair, and they were the same lavender as her robe. Navid's heart melted. He took her hands and looked into her eyes. "You have made me the happiest man in the world. Having you as my wife is the greatest blessing God has given me," he told her.

"I am the one who is blessed," said Ava, "there is no finer man in all of Asia than my Navid. I will always love you."

The Family's women rushed to the head table ending any chance of further conversation; everyone wanted to present their special dish first. The table was full of every delicacy imaginable in a matter of minutes. Curries, stews, tandoori meats, chickpeas, wild onions, roast goat and lamb, bread slathered in butter and garlic, fruits, sweet rice dishes, every food Navid loved was on that table. The aroma was overwhelming.

Fardad rose and called for silence and prayed, "Great God, Jehovah, maker of heaven and earth, the Sustainer and Redeemer of Israel; we bow down before you. You have called us and set us apart to go and worship the Lord of Lords and the King of Kings. We are honored and humbled that you have chosen your servants, the Magi. Some would stop us, who want to end our journey. We pray that You would cover us with your wings, that You would hide and protect us, and that You would fight for us. We are weak, but You are strong. Tonight we stop, and we celebrate. We give thanks to You, and we rejoice in the marriage of these four young people, whom You love. Bless them, guide them all their days, and make them fruitful that they may fill the earth. Amen."

The wedding party dug in with relish. Utana did the best he could with one hand, but he didn't need to bother. Fahnik stared at him with her large doe eyes in rapt adoration. Her man had killed the lion and had borne the brunt of the beast's charge. Utana was now a hero. She barely touched her food; she was so busy feeding him. Utana took full advantage of her adoration; he leaned back on his cushions, held his broken arm with his right hand, and periodically grimaced in pain.

Navid watched his friend's performance. Utana was playing the part perfectly, and Fahnik was buying the whole thing. He grinned at Utana and winked. Utana winked back and then moaned, clutching his arm. Fahnik immediately responded by adjusting his pillows, rubbing his back, and cooing to him. Navid looked over at his father, who was also enjoying this performance. Jahan rolled his eyes up in his head and shook his head, appalled at Utana's over-exaggeration but enjoying the skill of his performance.

When Fardad saw that the eating frenzy was slowing, he rose once again and walked to the center of the clearing. The four young people knew this was the signal for them to follow, and they stood and joined Grandfather in the clearing's center. The four of them formed a semicircle around Fardad, and a hush fell over the Family.

Fardad smiled at the two couples, then began, "We have gathered here tonight to join Utana and Fahnik and Navid and Ava in marriage. Scripture tells us they will become one flesh after tonight… they will leave their parents and cleave only to each other for all eternity. That is God's plan; that's how He designed us. We all have many weaknesses, and their journey together will not always be smooth. There will be arguments and disagreements over many subjects, but they must be united in one thing. They must worship the Lord together; He must be the center of their lives and their marriage. There is nothing they will not be able to resolve with God's guidance. I am now going to ask each of you some questions," Fardad said, looking at the two couples.

"Navid and Utana, do you promise to be faithful to your wives, and do you promise always to protect them? To protect them from all physical dangers and to protect them from those who would lure them away from God or you? Do you promise to love Ava and Fahnik and to build them up and nurture them? Do you promise to love the children born to this union and to raise those children in the knowledge and love of the Lord?"

"I do promise," responded both Navid and Utana.

"Fahnik and Ava," continued Fardad, "do you promise to love and be faithful to your husbands? Do you promise to support them and encourage them and lift them to God in prayer every day? Do you promise to make your home a place of peace and joy, a refuge from the turmoil of the world? Do you promise to raise the children born to this union to love God and respect their parents? Do you promise always to put your marriage first and your children second?"

Fahnik and Ava said, "I do."

"As the Family leader, I recognize your choice to be united, and I pronounce you man and wife. You may kiss your brides," Fardad said, looking at Utana and Navid.

For the first time in his life, Navid folded Ava in his arms and kissed her. He thought he would faint; he became so light-headed. Then pandemonium broke out; first, both mothers started crying, and then everyone rushed up and began pounding the two couples on the back. Everyone spoke at once, and everything became indecipherable. What was clear was everyone's joy and excitement.

The two couples were hoisted onto the men's shoulders and paraded around the clearing. For just a moment, Navid pictured himself and Leyla at their engagement party; then, quickly, that memory was gone as he looked at his wife.

The two couples were finally placed back on their feet, and they walked back to their table. Navid and Utana held their brides' hands as they walked—something they had never done before. Navid felt like the king of the world, and he had never felt like this in his life. He looked down at Ava, who looked lovingly up, and then she held his arm in both hands and nestled her head against his shoulder. Life didn't get any better than this.

They reached the table, and both sets of parents stood. The mothers rushed to their new daughters-in-law and began hugging, kissing, and crying simultaneously, which set off a similar response in both girls. The fathers pounded their sons-in-law on the back and shouted words of encouragement, no crying, just lots of grinning and eyebrow-raising. Now, Utana was actually grimacing in pain as the massive Jahan pounded on his back.

The party got into full swing. They quickly consumed the little wine they had brought on the trip; people broke out drums and stringed instruments, and they danced. The women formed into many circles, and the rings started to rotate as the women performed ancient folk dances. The music became faster, and it was the men's turn to dance. They jumped, twirled, and squatted on their haunches; it looked more like a prelude to war than a dance. The dancing, eating, and drinking lasted well into the night; the Family would be getting a late start tomorrow.

After what they thought to be a respectable period, the two couples made their way around the clearing, stopping to talk to everyone. They thanked them for coming and for the mountain of gifts they had received. The other Family members had given the couples everything they needed for their new homes; they would lack nothing. After they had thanked everyone, the couples headed for their new yurts to begin their married lives.

Jahan sat next to Fardad, watching the festivities, the two men at peace and enjoying each other's company. The men had not had a moment like this since the beginning of the trip.

Jahan leaned toward Fardad and nodded to the far corner of the clearing. "I have been watching that group for much of the evening. They have had their heads together, whispering for most of the night. I think dissent is finally beginning to surface. We both knew it was there, but this is the first time it has been this obvious. The leader of the group is Danial, Yusef's father; we expected that. It is the others that surprise me, Gohar, Heydar, and Reza. What's the connection?"

Fardad said, "I think it's relatively simple. Danial and Reza's wives are sisters. Gohar and Harydar are both on the right flank, with Danial. They will bear watching; we are reaching a critical point in the journey. I don't like it because I don't know what they intend, but it would be counterproductive to confront them. I'll visit with some of their friends the next few days to see if they have heard anything."

"What is wrong with you," Danial whispered fiercely to Gohar as he pounded his fist into the palm of his other hand. "We have to take some action to protect our families. It's going to be too late to negotiate when the Immortals show up. We have to find some way to convince Queen Musa that we are not part of this rebellion. When we reach Ur, Reza and I will find someone willing to carry a message to the Immortals. I have enough gold to buy someone, I'm sure. Gohar and Heydar, your responsibility is to find a way to create a diversion when the Immortals arrive. We have to find a way to disrupt things enough to get our families out before the fighting starts."

Gohar remained unconvinced, "Surely, there is another way. We have known these people all our lives. We need to convince Fardad and Jahan to surrender when the Immortals arrive, and they will listen to reason. We have to protect the Family."

Danial hissed, "Listen to me. There is no other way; the old boy has lost his mind. Angels visit him, and they talk to him. He talks to some mythical God to whom no one else has ever spoken. He has convinced everyone that God is making us go to Israel, and they are all mindless sheep. Wake up, Gohar; this is the only way to save our families."

Gohar slumped in resignation, "All right, all right; we'll do it your way. I hate it, but I don't see any alternatives."

Navid held the tent flap back, and Ava entered their new home. Navid lit a candle and took off his boots and outer robe. Even without bringing in their wedding gifts, the yurt had been nicely furnished. The rug on the floor was not new, but it still had a lot of wear left in it. There were two chests for them to each store their clothes and a thick sleeping mat. Navid sat on the mat and patted the spot next to him, and Ava sat.

"We don't need to rush anything, Ava. We have all the time in the world. This is the first time we have ever been alone together. We have a lot to learn about each other; what would you like to know about me or my expectations?"

Unable to control herself any longer, Ava threw herself into Navid's arms, kissing him passionately.

Navid broke the embrace, sat up, and blew out the candle. "We can talk later," he said and lay back on the mat next to his wife.

Fahnik didn't wait for Utana to take charge. After entering their new yurt, she threw Utana on the sleeping mat and took off her outer robe. "Shut up and get your clothes off," she commanded. "I have waited long enough."

Utana lay back and smiled. *My kind of woman*, he thought. *I'm a lucky man.*

Scene 3 Crossing the Euphrates - Day 50

It had taken the Magi two extra days to reach Ur. They had reached the city before the spring snowmelt and rains, and the river was not high or fast. The river's condition meant that the crossing was not impossible, but it was still challenging. Getting two hundred people across a river one hundred feet deep and five hundred yards across is a formidable task. The additional help or boats they expected to find in Ur was not there. The city had dried up and shrunk to a few hundred people, and there were no boats or ferries large enough to help. In actuality, they weren't in Ur at all. They had reached a small village at the confluence of the Tigris and Euphrates Rivers. When Navid had questioned one of the villagers he had met on the trail, the man confirmed this was Ur. Navid was unaware that the man hadn't understood a word he had said. He nodded yes to everything. Navid also was unaware that the river they were crossing was the Shatt al-Arab, formed by the Euphrates and Tigris Rivers.

Jahan broke everyone into working teams. One group of men he sent up and down river to harvest as many trees over ten feet tall as possible. Another group built rafts with the cut trees. The rafts would carry people, flocks, and equipment across the river. To address getting horses and camels across, Jahan had the women sewing bladders from skins. Two air-filled bladders would be tied together. The rope would be slung under the horse or camel and would help support it as it swam. The horses could swim, but camels were not known to swim. Jahan knew some horses might be strong enough to swim 500 yards, but the camels would need floatation help.

The Magi put the rafts and bladders into service as soon as they completed them. Jahan had been on the first raft to cross, accompanied by a group of horses and camels. As they neared the other bank, Jahan had seen several crocodiles on the bank, led by a large old bull. Jahan would warn the men swimming with the livestock to be on alert when they neared that bank.

They had been ferrying flocks and equipment across for two days. It had been slow at first, but as they constructed more rafts and floats, progress improved. The men propelled the rafts with two long oars, one on either side of the raft. They also fashioned a rudder, which they attached to the rear of the raft to help the raft move in a straight line. It took three men to propel and steer the raft; therefore, Jahan's work crews diminished every time they completed a raft. At their current rate, Jahan estimated they would finish crossing in two more days.

The steering and propulsion system kept the rafts from drifting too far downriver since the current was slow. The same was not true for the animals; their propulsions systems were not very good, and they had no steering system. The rafts landed about fifty yards south of their starting point on the other side of the river, but the animals landed almost half a mile below their starting point.

Jahan had assigned Danial and Reza tree-cutting duties, which provided the men freedom of movement. On the second day, they informed Jahan they would harvest trees north of their location. The other cutters all went south. When they were out of sight of the camp, the men spurred their horses and rode three miles to what they believed to be Ur. In the city, they found a run-down hostel that had no horses in its corral. The establishment also had no travelers housed there. The two men left their horses in the corral and went inside.

The light was weak, and there was no one in the main room. Shortly after entering, an older man in a filthy apron came out of the backroom. He rubbed his hands together in anticipation of gain as he approached the men. "How can I help you, fine gentleman?" He inquired, bowing slightly.

Danial spoke up, "We're traveling with the group located south of town. We're currently crossing the river, but our leader asked us to come into town to see if we could hire a local man to run an errand for us."

"What kind of errand would that be exactly?" the older man asked, not accepting this story at face value.

"We are meeting a group that's coming down from Babylon, but it looks like we will be across the river before they get here. We need someone to carry a message to them to tell them where we crossed," Danial lied.

"You have quite a few people; why don't you have a man ride north and tell them yourselves?" He asked, smelling the lie.

Danial pulled out a small gold piece from his pouch and showed it to the man. "We're all busy with the crossing. Do you have someone that can help us or not?"

Now, the hosteller knew he was in a bargaining position. "Of course, I know a lad who can help you; of course I do," he said, taking the gold piece from Danial's hand. "But you know riders don't come cheap. It could be a long, dangerous journey, and the lad's family will suffer horribly with him gone. But for the right price, I'm sure I can convince him to help."

Danial pulled out five more gold coins from the purse and stared at the man, "Do you think that's enough to convince the young man?"

"Oh, that should do nicely," the man said, grabbing for the coins.

Danial stepped back and closed his hand over the coins, "You'll get them after we meet the man."

The hosteller yelled into the back room for his wife and told her to fetch, Aghil. His wife appeared in a few moments with a slightly dirty but lovely sixteen-year-old young woman.

"Wait a minute!" shouted Danial, "You said 'lad'; you said you were going to send a 'lad.' This is no 'lad.' What are you trying to pull?"

The hosteller waved his arms, palms down to indicate everyone needed to calm down, "You said you needed a message carried. I said, 'lad' because I knew you would be concerned about sending a young woman, but there are few options here. She's the only one I know who could take the message. Don't underestimate her. She can ride, and she's tough. Do you want the message sent or not?"

Danial looked at the young woman and growled, "What do you call yourself?"

"I'm Aghil," she replied without hesitation, looking Danial in the eye, "and I can take your message. I can ride and fight as well as anyone in this village." She pointed to a bow standing in the corner of the room.

"All right," Danial replied, looking at the hosteller. He opened his hand and handed over the gold coins. "It appears I don't have an option, but if the message doesn't get delivered, I'll be back. You can count on that." He reached into his tunic and pulled out a parchment sealed with wax addressed to Sasan. Danial handed the document to Aghil, "You are looking for a large group of men, probably two or three hundred men. There will likely be a man with them named Sasan. These men are the Immortals, Queen Musa's guard troop. Deliver this message to Sasan if he is with them. If he is not with them, ask for their leader and deliver it to him. They should be somewhere between here and Babylon."

Aghil took the message from Danial. "I will find them. I know this territory well, and I know people who will have seen them if they are out there."

For the first time, Danial grinned, "Oh, they're out there. You can count on that."

Danial and Reza left the hostel and searched for useable trees along the river bank.

Fardad sat on his horse on a slight rise, overlooking the town. He watched as Danial and Reza left the hostel. A short time later, a young man dressed for travel and carrying a bow came out of the hostel. He walked up to a large white mule tied to a hitching rail. The man untied the mule and rode north. It was as Fardad and Jahan had feared. The conspiracy was now in the open, and they were taking action against the Family. He turned his horse and headed back to camp.

Fardad found Jahan when he arrived back at camp. The two men discussed Fardad's observation and walked to Navid's yurt. They stopped outside the yurt and called to Navid.

Navid and Ava both came out, "Good morning, Father and Grandfather. Ava and I are going to find Utana and Fahnik. We had talked about riding back to the beautiful glen we found yesterday and eating a meal together. Do you need something before we go?"

"Unfortunately, we do need something," said Jahan. "We told you about Danial and the three men with whom we believe he has formed a conspiracy, and they have confirmed those fears. Fardad just observed Danial and Reza visit an inn in Ur, and after they left, a rider came out of the inn and rode north on a white mule. We believe that rider is carrying a message to the Immortals. We need you to send two men after that rider and bring him and the message back."

Navid looked at Ava, "I'll find Esmail, and we'll go after the rider. We'll bring him back."

Fardad shook his head, "No, you will not go after the rider. You must learn to delegate if you want to be a leader. Send Esmail and Habib; they are competent, and they will be honored that you have trusted them with this mission. It will also reassure Esmail you haven't lost confidence in him after the incident with the lion."

Navid bowed to his grandfather, saying, "As usual, you are correct. I'll be right back, Ava. Esmail is building rafts; I'll give him instructions, and he can inform Habib as they ride."

Fardad and Jahan left to attend other duties, and Navid was right back. "Let's go find Utana and Fahnik; we told them yesterday we would ride back to the clearing by the river and have a picnic today."

As they reached Utana's yurt, Fahnik and Utana were just coming out. Fahnik was carrying a leather pouch filled with food, and Utana was bringing two rugs. They smiled as they saw Navid and Ava approach.

"Looks like we both had the same idea," Fahnik said as she hugged Ava.

Fahnik had shortened the splints on Utana's arm, so they started below the elbow and ended before the wrist. His strength in the arm was limited, but he had full mobility. Utana hugged Navid, and the two couples walked to the corral. As they neared the corral, two horses came thundering out at full gallop before leaving the camp.

"Where are those two going?" Utana inquired, seeing Esmail and Habib on the two horses.

"Long story," replied Navid, "I'll tell you when we reach the clearing."

Getting to the clearing was a short ride. Utana spread the rugs on the ground, and the two women spread a feast from the food in their bags.

As they ate, Utana inquired, "So what's the story?"

Navid looked at his sister and Utana, "This is not something you can discuss with anyone else. Danial is the head of a conspiracy that wants to stop the Family from reaching Israel. Grandfather saw Reza and him hire a rider in Ur. The rider is heading north on a white mule as we speak. We suspect the rider is trying to find the Immortals. Esmail and Habib are going to retrieve the rider and the message. Gohar and Heydar are part of Danial's group. We don't know their role, but it would be best if we kept a close eye on them."

"Great," said Fahnik, "as if this trip isn't difficult enough. I don't understand; they didn't have to come, and they swore an oath to uphold the Family. How can they do this?"

No one answered because there was no answer.

Ava decided it was time to change subjects. "We have been married a few days now. Tell us what you have learned about each other, and we will do the same."

Utana grinned, and Fahnik shot him a stern look. The stupid grin disappeared from his face. "I think a fascinating thing I've learned is how patient Fahnik is. She never becomes upset or nervous about something; she applies herself until she masters the task. She asked me to teach her to tie some of the knots we use to create a loop in a rope or secure a log so we can drag it. I taught her ten different knots, and she practiced them for hours until she mastered them all."

Fahnik smiled at Utana, "I now know how sensitive and gentle Utana is. Beneath the gruff exterior is a man who wants to understand people's thoughts and emotions and is upset if he causes hurt or offense."

Ava's turn: "I have discovered that Navid sees me as a partner and as an equal. He opens himself and his heart to me. He has shared many concerns about dealing with specific men in the Scouts, and he truly wants my opinions. I never suspected he had that much respect for me."

Navid bowed his head, temporarily overwhelmed by his emotions. "I have learned that I love Ava more than life itself. I had observed her for all of her life and knew about her kindness, wisdom, and dedication to others. She is truly selfless. I don't know how I could have been near her my whole life and not known that the love of my life was right there in front of me."

The two couples talked through the afternoon, laughing and sharing. It was an afternoon they would long remember. They were young and in love, and nothing could ever change.

It took another day of river crossings, and by day fifty-five, they made the last trips across the river. The Council and Fardad's family were the last to cross. Gohar, one of the conspirators, was an oarsman, and his family was also on the raft; his wife and ten-year-old daughter, Mahsa. They were within one hundred yards of the far bank when something spooked one of the sheep. The sheep leaped over the raft's railing. Mahsa grasped the sheep's lead rope, and the sheep pulled her over the side. Sheep and girl were both in the water, and the current was pulling them downstream away from the raft.

Without hesitating, Tiz threw off his outer wrap and dove into the river. He was a strong swimmer and had soon caught up with the girl and sheep. Mahsa was still clinging to the lead rope, and Tiz pulled the rope from her hand. Mahsa cried and struggled as the sheep drifted away from them. Tiz had one arm around the girl and spoke soothingly. "Mahsa, I need you to help me. I need both of my arms to reach the far shore. I want you to crawl onto my back and put your arms around my neck. Can you do that?"

Mahsa nodded yes; Tiz let go of her, and she crawled to his back and put her arms around his neck. Tiz swam with long, steady strokes and was gaining on the bank with every stroke. Tiz kept his eyes on the riverbank as he swam. They had had a few incidents in the crossing with animals and crocodiles, nothing too serious. Horses and camels were not easy prey, but a man and young girl might look like a tasty snack. As he feared, when he was within twenty yards of the bank, an older male crocodile slid into the water and disappeared. Tiz swam for a few more yards, then stopped and trod water. "I'm going to count to three Mahsa. Take in a big breath and hold it; when I reach three, I'm going to dive under the water. One, two, three."

Tiz ducked under the water. The water was murky, but Tiz could make out a dark form approaching them. He pulled his fighting knife from his belt and waited. Tiz made a deep slash across the crocodile's nostrils when the croc was within striking distance and then jammed the knife upward into the croc's throat. The croc rolled in its death throes and roiled the water. The thrashing crocodile soon attracted other crocs, and Tiz used the diversion to swim the rest of the distance to the riverbank and staggered from the water with Mahsa still clinging to his neck.

Mahsa's parents had already reached the riverbank and had watched the rescue. They and everyone else who had been watching rushed to aid Tiz and Mahsa. The men helped Tiz and Mahsa's mother extricate Mahsa from Tiz's neck. Gohar ran up and began crying, pounding Tiz's back and hugging him all at the same time.

Fardad and Jahan came over and hugged and thanked Tiz. "Come, Tiz," Fardad said, grabbing Tiz by the elbow, "they have lit cooking fires; let's go over and get you dry."

Gohar followed them over to the fire and stood there looking down at his feet.

Fardad looked at him; Gohar was uncomfortable, "Yes, Gohar is there something you would like to say?"

Gohar looked up, "Yes, I have something I need to tell you."

"Go ahead, Gohar; I'm sure it's nothing that Tiz and Jahan cannot hear."

Gohar hesitated for a moment and said, "It's about Danial. He wants to prevent the Family from reaching Israel, and I am supposed to help him."

There was a commotion on the riverbank, and the group turned and saw Navid and two other men taking one of the rafts back across the river. On the other side, sitting on their horses were Esmail and Habib and a man on a white mule.

Jahan turned to Gohar, "It appears the plan has already unraveled. The man on the mule is the messenger Danial hired to take a message to the Immortals. Now tell us about your participation."

Gohar confessed, "Danial and Reza were to hire a messenger, and Heydar and I were to create a diversion when the Immortals came. We were going to set fire to the food supplies, and that way, we couldn't continue to Israel."

Fardad stared at Gohar. "The others I understand; they have always been malcontents, but you Gohar. I don't know why you would do this?"

Gohar hung his head. "I feared for my family. Queen Musa won't send one or two hundred Immortals; she will send three hundred or more. We don't stand a chance against a force that size. I thought you and Jahan had made a mistake. I wanted to save the Family. I want to see the Messiah, but I don't believe we'll ever leave Persia alive."

Fardad looked at him. "We will banish the other three families today, we will give them food, but we will not give them any horses or camels. They will leave with food and the clothes on their back. I am giving you a choice, you may leave with them, or you may go to Israel with us."

"Do you believe we will make it to Israel?" Gohar pleaded.

Fardad looked him in the eye and said, "No, I don't believe we will make it. I know we will. God has called us, and He will take us the rest of the way."

Gohar smiled, and the two men grasped each other's forearm. "Then, I will stay and fight. When the Immortals come, we will make them sorry they left Susa."

The Magi spent the rest of the day preparing to travel. They disassembled the rafts and sent the logs downstream, and they deflated the bladders, dried the skins, and packed them on camels. They were ready.

Fardad called everyone to the evening meal and had Daniel, Reza, and Heydar stand before the Family, and he pronounced their banishment. They gave them food and sent them from the camp. The Family turned their backs on them as they left; no one spoke. The man on the white mule turned out to be a young woman, which embarrassed Fardad. She was given her mule and permitted to return to her family. Fardad then prayed and thanked God for the safe river crossing and blessed the food they were about to receive.

When the meal was over, Rahim called the children to the camp center, picked up the ancient scroll, and began to read...

Scene 4 Zaia - 702 BC

Much had happened over these past years, Zaia, son of Meesha, thought. Five years after Baildan had started his school, Tiglath-Pileser III had died of old age. Baildan had been wise in getting a grant in perpetuity. Not only had Tiglath-Pileser died, but also his two successors Shalmaneser V and Sargon II had only ruled for a combined twenty-five years. Sennacherib was now king and had been for three years. When Sennacherib took the throne, Hezekiah, now king of Judah, decided to stop paying tribute to Assyria. There was no doubt in Zaia's mind the King of Assyria was gathering an army to bring Judah back into submission.

Zaia reflected on the changes the years had brought. He was now forty-two years old, and his father, Meesha, was sixty-four. Zaia was ambassador to Judah. Meesha was traveling to Nineveh to spend his last years teaching at Baildan's school. He was bringing a whole new course of study, but it was not for the school. Meesha was taking a message of faith in God. He would only be teaching his immediate family and the school faculty whom they could trust. King Sennacherib would be incensed if he knew Meesha was teaching faith in Jehovah.

Zaia's wife came into his study as he was contemplating. "Come, food is on the table, and the children are starving."

His oldest son, Javed, was twenty-one, and his daughter, Negar, was sixteen. His wife, Abigail, still referred to them as children; it was difficult for her to let go. It was hard to imagine that he and Abigail had been married for more than twenty years. It had been a difficult marriage to arrange. Abigail was of the tribe of Benjamin. Her father was a member of King Ahaz's court, where Meesha and Zaia had seen her. After he had seen Abigail, Zaia could think of nothing else, and Meesha had finally approached her father. The first answer was no, never. Meesha pursued her father for months, and her father finally agreed to meet with Meesha and Zaia. He would approve the marriage on one condition: Zaia must convert to Judaism and be circumcised.

Zaia had agreed without hesitation and had never regretted the decision. They had circumcised Javed on the eighth day after his birth, as prescribed by Jewish law, to avoid complications for him in the future.

Everyone was seated in the central room when Zaia came in. Abigail had prepared fresh bread and a type of porridge she made with goat's milk and barley. She added honey to the porridge, and it was Javed's favorite, which is why they had it far too often. Zaia prayed and gave thanks for God's grace and goodness and the meal before them.

"Father, are we meeting with Hahn today?" Javed asked.

"Yes, I told him to come over this morning," Zaia answered. For years, Zaia and his father had met with Adin, another disciple of Isaiah, but he had gone home to be with the Lord five years before. Since then, they have met and studied with Hahn.

Hahn's visit was also something that had changed. When Meesha was head of the house, Hahn could not enter the home of a Gentile. Now that this was Zaia's home, Hahn could visit for the first time.

Meesha and Zaia had been copying the Hebrew Scriptures for years, but Meesha had not taken them to Assyria for security's sake. Zaia wanted to go over the copies and his notes one last time before sending them to Meesha. The Hebrew Scriptures, or Tanakh, consisted of the Torah (the first five books or Pentateuch given by God to Moses), the Prophets, and the Writings. The Writings contained the Psalms, Job, Proverbs, Ecclesiastes, Song of Solomon, and Chronicles. The Prophets include everything that wasn't in the Torah or Writings. The Scriptures were a live document. The scribes added to the Scriptures everything prophesied by Isaiah and his contemporaries, Micah and Amos. The scribes also recorded decisions and actions taken by King Hezekiah and would continue to record the actions taken by future kings and prophets of Judah. Israel, the northern kingdom, was no more. The last king of Israel had been Hoshea, and he was dead.

There was a knock on the door, and Abigail answered, "Hahn, it is good to see you again. Zaia and Javed are in the study; please go in." Hahn was five years older than Zaia and had been a disciple of Isaiah's since his youth. He was not physically attractive, was of medium height, and had a prominent nose, and a childhood disease had marked his face with pits. But what you noticed the most was not those physical things. When he spoke to you, he looked you in the eye, and you knew he was genuinely interested in you and what you were saying. That was his gift, and that's what you noticed.

Hahn entered the office and sat with Zaia and Javed. "What shall we speak about today, my friends?"

Zaia smiled at Hahn, "I have finished copying everything that you and Adin have given me these past twenty-two years. I will send these works to Meesha and need to make sure I haven't missed anything. I especially want to make sure I have everything Isaiah has prophesied."

Hahn took the pile of parchments from Zaia. "Based on the weight alone, it looks like you have everything. More important than the volumes you have written is your understanding of what you have written. May I ask you a few questions?"

"Of course," said Zaia, "and when you have finished, I may have a few of my own."

"Who is God?" Hahn began.

Javed said, "God is eternal; He has no beginning and no end. God is one; He is Holy, and He is a jealous God. God is Spirit; therefore, we are to make no images of Him or other gods. He is the creator and sustainer of everything. Life and death are His. God is present everywhere. He never learns—He has all knowledge, and He never sleeps. God is love. He is perfect in every way."

"Excellent, Javed. What is sin?"

"I'll take that one," said Zaia. "Sin is anything that falls short of God's standard. God's standard is perfection—perfect love, holiness, honesty, truthfulness, and anything less than that standard is sin. Adam sinned, and God expelled him from His presence, and since Adam, all people are born with a sin nature."

"Perfect, Zaia. One last question: How can people be brought into a right relationship with God?"

Zaia hesitated for a moment and then said, "That is what Isaiah has been trying to tell everyone. People think it's by observing the Law, attending the temple, making sin offerings, and going through the motions. Isaiah says God hates that, that he has no regard for those offerings. God doesn't care about the action. He cares about the heart and the motive behind the action. God cares about how we live our lives: Do we care for the widow and the orphan? Are we honest? Do we deal fairly with people? And are we just? We are to fear God and repent of our sins against Him. We cannot redeem ourselves; we must rely in faith on God's grace and mercy for our redemption. We must look to Him. The Law reveals our sin and weakness, but it cannot save us."

"Isaiah would be proud of that answer. Now, what questions do you have?"

This time, Zaia did not hesitate. "I have several questions. The last scroll of Isaiah we have deals with the ransomed of the Lord returning to Zion with singing.[16] Is that everything to this point in time? In the prophecy against Jerusalem in Chapter Eight, what does it mean, 'The water will reach up to the neck.' Lastly, I understand the prophecies against the nations in Chapters Thirteen through Twenty-three, but in Chapters Twenty-four and following, I do not understand the timing."

"The first two are easy," Hahn replied. "Yes, you have everything Isaiah has prophesied to this point. First, Jerusalem is the head, and Jerusalem houses the king, a descendant of David, through whose line the Messiah comes. Second, Jerusalem is the location of God's temple, and it is the head of Israel. Therefore, when Isaiah prophecies the waters will only reach the 'neck,' he means Judah will suffer punishment, but Jerusalem will not fall.

"The last question is the most difficult. God sometimes speaks to Isaiah, and sometimes He gives him visions. Sometimes, God gives Him specific dates, such as in Chapter Seven when Isaiah prophecies the northern kingdom will no longer be a people in sixty-five years, thirty-five years from now. Sometimes, we can come close to an understanding of when an event will occur based on its setting. If Isaiah says Assyria will execute a judgment, it will happen while Assyria remains in power. Isaiah has already seen Babylon coming to power, which means they are the successor to Assyria. Therefore, any involvement between Judah and Babylon is some future event, and we don't know a specific date. Lastly, prophecies, such as Chapter Twenty-four, have no predictable time frame. God did not reveal the time to Isaiah, and it is not for us to know."

"Thank you, Hahn. Your teaching and friendship have been invaluable. This knowledge is essential to the Magi. I will send this collection to Baildan by diplomatic courier with an armed guard. While I was praying this morning, God revealed something about Scripture to me. When I look at the Palace walls in Nimrud, the recordings are about the king and his victories. The artists record nothing negative concerning the king. His victories are recorded but never his defeats or failures. Everything revolves around the king's glory and power.

"The Jewish Scriptures are the exact opposite. They are about God's Glory and Power. The Patriarchs, Judges, and Kings have all been flawed men, and Scripture records their sins and repentance. A good example is when Nathan confronts King David, and David confesses that he committed adultery with Uriah's wife and then had him murdered. God's Scriptures are unique, as is the nation of Israel. Now, if you will excuse us, we are due at the palace shortly to meet with Hezekiah."

"The men embraced each other, and Hahn left. Zaia and Javed changed into formal robes and walked to the palace.

The steward was expecting them and ushered them into the throne room. King Hezekiah was there sitting on his throne. Zaia and Javed approached and bowed in respect to the king. In Israel, men bowed to the king; they knelt only in the worship of God. *Another difference between Assyria and Judah* thought Zaia.

"I see my two favorite Assyrians have been busy this morning. How was your meeting with Hahn?" the king inquired.

Zaia was stunned the king knew about a meeting that had happened just moments before, but he hid his surprise. "The king honors us by taking notice of ones so lowly and unworthy as us. Our meeting with Hahn was enjoyable. He is kind enough to tutor us in the ways of YAHWEH and the knowledge of Scripture, and he is a good friend of ours."

"I find it interesting the Ambassador of Assyria takes such an interest in YAHWEH.'" Hezekiah was wise, and Zaia knew that. "It seems like a conflict of interest to me."

"Great King, my focus is on what is in the best interest of Assyria. Knowledge of one's friends and allies is of critical importance. YAHWEH and the worship of Him are at the very core of Judah. I would be remiss if I did not study the Scriptures."

"You are an interesting man, Zaia. You bear watching. But I am sure you didn't come here today to discuss theology. How can I help you?"

"King Hezekiah, I have heard rumors that a delegation is carrying gold to Egypt to seek assistance against King Sennacherib. I know these rumors must be false, and I thought it essential that you hear them."

The king leaned back on his throne and merely stared at Zaia. "Is there anything else you came to discuss?"

Zaia continued, "King Hezekiah, King Sennacherib has been busy subduing his eastern territories since he took the throne three years ago. He has completed those campaigns. Next, he will turn his attention to the Levantine states, Philistia, and Judah. You have all taken advantage of his inattention to stop paying tribute. You mistook his inattention as weakness. That is an error. When he comes, he will bring 400,000 men. He will come with chariots and horses, siege engines, battering rams, archers, slingers, and a vast infantry. They will come wearing iron from head to foot. They will go through Judah like locusts, and death and starvation will follow in their wake. I am not making threats. My wife and my daughter-in-law are Israelites. My son and I have lived in Jerusalem our entire lives. Yes, I speak for King Sennacherib, but more importantly, I represent my family. Seek peace with Assyria, send your annual tribute. I beg you."

The king looked down at Zaia. "You have been here since I became king. You have seen how much we have strengthened our fortified cities. Lachish and Jerusalem are impenetrable. I have added more warriors, horses, and chariots. We can, and we will resist Sennacherib if he comes."

"I feared that would be your answer. If this is the course you choose, then listen to your prophet, Isaiah, oh king! Only God can save you from the king of Assyria."

CHAPTER 12

Final Battle - 701 BC

Scene 1 Magi Journey - Day 58

The Magi found themselves in unknown territory, so Jahan called a Council meeting at daybreak.

"That was a difficult crossing, but the teamwork and leadership of this group were exemplary. There is no way we could have crossed in less time. Thank you all. Navid, we have the desert to our west and the river and marshland to our east. We do not know the people in this area but err on the side of caution. Assume everyone is hostile until you are certain otherwise. You need to range wider to the west. I am not too concerned about the river, but I'm apprehensive about what's in the desert. Have your men scout at least five miles or more to the west of our route. If there are problems, we need to know.

"Kevan, I have a nasty assignment for you. Pick four good men and have them cross back over the river. We need to know the location of the Immortals. We will be hard to find, but not impossible. The men you send need to be invisible; no one can see them. We need an exact count, and if possible, we need to know who is leading them.

"Navid, that brings me to another point. As you scout, be on the lookout for defensible positions. We cannot fight the Immortals in open territory; they will undoubtedly outnumber us. Are there any questions?"

Navid spoke, "Please define 'defensible position,' father."

"Sorry, Navid, I should have been clearer. In order of preference—a canyon with a narrow entrance and high ground to place archers. There are several cliffs along the river, I recall. We may find canyons or ravines on the desert side. If you cannot find a canyon, then an isthmus in the marshland. Again, look for a narrow entrance with water on three sides. It leaves us exposed to their archers but protects us from horses and infantry. If you cannot find the first two, then woodlands. Someplace we can set ambushes and pick them off piecemeal."

"I understand," Navid replied, "we will mark every location we find using a pole with a colored flag. We will mark Canyons with a green flag, isthmus with a yellow flag, and woodlands with red. The family can fall back to a marked area based on the amount of notification we receive."

"Are there any other questions?" inquired Jahan.

There were none. Everyone headed to the corrals to start their day.

At the corral, Navid called the Scouts together and explained the plan Jahan had outlined. "I want four riders on camels today. Your job will be to scout the desert. Keep a parallel route to the river, but I want you at least five miles west. If there's anyone out there, we need to know. Stay in pairs and stay sharp. We have no idea what or whom we may encounter."

They rode until late morning with no issues. Navid had located two defensible positions so far, one an isthmus at the edge of marshland and the other a thick copse of trees. The trees grew so closely together it would be impossible for horses to maneuver. He had not found canyons, but ahead he could see formations that looked hopeful. He heard the thunder of hooves and turned to see Esmail riding toward him.

"Where is Habib?" Navid shouted as Esmail attempted to get his camel under control.

"I left him about three miles from here," Esmail replied. "We saw a trail in the sand and followed it to the camp of slavers. There are fifteen men, and they have thirty slaves chained together. They did not see us, and I left Habib to keep an eye on them."

Navid blew his Ram's horn, signaling an emergency. The Scouts responded to the horn and came to Navid. "Esmail and Habib have found a slaver camp about three miles from here. They saw fifteen armed men; others could be out gathering slaves, or that could be all of them. There is no way to know. So, we will deal with what we know. We can't pass them by; there is too great a chance they could come upon an outrider or herdsman. We're going to hit them in a two-man column. We will ride through the center of their camp at a gallop, firing as we go. We will wheel at the end of their camp and repeat the process. After two passes, proceed on foot and clean up what's left. Any questions?"

There were none.

Navid and Utana were at the front of the column. They rode at a walk, lying on their horses' backs to reduce their profile. When they reached the spot where Esmail had left Habib, they had a quick conference. Habib assured them nothing had changed. Therefore, Navid stayed with his original plan. Navid and Utana led them at a walk again until they could see the edge of the slaver's camp. They dug their heels in, and the column came to a gallop.

The slavers, startled, hesitated for a moment, a deadly mistake for many of them. The Scouts rode through the center of them, firing arrows at point-blank range. More than half of the slavers were down. When they reached the end of the camp, the column of Scouts wheeled and began a second pass. A few of the slavers stood their ground, and the Scouts killed them. Several escaped the camp, but they were on foot. Navid signaled for four men to follow those who had escaped. The rest of the Scouts checked the slavers and dispatched any who were seriously wounded. Two had minor wounds and would survive. The riders Navid had sent after those who fled returned with four prisoners.

Navid attempted to interrogate the prisoners. They appeared to be Arabian, dark, swarthy long-bearded, ill-kept, and ill-tempered. He tried several dialects but could not understand them. He finally gave up trying. Navid instructed his men to strip the Arabians and unchain the slaves. He put the slave chains on the Arabians and drove them naked and without food and water into the desert. A decision he would live to regret.

The slaves were in poor condition and were of mixed nationalities. Some were black and of a tribe Navid had not seen before. Some were Persian or Ethiopian, and Navid was able to communicate with them. Their stories were all pretty much the same; the slavers had raided their village or caravan. They had killed the weak and had taken everyone else captive. Some captives had already been sold or traded to other groups. These captives did not know where the slavers were taking them.

Navid fed the prisoners and distributed the clothing of the slavers to them. There wasn't enough for everyone; some got robes, some got trousers, some received shirts. But in the end, everyone was at least partially dressed and seemed satisfied.

The captives broke into groups depending on their destination, and Navid gave them the slavers' horses. He also gave them half of his horses; the Scouts could double up for the ride back to camp. Groups assembled to leave when suddenly, a young black boy with short, tightly curled hair and large dark eyes ran over and clung to Navid's leg. Navid talked to the captives and determined the boy didn't belong to any of the groups. The slavers had killed both his parents, and no one knew the boy's home.

Navid looked down at the boy clinging to his leg and shook his head in resignation. It seems like the Magi Family just grew by one. Navid pointed to his chest and said, "Navid." The boy just looked at him blankly. Navid pointed to his chest again and repeated, "Navid." Then he pointed to the boy's chest.

Recognition dawned on the child's face, and he smiled, "Nura," he said, pointing to himself.

Navid took Nura and walked over to his horse. He pointed to himself and said, "Navid—man," he waved his hand over his head to show he was tall. "Nura—boy," he said, again using his hand to indicate Nura's height. Then he patted his horse and said, "Horse."

Nura grinned wildly; he ran over to the horse and patted its leg, saying, "horse." Then he pointed to Navid and repeated, "Navid—man," then indicating himself, "Nura—boy."

Nura was like a sponge, thought Navid; he absorbed language. Navid mounted and reached down for Nura's hand. Nura stuck his little hand into Navid's, and Navid swung him onto the horse in front of himself. On the ride back to camp, Nura pointed at everything, and Navid patiently named them all, "rock, Utana, bush, snake, Esmail, bird, hawk, tree," etc., etc.

They arrived at the camp, rode into the corral, and dismounted. Nura ran over to Utana and patted his leg, "Utana," then he ran over to Esmail and patted his leg, "Email," *well, close enough*, thought Navid. Both men grinned down at the boy.

Navid took Nura by the hand and walked through the camp to his yurt. Ava was standing outside talking to Pari. They spent much of the day together; they were kindred spirits. Ava looked at Navid, then down at Nura. "Well, this should be an interesting story. Who is this young man?"

Navid recounted the story of the slavers, the released captives, and the orphan Nura. "No one wanted to take him," he told Ava and Pari, "and I couldn't abandon him. So, say hello to the newest Magi."

Ava patted Nura on the head, "Hello Nura, my name is Ava."

Nura looked up at Navid quizzically.

Navid patted Ava on the shoulder, "Ava—wife," and he pointed back and forth at themselves, indicating they were together. Nura nodded in understanding. Then, Navid patted Pari on the shoulder and said, "Pari—sister."

Nura let go of Navid's hand and ran over to Ava. "Ava," he said in his little voice. Then he walked over to Pari, and sadness came over him, "Pari," he said, and he patted her withered legs. Then he hugged her. Tears streamed down Pari's face.

Without hesitation, she looked at Navid. "I will raise him."

Navid felt this was a purely emotional reaction. "Are you sure that's a good idea?" he asked her.

A voice spoke behind him. Tiz had just come from the corral, and he took in the scene in front of him, "Yes, she's sure," he said. "We will raise him." Tiz had watched Navid with the boy on the ride back to camp and was amazed at how fast the boy learned. He walked over to Nura, pointed to himself, and said, "Tiz—father," and then placed his hand on Pari's shoulder, "Pari—mother."

"Father," "Mother?" *Whoa*, thought Navid. *I wasn't ready for that.* Tiz had never talked to anyone about his feelings for Pari. *I better have a conversation with Jahan tonight.* To punctuate the point, Nura plopped down next to Pari and grinned at everyone.

Tiz picked up Pari and motioned for Nura to come with them. They went off to introduce Nura to the rest of the family.

Navid looked at Ava. "Father-Mother, did you see that coming?"

"Men can be such boneheads," she said, shaking her head.

Wait just a minute, Navid thought, *that's what Asha had called Jahan.* If that was true, he and his father needed to work on their observation and sensitivity skills.

Navid could smell the evening meal on the cooking fires. "Come on, let's eat; we can talk about this 'bonehead' comment later."

They joined Fardad and the rest of the family. Asha had already gathered food for them. Tiz, Pari, and Nura were there. "Navid looked at his parents. Well, what do you think of our family addition," he said, pointing at Nura.

Before Jahan could respond, Nura patted Jahan on the knee and said, "Jahan—grandpa."

"Absolutely correct, Nura, Jahan—grandpa," Navid said, laughing and pointing at Jahan, "grandpa."

"One more 'grandpa' from you, and you'll be riding night watch for the next month," Jahan growled, patting Nura on the head affectionately. "And as for what I think of the new addition, I would say you did well today. You took on the slavers, didn't lose a man, and rescued people who needed saving. I would say you had a pretty good day. We are extremely pleased to welcome Nura to the family."

Navid hesitated, "What do you think of the parenting arrangement?"

"You don't think Pari is up to raising a child, do you? Don't beat around the bush, Navid. Say what you mean. But I'll save you the trouble. Yes, I think Pari and Tiz are more than capable of caring for Nura. Your sister has more than enough love for ten mothers, and there is no better teacher in the Family. Tiz can teach him what it means to be a man, and who knows, Nura may be the next great sculptor in the Family," Jahan said, smiling at Tiz.

Navid blushed and looked at his sister, "I'm sorry, Pari; I don't doubt your abilities, but I don't want to see you put under undue stress."

Pari looked affectionately at her brother. "I'm not offended, Navid. You have always looked out for me. I want to raise Nura and share God's love and His word with him. Raising him is what God was saving me to do. But right now, He's calling me to examine the candidates."

Each year, the boys and girls turning fourteen go through a rite of passage to adulthood in the springtime. This year's candidates had already passed all of the physical tests, which—to say the least—were grueling, and tonight Pari would examine their knowledge of Scripture and history.

The family finished eating and walked to the clearing, where the children and their families had gathered. The youngest children were seated in the front row, and Nura looked up at Pari. "Go ahead," she said, pointing to the other children. "You may join them." Nura ran to the other children and began hugging them one by one.

Pari laughed as Tiz placed her on her speaking cushions. "I can see Nura is already introducing himself to each of you. He is the newest member of the Family and is just beginning to learn our language. So please be patient with him if he doesn't understand you."

Pari looked at everyone and began, "Tonight, we have six children standing for examination. If they pass, today will be their last day as a child. Tomorrow, they will be adult members of the Family, with all the responsibilities and rights that membership entails. Will the candidates please come forward?"

Three boys and three girls came forward and stood before Pari, facing the children and their families.

Pari explained. "I will ask a series of questions; the candidate on the far right will answer first. The person on their left will take the next question. We will continue this rotation until the examination is complete. Are there any questions?"

There were no questions. Pari began the examination on their knowledge of Scripture. Who is God? Who were the first man and woman, and what was their sin? Who were the Patriarchs of Israel? Who was Moses, and how did God use him? Name the Ten Commandments. How long was the period of the judges, and what happened during that period? The questions covered every significant event of Jewish history and God's revelation about His Holiness, Love, Judgment, and Redemption.

"That brings us to the prophet Isaiah," announced Ava. "What was his prophecy to Israel and Judah in the first five chapters?

The third girl in line answered the question. "He announced that God would judge Israel and Judah because they were thoroughly corrupt and worshipped other gods. Israel would cease to be a nation, but He would redeem a remnant from Judah. Isaiah called them to repent, but they would not listen."

"Very good. How was Isaiah called to be a prophet?"

The next candidate answered, "'In the year that King Uzziah died, I saw the Lord.'[17] God called Isaiah, Isaiah confessed his sin, and God cleansed him, and commissioned him to take the message of judgment to Israel and Judah."

"Excellent. Does God bring his judgment on only Israel and Judah?"

"No," said the last candidate, "God pronounces judgment on all of Israel's enemies: Babylon, Assyria, Philistia, Moab, Syria, Ethiopia, Egypt, Edom, Arabia, and Tyre. All of these nations God judged."[18]

"One last question. Were these prophecies fulfilled?"

The girl who had started the responses now received the final question. "We now know that all of the prophecies of Isaiah, Micah, and Amos against these nations were fulfilled."

Pari probed the candidate further. "Isn't there a problem in Isaiah when he prophesies Israel will cease to exist as a nation in sixty-five years? Hoshea is the last king of Israel; Shalmaneser V removed him 724 years ago and destroyed Samaria. King Hoshea was removed ten years after Isaiah's prophecy."

The candidate turned her head and grinned at Pari, then turned and addressed the children. "That is true; Hoshea was removed and was the last king of Israel, but the final deportations of Israel did not take place until Esarhaddon was the king of Assyria 669 years ago.[19] Sixty-five years after Isaiah's prophecy—'And within sixty-five years Ephraim will be shattered from being a people.' After the final deportation, the tribes of the northern kingdom were no more."

"Excellent work, candidates; that completes your examination. May I be the first to welcome you as adults into the Magi Family?"

The Magi Family greeted Pari's announcement with loud applause and cheers. The new adults rushed to their families, who greeted them with hugs and congratulations.

Tiz carried Pari from the podium, and Rahim replaced her.

Rahim stood on the podium and said one word, "Sennacherib."

A hush fell on the Family as Rahim unrolled the scroll to read the last Assyrian campaign against Judah…

Scene 2 Sennacherib - 701 BC

Benjamin sat by his mother's bed, holding her hand. Baildan, who was fifty-nine and showed advanced age, sat on the other side of the bed. Rachael's skin was feverish, and there was perspiration on her brow. Her breathing was labored. She had gotten progressively worse the last two days. The healers had been unable to do anything to help her.

Baildan wet a cloth and bathed her forehead, trying to cool her. Rachael's eyes fluttered open, and when she saw Benjamin and Baildan both there, she smiled.

Rachael gasped, "I'm glad you are both here. I was afraid I wouldn't get to say goodbye to Benjamin before he left. I want to tell you both how much I love you. The greatest joy in my life has been to be Baildan's wife and your mother, Benjamin. I could not have wished for more. Benjamin, Meesha is aging, but hopefully, Zaia will be home soon. It will fall on you two to ensure the Word of God is preserved and taught to the family. The survival of this family will depend on their faith in God. This is clear to me. Say goodbye to Naomi and the children for me; tell them I love them."

"Mother, they will be in shortly, and you will be able to tell them yourself." Benjamin pleaded.

"Just do as I tell you, Benjamin. One last thing: when you are in Judah, go to Mizpah, to our old family home. Do you remember where it is?" Benjamin nodded yes. "There is a treasure in gold hidden in the wall. Do you remember how to open the wall?" Again, Benjamin nodded yes. The gold is yours; it's time to retrieve it." Benjamin nodded yes, not wanting to argue and upset his mother, but the gold was the last thing on his mind.

Rachael looked at Baildan, "Will you kiss me goodbye, my love?"

Tears were streaming down Baildan's face. "What's this nonsense about goodbye? You are getting better. You're much stronger this morning."

"Baildan, we both know that is not true. I have seen this fever before, and few, if any, survive. Now kiss me goodbye."

Baildan held Rachael's head gently in his big hands and kissed her tenderly. When he looked at his wife, her eyes were closed. She let out a long sigh and lay still. She was gone. Both men sat there, crying and holding her hands. The woman they had loved and who had loved them was gone. She had cared for and nurtured them. She had been the home to which they always returned after every campaign.

Naomi, Benjamin's wife, entered the room and saw the two men weeping. She knelt beside them at the bedside and mourned with them. Her mother-in-law had been a great woman and a great friend. Naomi was of the tribe of Naphtali in the kingdom of Israel. The Assyrians deported her to Nineveh after Tiglath-Pileser III defeated the northern kingdom. Rachael had seen her working for a merchant in Nineveh as a slave. She talked to her whenever she visited the merchant, and Rachael became convinced this was the right woman for Benjamin. Rachael approached the merchant and inquired what his price would be for Naomi. At first, the merchant insisted she was invaluable and priceless. Rachael was insistent and continued to pursue the merchant. Frustrated, she finally played her trump card and informed him she wanted Naomi to be Benjamin's wife. The merchant paled, stammered, and apologized profusely. Everyone knew Benjamin, the king's champion. The merchant insisted he could not accept payment from the mother of Benjamin and released Naomi to Rachael.

Rachael had taken Naomi home. Naomi bathed and put on the new clothes Rachael had given her. She was beautiful—tall for an Israeli woman, with light-brown skin and long eyelashes. Rachael adorned her in gold necklaces and armbands and brought her to the evening meal, seating her next to Benjamin. Benjamin was speechless; Naomi was beautiful, graceful, and eloquent. They were married shortly after that and had three children in the years following. You could tell the length of each military campaign of Assyria by the ages of the children.

The children heard the mourning and gathered the Magi Family's women, who prepared Rachael for burial. Following the Law and Traditions, Rachael was to be buried that day before sunset. There were many caves in the family's canyon, and Baildan had chosen one several years ago to serve as his and Rachael's tomb. The women prepared Rachael, and the Magi Family gathered. The men lifted her body and carried her to the cave. They gently placed her on a rock shelf inside the cave and rolled a large stone across the cave entrance. The Magi knelt outside the cave, praying and mourning the loss of Rachael. Baildan and Benjamin had put on sackcloth and covered their heads with ashes.

Baildan and Benjamin mourned until sunset. Then they went home, cleaned up, and sat down to eat.

Baildan looked at Benjamin and quoted from memory 2 Samuel:

"And David said to his servants, 'Is the child dead?' They said, 'He is dead.' … He then went to his own house…He said, 'While the child was still alive, I fasted and wept, for I said, "Who knows whether the Lord will be gracious to me, that the child may live? But now he is dead. Why should I fast? Can I bring him back again? I shall go to him, but he will not return to me.'"[20]

"I believe what God has revealed, Benjamin. Rachael will not return to us, but we will go to her. Praise God that will be true of all of us," Baildan said, looking at Naomi and the children, "Death is not the end for us. We have faith in God's grace and mercy, and we place ourselves in His hands. Regardless of what happens to us in this world, we will be together again if you seek God with all your heart."

They had finished eating when the household steward came in, followed by one of King Sennacherib's messengers. The messenger delivered a sealed document to Benjamin, and Benjamin opened the document and rose.

"It looks like I will be returning to Judah sooner than Mother thought. The king has called for me." He stood to leave, and Baildan rose and followed him out of the house.

"Father, where are you going?" Benjamin asked.

"With you to the palace, of course. Did you think I would let you go alone?"

"Father, I don't want to seem rude," Benjamin said, "but the king did not call for you."

"An obvious oversight on his part," Baildan replied. By the time they reached the courtyard, the servants had brought two horses from the corral. *It looks as if I'm the only one who thought I was going to the palace alone*, Benjamin thought. The men rode the rest of the way to the palace in silence. Sennacherib had built a new palace in Nineveh just last year on the southwest side of the city. And the palace was not the only construction project. Sennacherib had decided to turn the city of Nineveh into a city fit for the king of kings. The city walls were extended and thickened, and he built many new public buildings.

The two men arrived at the palace and entered the throne room. They made obeisance to the king and waited for him to speak.

"I only called for Benjamin, Baildan. Why are you here?" demanded the king.

"My lord, it is obvious you are preparing for war, and you will need all of your generals."

"Baildan, we are going to war, but you have earned your rest. You have fought enough campaigns. You are getting a little long in the tooth for this. War is a young man's endeavor."

"My king, I do have a few gray hairs, which is why you need me. According to Zaia, King Hezekiah has been preparing for war for the past three years. You will need your best generals to defeat both Lachish and Jerusalem. My King, it would be an honor to lead one of the armies on this campaign."

"Very well, Baildan, if anyone has earned the honor, it is certainly you. You and Benjamin will each command an army of 100,000 men. There will be two more generals; we will take a force of four-hundred-thousand men on this campaign, and I will lead the attack."

Baildan and Benjamin both dropped to their knees and placed their heads on the marble floor. The king had done them a great honor.

"Arise, gentlemen, and see to your armies. We leave in two weeks, and you have much to do."

The two men did as instructed and backed out of the throne room.

"What are you doing, Father? You know how difficult this campaign will be. Why are you doing this?" Benjamin pleaded.

Baildan looked sadly at his son, "I have lost Rachael, the love of my life, my north star. I cannot sit in that house thinking of her, seeing her things every day, and grieving with each reminder. I will do what I have always done. I will go to war, and I will crush the enemies of Assyria. That will be my focus. I also have a second reason; we are going up against King

Hezekiah. He is a king like King David, they say. He has taken down the altars to foreign gods and worships only Jehovah. God will fight for him. I have a feeling before this is over, you will need me, and I will be there."

The following two weeks went by quickly. They appointed division commanders and company commanders. Faithful Samir was still with them and would lead the cavalry. Ashur was still alive, but his memory was diminishing. Many days he did not recognize his old friends. At other times, he remembered the details of past battles in great detail. He lived at the Magi compound and had someone to care for him at all times. Before he left, Baildan went to see Ashur one last time.

Ashur was having a good day and recognized Baildan instantly. Baildan hugged him and said his goodbyes. He knew that at least one of them would not make it to the end of this campaign. With tears in his eyes, he went to the corral. He and Benjamin rode out of the compound. They were going to war!

They followed the same route they had followed thirty-three years earlier. They came to Byblos, and the city submitted without resistance. At Sidon, the king of Sidon foolishly chose to resist. The Assyrians defeated Sidon, and the city paid the usual penalty for resistance. King Sennacherib beheaded the leadership and other leading citizens and piled the heads in two mounds on either side of the city gate. The same thing happened in Ashkelon. After Ashkelon, the army continued down the coast, subduing Ashdod without resistance. After Ashdod, the army swung inland and came down the east side of the Jordan River and subdued Moab and Edom, also without resistance. The cities that did not resist paid tributes; people were deported and replaced, and Sennacherib left Assyrian officials in charge of the city or region.

After Moab, the army turned west again, and once past the Salt Sea, they traveled north, heading for their real objective, Lachish. Lachish was the second most fortified city in Judea, and King Sennacherib did not want the warriors from Lachish at his back when he attacked Jerusalem.

Baildan arrived with his army at Lachish and went to the king's tent. Benjamin and King Sennacherib were already there. Also present was the Tartan, the second-in-command to the king, the Chief Eunuch, and the

Chief Cupbearer or Rabshakeh. These were powerful men in Assyria. Two more generals came, and the war council was complete.

"Before we plan the attack on Lachish, your nephew, Zaia," the king said, nodding at Baildan, "has sent a messenger with a plea from King Hezekiah. It appears the king has had a change of heart and is seeking peace. I sent him a response telling him I required three hundred talents of silver and thirty talents of gold. I am sure he will reject such a ridiculous amount, but it doesn't matter. We will lay siege to Lachish and Jerusalem, and we will put an end to this Hezekiah once and for all. I want the Tartan to take the Rabshakeh, the Chief Eunuch, and half the army to Jerusalem, blockade the city, send a message to Hezekiah, but they are not to attack. When we have finished with Lachish, the entire army will lay siege to Jerusalem. Take Baildan and Benjamin's armies with you. I will attack Lachish."

This was the moment Baildan had feared, "Great king," he intervened, "I will accompany the Tartan to Jerusalem, but keep Benjamin with you. When you breach the walls, the fighting will be fierce. You will want Benjamin with you; his army should be the first through the breach."

The king studied Baildan for a moment before responding, "Very well, Baildan, it shall be as you say. Benjamin will stay with me. The Tartan may choose the other general who will go with you. Benjamin, I want your cavalry scouts ranging as far as Ekron. I do not trust the king of Egypt, and I believe he will seek to take advantage and combine forces with either the Judeans or the Philistines."

Everyone had their orders, and the king dismissed the generals. Once they were out of the tent, Benjamin approached Baildan. "What was that? Why did you want me at Lachish?" he asked.

"Have you forgotten the premonition I had in Nineveh? I do not want you anywhere near Hezekiah or Jerusalem. And the king will need you here. Lachish will be a tough city to take, and I believe the Egyptians are on the move. I am sure that when your scouts get to Philistia, they will find the Egyptians already there. The king will find himself up against one or two other armies, and he will need you."

Benjamin could only nod in agreement; as usual, Baildan was way ahead of him. He may not be the warrior he had been, but his tactical skills were undiminished.

The Tartan left with his two armies. Benjamin sent out his scouts and then toured the walls of Lachish, looking for the best place to build the siege ramps. There were too many archers and slingers at the main gate, and the grade was too steep. Benjamin decided to build two ramps, one against the west wall and the other at the northwest corner. He had the army begin work at once. He brought the mobile missile platforms forward and began clearing the walls of enemy archers and slingers. The massive army began loading and delivering wagon loads of dirt, which they dumped against the wall. They deposited load after load of dirt. Periodically, they placed a layer of trees to increase the rise rate and add stability to the loose soil. The work went well the first day, and Benjamin was confident he would bring siege engines forward tomorrow.

The Tartan and his armies marched on Jerusalem. The Tartan marched the army to the city's southwest corner and encamped in the fuller's field. Coincidentally the same fuller's field in which Isaiah had confronted King Ahaz thirty-three years before. As they neared Jerusalem, an armed guard came out of the gates and boldly marched up to the Assyrians. The guard commander informed the Tartan, they were escorting the silver and gold demanded by King Sennacherib. The Tartan smirked at him and allowed him to pass. He sent a messenger forward who yelled to the men on the wall that the Tartan would speak with King Hezekiah. Offended Sennacherib himself had not come, the king sent a delegation to meet with the Tartan. The Tartan sent the Rabshakeh forward to deliver King Sennacherib's address:

"Say to Hezekiah, 'Thus says the great king, the king of Assyria: On what do you rest this trust of yours? Do you think that mere words are strategy and power for war? In whom do you now trust, that you have rebelled against me? Behold! You are trusting now in Egypt that broken reed of a staff, which will pierce the hand of any man who leans on it. Such is Pharaoh King of Egypt to all who trust in him. But if you say to me, 'We trust in the Lord our God,' is it not he whose high places and altars Hezekiah has removed, saying to Judah and to Jerusalem,

"You shall worship before this altar in Jerusalem. Come now; make a wager with my master, the king of Assyria: I will give you two-thousand horses, if you are able on your part to set riders on them. How then can you repulse a single captain among the least of my master's servants when you trust in Egypt for chariots and for horsemen? Moreover, is it without the Lord that I have come up against this place to destroy it? The Lord said to me, 'Go up against this land and destroy it.'"[21]

The envoys of King Hezekiah begged the Rabshakeh not to speak in the standard Hebrew of the people. Still, the Rabshakeh spoke even louder, telling the people on the wall not to trust Hezekiah, telling them if they surrender, the Assyrians will deport them, but the king will place them in a land just like this full of grain, vineyards, and fruit trees. If the Judeans resisted, they would die; if they surrendered, they would live. Deportation will be inconvenient, but at least they will be alive. The Rabshakeh then taunted Hezekiah and God. He said no god had ever saved a people from the king of Assyria, and no god ever could. All gods were powerless against King Sennacherib.

King Hezekiah's envoys shredded their clothes in anguish over the words of the Rabshakeh and reported the words of the Rabshakeh to their king.[22]

Upon hearing the message, King Hezekiah tore his clothes and went to the house of the Lord to seek God. After some time, he sent his representatives and the senior priest to speak to Isaiah. They dressed in sackcloth and went to see the prophet.

Isaiah was in his inner chamber praying. Zaia and Hahn were in the outer chamber of the prophet's home, discussing the message delivered by the Rabshakeh.

"What are your thoughts?" inquired Zaia.

"There are several lies and some misconceptions," replied Hahn. "King Sennacherib has assumed that King Hezekiah formed an alliance with Egypt and relied on the Egyptians to rescue him. This is not true; King Hezekiah is not relying on Egypt. The Rabshakeh also stated that the Lord God had called King Sennacherib to destroy Jerusalem. That is a lie. God called the king to punish Judah with a rod. He never called him to destroy King Hezekiah or Jerusalem. The greatest misconception of Sennacherib is that YAHWEH is the same as his gods of wood, stone, and gold. He believes God is powerless against the army of Assyria. That is a misconception he will not live to regret. He will pay a heavy price for taunting the God of all creation."

There was a commotion as the king's envoys and the senior priests entered the outer chamber. Isaiah heard the noise and came from his inner room. The envoys took a circuitous route to their request and asked Isaiah if he thought God had heard the words of the Rabshakeh. They then asked Isaiah to pray to God to rebuke King Sennacherib.

Isaiah said to them, "Say to your master, 'Thus says the Lord: Do not be afraid because of the words that you have heard, with which the servants of the king of Assyria have reviled me. Behold, I will put a spirit in him, so that he shall hear a rumor and return to his own land, and I will make him fall by the sword in his own land.'"[23]

Meanwhile, in Lachish, the siege mounds were complete but at a terrible cost. Benjamin had lost five- thousand men to the Israeli archers and slingers. Benjamin used the darkness to help diminish the archers' effectiveness and rolled the siege engines into place. In the top of the forty-foot tall siege engines were archers and slingers. They were now on an even footing with the defenders on the wall. Four siege engines went to work, and the incessant hammering began. Inch by inch, stone by stone, the wall lost the battle with the machines. The machines hammered away for two more days before scouts rode into camp and reported to Benjamin.

"It is as you feared, General," one of them said. "The Egyptians are in Libnah. The Ethiopians are also there, and King Tirhakah of Ethiopia is leading the army."

Benjamin instructed the scout to come with him, and he went to the tent of the king.

The two men entered the tent, made obeisance, and knelt before King Sennacherib.

"Stand," ordered the king. "What news do you bring me?"

"My King, you were right in telling me to send scouts into Philistia. The scout has seen the combined armies of Egypt and Ethiopia in Libnah, under King Tirhakah."

"What is their strength and disposition?"

The scout looked at Benjamin, who nodded. The scout never looked directly at the king as he spoke, "I estimate their strength at just over two-hundred thousand. They have a large core of chariots, as the Egyptians usually do. The chariots are two-man chariots, smaller, lighter, and faster than ours, but only half the firepower. They have a sizeable cavalry, but most of their infantry is light infantry. They will not be able to stand up to our heavy infantry once we are in close."

"Excellent work," the king said, pointing to his steward. "Reward this man; he has faithfully served his king." With that, the king dismissed the scout, and he backed out of the tent. "Benjamin, send a messenger to the Tartan. Have him send us fifty-thousand men. The men from Jerusalem will continue the siege work while I lead this army to Libnah to destroy the Egyptians. We will force-march through the night and attack him before dawn tomorrow."

Benjamin sent a messenger to the Tartan in Jerusalem, and by mid-afternoon, reinforcements arrived from Jerusalem. Benjamin had hoped to see Baildan leading the troops, but a division commander led them. He prepared the army for the night march, and the king led 200,000 men north to Libnah. They arrived just before dawn.

The king moved the chariots and cavalry forward and sent them at a gallop at the center of the Egyptian camp. The archers, slingers, and infantry followed at a steady jog in perfect formation. They had practiced this formation many times, and the army executed it flawlessly. Benjamin was in one of the lead chariots. Baildan had taught him long ago to lead from the front. As the charging mass neared the camp, alarm bugles sounded, and men scurried from tents. The leading edge of the chariots and cavalry loosed their arrows. A storm of arrows greeted the men emerging from their tents. Benjamin could see this battle would not last long. He pointed his spear at a large tent in the camp center, and his chariot driver aimed for it. The back half of the Egyptian camp had gotten organized, and a wall of infantry, led by King Tirhakah's guard, had formed before the tent. The chariots smashed into the infantry at many points, and the Assyrians dismounted and fought as infantry. The fighting was fierce, and men on both sides died. Benjamin's chariot delivered him in the very center of the king's guard. These were the finest warriors in Egypt. Facing Benjamin was five Ethiopian warriors, all well over six feet tall, with plumed headdresses. The warriors carried spears and shields made from various animal skins— leopard, lion, or rhinoceros. Undaunted, Benjamin faced the warrior in the center while his chariot mates faced the other four warriors.

The giant warrior was skilled, but he was soon bleeding from numerous wounds, and Benjamin finished it by neatly slicing off the man's shield arm at the elbow. The Assyrian next to Benjamin was down, and Benjamin turned his attention to the man who had killed him. This man was equally skilled and managed to dent Benjamin's helmet, but Benjamin was unfazed. He pressed the attack and shattered the man's spear. Benjamin dropped his sword, caught the broken spear in mid-air, reversed it, and drove it through the Ethiopians' right eye. He squatted and retrieved his sword, his eyes never leaving the battle in front of him.

Benjamin saw motion in front of the king's tent—it was Tirhakah and his court jumping into waiting chariots and fleeing toward Egypt.

When the Egyptians saw their fleeing leaders, the rout was on. The Assyrians smashed the Egyptian wall of infantry. Leaderless men sought to evade the onrushing Assyrian infantry. They had no support from the rear, and as Egyptians died, there was no one to step into their place.

The Assyrians forced their way into the gaps in the Egyptian line, surrounding each cut-off group, killing them quickly and easily. The remainder of the Egyptian army was in full flight. King Sennacherib's signal core sounded halt, and the army stopped in place; not a man moved. The king saw nothing to be gained by chasing the fleeing Egyptians; he had more pressing business in Lachish. The King turned the army around, and without rest, marched them back to Lachish.

The army arrived in Lachish by late morning. The siege engines had worked through the night, and holes appeared in the wall. The gaps widened, and soon upper sections of the wall and parapet crumbled. Defenders on the top of the wall had to abandon their positions. Assyrian infantry and archers rushed forward. The infantry removed rubble to access the widening gaps, and the archers poured fire through the openings into the city. All four siege engines had breached the wall, and Benjamin had his forces poised to rush into the gaps.

When Benjamin was satisfied that the breach was wide enough, he removed the siege engines and attacked. The Judeans fought bravely and to the last man, but there was no stopping the relentless Assyrians. They killed, sacked, and raped, taking many prisoners they would deport to other areas of the empire. The Assyrians cleared the city of anything living or valuable. Then the army tore it down stone by stone until Lachish was no more than a pile of rubble. The army had been marching and fighting for forty-eight straight hours, and men dropped where they stood. Exhaustion overtook the army.

Baildan stood before the wall of Jerusalem and turned to watch the sunset behind him. It was a typical high-desert sunset. Heat still shimmered from the cooling rocks, and the sky turned a dark crimson as the moon showed itself in a barely visible silhouette. He continued to watch the sky as the first stars appeared, and the sky became even blacker. The stars took on life and movement. Comet tails appeared; night predators flew. God's creation never ceased to amaze Baildan, and he thanked God for allowing him to be a part of this moment.

The king had sent some of the troops back this afternoon from Lachish. As night fell, the army in front of the walls of Jerusalem numbered around 185,000 men. Baildan went to his tent, stripped off his armor, and lay down. He had barely slept when he felt someone touch his chest. He snapped awake, grabbed his fighting knife, and sat up. In the tent was the shadow of a man. The man had something like hyssop in his hand, and Baildan felt wetness on his chest.

The man in the shadows said, "Fear not; the Lord is with you." And the man in the shadows was gone. Baildan's heart was hammering in his chest. He could barely breathe, and yet at that exact moment, he felt peace like he had never known before. He calmed and sat there for a moment. He tasted the fluid on his chest; it had the coppery taste of blood. Baildan was confused at first, and then, for no explainable reason, the story of the Jewish Passover came to his mind. In Egypt, the Israelites had put lamb's blood on the doorposts of their homes, and the Angel of the Lord passed by them. He heard the sound of rushing wind coming from south of the camp, not like the onrush of a storm but more like a steady sighing. Baildan leaped up and ran from the tent. He watched the guards standing watch on the camp's perimeter, and one by one, they dropped. There were no sounds, no screams, no panic or alarm. Men simply dropped where they stood. The sighing of the wind continued for some time, and then it stopped. Baildan walked through the camp. Men lay on their sleeping mats; some sat slumped next to the night fires, the night guards lay in heaps. They all had one thing in common—they were dead.

The story of the Angel of the Lord killing the firstborn of Egypt came to Baildan's mind, and he knew that was what he was seeing. "Life and death are mine, says the Lord," and before Baildan was visual evidence. One moment these men had been alive, and in a moment, with no violence or bloodshed, the Lord had removed their life force and their souls. Baildan stood there and trembled at the mighty power of the Lord.

He walked to the leadership tent and found the Tartan and the king's staff all dead. Lastly, he looked to the edge of the camp where the cavalry had camped and forced himself to face what he dreaded. When he reached the area, the first person he saw was Eilbra, lying with his hand on top of his ram's horn. He walked looking at men he had ridden with for years and others new to this campaign. He stopped walking and knelt next to Samir. He bowed his head and prayed for his old friend and all the men he loved who lay dead all around him. This slaughter was the hand of God, and God had used these men to show His Power and Glory, but that did not ease the pain. His legs were weak and shaking, but he willed himself to stand. He walked toward the corral and, when he arrived, found three other men standing by the horses. They all had one thing in common; they had blood in the middle of their chests. Baildan questioned them and found they were all from northern Israel and had joined the Assyrian army during the deportations. They were men who believed in and worshipped YAHWEH, and they had been saved by the Lord this night. Baildan and the men rode to Lachish. Someone had to tell the king. Baildan thought of the sight the Judeans would see in the morning when they woke and saw 185,000 dead Assyrians lying outside the walls of Jerusalem.

Baildan and the men arrived at Lachish just as the sun was beginning to rise. Baildan sought Benjamin and found him sleeping with his men outside the breach in the wall on the west side of what had been the city. Baildan woke Benjamin and told him to follow him. Benjamin was confused in his sleep-deprived state but did as Baildan asked.

Baildan found the king's steward and had him wake the king. The king entered the command tent; furious Baildan had woken him.

"Baildan, what is the meaning of this?" the king bellowed.

"Great King, I barely know how to tell you this. Your army in Jerusalem is no more."

The king was dumbfounded; his mind could not process what he was hearing. "You mean there has been a battle? How many men did we lose? What happened?"

Baildan shook his head. "There was no battle, my king. The Angel of the Lord passed through the camp during the night and took the life of all 185,000 men. He left four people alive, of whom I am one, so that we might tell you what happened. I walked through the camp after the angel passed through. Everyone lay there as if they were still sleeping. There had not been a sound: no struggle, no sign of violence, and no blood. The Angel of the Lord had extracted the life force of every man. The Tartan is dead, and so is the rest of your staff."

Madness came over King Sennacherib; he looked wildly around the tent, expecting to see the Angel of the Lord coming for him. He screamed at his steward to pack everything; the army was leaving immediately. The king yelled at Baildan to get the army on the move. He rushed from the tent, dressed, and was in his chariot in moments. Baildan did not even recognize the king. This was not the man he had known all these years.

The army had subdued the western states; they had defeated the army of Egypt and had destroyed Lachish. Yet they slunk home like a defeated army.

As Baildan rode next to Benjamin on the long ride home, he asked, "Do you realize what we have seen?"

Benjamin wasn't quite sure what Baildan was talking about, "In the past mile? In the past week? I don't know what you mean."

"You and I, we have seen it all. We have heard it all. We heard the prophecies of judgment from Isaiah, and then we saw them all fulfilled. We were there. We weren't just there; we were a part of the arm of God's judgment. Can you imagine?"

The weight of Baildan's revelation dawned on Benjamin. He said, "We have a responsibility now, Father. We must record it, all of it. The Magi who follow us must know, and they must never forget. The judgments are not over; they will continue. Isaiah has said Assyria would fall and Babylon would rise. Then Babylon will fall."

Baildan nodded, saying, "My thought exactly. I didn't realize when I started the school what I was creating. It's not just a school; it will be an enclave of believers. A Family inside Assyria, Babylon, and whatever empire follows that knows the truth and understands that it comes from God. We must teach our children what is to come and Who it is who brings judgment and redemption. We must record everything we have seen these past thirty-four years, and we must continue to record everything as God unfolds his plan of judgment and redemption. That is our responsibility."

Benjamin smiled at his father and said, "When we get home, we will sit with your brother, Meesha. We will tell him all we have seen, and he will write it all down. This is not the end of the Magi journey; this is just the beginning."

Scene 3 Magi Camp - Day 58

Rahim closed the scroll and looked at the Magi Family in front of him.

"Tonight, we have finished the story of Assyria. Assyria was the first great empire and reached its peak under King Esarhaddon. Assyria destroyed and dispersed Israel, just as foretold by the prophets, and they punished Judah. Every nation upon whom the prophets pronounced judgment, that judgment was executed by Assyria. The kings of Assyria overstepped the bounds of their authority, as laid out by God, and Assyria will pay a severe price, but that is a story for another day."

"Baildan and Benjamin did stop at Mizpah on the way back to Assyria and retrieved the gold belonging to Benjamin's family," said Rahim, who nodded at Fardad. "Much of that gold is still with us today. A few years after their return from Judah, Baildan passed away quietly in his sleep. Benjamin said he was still healthy, that he died of a broken heart, and Ashur also died peacefully.

"Benjamin and Zaia took on the leadership of the Magi Family, but that is also a story for another day."

Then, Rahim looked around the clearing and saw young heads nodding. "It has been a long day, and we still have far to go. I think it's time we all got some sleep." He stepped down from the platform and went to his tent.

CHAPTER 13

The Immortals

Scene 1 The Immortals - Day 57

Sasan rode next to Parviz, the leader of the Immortals. Parviz had a dark complexion, a thick beard squared off below his neck, and deep-set eyes. He was massively built, not tall, just thick. He was brutish, heavily muscled with a layer of fat on top of the muscle.

Men had sometimes mistaken Parviz as fat and sedentary and challenged him to combat. In all cases, it had been a fatal mistake. He only loved two things—to see people suffer and to inflict pain.

Combat was the only subject he knew. And riding next to him day after day was the worst thing Sasan could imagine. Parviz sensed how uncomfortable he made Sasan and reveled in doing anything he could to increase that discomfort.

Six days previously, the Immortals had reached a point on the Tigris river, south of Babylon, and then traveled southeast on the east side of the Tigris River. Parviz believed it was the most logical route for the Magi. But Sasan knew it was a waste of time, and it was the last thing Jahan would do. Sasan believed the Magi were between the Tigris and Euphrates, but it was also likely they may have crossed to the west side of the Euphrates.

Either of those scenarios was possible, but Parviz had ignored Sasan's input. So, they had wasted six days. They were now forty miles north of the confluence of the two rivers, and Parviz brought the column to a halt.

"It is obvious the Magi are not on this side of the Tigris. Are you trying to aid your family by deceiving me, Sasan? Why did you suggest this route?"

Sasan was dumbfounded, "Commander," he said calmly, "I believe I told you that Jahan would not stay east of the Tigris."

"You said no such thing, and if the Magi escape, I shall make sure the Queen is aware of your deceit."

Sasan flushed red but remained calm. Then he said, "The Magi cannot move as fast as cavalry, with their flocks and herds of animals. They cannot escape, but we cannot waste any more time. I suggest we cross the Tigris, divide the force, and proceed north along the east bank of the Euphrates and the west bank of the Tigris. It remains possible that Jahan has crossed the Euphrates and is moving up through the edge of the desert. If he has, we will position ourselves in Babylon and wait for him there. We must keep ourselves between him and Ctesiphon. Once the Magi reach Parthian territory, we cannot pursue. As you know, our peace treaty with the Parthians is tenuous at best. They are prickly people. The Queen has forbidden us from entering their territory."

Parviz stared at Sasan as if he had not even spoken. Turning, Parviz looked back and waved for his second-in-command to come forward. The man rode up, and Parviz gave instructions. "Turn the troop; we will cross the Tigris here. You will take half of the men and proceed north along the east bank of the Euphrates. I will take the rest and sweep north following the west bank of the Tigris. We will halt when we reach Babylon. You will ride from sunup to sundown, with minimal rest breaks. Time is becoming critical. Is that understood?"

The junior officer nodded yes, turned his horse, and led the force across the Tigris. The party split into two, as Parviz had commanded, and they proceeded north. They had ridden for two hours when they came upon a party of five hunters from a local village.

Parviz questioned the five men, "We are looking for a large caravan of two hundred people who passed this way. When did you see them?"

The leader of the men said, "Commander, we have seen no caravans, nor have we heard any discussion of one."

Parviz glared at the man. "I will ask you one last time. When did you see them?"

The villager saw the look on Parviz's face and stammered, "Commander, if we had seen such a party, I would gladly tell you, but we have not seen anyone."

Parviz dismounted and ordered the men stripped and bound. Leyla was next to Sasan. She turned her horse and rode away from the scene. Sasan began to follow when Parviz commanded, "Stop. Leyla may go, but you will stay. I want you to see what happens to traitors."

Parviz personally tortured the men, slitting the skin on the soles of their feet, skinning parts of their arms and legs, lighting small fires under them, and scorching large portions of their bodies. Parviz was sweating heavily and had a look of ecstasy on his face. Sasan retched; he didn't know how much more of this he could take.

The men screamed and begged; they said anything to make the torture stop, but it did not stop until the last of them was dead. It had taken hours. The Immortals stood at attention through the entire process. This was not the first time they had seen Parviz enjoy himself. They were disgusted by the man, but they knew better than to show any emotion.

Parviz walked to the riverbank and washed. He walked back with a look of complete satisfaction on his face. "We have wasted enough time here; mount up." They continued north, following the Tigris.

Sasan stared at the man. Some men occasionally did evil things, but a few men were genuinely evil. Sasan knew he was in the presence of evil. This man was a monster.

Scene 2 Magi Route - Day 60

The Scouts rode out of the camp to lead the Family north. Esmail was not with them, he had some intestinal issues, and Navid ordered him to stay in camp. Habib would lead the camel riders to scout the desert, but he was no Esmail.

"Are you certain about this Navid?" inquired Utana. "Habib is not known for having the best sense of direction. Do you think he can find his way back?"

"I doubt it," said Navid. "That boy is as lost as a duck in the desert, but he has good men with him. They will get him back." Both men laughed as they watched Habib and the camel team head into the desert.

Navid and Utana rode in silence for a while. Navid finally spoke, "How is Fahnik doing? Is she concerned?"

"I would be lying if I said she wasn't concerned, but she is not afraid. She believes what Grandfather Fardad has told us. 'God has called us, and He will get us through.' This she firmly believes. But God never said we would all get through. She is concerned how many we may lose before this journey is over."

Navid nodded in agreement, "That is Ava's and my concern also. I think you know I was not happy when this trip began. I was mad at God. I had been angry at Him for a long time. When we were going to bed last night, Ava asked me if I would pray. I told her that her prayers were much sweeter than mine and asked her to pray. She said I was the head of our household and that if I did not lead us spiritually, we would never be whole and complete. She shamed me, Utana. I have been a selfish fool. All I could see was what I wanted, what I needed. I didn't think how my actions would affect everyone around me. Forgive me, Utana; I have not been the friend I should be. I have not been praying for you and Fahnik, but all that changed last night. I prayed with Ava last night; it was like a dam bursting, words flowing from me like water. God lifted the scales from my eyes, and He lifted me. We are here because He wants us to be here. What a privilege. We may not all make it, but we will all triumph, either in this life or in the life to come."

Utana looked at his friend; tears were streaming down his face. "You have no idea how badly I needed to hear that. Thank you for opening your heart to me. I will lead Fahnik in prayer tonight. I want to be the man God wants me to be. Now, I know I will follow you anywhere, Navid. You have always been my friend, but today you became a leader worth following. When the Immortals come, we will make them pay, and this Family will survive."

Scene 3 The Immortals - Day 62

Leyla rode to the corral that Mirza, now in charge of the animals, had recently constructed. They were south of the ruins of Babylon, and Mirza had driven the stock ahead of the Immortals. He and his wranglers had the corral up and ready for the riders when they arrived. Leyla had also ridden ahead of the troop to have a word with Mirza in private.

Mirza saw her coming and walked over and took her horse from her. Leyla had avoided him since leaving Susa, and Mirza had no idea what their relationship was, if any. He waited for Leyla to speak.

"I'm sorry if I have avoided you, Mirza, but believe me; it was for your protection. Parviz is a mad man. He watches me constantly; if he thought for an instant we were friends, your life would be in danger. That's why I need to talk to you."

Mirza's face brightened. "We're friends?"

"Of course, we're friends. What a foolish question! So, we will do what friends do; we're going to figure a way to get out of this place."

Mirza was concerned. "Where will we go? What will we do? How will we survive?"

"Listen to me, Mirza. My father's Satrapy is vast, and he has many villages and headmen who are loyal to him. We will hide in one of the villages, and we will be safe there. When the Satraps overthrow Queen Musa, we will be able to return to the Compound and resume our lives."

Mirza shook his head no. "It's an excellent plan for you. We risk death, but if we are successful, you will have everything you ever wanted. You will be Satrap of a large holding, and I will be a stable boy, and I want more than that."

"Of course, I should have thought," replied Leyla. "As I have said, our Satrapy has many villages. You may pick the best of them, and my father will make you a headman. You will have income, power, and respect. You will lack for nothing."

"That is not what I want."

Leyla was becoming frustrated, "Well, what do you want?"

"I want you. All those days we rode together, talking at night about our lives and lying next to you, I fell in love. I am a man, Leyla. I want you to see me as a man, as someone of worth. I want you."

Leyla put her hand on his forearm and looked him in the eye, "You think you want me. You have fallen in love with the person you want me to be. I am a terrible person, Mirza. I may have condemned an entire group of people to their deaths. What kind of person does that?"

Mirza looked into her eyes. "A person who acted rashly and without forethought. That is the person who did that. I know a different Leyla, and so did Navid. Are you going to let that one moment define who you are? You have a choice. Which Leyla do you want to be?"

She whispered, "I want to be the woman you fell in love with."

He grabbed her by both shoulders and smiled at her. "Then I'm going to get us out of here tonight. When you lie down, be fully dressed for travel. I will come for you."

Parviz and Sasan rode into camp. The troop that had scouted the Euphrates had already arrived. Parviz called for a quick council of his captains.

"We know where the Magi are not. As I suspected all along, they have come up the west side of the Euphrates, but they will not get past us. We will cross the Euphrates in the morning, and teams of scouts will ride south to find the Magi. We are about to bring the quarry to bay."

Leyla had been unable to sleep, starting at every slight sound, her heart racing. Only a few hours had passed since she lay down, but it felt like morning would dawn any second. She heard a rustling at the back of the tent, and the sound of the hide coverings being slit, and Mirza's head appeared through the opening. He signaled to her. She leaped out of bed and ran to him. She hugged him and then ran from the tent. He did not lead her to the corral; he had picketed four horses outside the camp and away from the posted guards. They led the horses away from the camp. Leyla walked beside Mirza and whispered, "What about the pickets?" She could see his white teeth as he grinned in the dark.

"Those men are about to get a nasty surprise. I dosed their horses, and any minute now, things will get pretty exciting for them." Mirza had no sooner finished speaking when they heard a horse neighing and saw the silhouette of a man flying through the air. They heard several horses neighing and the shouts of riders as they fought for control.

Time for stealth was over. "Mount," Mirza yelled. They jumped on their horses, kicked them, and were at full gallop. Quite naturally, these were the four fastest horses in the remuda. Mirza was pretty sure Parviz would not be happy when he found out his two prize stallions were missing.

Scene 4 Magi Camp - Day 63

The Magi were fifty miles south of the ruins of Babylon. Fardad's newly extended family were all sitting at the morning meal when a rider came thundering into the camp. One of the four men Kevan had sent back across the Euphrates to scout out the Immortals.

He jumped from his horse and ran to Fardad. He leaned over for a moment with his hands on his knees, trying to catch his breath. "The Immortals," gasp, gasp, gasp, "the Immortals," gasp, pause.

Jahan jumped up, "The Immortals, for heaven's sake. Okay, we got that part. Where are they?"

The man stood upright. "They camped east of the river last night, but they will cross it this morning. We probably don't have more than six hours until their scouts find us, and probably eight hours until they get organized."

"Good job, good job," Jahan yelled, pounding the poor man on the back. "Where are the other scouts?"

"We split up days ago to cover more ground. I haven't seen them since. I came on the trail of this group after I found five men tortured to death, over by the Tigris."

Jahan wasn't happy. "Is Parviz leading this group?"

"I watched their camp for a while, and yes, it's Parviz. I'd know him anywhere."

Jahan cringed. He was a nasty, vile student when he went through Immortal training. Jahan should have washed him out, but he hoped the years would change the young man. Obviously, they had not. "Get yourself something to eat; you're going to need it."

Jahan looked at Navid. "Go get the Council, Son."

Navid gathered everyone, and they sat in a semicircle around Fardad, just as they had fifty-six days ago when they had decided to make this trip. Fardad sat at the head; next to him was Jahan, then Ram, Kevan, Marzban, Rahim, and on Fardad's left sat Navid.

Navid felt humbled as he looked around the circle. These were men of strength and conviction, whose word was iron. They were men of great faith who loved the Lord and who lived selfless lives. Caring for the Family was the only thing that mattered to them.

Fardad opened the Council. "The Immortals are north of us and will be on this side of the river by mid-morning. We need to get ready to receive them. Navid, where is the most defensible position we can reach?"

"There is a good canyon three hours south of our position. The walls aren't as tall as I would like, and the mouth is a little too wide, but it's the best we can do. We should be able to hold out there for quite a while. There is a spring in the back of the canyon; we will have water."

Fardad scanned the group, "Are we in agreement? We will make our stand in the canyon."

Kevan stood. "We are God's warriors today, and He will fight for us. No man can stand against the mighty hand of the Lord." Kevan turned and left to get the people ready to travel.

The Family, spurred on by the news of the Immortals, broke camp quickly and arrived at the canyon in less than three hours. Kevan moved the animals, food, and other stores to the back of the canyon. He put the children under thirteen in the back too. Everyone else would fight. The men put on full combat armor, and women put on lighter armor but with larger shields. The women would be archers and slingers, with one woman shooting and the other covering them both with the shield. The men began the process of preparing the defenses. A copse of trees was close to the canyon, and half of the men dragged dead and fallen trees to the canyon entrance. The remaining men built a wall across the canyon entrance, ten feet tall and four feet thick. On the canyon side of the wall, they made a five-foot elevated platform. The Magi would be able to stand on the platform and shoot arrows or hurl Javelins. It wasn't perfect, but it might be enough to survive.

They were ready; now they waited.

Scene 5 The Immortals - Day 63

When Parviz discovered that Leyla and Mirza had deserted, he screamed for his aide to get one of the grooms. He questioned the man, knowing that he must be part of the conspiracy, but discovered nothing. Needing a way to vent his fury, Parviz beat the man to death with his bare fists. Then, he questioned Sasan about the relationship between Mirza and Leyla. Sasan replied that all he knew was they had spent eight days alone on the trip to Susa. He was a groom of Baraz, and Sasan had never thought for a minute that there could be a relationship between the two. Sasan said if he had to guess, there was probably coercion involved. There was no way this could have been a mutual decision.

Parviz didn't care who had decided what. When he finished with the Magi, he would track Leyla and Mirza. When he thought about the things he would do to them, he began to sweat.

The Immortals finished fording the Euphrates by mid-morning and set up camp. Parviz had sent out scouts earlier, and they were coming back with reports. He learned about the canyon and the defenses the Magi had built. He was not worried. He would lose some men, but with his numeric advantage, the outcome was inevitable.

Sasan had other plans. He walked up to Parviz, "Commander, might I suggest that you and I ride to the Magi camp and offer them the opportunity to surrender."

Parviz sneered at Sasan. "They have all the opportunity they need. If they want to surrender, they can ride out of the canyon unarmed, and we will take them to Susa. If they stay where they are, we will kill them all."

"I understand your logic, and you are correct. The burden is on the Magi to surrender. The only problem is Queen Musa. She views the Magi as a possession, a valuable possession. She wants me to kill the leadership, and she wants the rest of the Family returned. When she finds out we didn't attempt to negotiate, she will be highly displeased. I don't want to go back and tell the Queen we didn't even attempt to bring them home. But you are the commander, and, of course, it is your decision."

Sasan had cornered Parviz, and he knew it. He scowled at Sasan and growled, "When we get there, I'll do the talking."

"Of course, you are the commander, and it is your right."

They rode to the camp of the Magi.

The two men arrived in the late afternoon under a flag of truce. The defenders called for Fardad, and he and the Council came out from behind the wall and walked up to Sasan and Parviz.

Fardad looked at Sasan. "Son, I am surprised to see you here."

Parviz didn't give Sasan a chance to answer. He grinned at Fardad. "Why, he's the reason we're here. He made a deal with Queen Musa. If he brings the Magi Family back to Susa, he gets to take over Family leadership and kill you and your descendants. Isn't that correct, Sasan?"

Sasan looked at his father. "That was not my intent, but those are the Queen's orders," he said.

Parviz raised his voice to make sure everyone on the wall could hear. "Those are the Queen's orders. If you surrender without resistance, I will escort you to Susa. You will resume the school exactly as it existed in Persepolis. No one will harm you. Sasan will execute Fardad and his descendants for inciting rebellion against the Queen. Those are the Queen's orders."

Sasan held his arms out and took a step toward his father, "Father…" he never finished the sentence. Sasan reached down, grabbed the hilt of his father's sword, and pivoted on one foot. He took a step forward with his rear foot and stomped down as he lunged. All his weight was behind the blade, and he drove it through Parviz's chest and severed his spinal column.

Parviz looked down in shock at the blade sticking out of his chest. He raised his head and looked at Sasan as if he had a question, but the words never formed.

Sasan placed his foot on Parviz's chest and said, "Now, will you finally shut up?" Sasan shoved with his foot and extracted the blade. Parviz landed flat on his back, and he did not move. His dead unseeing eyes stared up at the blue sky.

Sasan turned and knelt in front of his father and extended the hilt of the blade. Fardad took the sword and looked at his son. "Well, what would you like to do now?"

Sasan looked up at his father. "Parviz is dead because he is an evil man, but nothing has changed. There are still 500 Immortals out there, and the second-in-command will not go back to Susa without the Family. The Magi must either go back or face overwhelming odds."

Fardad turned and looked at the men and women gathered on the walls and the overlooking cliff. He raised his voice, "You have one last chance; anyone who wants may step forward and go to Susa to resume the school. I will not think less of anyone who decides to go. If you want to leave, step forward now."

No one moved.

Fardad turned to Sasan and said, "We will fight. What will you do?"

Sasan said without hesitation, "If you will have me. I will fight next to you and my brother," he said, nodding at Jahan.

Fardad reached out and put both hands on Sasan's shoulders, "Do you remember the story of Joseph and his brothers. They were jealous of him and sold him into slavery in Egypt. Joseph suffered much, but in the end, he became second only to Pharaoh. He was in a position to save his family from starvation when the famine came. Because of the evil actions of his brothers, he ended up in a powerful position in Egypt. When he confronted them in the end, he said, 'What you meant for evil, God meant for good.' We will glorify God when we defeat the Immortals. It was not your intent, but that will be the result. Welcome home."

Jahan tied Parviz to his horse and sent it back to the Immortals. He figured they would get the message. Then he walked up to Sasan and hugged him, "Welcome home, brother. I'll find you some armor."

Scene 6 Final Confrontation - Day 64

The Immortals decided it was too late to begin an attack after Parviz's body came back to camp tied to his horse. As soon as the sun rose the next day, they rode to the Magi camp.

Pari and Tiz were finishing the morning meal, and Pari heard the advancing horsemen. "Tiz," she asked, "carry me up to the clifftop. I must help with the battle."

Tiz looked at her in horror, "I cannot do that; you cannot handle a weapon. The cliffs are not where you need to be today."

Pari put her hand on Tiz's forearm, "Do you believe in God, Tiz? Do you believe He will fight for us today? I do. Grandfather and the others have always said it, but I believe it. We will not win this battle with swords and arrows. The God of all creation will fight for us, and His will be the glory. I must be there, Tiz. The Family needs me, and I will call upon God."

Tiz stared in amazement at this woman he loved more than anything in the world. Then with his eyes misting, he picked her up and carried her to the top of the cliff.

Navid saw Tiz ascending the cliff, carrying his sister, and ran after them. "Tiz, what are you doing?"

Pari looked at her brother, "Tiz is doing God's will. I am going to the clifftop to speak to Him. I must do this for the Family."

Navid pleaded with his sister, "Please, Pari, please don't do this. I couldn't stand it if anything happened to you."

"Navid, go back down. I know what I'm doing. I will be fine, and so will the Family. Tiz, take me up."

Tiz looked at Navid, shook his head, and then carried Pari up to the top, giving her a view of the Family and the Immortals. Tiz sat her on a small, flat-topped boulder and then stood there with his shield over her.

The Magi were on the wall and cliffs overlooking the Immortals. The two forces stood facing each other, and finally, the new commander of the Immortals rode forward and spoke to everyone. "I know many of you. I ate at your tables; I grew up with your children. You educated me, taught me to be a man, and you made me a warrior. I beg you to give this up and return with me to Susa. I cannot bear the thought of fighting you, but I will if I must."

There was no response, except for a single arrow that arched high and landed at the commander's feet. He shook his head and ordered his men to dismount. The horses would be useless against the fortification. This would be an infantry attack.

They lined up two ten-wide-by-twenty-deep phalanxes. One would attack the left side of the wall, and the other the right side. The commander kept one hundred men in reserve. The men on the perimeter of the phalanx faced their shields outward, and the men in the center of the formation held their shields over their heads. It would be difficult for the Magi to find targets in the massed formations attacking them.

The Magi held their fire. It would be a waste of arrows to attack the moving phalanx. When they stopped marching, they would open the top shields so the archers could fire. That is when the Magi would attack. The commander yelled halt and called archers. The men who had been so designated put down their shields and drew their bows. Now there were openings in the top of each phalanx. The archers on the wall and the archers on the cliffs drew their bows and aimed them skyward.

The Immortal archers drew their bows and aimed them skyward, waiting for the command to release.

Pari looked up to the heavens, but all she could see was Tiz's shield. "Tiz, lower your shield. I must be able to see the heavens."

Tiz hesitated but then lowered his shield. Pari turned her face up and raised both arms with her palms up, and she began to pray. Words poured from her like water from a spring, calling upon God to stop this battle to save the Magi and the Immortals. Pari called upon Him to show His Power and His Glory. Her face began to glow, and her voice grew stronger.

The commander of the Immortals fixated on the young woman sitting on the top of the mountain. He saw her raised hands and her face pointing skyward. For some reason, he could not take his eyes off her. Her face seemed to be glowing. The Immortal archers' arms began to tremble from holding their war bows at full pull for so long. Before the commander could speak, there was a blinding light that shocked everyone. The Magi lowered their bows and looked down at the Immortals. They were staggering as if they were drunk. Men bumped into each other. Men fell, and others walked on them. It was chaos. Then one of the Immortals yelled the Magi were attacking. Everyone pulled their swords, and Immortals began killing each other. They were all blind. The Magi were unfazed by the light, but the Immortals, in their blindness, were slaughtering each other.

Jahan had trained the Immortals and knew their signal calls. He grabbed a ram's horn and blew Halt. Thankfully, the Immortals training kicked in, and everyone stood at attention. Jahan spoke to them, "Immortals, the Lord God almighty has blinded you. It is temporary, and it is for your protection. Do not be concerned; no one will harm you. Drop your shields and your weapons, and the Magi will collect them."

Immortals dropped their weapons except for a few men. "This is the last warning. If you are still holding a weapon, I will order the archers to kill you. I will not take a chance with the safety of my people." The few men who held onto their weapons dropped them.

The Family looked up at the clifftop and saw and heard Pari, still facing heaven, giving thanks to God for the victory and thanking Him for allowing the Magi to see His Glory. Then, the Magi came out from behind the wall and passed through the Immortals. Some collected weapons, and others led the uninjured to a nearby clearing. The Magi bandaged the wounded and carried the dead to a pile to burn them later. The Magi led the wounded to the clearing after tending to them. The Magi women took off their armor and lit cooking fires. When the food was ready, the Magi spread out through the Immortals and fed them. The Magi felt at peace for the first time since leaving Persepolis. They kept guards over the Immortals that night, but there were no incidents.

The sun rose, and Jahan walked to the clearing where they held the Immortals. The commander of the Immortals walked up to Jahan. He explained that his sight returned that morning. Jahan knew everything had a purpose. He gave the commander options, to remain in the canyon until everyone's sight returned, or he could lead the blind men home. The commander did not intend to take this blind herd anywhere. Jahan promised to stop by the Immortal camp when they left and tell his supply train where they were. They should have food and water by noon.

Jahan walked back to the Magi camp, everyone was ready to travel, but first, they would eat. Fardad called everyone together before they ate and gave thanks.

"Heavenly Father, you are faithful. You protected us yesterday, and you allowed us to see Your Might and Your Glory. We have far to go, but we do so in confidence. The Lord God Almighty goes before us. Great Jehovah, our eyes are focused on You and Your Son. This is Day 65, Father, and we have far to go, but you know the way and will lead us safely to the Messiah."

Amen

APPENDIX

Credits

To Sherry Garner, my wife, whose love, care, and support made this book possible.

Retired Lt Colonel Marvin (Bill) Terry, whose content reading, recommendations, and insight greatly improved the book.

Pete VanDyke, whose early recommendations gave the book structure and whose edits and proofreading were invaluable.

Cheryl Clayton pushed me to write to the best of my ability and not settle for anything less.

Ronnie Rogers, pastor of Trinity Baptist Church in Norman, Oklahoma, God used to disciple me, teach me, and pray for me. Without him, there would be no Magi Journey – Assyria.

Maps

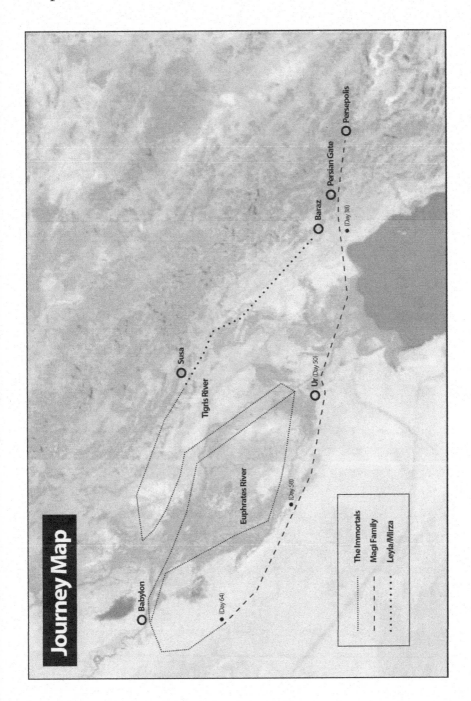

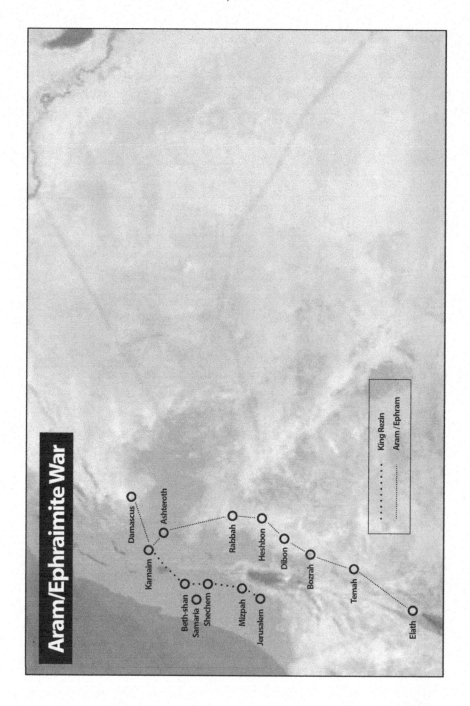

Aram/Ephraimite War

Damascus

Ashteroth

Karnaim

Rabbah

Heshbon

Dibon

Beth-shan

Samaria

Shechem

Bozrah

Mizpah

Temah

Jerusalem

Elath

King Rezin

Aram / Ephram

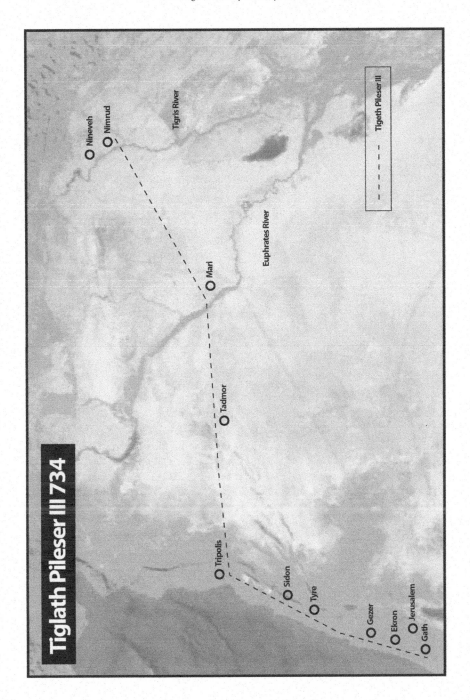

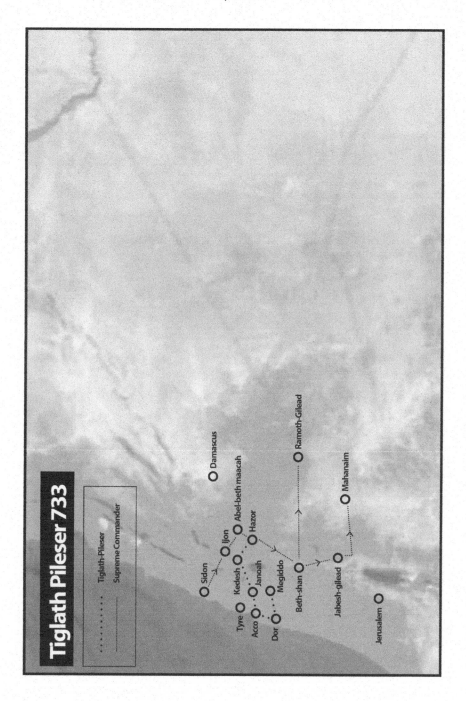

Tiglath Pileser 733

.... Tiglath-Pileser
——— Supreme Commander

Damascus
Ramoth-Gilead
Mahanaim
Abel-beth maacah
Hazor
Ijon
Sidon
Kedesh
Janoah
Tyre
Acco
Dor
Megiddo
Beth-shan
Jabesh-gilead
Jerusalem

Sennacherib 701

Characters

Persians

Alibai – Uxian shepherdess
Baraz - Satrap of southeast Persia, father of Leyla
Leyla - daughter of the Satrap Baraz
Mirza - servant of Baraz, horseman
Musa - Queen of Persia from 2 BC to 4AD, co-ruler with her son Phraates V
Omid – sister of Satrap Baraz
Parviz – leader of the Immortals
Phraates V - King of Persia from 2 BC to 4 AD, co-ruler with his mother, Musa
Taghi – leader of the Uxians
Zard – Uxian shepherd

Magi Family - Major Characters

Asha - wife of Jahan and mother of Navid
Ava - wife of Navid
Fahnik - Daughter of Jahan and Asha, wife of Utana
Fardad - Leader of the Council, father of Jahan
Hosh - Military leader and father of Ava
Jahan - a member of the Council, son of Fardad
Marzban - a member of the Council, son of Kevan
Navid - a member of the Council, leader of the Scouts, son of Jahan and Asha
Pari - daughter of Jahan and Asha
Rahim - a member of the Council, teacher of the children
Ram - a member of the Council, livestock manager
Sasan - son of Fardad, chief counselor of Queen Musa
Tiz - a member of the Scouts and caretaker of Pari
Utana - a member of the Scouts, husband of Fahnik
Kevan - a member of the Council, head of military training

Magi Family - Minor Characters

Adel - leader of the right flank on the march
Aref – a member of the Scouts
Danial - leader of the dissidents
Dara - Father of Utana
Delara - 5-year-old girl, very energetic
Esmail - a member of the Scouts
Farida - one of Rahim's best students, highly energetic
Gohar – dissenter, father of Mahsa
Gul - a servant to Asha
Habib - a member of the Scouts
Heydar - conspirator
Jangi - subordinate to Hosh
Mehr - Mother of Utana
Reza - Dissenter
Yusef - a 12-year-old boy, son of Danial

Assyrian - Major and Minor Characters

Abigail – wife of Zaia
Ali - Judean who rode with Eliya
Ashur - second in command under Baildan
Baildan - leader of a troop of 100 cavalry, son of Domara
Benjamin - Judean, son of Rachael, rescued by Baildan
Domara - Patriarch of the Magi Family, counselor to Tiglath-Pileser III
Eilbra - signal caller under Baildan
Eliya - servant of Meesha
Hano - wife of Meesha
Jamal - a member of Baildan's cavalry
Javed – son of Zaia and Abigail
Karim - servant/armor-bearer of Baildan
Khannah - wife of Domara, mother of Baildan and Meesha
Mardokh - Member of Baildan's troop
Meesha - son of Domara, representative to the court in Jerusalem
Naomi – Benjamin's wife
Negar – daughter of Zaia and Abigail
Pera - a member of Baildan's cavalry, wrestling champion
Rachael - rescued by Baildan and married to him, Judean

Safa – a friend of Leyla, father a court official
Samir - commander of fifty under Baildan
Samuel - Judean who rode with Eliya
Tiglath-Pileser III - King of Persia from 745–727 BC
Zaia - son of Meesha and Hano

Judeans - Major and Minor Characters

Adin - a disciple of Isaiah
Ahaz - King of Judah
Hahn – a disciple of Isaiah
Hezekiah – King of Judah
Isaiah - the Prophet

Ephraimites

Pekah - King of Israel, Northern Kingdom from 737–732 BC
Zichri - military champion of Ephraim

Syrians

Rezin - king of Syria, ruled from 754–732 BC
Nabil - commander of the Syrian forces combined with Ephraim

Arabians

Samsi - Queen of Arabia in the 730s and 720s (exact dates are not known)

Animals

Anosh - Navid's warhorse
Arbella - Baildan's favorite horse
Arsha – Navid's war dog
Bendva – Navid's war dog

Extras, minor characters with a single appearance, have not been listed.

Bibliography

Freeman-Grenville, G.S.P. *Historical Atlas of the Middle East.* New York, NY.: Academic Reference Division Simon and Schuster, 1993

Isbouts, Jean-Pierre. *Atlas of the Bible.* Washington, D.C.: National Geographic Partners, LLC, 1974

Herzog, Chaim & Gichon, Mordechai *Battles Of The Bible,* New York, NY.: Fall River Press, 1978, 1997

Wood, Leon J. *A Survey of Israel's History.* Grand Rapids, MI.: Zondervan Press, 1970, 1986

Gabriel, Richard A. *On Ancient Warfare.* South Yorkshire, England, Pen&Sword Books Ltd, 2018

Persian Empire, History, 23 May 2021 https://www.history.com/topics/ancient-middle-east/persian-empire

Persian Gate, Livius, 15 Dec 2020 https://www.livius.org/articles/battle/persian-gate-330-bce/

Assyria, BibleHub, 14 May 2020 https://bibleatlas.org/assyria.htm

Assyrian Warfare, World History Encyclopedia, 1 July 2020 https://www.worldhistory.org/Assyrian_Warfare/

The Iron Army: Assyria - Terrifying Military of the Ancient World - Part 1, Camrea, 10 July 2020 http://www.camrea.org/2017/01/06/the-iron-army-assyria-terrifying-military-of-the-ancient-world-part-i/

Assyrian Archers, Ancient Replicas, 10 Jan 2021 https://www.ancientreplicas.com/assyrian-archers.html

Tiglath Pileser III, World History Encyclopedia, 04 April 2020 https://www.worldhistory.org/Tiglath_Pileser_III/

Assyrian March Against Judah, History Net, 05 May 2021 https://www.historynet.com/assyrian-march-against-judah.htm

Excavations Reveal Idol Worship in Ancient Jerusalem, WatchJerusalem, 15 November 2020 https://watchjerusalem.co.il/788-excavations-reveal-idol-worship-in-ancient-jerusalem

The Syro-Ephraimite War: Context, Conflict, and Consequences, BYU, 16 February 2020 https://scholarsarchive.byu.edu/cgi/viewcontent.cgi?article=1019&=&context=studiaantiqua&=&sei-redir=1&referer=https%253A%252F%252Fwww.bing.com%252Fsearch%253Fq%253Dsyro%252520ephraimitic%252520war%252520map%2526qs%253Dn%2526form%253DQBRE%2526sp%253D-1%2526pq%253Dsyro%252520ephraimitic%252520war%252520map%2526sc%253D1-2

4%2526sk%253D%2526cvid%253DE519DFEA5EF845A59758429B-
DC0216DF#search=%22syro%20ephraimitic%20war%20
map%22

The Deportation of Judah, Bible History, 25 February 2020 https://www.
bible-history.com/map_babylonian_captivity/map_of_the_deportation_
of_judah_the_deportation_of_judah.html

Prophecies of the First Coming and Their Fulfillments, EndTime Ministries,
23 May 2021

The MacArthur Study Bible English Standard Version. Wheaton, IL.:
Crossway, 2010

Magi from the East, Gates of Nineveh, 27 May 2021 https://gatesofnineveh.
wordpress.com/2011/12/24/magi-from-the-east/

Crossing the Euphrates in antiquity: Zeugma seen from space,
JSTOR, 30 May 2021 https://www.jstor.org/stable/pdf/3643016.
pdf?refreqid=excelsior%3Ac7a8c003422a979b4dbc28e836bd78f9

Keil, C. F. & Delitzsch, F. *Commentary on the Old Testament - Volume 3*,
Grand Rapids, Michigan: William B. Eerdmans Publishing Co., 1978

Keil, C. F. & Delitzsch, F. *Commentary on the Old Testament - Volume 7*, Grand
Rapids, Michigan: William B. Eerdmans Publishing Co., 1978

Tiglath-Pileser III Campaigns 734–732, JSTOR, 13 June 2021 https://www.jstor.
org/stable/42614666?seq=1#metadata_info_tab_contents

Endnotes

1 **Numbers 24:17** "[17] I see him, but not now; I behold him, but not near: a star shall come out of Jacob, and a scepter shall rise out of Israel;"

2 **Isaiah 9:2** "[2] The people who walked in darkness have seen a great light; those who dwelt in a land of deep darkness, on them has light shone.

3 **Isaiah 49:6** "[6] he says: "It is too light a thing that you should be my servant to raise up the tribes of Jacob and to bring back the preserved of Israel; I will make you as a light for the nations, that my salvation may reach to the end of the earth.""

4 **Isaiah 13-23**

5 **Isaiah 44:28** "[28] who says of Cyrus, 'He is my shepherd, and he shall fulfill all my purpose'; saying of Jerusalem, 'She shall be built,' and of the temple, 'Your foundation shall be laid.'"

6   **Matthew 2:1-2** "Now after Jesus was born in Bethlehem of Judea in the days of Herod the king, behold, wise men from the east came to Jerusalem, ² saying, "Where is he who has been born king of the Jews? For we saw his star when it rose and have come to worship him.""

7   **Genesis 18:17-18** "¹⁷ The LORD said, "Shall I hide from Abraham what I am about to do, ¹⁸ seeing that Abraham shall surely become a great and mighty nation, and all the nations of the earth shall be blessed in him?"

8   **Isiah 7:14** "¹⁴ Therefore the Lord himself will give you a sign. Behold, the virgin shall conceive and bear a son, and shall call his name Immanuel."

9   **Isaiah 9:6-7** "⁶ For to us a child is born, to us a son is given; and the government shall be upon his shoulder, and his name shall be called Wonderful Counselor, Mighty God, Everlasting Father, Prince of Peace. ⁷ Of the increase of his government and of peace there will be no end, on the throne of David and over his kingdom, to establish it and to uphold it with justice and with righteousness from this time forth and forevermore. The zeal of the LORD of hosts will do this."

10 **Isaiah 53:10-12** "¹⁰ Yet it was the will of the LORD to crush him; he has put him to grief; when his soul makes an offering for guilt, he shall see his offspring; he shall prolong his days; the will of the LORD shall prosper in his hand. ¹¹ Out of the anguish of his soul he shall see and be satisfied; by his knowledge shall the righteous one, my servant, make many to be accounted righteous, and he shall bear their iniquities. ¹² Therefore I will divide him a portion with the many, and he shall divide the spoil with the strong, because he poured out his soul to death and was numbered with the transgressors; yet he bore the sin of many, and makes intercession for the transgressors."

11 **Isaiah 7:3** "³ And the LORD said to Isaiah, "Go out to meet Ahaz, you and Shear-jashub your son, at the end of the conduit of the upper pool on the highway to the Washer›s Field."

12 **Isaiah7:4-17** "⁴ And say to him, 'Be careful, be quiet, do not fear, and do not let your heart be faint because of these two smoldering stumps of firebrands, at the fierce anger of Rezin and Syria and the son of Remaliah. ⁵ Because Syria, with Ephraim and the son of Remaliah, has devised evil against you, saying, ⁶ "Let us go up against Judah and terrify it, and let us conquer it for ourselves, and set up the son of Tabeel as king in the midst of it," ⁷ thus says the Lord GOD: "'It shall not stand, and it shall not come to pass. ⁸ For the head of Syria is Damascus, and the head of Damascus is Rezin. And within sixty-five years Ephraim will be shattered from being a people. ⁹ And the head of Ephraim is Samaria, and the head of Samaria is the son of Remaliah. If you are not firm in faith, you will not be firm at all."' ¹⁰ Again the LORD spoke to Ahaz: ¹¹ "Ask a sign of the LORD your God; let it be deep

as Sheol or high as heaven." [12] But Ahaz said, "I will not ask, and I will not put the LORD to the test." [13] And he said, "Hear then, O house of David! Is it too little for you to weary men, that you weary my God also? [14] Therefore the Lord himself will give you a sign. Behold, the virgin shall conceive and bear a son, and shall call his name Immanuel. [15] He shall eat curds and honey when he knows how to refuse the evil and choose the good. [16] For before the boy knows how to refuse the evil and choose the good, the land whose two kings you dread will be deserted. [17] The LORD will bring upon you and upon your people and upon your father's house such days as have not come since the day that Ephraim departed from Judah—the king of Assyria!'"

13 **2 Kings 16:7-9** "[7] So Ahaz sent messengers to Tiglath-pileser king of Assyria, saying, "I am your servant and your son. Come up and rescue me from the hand of the king of Syria and from the hand of the king of Israel, who are attacking me." [8] Ahaz also took the silver and gold that was found in the house of the LORD and in the treasures of the king's house and sent a present to the king of Assyria. [9] And the king of Assyria listened to him. "

14 **2 Chronicles 28:6-7** "[6] For Pekah the son of Remaliah killed 120,000 from Judah in one day, all of them men of valor, because they had forsaken the LORD, the God of their fathers. [7] And Zichri, a mighty man of Ephraim, killed Maaseiah the king's son and Azrikam the commander of the palace and Elkanah the next in authority to the king.

15 **Isaiah 6:1** "In the year that King Uzziah died I saw the Lord sitting upon a throne, high and lifted up; and the train of his robe filled the temple."

16 **Isaiah 35:10** "[10] And the ransomed of the LORD shall return and come to Zion with singing; everlasting joy shall be upon their heads; they shall obtain gladness and joy, and sorrow and sighing shall flee away."

17 **Isaiah 6:1-9** "In the year that King Uzziah died I saw the Lord sitting upon a throne, high and lifted up; and the train of his robe filled the temple...[8] And I heard the voice of the Lord saying, "Whom shall I send, and who will go for us?" Then I said, "Here I am! Send me." [9] And he said, "Go, and say to this people:"

18 **Isaiah 13-23**

19 **Ezra 4:1-2** "Now when the adversaries of Judah and Benjamin heard that the returned exiles were building a temple to the LORD, the God of Israel, [2] they approached Zerubbabel and the heads of fathers' houses and said to them, "Let us build with you, for we worship your God as you do, and we have been sacrificing to him ever since the days of Esarhaddon king of Assyria who brought us here."

20 **2 Samuel 12:15-23** "And the LORD afflicted the child that Uriah's wife bore to David, and he became sick. [16] David therefore sought God on behalf of

the child. And David fasted and went in and lay all night on the ground... And David said to his servants, "Is the child dead?" They said, "He is dead." [20] Then David arose from the earth and washed and anointed himself and changed his clothes. And he went into the house of the LORD and worshiped. He then went to his own house. And when he asked, they set food before him, and he ate. [21] Then his servants said to him, "What is this thing that you have done? You fasted and wept for the child while he was alive; but when the child died, you arose and ate food." [22] He said, "While the child was still alive, I fasted and wept, for I said, 'Who knows whether the LORD will be gracious to me, that the child may live?' [23] But now he is dead. Why should I fast? Can I bring him back again? I shall go to him, but he will not return to me."

21 **2 Kings 18:19-25**

22 **2 Kings 18:26-37**

23 **Isaiah 37:6-7**